LISHING

7/23

Our Father, Who Art Out There...Somewhere

AJ Taft

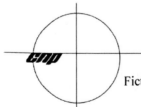

Fiction aimed at the heart and the head...

Published by Caffeine Nights Publishing 2011

Published in Great Britain by Caffeine Nights Publishing

www.caffeine-nights.com

British Library Cataloguing in Publication Data.
A CIP catalogue record for this book is available from the British Library

ISBN: 978-1-907565-06-9

Cover design by
Kirsti Robinson
&
Mark (Wills) Williams

Everything else by
Default, Luck and Accident

For Esme

ACKNOWLEDGEMENTS

Thanks to everyone at YAC and Ink especially Phil, Liz, Chris, Lucy and Danuta Reah.

Big thanks to Katie and Justine for reading the early drafts and Steve, for his fine attention to detail and inability to hide his wincing.

Thanks to Rose for her great idea, Ron Strong for the web-site, Kirsti Robinson for the art work and Darren at Caffeine Nights for making it all happen.

And Sandra, thank you so much for helping me along the way.

Special thanks to my mum for not being anything like Lily's mum and for never giving up.

And to Uncle Keith, see I told you, in my book and in my heart forever.

It is wise to disclose
what cannot be concealed

Johann Friedrich von Stiller (1759-1805)

Our Father, Who Art Out There... Somewhere

Born and raised in Burnley, Alison Taft dreamed of becoming a writer ever since reading Harriet the Spy by torchlight under the bedcovers, aged eight.

After completing a degree, Alison lived in Crete and spent time in the Middle and Far East. In the mid-nineties she was a keen supporter of the free party network. She has worked in a variety of jobs but after being sacked once too often for gross insubordination, Alison decided to heed the words of one employer who described her as 'unmanageable', and became a full time writer.

Alison now lives in Leeds with her partner and two children. She spends her evenings at the computer, sipping mint tea and plotting her revenge.

Our Father, Who Art Out There... Somewhere is Alison's first novel.

Prologue

It's not a pretty sight, even to the uncynical eye. Ten minutes to go until last orders, Happy Tuesday of Fresher's week (like happy hour but without the constraint of time). The crowd at the bar is at least five deep; everyone jostling to get another one in before the lights come up, and the grim reality of the surroundings can no longer be ignored. The air is so heavy with cigarette smoke, it's difficult for Lily to locate her friend as she emerges from the scrum, head bent, arms at right angles, with two plastic pints of luminous vodka and orange. Her DMs stick to the floor each step she takes. Luckily, Jo's bleached white flat-top helps her stand out from the crowd.

"God, some bloke just threw up behind me, is it in my hair?" Lily has to shout to be heard above the strains of 'Walking on Sunshine' by Katrina and the Waves. She turns round and Jo inspects her dirty blonde dreadlocks, which hang down her back like rope.

"Can't see anything." Jo spins her back round and takes a drink from her, "Cheers."

Jo stubs out her cigarette in a convenient, but overflowing ashtray on the table next to them, and raises her plastic pint to her mouth. As she does so, a hand gropes her well rounded bottom, which jolts her, causing her to miss her mouth and to tip a hefty slug down the front of her Ramones T-shirt.

"Do you mind?" She turns on the bloke standing behind her. He's six foot tall, and so drunk he's swaying. He leers at her as he tries to focus.

"Hey gorgeous. Want to come back to mine? We're having a party. You can bring your mate."

"I'd rather stick pins in my eyes," Jo snarls at him. "So leave us alone." She turns back to Lily.

1

He isn't easily deterred, "Oh wow, lezzers." Jo shakes her head in disgust. "Can I come back to yours then, please? I could just watch," he adds hopefully. Jo's arm jerks and then she watches him slowly come to terms with the fact that he is now wearing the remains of her vodka and orange. "You frigging cow," he splutters.

"Yeah, what you going to do about it?" asks Jo. As she speaks a large hand clamps onto her shoulder from behind. Jo turns to face the security beefcake, whose rippling, black muscles bulge out of a tight green T-shirt.

"Come on, time to go," he says, with the air of someone who has done this once too often.

"He's just been feeling me up," says Jo, pulling herself up to her full five feet one and a half inches. "I believe this Students' Union has an equal opportunities policy. He's a sexist. If he'd been racist you wouldn't be throwing out the victim."

The bouncer steers her towards the exit as she continues her tirade. Lily follows a couple of steps behind, throwing back the rest of her drink in urgent bursts. The bouncer opens the door. "Don't be walking home, girls."

"It's women. Do we look prepubescent?" Jo cups her breasts in both hands, her cheeks flushed with rage.

He refuses to be drawn into an argument. "Have you got enough money for a taxi?"

" Haven't you heard?" says Jo. "All men are rapists. That includes taxi drivers."

He shrugs his shoulders and shows them the palms of his hands, as if to say he's done all he can.

Lily sways as she steps outside, "I think I'm going to be sick," she mumbles. The bouncer shakes his head. She's such a pretty thing, but always so wasted. Skin and bones too. He closes the door behind them.

"Come on," says Jo, "the air will do you good." She grabs Lily's arm, tucks it into hers and starts marching her up the road. It's uphill all the way to their shared student flat, 'the rat run'. As they walk, students spill out from The Fenton, The Packhorse, The Eldon; some in worse states than Lily.

Halfway home, they take the short cut through Hyde Park, a breath of fresh air between the grey/white high rise buildings of Leeds University and the red brick student slums of Headingley. They hear the familiar sound of other groups of students wandering home; singing, shouting, stealing traffic cones, as they make their way through the darkness. At the playground on the edge of the park, close enough to the road to be illuminated by the street lamps, Lily sits down on a swing. She pushes herself high into the air, while Jo opens her bag and pulls out a bottle of vodka. They stop off here on their way home most nights. Jo finds her pack of cigarettes, puts two in her mouth, lights both and then passes one to Lily.

Lily slows down to reach the cigarette and sits on the swing, gently swaying. After a couple of drags she turns to Jo. "Do you really believe that?" They haven't spoken all the way home. "That all men are rapists?"

Jo considers the question, "I think they all have the potential, it's there in them. If they knew they could get away with it I reckon any man would. Don't you?"

"Dunno, never really thought about it." Lily takes another deep drag on her cigarette, "I'm always too drunk to say no."

"Seriously? You've never had sex sober?" Jo asks. Lily stops swinging. It's hard to remember. "How about your first time?"

"No, I was definitely pissed then." Lily takes a swig from the bottle that Jo is offering. "Thank God."

"How old were you?"

Lily wipes her mouth with the back of her sleeve, "Thirteen, actually twelve."

"Christ."

"I know. It's not good, I know." She flicks her cigarette as far as she can and watches the sparks blaze a small trail, as the stub hits the ground. "Give us another fag."

Jo passes her another Marlboro and Lily takes a lighter out of her pocket. She cups her hand around the lighter, bending her head towards it. It shoots a jet of flame that rises a couple of feet, taking with it Lily's eyebrows and most of her fringe. Lily screams.

"Shit, are you ok?" Jo grabs her and looks at her face. She pats out the smouldering ends of her hair. "Jesus, good job you don't wear hairspray. You could have been a goner."

Lily adjusts the gas flow on her lighter and tries to relight it, but this time it doesn't work at all. "Aargh!" she bellows, as she hurls the lighter into the darkness. She stands up, "I want to go home."

Chapter 1

The magpie sits on the head of the statue of Robert Peel and cackles. A shudder runs all the way down Lily's spine. She doesn't know whether it's the same lone magpie that greeted her as she opened the front door that morning; spreading its large black wings and scaring the bejesus out of her, or whether it's the same one that was sitting on the lamp post as they rounded the corner to the edge of the park. She recites the rhyme silently to herself, "One for sorrow, two for joy, three for a girl, four for a boy." If she has seen three separate single magpies in the space of ten minutes, can she add them together and count three for a girl? Or is it three helpings of sorrow? Or sorrow multiplied to the power of three? Lily shakes her head, salutes it, and for the third time, mutters, "Morning Mr Magpie, where's your wife?"

Jo screws up her face, "Will you quit with that. It's just a bird." She looks up at the magpie. "An ugly, noisy bird."

The magpie cackles again and flies off.

Lily can't shake the queasy feeling. It's still there in their 'Development of the Welfare State' lecture, and she knows it's more than a hangover. Her charred eyebrows itch. She rests her chin on her forearms and stares at the piece of paper in front of her. "P?" she whispers.

Jo shakes her head and draws an arm onto the stick figure hanging from a noose at the bottom of the page.

Lily tries again. "K?"

Jo wrinkles her nose and fills two of the blank spaces with the letter K.

Lily shuffles further forward on the bench. "I?" she says, her voice gaining confidence.

Tutting, Jo adds six I's to the nine word sentence.

Lily raises her chin, forgetting, in her excitement, to keep her voice down, "I'm so bored I think I might kill myself?"

Jo fills in the missing letters as they both start to laugh. Mr Wardle raises his hairy eyebrows from the podium at the front of the class. "Quiet there at the back, please."

Lily bites the skin on the inside of her cheek to try and stop herself from snorting with laughter. She daren't look at Jo. As Mr Wardle clears his throat and rustles his notes, the door opens and a woman in a grey suit enters the room. She doesn't glance up at the ten or twelve rows of students, but goes straight across to Mr Wardle. The room falls silent, so that Lily, even from her position on the very back row, can hear the sounds of the woman's urgent whispering. Adrenaline starts to seep into Lily's stomach, heightening the waves of nausea she's been fighting all morning. As she watches Mr Wardle nod, Lily glances out of the window just in time to see another lone magpie sailing across the sky, its tail feathers like an arrow behind it.

Mr Wardle glances up, his eyes searching the rows of students. He clears his throat again, "Lily Appleyard?"

Lily jerks her head up and he spots her. As soon as he makes eye contact he averts his gaze. "Could you go to Student Services please?"

She stumbles her way along the row, tripping over another student's satchel as she does so, before making her way down the steps at the side of the theatre. Her dreadlocks bounce off her shoulders as her heart hammers against her skinny ribs.

The woman in the grey suit waits for her, holding the door ajar. She doesn't say anything to Lily. Lily follows her out of the room, down a flight of stairs, and then down the corridor at a brisk pace, until she stops at a door with a sign that says, 'Stuart Strange, Head of Support Services'. The woman nods at her to open it. Lily knocks, the heavy wooden door making her knuckles sting. She pushes it open and steps inside.

A man in his early fifties, with a greying beard and black rimmed spectacles, presumably Mr Strange, stands to greet her. A large black topped desk lies between them.

"Ah, Lily," he says, rubbing his hands together. "Thank you for coming." He takes a deep breath, puts his finger tips on the edge of the desk, as if to support himself. "I'm terribly sorry to have to tell you, Lily that your uncle has telephoned the polytechnic this

6

morning with the news that your mother has passed away. She died last night, peacefully in her sleep. She didn't suffer." He takes another breath, looks her straight in the eye, counts to five and says, "I am very sorry."

Her hangover helps in some strange way, cushions her from too much reality. She stands looking at the bookcase behind him. The colours are all wrong. Three large books with bright red spines, are stacked next to each other on the right hand side, without any thought to counterbalance. It makes it look like the bookcase could fall over at any point.

"Would you like to sit down?" He points to the two leather armchairs and small coffee table in the corner of the room.

Lily takes a moment to register she's being asked a question. "No, no thank you." Even a purple cover or a dark blue tome in the bottom left corner would have sufficed. *Working with the Problem Drinker*, she reads down the spine of one badly sited yellow textbook, that's half the size of the book next to it. She adjusts her weight onto her left leg and tries to pull her mind back to the man in front of the bookcase.

They stand in silence across his desk, facing each other. Mr Strange is the first to crack. He looks across to the door as if he's heard someone knock at it. Lily tries to search for any useful clues in her head for what to say in a situation like this. She tries to think of a film she's watched, or a book she's read where this same thing has happened because she is at least aware that questions should be asked. But the only question in her mind is why he has ordered the bookcase the way he has? Her breathing starts to quicken. Mr Strange looks at her with concern.

"I don't have an uncle," she says at last.

This news takes him back a bit, "Oh," he says. He picks up a piece of paper from his in tray and peers at it. "He said he was your uncle."

Lily sees the phrase, 'died peacefully', with the peacefully underlined. More than how she lived, she thinks.

"Ah, yes Uncle, Bert?"

"He's not my uncle."

Stuart Strange looks at her questioningly, waiting for her to expand. He's also trying to work out what's wrong with her face. Lily tries to engage in conversation, "He's just the perv who lives next door to my mum. He's always trying to get me to call him uncle, and look at his puppies," she adds as a joke.

7

Mr Strange looks alarmed. "Is there someone else I can call, someone who could collect you?"

Lily shakes her head quickly. The last thing she wants is to have this man feel any more concern for her. "No, there's no one else. It's alright. He's harmless."

Mr Strange looks at the wall behind Lily. "He said he'd arrive at 2 o'clock to pick you up. He said to meet at your flat."

Lily becomes aware of a clock ticking. She turns to look. It's half past eleven. She watches the hand of the clock tick off the seconds; jerking so violently each time one passes, it appears the clock might fall from the wall and Lily starts to worry for its safety. She watches twenty-eight seconds jolt past without incident and calms herself.

"Should I go back to my lecture?" she asks. She wants to get out of this too warm room. She's not up to this kind of scrutiny; not without eyebrows.

"Have you a friend who could wait with you?"

Lily's face lights up with relief, "Jo." Jo will know what to do.

"I'll go and get her for you." Mr Strange starts towards to door.

"No it's ok. I'll go," says Lily, throwing herself at the door handle. She runs down the corridor before Mr Strange has time to argue. She opens the door of the lecture theatre and sees Jo stand immediately. Leaving her books on the bench, Jo runs down the steps to Lily. No one inside the theatre says a word. Jo takes Lily's hand and together they hurry from the building.

It's only when they get outside that Jo asks, "What's up?"

"Me mum's dead," says Lily.

Jo pulls a packet of cigarettes from her pocket. She lights two and holds one out to Lily. "Shit." They start walking, neither knows where. "Pub, or home and a spliff?" Jo eventually asks.

Lily sighs, "Spliff I guess, I've got to pack some stuff. My, er uncle's coming to get me."

They've been inseparable for over a year, and yet Jo knows so very little of Lily's life, beyond the fact that she doesn't like to talk about it. She knows Lily hardly ever goes home to Accrington. "I'm really sorry, Lil."

"Yeah, it doesn't matter. She died a long time ago, before I was born. Her soul I mean. It's just taken nineteen years for her body to get the message."

Jo links arms with Lily as they make their way up the hill, past the polytechnic and its university neighbour, until they come to the park. The September sunshine is still warm enough for there to be groups of students lounging around, some reading; the more energetic playing Frisbee. Lily breathes in deeply as they pass one brightly coloured group, savouring the sweet smell of hashish.

"I hope Tim and what's-his-face aren't in," says Lily, as they walk up the path to their front door. Two bedroom houses were hard to find, so when they'd first start looking for a flat, Jo had suggested them getting two rooms in a shared house. When the landlord had shown them round, they'd met the two final year chemistry students; Tim with his jam jar glasses, and been immediately satisfied they wouldn't impinge on their lifestyle.

"If they are, they can fuck off," says Jo.

At a quarter to three, Bert pulls up in a pale blue Vauxhall Chevette, circa 1976, his pot belly nestling the steering wheel. As Lily climbs into the car she turns to Jo, "Do me a favour, post this for me?" She takes a battered envelope from the side pocket of her holdall. It's addressed to the Salvation Army, written in a childish scrawl; the I's have circles over them.

Jo looks at her questioningly. "You're not going to get God on me now are you?"

Lily smiles, "The next best thing." She ducks into Bert's car, "Please? You won't forget? It needs a stamp."

Jo puts it inside her coat. "Course."

Chapter 2

Standing above the open dirt pit, Lily watches as ten black suited men bear her mother's coffin aloft through the headstones. She can see beads of sweat running down the red faces of the front two; Bert and Mr Peterson. What they are carrying looks more like a boxed sofa than a coffin, appropriate really as her mother had hardly left the settee in the last few years. The funeral parlour had offered the use of a steel-framed trolley, but Lily had insisted. The coffin was to be carried.

Finding ten men ready, willing and able to carry the coffin had been no mean feat. A real 'Challenge Anneka'; Lily could almost hear the voice-over, "You have six days, no living male relatives (leastways none you've ever met), and a dead, agoraphobic mother who weighs more than a carthorse." Volunteers were going to be thin on the ground. Luckily Mr Peterson across the road had two sons, and the bloke from the chippy was duty bound. And Bert of course. The funeral home had made up the rest. It's hardly nearest and dearest, but at least she's in the ground. As the vicar brings proceedings to a close with a solemn rendition of the Lord's Prayer, Lily takes a seat on a conveniently sited gravestone and lights a cigarette. Relief floods her body, making her feel like she can breathe again, really for the first time since Mr Strange had told her of her mother's death. Her mother is safely in the ground; in a way her whole life has been in anticipation of this moment. Lily has fulfilled her birthright.

Bert sidles up to her, still sweating from his earlier exertions, his hair slicked back and wearing a shiny dark grey suit that fits badly, where it fits at all. "How you doing, Lil? Crash us a fag, will you?"

She pulls a Lambert and Butler from her packet and hands it to him, trying her best to avoid any physical contact as she does so.

Technically she's giving away her inheritance (she found 100 packets of them in the dresser, the warning printed in Arabic or something, probably the most valuable asset in the house), but what the hell. She's guessing there won't be any fighting over the will.

"Do you know, no one here's said sorry?"

Bert lights his fag, and wiping the sweat from his forehead with his sleeve, he looks at her, like he doesn't understand. She spells it out for him, "I'm nineteen years old, me mum's died, I have no other living relatives, no money and no one's said to me, "I'm sorry your mum's dead." Everyone murmurs inane crap like, "at least she's at peace." Even the vicar said he hoped she'd be happier where she is now. No one's sorry for me. I'm completely alone."

Bert coughs, a cough that comes from deep within his lungs. Lily can hear the mucus rattle in his windpipe. He bends over and puts his hands on his knees for a moment until he recovers. He takes another drag on his cigarette and then says, "You can move in with me."

Lily laughs, momentarily taken out of her self-pity. "I'm not that alone, thanks anyway, Bert. I meant I don't have any family left, look at this lot." She gestures at the sparse funeral congregation. Mr Khan from Passage to India mistakes her gesture for a wave and returns it. The woman he's talking to turns round to see who he's waving at and smiles across at Lily. Lily hasn't noticed her before and she frowns as the elderly woman bustles her way across the grass, over to them. She's small, with an ample bosom cradled tightly in a floral print.

"Lily," she says, taking Lily by both arms and pulling her up to her feet. "I'm so sorry." Concern brims over in the woman's eyes as Lily stares at her, trying to place her. "You don't remember me, do you?"

Lily opens her mouth to protest, but then closes it again.

"You used to call me Aunt Edie, you poor lamb."

"Aunt Edie?" Lily puts out a hand onto the headstone next to her, as standing up so quickly seems to have made her light-headed. "I thought... I mean... I haven't seen you for years."

"I saw the notice in the paper and thought I'd come." Aunt Edie speaks slowly, each word laced with sympathy. "I hope you don't mind. I know we didn't see eye to eye in the end, but, well, you know. Hopefully she's found some peace at last."

Lily senses a response is required, but the words aren't coming to her. Aunt Edie watches her for a moment and then continues, "You

11

were eight years old last time I saw you. Do you remember? You used to come round for tea every Thursday? You don't look like you've had a decent meal since, look at the size of you." She turns Lily from side to side. "There's nothing of you, and what's going on with your hair? You used to have lovely hair."

Lily's mind fills with memories of beef paste sandwiches and wagon wheels. "But what happened? I mean Mum told me you'd ... well." Lily's cheeks start to flush as she tries to run a hand through her dreadlocks.

"What did she tell you?" Aunt Edie cottons on. "She told you I died? She never. Bloody hell. You wouldn't put anything past that one. She always was a-" The vicar walks up to them and smiles. Aunt Edie almost curtsies. She doesn't complete her sentence.

"I'm going to have to dash, I'm afraid," says the vicar. "I have another, engagement."

"I actually went to your funeral," says Lily, once the vicar has moved on. She stubs her cigarette out on the nearest headstone. "I knew something was odd at the time, but I was only eight. Mum told me not to speak to anyone; she said it was rude to talk at funerals. And then we left straight after you, well, after someone was cremated."

Bert pulls heavily on the stub of his borrowed Lambert and Butler. Lily chews the inside of her mouth. "Well, there was me saying to Bert I didn't have any family, and now I've got an aunt I thought was dead." She lines the extinguished cigarette up between her thumb and middle finger nail.

"You've still got a dad as far as I know," says Aunt Edie.

Lily flicks the stub and watches it sail through the air and land in the grass between the headstones. She wipes the sweat from her palms onto her black canvas trousers. "I was just coming to that."

Chapter 3

Lily props Bert up against the privet hedge while she fumbles with the latch on his garden gate. The nearest street lamp is broken, the light burning a dull orange, too low to make any impact on the surrounding dark. It fizzes as it burns. Lily pulls Bert's arm around her shoulder again and drags him up the path to the front door, "Key?"

"It's in me pocket," says Bert, trying to stand up straight to allow Lily to reach into the front of his suit trousers.

"I'm not that pissed," says Lily, holding out her hand for the key.

Once inside, Lily leads him into the front room and drops him into the fake leather armchair. The covering on the arm has peeled off, leaving a scorched bald patch where the ashtray would normally sit. Lily glances around and sees it on the floor, its contents spilled. She picks it up and returns it to its rightful position. "See you then, Bert."

"I miss her, Lil."

Lily doesn't reply. She lets herself out of his house and back down the path.

In some ways the estate feels like toy town. As a teenager Lily used to walk home, pissed, at all hours of night, past the rows of identical 1940s council houses, each window trimmed with net curtains. Front lawns the size of handkerchiefs edged with matching privet hedges. She never once felt threatened.

Everyone knows everyone. If it weren't for the occasional burnt out wreck of a car, you could almost imagine the original vision, 'Homes fit for heroes'. Lily lets herself into the house next door. The smell makes her retch as soon as she steps over the threshold.

She's spent the last six days here, but the smell won't go, no matter how many tins of Floral Harmony she sprays.

She turns into the front room and flicks on the light. A bare bulb illuminates the room, which looks even smaller without furniture. When her mother was alive, a reinforced settee had taken up almost all the floor space, but it wasn't here when Lily arrived and no one has mentioned it since.

Lily sits on the floor and pours herself a vodka from the half empty bottle. She uses the same glass she's used for the last six days. She rests the back of her head against the wall behind her and wonders for a moment what her mother would have made of her wake. Stupid question, seeing as how her mother hadn't left the house in ten years. There would have been more chance of getting her mother to the moon than to the back room at the Dog and Duck.

Lily opens her eyes and focuses on the pair of bolt cutters leaning against the side of the gas fire. She bought them three days ago from Mr Bhopal's Tardis-like hardware store, and they've stood, unused, in their current position ever since. Lily takes a mouthful of vodka and crawls across the room to them. She kneels and picks them up, the weight of them pulling on her biceps. She makes a cutting gesture with them, as if practising for the task that lies ahead. She's told herself, as a mark of respect, she'll wait until morning; the dawning of a new, motherless, era.

Lily stands and closes the curtains. The minutes tick past on the small carriage clock on the mantelpiece. It's almost 2 a.m. Occasionally she hears the sound of a car engine on the estate, or the distant echo of a police siren, but mainly there is silence. The only furniture in the front room now is the dresser, its centre drawers on the verge of collapse, and the television. It's difficult to stand and watch television. Lily drains her glass and reaches again for the bolt cutters.

The metal padlock on the loft hatch has rusted over the years. To Lily's knowledge it has never been opened. She spent the first two days she was here, ransacking the house for a key, but at the back of her mind she had known she wouldn't find one. For as long as she can remember she's fantasized about getting past that padlock, knowing the secrets of her past must lie up there.

Her old desk chair wobbles beneath her as Lily holds up the bolt cutters and snips at the thick metal. The cutters slice through it, just as Mr Bhopal had told her they would, and the padlock falls to the floor, narrowly missing Lily's head on its descent. Lily pushes against the wooden trap door and sees a set of metal stepladders. They make such a racket as she pulls them down, she's afraid they will wake the dead.

It's pitch dark in the loft. Lily flicks the light switch but nothing happens. She climbs back down the ladder and takes the bulb from her mother's bedroom, standing on piles of yellowing *News of the Worlds* to do so. Back in the loft, Lily has to replace the bulb by the light of her cigarette, her hand shaking. She switches on the light and is momentarily blinded. It takes a while for her eyes to adjust and allow her to focus on the contents of the room. Cobwebs hang from the ceiling, which is so low Lily cannot stand up straight. Two suitcases and a couple of boxes, the proper, old-fashioned, tea chest kind, are grouped together in the centre of the gloom. Lily guesses they were put up there when they first moved in, when Lily was just a baby. Lily reaches for the nearest suitcase and flicks open the catches.

Inside are clothes, men's clothes. She pulls out the first item, a brown shirt with thin white stripes, ironed and neatly folded on the top of the pile. The buttons are done up. She holds it to her face and smells mustiness, mixed with a hint of pine aftershave. Lily holds up the shirt in front of her and as the folds drop out so do the arms, falling onto her lap, each neatly cut off at the shoulder. She pulls out a pair of trousers, with creases like tramlines, and a hole where the crotch should be. Lily doesn't know what makes her feel saddest; the thought of her mother neatly ironing and folding her husband's clothes after she's hacked them to pieces, or the fact that her father obviously never returned to notice.

She reaches for one of the wooden packing crates. Inside are books. Her mum was never much of a reader, unless you count Mills and Boon, which Lily didn't. She picks up the top one; it has a picture of a fat frog and a pink flower on the cover, *You only live twice, Ian Fleming* is written on the front. Lily's seen the film. She holds the book up to her face and smells the paper as she flicks through the pages. Then, with her hands trembling, she turns to the front page, hope making her hold her breath. But if a name was written there, and it probably was, it has been cut out; a small, neat rectangle of paper missing in the top right hand corner. Lily turns to the back page and realises it's missing.

Lily swears under her breath and reaches for the second box. It contains a record collection: The Rolling Stones, The Beatles, a seven inch copy of *Leader of the Pack* by the Shangri-Las, and *I*

Got You, Babe by Sonny and Cher. The box is full. Lily had always thought the theme tune to Coronation Street was the closest her mum had ever come to music. Simon and Garfunkel, The Kinks, Dusty Springfield. Lily bites her lip as she slides *Sgt. Pepper's Lonely Hearts Club Band* out. It comes out of its sleeve in three separate pieces.

Lily notices through the cracks in the airbricks that it's getting light. The bottle of vodka she brought with her is empty, and the heap of clothes feels slightly damp. She stands up too quickly, hitting her head against a low beam and falls to her knees, momentarily stunned. When her head stops hurting, she goes downstairs. She rummages through her pockets and finds, scribbled on a piece of paper, in old lady handwriting, Aunt Edie's telephone number.

As she listens to the ringing phone, she has a flash of memory of Aunt Edie's funeral. Her mother, already gigantic, in a black tent of a dress, hurrying her out of the churchyard as an elderly couple had approached them. The man had a gold ring on his finger with a red jewel that had sparkled in the sunlight. Lily had wondered whether he was the Pope. She had opened her mouth to ask, but her mother had pushed her out of the gate so hard she had almost fallen over.

"Hello?" A tremulous voice answers the phone.

"Aunt Edie? It's me, Lily."

"Heavens child, what time is it?"

Lily glances across at the carriage clock on the mantelpiece. It takes her a moment to work out that it's half past five. "Shit, I mean sorry, I didn't realise," Lily takes a breath. "I need to see you."

Chapter 4

Aunt Edie's house smells of vinegar, perfectly preserved, it's exactly how it was the last time Lily visited. Memories assault her from all angles. The china dogs that she'd pretended to feed and take for walks are still on the hearth; the ashtray with a black cat in the centre, that Lily's mother had painted when she was a child, is still on the windowsill.

Aunt Edie is bustling around in her kitchen, wearing her floral pinny, delighted to have company. She hands Lily an American Cream Soda. The glass is the same glass Lily drank out of twelve years ago, with glass bubbles in the bottom. Aunt Edie sings along to Andy Williams on the radio, out of tune and about four words behind.

They sit down at the small wooden table in the corner of the sitting room, where Aunt Edie has laid out lunch. "Oh, it's so nice to see you, Lily."

"I need to find my dad," Lily blurts

"Would you like salmon or beef paste? I got the beef special this morning."

"I want to find my dad." Lily says, louder this time.

"Of course you do pet, no need to shout. I take it you've not seen him? Not ever?" Lily shakes her head and tries to stop herself ripping the skin from the sides of her thumbs. "What did your mother tell you?"

"Nothing, I don't know anything about him. I looked in the loft last night. Found some old clothes and his record collection, but..." she hesitates at telling Aunt Edie what her mother had done, "but there was nothing that would help me find him."

"She was a different woman altogether in those days, Lil. She loved him so much. Never looked at another man. She got with him

17

when she was seventeen. Always said she was going to marry him. He didn't stand a chance." Aunt Edie chuckles to herself. "Ay, she was determined, stubborn as a mule. Always was. The happiest bride I've ever seen."

"So, what happened?"

"He ran off with another woman," says Aunt Edie, as she tears the cellophane lid off the beef paste. "And it broke her heart, simple as that. She swore she'd never recover and she never did. Like I said, stubborn as stubborn." Aunt Edie stands up and fiddles with the teapot. "That's what I told her in the end. She was determined not to get over it and it wasn't fair, Lil. It wasn't fair on you, or on anyone around her. I told her she had to move on and that was that. She never spoke to me again. Once she made her mind up about something. Well you know what she's like, was like." She sits down heavily in her chair again. "Oh dear, I still can't believe she's passed over."

"What was he like," Lily asks, "my dad?"

Aunt Edie spreads a dollop of butter as thick as clotted cream on her bread roll, while she considers the question. "He was handsome," she says after some time. "But never trust a handsome man, that's what I always say. Thank the good Lord my Arthur wasn't anything to look at." She pauses for thought and to spread a broad smear of salmon paste on her barm cake. "He were carrying on, course, but no one knew a thing about it. He used to play snooker with our Terry and he didn't have an inkling. And there was your mum, all pregnant, just about to have you. Terrible really." She takes a large bite out of her creation. "It did for your grandmother," she adds with her mouth full, "Sent her to an early grave."

"I need to find him, Aunt Edie. I need to get some sense of where I'm from. I want to know about my past."

Aunt Edie looks her up and down as she chews. She finally swallows. "I have something for you. Your granddad gave it to me for safekeeping when your granny died. I think he knew he wouldn't last long without her. I didn't really know what to do with it while your mother was alive. She'd have had my guts for garters if I'd given it to you." She stands up again. "Mad as a wasp she'd have been. Wait there."

A few minutes later Aunt Edie returns carrying a rectangular box. "I don't know why he wanted you to have this. You see, your granddad never did like David, your dad. Always said he weren't to be trusted. And turns out he were right, of course. But I think your granny must have wanted you to have it. I think she knew you'd be curious one day." She hands the box to Lily. "You have a look at it love, while I check on the custard."

Lily takes the box. She puts it on the table in front of her and eases off the cardboard lid. Inside she can see a large, cream coloured book, with a sheet of see-through crepe paper laid over the top of it. Lily's hands start to shake. She slides off the crepe paper and reads the gold lettering on the front, 'Wedding Album'. She'd often wondered whether her parents were married. She opens the first page:

In celebration of the marriage of David Winterbottom
and Miss Pamela Lillian Tattersall
16th May 1965
At the Church of our Virgin Mary, Clitheroe

Lily holds her breath and turns over the page, ready for her first glimpse of her father.

But the first picture is of the bride, and Lily's first thought is that Aunt Edie's given her the wrong wedding album. That wasn't her mother. Confused, Lily turns back to the front page. Her father's name was David Winterbottom. She only knew that because she'd ransacked the house eight or so years ago, when her mother had been admitted to hospital for a few days. Lily had found her birth certificate hidden in an old teapot. Remembering a news item she'd seen, about a child whose estranged father had abducted him from school, she'd stashed the birth certificate inside the lining of her school bag just in case. Pathetic really.

Lily brings her mind back to the page in front of her. Her mum's name was Pamela. Lily had long suspected Appleyard was neither her maiden, nor her married name. Lily turns the page again. The photograph is of a slim, beautiful bride with long blonde hair, laughing as she runs along a stone path. Slim, like Marilyn Monroe slim. Six men line the way, holding umbrellas up to protect her from the pouring rain. She's holding her skirts up as the rain bounces on the ground around her. The men are smiling at her, admiring her verve. The rain is torrential; Lily can almost make out the individual drops. She squints at the picture again. The woman laughs back at her, attractive, happy and slim.

Lily doesn't recognise any of the men holding the umbrellas. Could one be her father? It's not even important at this moment.

19

The thought strikes Lily that she never saw her mother laugh. A wave of jealousy sweeps through her body, someone else could make her laugh. She wants to know this woman in the picture. For the first time since her mother died she feels a sense of loss.

She turns the page and gets her first sighting of the bride and groom. Hands clasped together, gazing into each other's eyes, grinning inanely. Her mum appears enraptured, lost in love, alive. Her father is tall and slender, and rock star handsome.

She wants to close the book, but like a scab that shouldn't be picked, she can't leave it alone. They look so young and hopeful. All Lily's life she's been longing to know her father. It had never once occurred to her that she didn't know her mother either.

The bride is wearing a sleek satin dress, no frills or ruffles, beautifully skimmed across the front to emphasize her tucked in waist. Lily compares her to the mental image she has of her mother, fat hanging off her legs like saddlebags. The woman in the photo has long blonde hair scooped up on the top of her head, the occasional strand curling down past her neck. The groom wears black rimmed spectacles and a dark suit. His hair is slightly spiked. Lily wonders what it would have been like to have had these two as parents.

In the next picture are two people she does recognise. Her grandparents standing either side of the bride and groom. Lily's father is staring straight at the camera, and Lily notices his deep brown eyes, same as her own. Granny is smiling, with David's arm loosely around her shoulders. Lily's grandfather stands straight-backed, not touching his daughter. Lily senses that his smile doesn't reach his eyes.

Another photograph shows the groom, her father, with his ushers. She doesn't recognise any of them. Frustrated, she turns through the pages until she comes to a guest list at the back. Lily's eyes flick down the list. The wedding was overrun by Winterbottoms.

The gas fire is on full, despite the autumn sunshine pressing on the windows. Lily tries to open a window, banging against it with the palm of her hand. It doesn't budge. Aunt Edie appears behind her, carrying two plates. She puts the plates down on the table and fetches a box of tissues from the mantelpiece. "Here pet."

Lily takes a tissue and scrunches it up into a ball in her fist. "Do you know, I never saw her laugh?"

Aunt Edie tuts and shakes her head, "Would you like a Mr Kipling with custard?"

"I spent my life growing up with someone who wasn't actually there. Can you imagine what that's like?" Lily's voice rises by an octave. "Knowing no matter how hard you try, you're never going to make her happy?"

"Come on love." Aunt Edie starts ladling custard. "You need some meat on your bones."

"I don't mind him leaving so much, shit happens, I know that, but it's like I lost both my parents because of him. Do you know what I mean?"

Aunt Edie heaves herself up from her chair and comes to Lily's side. "There, there pet." She pulls Lily's head against her ample bosom. "I know. I know. You let it all out."

Chapter 5

It's dark by the time Lily gets home, and the electric meter has run out of credit. She didn't notice the drizzle during the forty-five minutes she spent waiting at the bus stop, but she's soaked to the skin. She lights the gas fire and draws the curtains, before stripping her sodden clothes from her body and wrapping herself in her duvet. Once she's poured herself a drink, she opens the wedding album but she can hardly make out the people by the glow of the gas fire. The local Spar sells electricity tokens, but Lily hasn't the energy. When morning pushes through the cracks in the curtains, Lily is asleep on the floor. The gas fire is still burning.

Four days pass in a blur, until the silence that shrouds the house is broken by a bell sound like an alarm. It takes Lily a moment to connect the noise to the telephone.

"Could I speak to Lily Appleyard?" asks a pleasant female voice.

"Who is it?"

"I'm calling from Leeds Polytechnic."

"She's not in," Lily mumbles.

"Oh, do you know when she'll be back? Or if she's planning to return to her course?" Lily leans against the wall for support and closes her eyes. When will Lily be back? For some reason the Whitesnake song, *Here I Go Again,* starts to play in her head. The woman on the phone coughs politely. Lily wants to say Lily will never be back. Lily no longer exists, but that may lead to awkward questions.

Lily casts around the room, searching for clues. Her eyes fall on the pile of unopened letters, junk mail and free newspapers that have built up by the front door. On the top of the pile is a copy of the *Accrington Weekly News*. It's dated Thursday 20th October. "Next Wednesday?" Lily suggests.

"Ok," says the woman cheerfully. "I'll call back then. Would you just tell her I called? Thank you."

Lily doesn't sleep that night. She lies awake, mulling over the scraps of information she'd been able to glean from Aunt Edie about her father. "I don't know where he is, could be on the other side of the world for all I know," Aunt Edie had blustered, fiddling with the plastic place mats. But, she had admitted when pressed, she had heard a rumour he might have moved to Skipton. "I suppose he probably moved in with his fancy woman, leastways that's what Patsy Smith said in the butchers." Some eighteen or nineteen years ago. "I think it was Skipton," she added vaguely. "In Yorkshire." Like it was the other side of the world.

As soon as it gets light, Lily pulls on her black canvas trousers and a dark green sweatshirt, which some bloke had once left at her flat after a particularly awful one-night stand, and wanders down to the bus station. She finds the bus that will take her to Skipton and asks the driver to shout to her when it's time to get off. It's market day and the stall-holders are out in sheepskin coats. Lily wanders through the cobbled streets, paying particular attention to any white man in his late forties, early fifties. She spots three possibilities in the space of seven minutes, including a man in a black bomber jacket who has a dimple in his cheek, just like Lily's. She buys a peach and sits down on the steps of the stone cross to eat it.

As the coldness seeps into her bones, she notices a sign on the building opposite, Public Library. The building is old and built out of sandstone, and Lily pushes through the revolving doors. She stands in the doorway, unsure in what direction to head.

An elderly librarian wanders over and asks if she needs any help. "I'm looking for someone who used to live here, maybe nineteen years ago."

"Have you tried looking in the local paper? We keep every copy there ever was, on microfiche." Twenty minutes later, Lily is reading her first ever copy of the *Craven Herald and Pioneer*, 'The Voice of the Dales since 1853'. As she reads stories about Sheep Day, and whether the public toilets in Coach Street should be cleaned more regularly, she loses track of time. Her head starts to ache and her eyes are sore as she flicks through the 1970s. The Births, Marriages and Deaths columns start to swim before her eyes.

Abruptly, she stands up, pushing back her chair so hard its legs scrape the wooden floor, causing everyone in the library to raise their heads and stare at her. She runs for the door. On her way through the town centre she sees the bus for Accrington, standing waiting at the bus stop. She runs as fast as she can and manages to throw herself between the closing doors.

One morning she wakes up on the floor of the living room, fully clothed. The pressure on her bladder is what's caused her to wake. She tries to stand but her legs are so stiff, she finds it easier to crawl along the carpet into the hall. It's there that she notices a letter on the doormat, addressed to her. How long it's been lying there is anybody's guess. The urgent need to urinate seems to leave her body as she picks up the letter and sits on the bottom stair. The quality of the envelope sets it apart from the mound of junk mail by the door. It's from the Salvation Army. Lily stares at the envelope, turns it over in her trembling hands, before peeling it open:

> *'Dear Lily, We have received your letter regarding your father, David Winterbottom and our enquiries regarding his whereabouts are now underway. Please be assured that we will contact you as soon as we have any information. In the meantime, if you could refrain from contacting the office, we would be grateful. We are a charitable organisation and dealing with telephone enquiries can severely limit our resources.*
> *Signed on behalf of Major Farley-Greystone.'*

Lily reads it four times, her eyes watering at the strain of focussing on the print. She sets it to one side while she eventually remembers to go to the toilet, and then picks it back up again and reads it another three times. She tidies away the empty bottles, stacks them neatly outside the back door, before picking up the phone. A woman answers on the second ring.

"Hello?"

"Can I speak to Major Farley-Greystone?"

"I'm afraid he's not in right now. May I help?"

"S'complicated." Lily realises her words are slurred. She wonders whether the two vodkas she had to try to steady her nerves were a good idea. She stands straighter.

"Oh. It's only my second week but I can try."

"It's just; I'm trying to find my dad and I've had this letter saying that you've started, I mean I know I'm not supposed to ring it's just..." She bites her lip until she can taste blood. "It's just I really need to find him."

The woman tuts sympathetically. "When did you last see him?"

"I've never met him, well, not that I remember. He…" Lily thinks quickly and revises the version of events Aunt Edie gave her. "My mum left him, and my Aunt says he was heartbroken, because he loved me so much. And now my mum's died. And I'm all alone."

"Oh, I am sorry."

"I've been trying to find him myself and I don't know how to do it. And I really need, I really need somebody to help me."

"Well, I'm not really supposed to give out any information." Lily closes her eyes and doesn't speak. "How old are you?" the woman asks.

"Seventeen," says Lily, shaving a couple of years off. "And the thing is, I'm not very well. The doctors say I shouldn't be under stress but I'm all alone, I don't have any money, anywhere to live-"

"What name is it?"

"Lily."

"I meant your father's name?"

"David, David Winterbottom."

"Oh."

From the tone of the woman's voice, Lily knows she knows something. "What? Oh please," she begs. "I can't take the not knowing."

"Well, like I say, I'm not really supposed to say anything but," Lily can almost sense the woman looking over her shoulder. "Major Farley-Greystone went through your case as part of my induction last week."

"And?" Lily holds her breath.

"All I can say is, I think you'll be hearing from him soon."

"You mean they've found him? He's not dead?"

"He's not dead." The woman's voice is gentle and Lily can tell she's smiling. "But don't say I told you so. Ok?"

"Thank you. Thank you so much." Lily puts down the phone and lets out a loud screech.

Sitting in a dazed heap under the windowsill, Lily experiences a new feeling. She has something to go on for. She lifts her head and sees the front room through new eyes. And the thought strikes her that she can't let her father see the house like this. It must be cleaned and she hasn't got long. She hurries through to the kitchen to find a pen and some paper and starts to make a list. Furniture polish, bleach, bin liners, cloths, rubber gloves. She chews the end of her pen thoughtfully and gazes out of the kitchen window. The small back garden is completely overgrown. The rusting springs of an old mattress poke up through the grass. Lily used to have loads of bonfires out there, just to get out of the house. It's getting dark now. The kitchen clock shows it's almost five. Not really time to start now. What she needs is a new day, a clean slate to symbolise the new life she's about to begin. She pours herself another vodka from the bottle on the kitchen table.

Chapter 6

The next morning Lily's first thought is of her father. A smile eats its way across her face and she springs out of bed. She makes herself a slice of toast and a cup of black tea, adding butter and milk to the shopping list as she does so. Then she goes up the steps into the loft and pulls the suitcase of her father's clothes down the ladders. In her mother's bedroom, she opens the suitcase and spreads the clothes out carefully on the bed, trying to gain some sense of the man. Lily finds a roll of Sellotape and tries to attach the arms on as best she can, and then hangs whole outfits on coat hangers on the front of the fitted wardrobes. They look like headless scarecrows; some crazy kind of art installation. Lily wants to stuff the trouser legs to give them substance, but the Sellotape is barely holding them together as it is. Downstairs she adds safety pins to the shopping list.

At lunchtime, as Lily is getting dressed for the shopping trip, the doorbell rings. She almost falls over as she struggles to get her trousers on. It couldn't be him already, surely? They wouldn't give him her address without some warning, would they? She jumps down the stairs, her hands shaking as she opens the door. A large man wearing a dark suit and sunglasses stands before her. Lily's mouth is dry.

"Pamela Appleyard?" he asks. Lily shakes her head, disappointment floods her body. "Is she in?"

Lily shakes her head again. "Well, she hasn't been paying her account. She's overdue. I'm here to collect the telly." He shrugs as he pushes past her. Moments later he returns with the giant black box in his arms, its flex curled like a snake on the top. "Have a nice day," he says, as he strides towards the gate. Lily nods.

The next morning the sun shines down from a clear blue sky. The leaves on the stray Sycamore have turned golden. Lily knocks on Bert's door and asks to borrow his lawn mower and hedge cutters. "Mine could do with a trim." He nods at his patch of dandelion clocks.

"Sorry, Bert. Haven't got time."

He scratches his groin. "Aw, come on, you've got time for a drink with me, haven't you?" he wheedles. "I've not seen you since the... you know."

Lily shakes her head. "Sorry, Bert. I've got stuff to do."

He watches her lug the rusty old lawn mower down his path. "Why don't you come round later? I've got steak and kidney pudding."

"I'm vegetarian," she calls back from the street, which isn't strictly true but she does draw the line at Fray Bentos. "But thanks."

The grass is too long for the lawn mower and also appears to be full of stones, so Lily fetches a chair from the kitchen. She stands on it to cut the hedge in the still warm sunshine and snaps at a few leaves, but her arms are screaming at the effort required to hold the shears aloft.

At the local SPAR, Lily refuels with a cheese and onion pasty and a packet of prawn cocktail Skips. She wanders around the shelves, trying to visualise what else is written on the shopping list, which is sitting at home on the kitchen worktop. She adds a loaf of bread and tub of margarine to her basket. As soon as she gets home she puts the kettle on, but then realises she's forgotten to get milk, so she pours herself a very weak vodka and orange instead, to help the pasty go down. Fortified, she has another chop at the garden, but the sun has lost its warmth and Lily's breath hangs like icicles. She goes inside and lights the gas fire.

Lily spends another evening staring at the wedding album, tracing her father's face with her finger, unable to believe that soon this face will be fleshed out for her.

The next two weeks slip quietly past, Lily content in her domesticity. She borrows a wheelbarrow from Mr Peterson and spends three days wheeling her mother's empty Coca Cola bottles to the recycling bins in the supermarket car park. The Special Brew tin cans, she bags up in black bin liners in the back garden. As soon as she can face spending any time with him, she's going to ask Bert if he'll drive her down to the tip. She bought a pack of safety pins too, so her father's arms and legs are hanging on with more confidence in her mother's bedroom.

Lily wakes to the sound of the postman whistling as he closes the gate. She runs downstairs, as she does every day now, to check what has arrived. And today it beams up at her from the doormat, a slim, white envelope with her name on the front. She jumps down the last four stairs in one swoop and pounces on it:

> *Dear Lily*
> *We are writing to advise you that we have now concluded our enquiries with regard to your father, David. Unfortunately, it has not been possible for us to reunite you with your father, and we are left with no alternative but to bring our investigations to a close. We do understand that you will be disappointed at the outcome of this enquiry, but can only assure you that everything possible has been done on your behalf.*
>
> *May God bless you.*

For a while the silence is only broken by a strange throbbing in her ears, where she swears she can feel the membranes of her brain. Her head swims as she tries to understand. Her first thought, her worst fear, the one that's festered since she was a small child, is that her father is dead. Did the stupid receptionist get it wrong? Is that why she needs God's blessing? Is she an orphan, destined to know neither her mother nor father? The days are getting shorter and the light is already starting to fade by the time she rings the number written on the top of the letter.

"Good afternoon, Major Farley-Greystone speaking. How may I be of assistance?"

He coughs when she tells him her name. "I just want you to explain what your letter means…" Lily starts. The Major doesn't speak. "I mean, can't you find him? Has he emigrated?" Lily chews a fingernail. "What does that mean, 'It has not been possible to reunite me'?, It could mean anything."

"Yes." His tone is slow and deliberate. "I can see where the confusion arises." Another lengthy pause but this time Lily rides it out. "I, er, I was trying to break the news gently."

Lily closes her eyes. "Is he, is he dead?"

He coughs again, clearing his throat. "No. I, well, we did manage to ascertain his location. He isn't dead, but, well there isn't an easy way to tell you this. He doesn't want to get in touch with you."

Lily counts the flower petals on the wallpaper and wonders why she's never noticed how uneven the pattern was; the ink doesn't run to the edges of the outlines, cheap crap. She becomes aware that she's holding the phone to her ear but no one is speaking. "Is he allowed to do that?" Her voice rises in pitch. "I mean, doesn't he, don't I have a right..."

"We have to respect his wishes." The Major seeks to stamp out this line of enquiry. "If the boot was on the other foot, as it were; if he'd tried to contact you, we would respect your right to say no."

"But that's totally different," Lily is confused, "I never left him, I've never even met him." She tries to breathe, collect her thoughts. She presses her forehead against the cool glass of the front room window. "I have questions. What about..." she casts wildly around, trying to think of some justification as to why it is her right to meet the man who fathered her, "my health. When I registered at the doctors, I couldn't even complete the form because I don't know anything about my genes."

The Major doesn't respond. Lily senses she's not going to win this man over with mention of her rights. Her body sags. "Did he say why?" a small voice, a little girl's voice she doesn't recognise, asks.

"I'm afraid I am unable to give you details."

"Has he a heart complaint? Or..." Her mind flails around, trying to think of valid reasons for a man not to want to meet his daughter, his only child.

The Major sighs heavily. "He says he has never been in contact with you. Is that correct?"

"I have no idea, that's the point. Did you explain my circumstances to him?"

"Look..."

"Does he know my mother's dead? Did you try to persuade him? Couldn't you..."

Major Farley-Greystone sighs again, even louder this time, so it sounds like a gust of wind whistling down the phone. "Can't you accept…"

"Will you ask him if he'll meet me just once? If you explain…"

"Listen, I can tell you he wrote us a letter and it says... bear with me." As she hears the rustle of paper, Lily hates this man for the power he holds over her; for the fact he's holding a letter from her father in his hand; that he knows what it says, what his handwriting is like, he knows where he lives and... "Yes, here we are." His words are fired as if from a machine gun. "He's written, and I quote, 'I have no…'" Major Farley-Greystone stresses the word no, makes it last several seconds, "wish to communicate.'" The Major pauses, allows the weight of the sentence to hit home before continuing. "The word 'no' is in capital letters…" there's a dramatic pause, as Lily feels the hairs on the back of her neck stand to attention, "and underlined."

He finishes with a flourish; as if confident he has now demonstrated to her that there is no possible way in the whole world that her father would ever want to meet her. How much more definite can a man get; capital letters and underscoring.

Every childhood fantasy Lily's ever entertained dies in that moment. The hours, weeks, probably even years of her life she's spent dreaming of him and their eventual meeting. Everything dies, collapses. Lily slides down onto the floor, her back against the wall and bumps the back of her head against it to try to ease the pain.

The Major sighs again. "You see, this is why we tell people not to trace people if they can't handle rejection," he blusters. "Don't start getting all upset now. It won't do you any good."

Lily hangs up, because the receiver is making her ear ache. She curls up in a ball, like a kitten, hugging her knees to her chest. When she comes to she isn't sad anymore. She stands up and kicks out at the wall and then winces in pain as she realises she's not wearing shoes. Anger and despair collide. She wants to run out into the street, grab her father, hold him against the wall and force him into a conversation. Hold a gun to his head. Why didn't he want to see her? Did he know something about her? Something that made him know he didn't want to meet her? Did he know anything about her? If he didn't then why wouldn't he at least be curious? She wants his address, wants to turn up on his doorstep, to lie in wait for him. No way is this the end.

Nights merge into day, with no distinguishing features. She stops dressing, cleaning her teeth, caring at all. She's drinking heavily and existing solely on toast and Marmite. The house slowly reverts to its normal state. The empties start to pile up again.

And then one day the phone rings. Lily is sitting next to it as it suddenly bursts into life and she picks up the handset automatically, to stop the noise, without thinking whether she wants to speak to anyone. Her voice is hoarse.

"Hello?"

"Lily!" A female voice screeches at her.

It takes a moment for Lily's brain to process the information. Her brow creases, making her eyebrows ache. "Jo?"

"Why haven't you rung me? I've been going out of my mind worrying about you. I had to steal your phone number from student services."

"You didn't?"

"Why haven't you rung me, you cow? I was worried I was never going to see you again. It's been over a month, Lily. Where the fuck have you been? What are you doing? Are you coming back? You room's still here you know."

"Oh Jo, I didn't, I can't, I don't know..." Lily closes her eyes.

"Tell me where you live, Lily. I'm coming to get you."

Chapter 7

It takes less than three hours for Jo to appear on Lily's doorstep. "Jesus Christ girl, look at the state of you," says Jo, as she grabs hold of Lily and hugs her tightly. Lily nearly faints at the intensity. Jo steps inside, into the front room and, without meaning to, recoils slightly. Lily looks around at the small, chocolate brown room, and sees it for the first time through a stranger's eyes. Dark brown curtains, that may or may not have been patterned once upon a time, hang haphazardly at the window. The walls are streaked with nicotine stains and the gas fire burns yellow in the centre of the room. The floor is littered with chip wrappers, polystyrene boxes, empty bottles and full ashtrays. "Like what you're doing with the place, Lil. It's bold, it's uncompromising..."

"I'm a mess. You shouldn't see me like this. No one should see me like this."

"Shut up." Jo climbs over a couple of boxes full of newspapers. "I'm your best mate. What's the smell?"

"Don't ask."

"Where's the sofa?"

"Oh I... I think probably, I don't know, probably my mum rotted onto it."

"Ok." Jo stretches out the 'K', making it last about seven seconds. She looks around the room sizing up their options. "Let's clear a bit of space in front of the fire. I've brought food and spliff."

Jo's wearing a T-shirt that says, 'fuck the right to vote', but for all her revolutionary politics, she has never witnessed such squalor first hand. The house they share in Leeds could never be described as posh, but it's an old Victorian terrace with high ceilings. Neglected for the past twenty years by successive landlords, it still contains a hint of former glory. Here, in this 1950s council house, the walls tell of cheapness and mundanity. Nothing great ever happened here. No one ever cared for this place, not the architect who designed it, the builder who built it, the council who own it, nor any of its inhabitants.

Jo starts clearing a space with her feet, kicking the rubbish to one side. Underneath, the carpet is cheap, brown nylon with deep ridges that look like they would cause pain if sat upon. "There must be something we can sit on, Lil. What about a mattress?"

"There's one on my mum's bed upstairs," Lily ventures. Jo hesitates, images of Lily's rotting mum, still at the forefront of her mind. "She hasn't slept... hadn't sleep in it for years. She couldn't climb the stairs."

"Come on then, let's get comfy. Let's pile all this stuff up against the wall and then we can carry it downstairs."

It is not until Lily opens the door of her mother's bedroom that she remembers her father's clothes hanging from the fitted wardrobe door handles. Jo looks at her quizzically. Lily shrugs her shoulders. "It's a long story."

Together they lug the mattress, half throwing it down the stairs, and lie it on the floor in the front room, one side against the wall, to form a makeshift settee. Lily gathers as many pillows, cushions, and duvets as she can find, and they then both collapse on top of it, exhausted from their exertions.

"Tomorrow, you and I are going to get this place looking great, but this will do for now. Now, get your laughing tackle round this," she passes her a huge joint she's pulled from her canvas bag, "and then we'll eat." Jo's been through the kitchen while Lily was upstairs fetching blankets, and found a couple of small bottles of Coke and half a pint of suspect milk in the fridge. In the cupboards, a couple of ancient looking pot noodles, a few tins of baked beans and half a packet of chocolate hobnobs, stare back at her. "You've got way too skinny, Lil. You look like Lena fucking Zavaroni."

Lily takes a deep drag on the spliff. She's missed her dope; she's been drinking more to compensate, and the hangovers have been getting her down. But she finds drink better for holding onto anger and she so much prefers the anger; afraid the sadness might kill her. Even the smallest acts of kindness are now enough to send her completely over the edge. The man in the corner shop had let her off 20p yesterday. She'd run out, her face so red she might have been slapped.

"I'm really sorry about your mum, Lil."

34

"Thanks." Lily lies back on the mattress and closes her eyes. "I always thought I'd be pleased, not, 'oh hurrah, she's dead, but thank God I don't have to worry about her anymore' you know?" She opens an eye, Jo nods but she has no idea. "But there's more than that. A lot's happened."

Jo pulls packets of salt and vinegar crisps from her bag. She opens a bottle of Thunderbird and pours it into two chipped tea cups she finds in the kitchen.

"You know that letter you posted for me? I wrote that when I was thirteen. It wasn't really a letter; it was an application form, to find my dad. I could never find him before; my mum would have killed me. I had to wait for her to die."

"Here," says Jo, handing her a teacup. Lily sits up to take it, she takes a mouthful.

"I got so impatient at times, I thought of killing her myself." A memory forces itself into Lily's mind. She shudders and pushes on. "And then finally she dies and my first thought is 'I'll get to meet my dad'. I know that sounds bad, but you don't know what my mum was like." Lily stares at the gas fire, smoking.

"Lily? What was she like?"

Lily looks up, almost surprised to see Jo. "She was..." she searches for the right word. "Fat. I mean really, hugely fat. She must have weighed fifty stone. She didn't leave the house for the last ten years. She sat on the sofa, eating crap and watching telly." Jo looks around the room. "They repossessed it," Lily explains. "And she drank about ten cans of Special Brew a night. I was so scared of anyone coming to my house, I used to leave school and head in the opposite direction until all the other kids went home, and then I'd sneak back here. She was so fat she couldn't climb the stairs, so she used to shit in a bucket. When I left home the council finally put in a downstairs toilet."

"So, did they find your dad?"

Lily nods her head and bites her lip. She goes back to the gas fire. "He doesn't want to know. He has <u>NO</u> wish to communicate with me. Capital letters, underlined."

Jo looks confused.

"That's what he wrote back to them."

"Prick." Jo bends a pepperoni until it snaps in half. "Men; emotional sodding retards. Every single one of them; his loss." She bites into the salami. "He's not worthy, Lil."

35

"Do you see your dad?" Lily knows Jo's parents are divorced, but they hardly ever talk about their families.

"Yeah, about three times a year to take delivery of his guilt offloading presents. Mind you, I see him more now than I ever did when he lived with us. He was this guy in a suit that I occasionally use to pass in the hallway. He was always either at work or screwing his secretary. He's married to her now. She's three years older than me."

Jo nods her head as she watches Lily absorb what she is saying. "She was seventeen when he started having an affair with her," Jo continues. "He's 52. Pathetic."

Jo picks up the packet of Rizlas and takes three papers out. She lines two of them up and sticks them together, and then adds the third along the bottom. Lily feels her shoulders relax and her stomach gurgles away some of its tension. For the first time since she came here, she wants to go back to Leeds. Escape the memories of this house and its hold over her.

Lily tries to comfort herself with the facts. For years she had tried to get her mother better. On her first day at school she'd asked the teacher if he wanted to come home for tea. She knew then, aged four, that her mother needed saving. He didn't come. Then as her mother grew larger and the house grew more revolting, she'd stopped trying to get people to come; had concentrated more on trying to get her mum out. Nothing had worked. The day Lily left for university her mother had asked her not to go and Lily had lost it with her. She had screamed, "I am sick of watching you die. I've been doing it my whole life. Do it on your own if you're determined to do it," and slammed the door behind her.

Lily turns her attention back to Jo, pink tongue stuck out, sealing the spliff. "I went to see my Aunt," says Lily. "I thought she was dead but she showed up at my mum's funeral. And she gave me this photo album of my mum's wedding day. I'd never seen a photo of my mum from before I was born. I didn't recognise her, look." She pulls the album out of the top of one of the boxes for the tip. "I never saw her smile, not once." Lily takes the spliff Jo is offering and lies back on the mattress. She smokes in silence, while Jo leafs through the album.

"He's got your eyes."

"Do you know what?" says Lily, propping herself up on her elbow. "I can't believe it's legal. I can't believe that you can have a child and then leave it, abandon it to whatever life, without checking up on me... it, at all. He has no idea what kind of life I've had. He's never checked that someone's taking care of me. What if my mum had died fifteen years ago? Do you know what I mean? And now, he can refuse to meet me or give me any explanation? It should be against the law."

Jo nods. "It's called something like breach of promise." Jo had studied law for a year at polytechnic, before switching to the same politics degree as Lily. "Breach of contract, that's it. He was supposed to be a father but instead he turned out to be a useless prick."

"I should sue him."

"For damages."

"For the life I could have had if he hadn't left and taken me mum's heart with him." Lily smiles to show she's half joking. Jo takes the spliff from Lily's fingers.

"What do you think your life would have been like?"

"What, if my mum would have been as happy as she was then?" Lily nods towards the album. "God, it would have been completely different. I would have had clean clothes and learnt to play guitar. I used to hate kids with two parents; you know the ones that both turned up at parents' evening, sports' day. My mum never went to one. I used to make up all kinds of excuses for her, she was ill, my granny had died, she'd got a new job. They must have known I was lying; I got through about fifteen grandparents, but no one ever said anything. I used to fantasize about my dad taking me to football matches. I worried that he'd left because he'd wanted a boy not a girl. Stupid huh? But then why did he leave as soon as I was born? What was so disappointing?"

"He'll just be another sad ass bloke."

"I would have been normal. I'd be at the uni, living in halls of residence; one of those ones like what's-his-face lived in, with wardens on hand in case I couldn't work out how to use the tin opener. I'd have a big gang of friends with names like Tamara, we'd all be about to move into a house with central heating and a washing machine." Lily's spent a great deal of her time at polytechnic observing such students. She starts to laugh. "I could have been ordinary."

"We wouldn't be friends though, Tamara."

"And you know, it's not just him." Lily sobers up for a moment. "It's everyone. Where are all my relatives; his side of the family? I had no one growing up. My grandparents, my mum's mum and dad, died when I was little. I had Aunt Edie, but my mum pretended she was dead." Her anger surfaces again and Lily feels sick. "And the least my 'dad' could have done was to meet me, just once. Or at least write me a letter. The Salvation Army would have passed it on to me. Why didn't he at least explain why he didn't want to see me? He hasn't considered my feelings at all, ever. Not one moment in my whole life."

They are down to the last candle and it flickers bravely on. The Ginsters cheese and onion pasty has been at least nibbled and another bottle of vodka lies empty on the floor. Lily reaches for her cup, and as she does so, Jo notices the grubby bandages on her wrist. Lily catches her looking and pulls at her sleeves self-consciously.

"You're right Lily," says Jo a few moments later. "He owes you a meeting. So, let's set it up."

"What do you mean?"

"If he doesn't want to see you, let's go see him."

"We can't," says Lily, at the same time as a feeling of excitement floods her belly.

"Yes we can. Otherwise you're just another victim. Another woman who's let a man walk all over her and then beat herself up about it, rather than the arse that's responsible. This is a war, Lily." Jo's radical feminism has become legendary at polytechnic. She handed out photocopies of Solanas' SCUM manifesto on their first Sex and Gender tutorial. "It's time to start fighting back."

Lily stands up. "But what's the point? He doesn't want to see me. What would I do? Chase him down the street shouting, 'please be my dad?'" Standing up has made her light headed. She starts to giggle.

"He owes you an explanation, Lily." Jo is deadly calm. "He's a spineless bastard, and he owes you an apology at the very least. If the Salvation Army can find him, I'm damned sure we can. What the fuck made you pick them?"

"There are not exactly thousands of people out there queuing up to help reunite you with your birth family, you know. It was either them or Cilla and 'Surprise, Sur-bloody-prise'. Their motto is blood and fire." She shrugs. "I thought it sounded good."

She sits back down on the edge of the bed settee. "I've tried to find him. I got the bus to Skipton, that's where Aunt Edie said he lives, well she thinks. I went to the library and read about a million old copies of the local paper, I went back over ten years, nothing. I looked in births, marriages and deaths, everywhere. I spent all day there, 'til I went bog eyed."

"Did you try the phone book?"

They look at each other. Lily opens her mouth to speak but no words come out. They both burst out laughing. Lily laughs so hard she worries she may choke.

Chapter 8

Two men are chasing Lily; one is wearing a trilby hat and a long dark raincoat, the other is dressed in jeans and a black bomber jacket. Lily knows him from somewhere but she can't remember where. She runs down a dark side street, her lungs screaming at the effort. She's halfway down the street before she realises it's a dead end. She starts trying to climb the wall, but the man in the bomber jacket reaches her and grabs her ankles.

Lily sits up with a jolt, as a police car passes the house with its sirens screeching. Sweat makes her T-shirt stick to her skin. The pile of duvet next to her moves, making her jump. Then she remembers. She takes a few deep breaths and then lays back down, smiling up at the ceiling.

Jo lifts her head an inch off the pillow. "What you grinning like that for? God, my head hurts. Roll me a fag and stop smiling."

Lily absent-mindedly sticks two cigarette papers together. Then she realises what she's doing and looks across at Jo. "Don't let 'em go to waste," says Jo, flinging her the dope tin.

"You know, it's Saturday," says Jo thoughtfully, as she inhales the last of Lily's spliff. "The library probably closes early. We should get going, we can clear up later."

Lily has never been to Accrington library. The lady at the desk directs them upstairs, to a shelf that bows under the weight of a complete set of phone directories.

"I can't believe you've spent all this time wondering where he is and never once picked up a phonebook." Jo scans the shelf for the Skipton edition. "I mean, Winterbottom. It's not exactly John Smith."

Lily starts to rearrange the poetry section, starting with shades of red. "Hey, so I've not been thinking straight. I never knew they kept phone directories in libraries."

Jo pulls out a directory, slings it on the table and flicks through the pages. "Here we are," says Jo, "David Winterbottom. There's only one."

Lily grabs the directory from Jo. "Let me see."

"Have you got a pen on you?" asks Jo.

Lily shakes her head. "There's seven other Winterbottoms. They might be my relatives too. What if I have a massive family out there?"

Jo glances around the room and then carefully rips the page from the telephone book. "Come on, let's get out of here."

They go to the pub across the road, and despite the drizzle, sit outside. "We could just ring him. Ask him if he used to be married to your mum."

Lily smokes in silence. She's spent nineteen years imagining meeting her father; she can't help experiencing a feeling of anticlimax.

"Or, we could pretend to be solicitors, trying to track him down because he's inherited something."

The drizzle turns to raindrops. The majority of them bounce down on the green umbrella fixed to the table. A few hit Lily's back. They drink in silence. Lily lights another cigarette from the butt of her first. "He's going to be suspicious. He's just had the Salvation Army on his case."

"What about if we said we were doing some market research? We could ask him if he's got any children…"

"He doesn't want me to find him, remember?" Lily looks up at Jo for the first time since they arrived at the pub. "He's hardly going to say, 'oh yes, I've got a nineteen-year- old daughter I abandoned at birth.' Is he?"

"Well, there's only one thing for it then. We'll have to go and see for ourselves. We've got a photo."

"It's twenty years old."

"So what? We'll still be able to tell if it's him. We'll just have to camp outside his house. We could do with a car." Jo takes a drink and then almost chokes. "I can get us a car. I'll borrow our Ste's, my brother's. He never uses it; it's rusting on my mum's drive. She'll be well pleased to get rid of it."

"What about poly, Jo?"

"What about it? It's hardly rocket science. We break up in a few weeks anyway. I told them you needed some compassionate leave. I talked to Wardle, he said fine, so long as we promise to get the lecture notes copied up. Oh and he gave me a couple of essay titles we have to hand in by January. I'm sure we'll both be able to catch up." She emphasizes the both. Lily looks uncertain. "We're both going back, Lily. We'll get this sorted out and then we're both going back, to continue our fabulous education and then get on with our fabulous lives."

Lily wishes she had Jo's optimism. She has a sense of foreboding that she can't shake.

The bus to Manchester arrives half an hour late, and they almost miss their connection to Liverpool. Lily sprints down the bus station with Jo lagging behind, and just manages to catch the driver's attention. From Liverpool they catch another bus to Kirby where Jo's mother lives on a housing estate, one of those Barratt ones Lily's seen advertised on television, the one where the helicopter flies in.

A Mini is parked on the drive. It has a white roof and red sides. "What do you reckon?" asks Jo. "Thank God he stopped short of painting a Union Jack on the bonnet."

Jo's mother opens the door, dressed in a pale blue, velour tracksuit. "Why didn't you tell me you were coming? I've got nothing in for tea. Why can't you ring like normal people?" She mock cuffs Jo round the back of the head and smiles at Lily. "I don't know what your friend's going to think of me, and look at the state of you," she says, drawing Jo in for a hug. "When are you going to get your hair cut? You look like no one cares for you. Oh it's so good to see you." Lily looks at the floor as Jo hugs her mother again.

"You must be Lily." Jo's mother puts her hand on Lily's shoulder. "I'm Wendy. I've heard so much about you. How are you doing? I'm very sorry about your mum. How was the funeral?"

"Fine. Could I use your toilet?"

"Upstairs, first on the left."

When Lily comes back downstairs, Jo and Wendy are in the kitchen. They both stop talking as Lily enters the room. "Anyway," says Jo looking at Lily, "we're not stopping. We just want to borrow the Mini for a few days. Our Ste won't mind. Well," she corrects herself, "he won't know. We'll have it back by the weekend."

"Oh take it away for good, can't you? He hasn't mentioned it in weeks. He's all caught up in this new woman." Wendy raises her eyebrows skywards. "I don't think they've got out of bed since he met her. If you can get it started, it's yours. Now, come on," she claps her hands, "Let's open a bottle of wine. Lily, if you can get the corkscrew from that drawer over there, Jo can get on with finding us some glasses, and I'll go and see what I've got in the freezer."

They sit together at a table in the kitchen eating homemade fisherman's pie. Lily has never tasted such deliciousness. She forks in mouthfuls, while Jo and Wendy gabble away like a pair of teenagers who haven't seen each other for months. After a second bottle of wine, Wendy says they'd better spend the night.

Jo's bedroom gives the impression that Jo the teenager has just gone to get a glass of water and will be back soon. As Jo opens the wardrobe door to find them both a pair of pyjamas, Lily spots a small picture of Simon Le Bon pinned to the inside. On the bedroom wall is a large poster that proclaims, 'Protect me from what I want'. Lily wants to ask if Jo wants Simon Le Bon, and if that's what she needs protecting from.

They lean out of the bedroom window and smoke a spliff in silence. It's a clear night and Lily watches the stars. When they pull their heads back into the room, Lily notices a photograph framed on the windowsill. A boy with a long, dark fringe stares sullenly at her. "Who's that?"

Jo sighs. "That's William. He, well, we used to go out."

"He's good looking."

"Yeah, too good looking. He got off with my best friend at a party. I went to get a drink and when I came back they were sat together on the stairs, snogging, with his hand up her jumper."

"Oh."

"Yeah. She told me afterwards that he'd been trying to get off with her for weeks." Jo pulls on a pair of pink candy striped pyjamas and climbs onto her bed. An old Snoopy, with only one ear, rests lopsidedly against her pillow, and CND badges adorn her curtains. "That's men for you." She sniffs. "He did me a favour really." She glances at the empty photo frame next to her bed, which used to contain a photograph of her father, swinging her up in the air when she was a kid. She threw the photo years ago, but for some reason she didn't fully understand, she'd kept the empty frame. She forces her attention back to William's transgressions. "He made me

43

realise men just can't be trusted. If he wasn't for him I'd probably still be wearing lipstick and hoping my ass didn't look too big."

Lily climbs into the put up bed. The duvet has a faded picture of a black and white Pierrot clown on it, and smells of fabric conditioner. Lily's wearing an old nightshirt of Jo's, that's about three sizes too big and has been mended with a patch on the front.

Jo turns off the light and lies on her back, her head resting on her arms. The glow stars she stuck to the ceiling when she was twelve years old, radiate back at her. She recites all the constellations to herself. "Did you ever love anyone, Lil?"

Lily doesn't answer. She's fast asleep, her swollen belly warming up the bed sheets like a hot water bottle.

They wake to the smell of frying bacon. "I don't know, you students." Wendy says as they enter the kitchen. "Spend half your lives asleep, while us hard working, taxpaying folk pay you for the privilege. I hope you were having deep and profound dreams at least. Come on, Lily; get your feet under the table. Tea or coffee?"

Lily, if given the choice, would stay at Jo's mum's house forever. She's never experienced freshly laundered sheets or real coffee, but Jo is anxious to get moving. She starts piling bags into the boot of the Mini. "I'm just borrowing a few bits. I'll bring it all back."

They have to push start the Mini down the road; Lily and Wendy at the rear, Jo running alongside, one hand on the steering wheel. It finally kicks into life and Jo dives headlong into the front seat. The car makes a throaty sound, coughs and splutters for the first few hundred yards but then finds itself. Jo pulls into the kerb, revving the engine, plumes of smoke billowing from the exhaust.

"Bye, thanks for having us." Lily says, standing stiffly as Jo's mum tries to give her a hug.

"Make sure you eat properly," Wendy shouts after her, as Lily pulls away and runs down the street towards the Mini.

"We've got wheels," Jo shouts, as Lily jumps into the passenger seat. Lily laughs. The car has a stereo system that looks more valuable than the car itself; thick speaker wires like liquorice shoelaces, hanging out from under the dashboard. Jo rummages through the glove compartment, one hand on the wheel, and pulls out a tape. Moments later both girls are singing along to Whitesnake. The amazing thing about Jo is, when Lily's with her, she gets this feeling she could do anything.

Lily's euphoria evaporates on the doorstep in Accrington. The house is dark and the smell seems to have intensified. She opens a window, despite the cold. How come, despite being left by her husband, Jo's mum had made such a go of life?

Jo is unloading bags from the car. She steps through the front door. "I've brought joss sticks." Her cheeks redden, "I just thought, you know…"

"Yeah, I know."

"Come on, look lively. Let's get the rest of the bags and then I'll skin up."

Chapter 9

Lily smokes thirteen cigarettes as she watches the sun rise from her position on the back door step. 'Red sky in the morning, shepherd's warning', the words go round and round her head as the bright pink dawn spreads over the horizon. She helps herself to a small glass of vodka, to try to settle the unease in her stomach.

The Mini must have enjoyed its journey from Liverpool to Accrington, because it starts first time. They stop at a petrol station on the outskirts of Skipton and buy a street map. Lily navigates, turning the map three hundred and sixty degrees on her lap as she follows their route with her finger. They follow the one way system round the town centre, before snaking their way up to the north, as the streets widen and become tree-lined, until finally they turn a corner.

"This is it, Primrose Glen." Lily looks up from the map and her brow creases. The street is devoid of parked cars and the houses are all set far back from the road.

"What number is it?" Jo slows the car to a crawl.

Lily looks at the scrap of paper in front of her. "Twelve."

"What number's that one?"

Lily leans the top half of her body out of the window. "Oak Dene." She pronounces it 'denny'.

"Oak Dene, la-di-fucking-da. Can't have something as ordinary as a number, dahling."

Lily comes back into the car and turns to Jo. "This can't be it."

"Hang on, that's number ten, it must be the next one." They edge another few hundred yards down the road, and Jo pulls the Mini into the kerb. She points to the large sandstone building, peeping over the mature trees and privet hedge that defend it from the road. A black, wrought iron gate, with the word, 'Newlands' fashioned in the middle, rises high above the boundary. They can see the windows on the first floor; all made from stained glass and there are a lot of them. "That's it."

There is silence in the car. "Do you think it's flats?" asks Lily, eventually.

Jo sucks in air through her teeth, "No."

Lily scratches her head. She doesn't know what kind of house she had thought her father would live in, only that this isn't it.

"Of course," says Jo. "He's probably at work – what day is it?" Lily scratches her head again. "It's Wednesday. We went to my mum's on Sunday, back Monday." Jo ticks the days off on her fingers. "Yesterday was Tuesday. It's Wednesday and it's half past twelve. He'll be at work."

Lily puts her feet up on the dashboard and lights a cigarette.

"Come on, Lil. Let's take a closer look."

"But what if someone comes? What if ... You don't think he's married do you? I mean, remarried?"

Jo shrugs her shoulders. "Well, it's big for a bachelor pad. Unless, maybe he's a rock star or something."

Lily doesn't want to admit to the fantasy she used to entertain, built from the time her mother threw the radio out of the kitchen window when 'Let It Be' by The Beatles came on. "Maybe he's gay? Maybe that's why he didn't want... Maybe he's ashamed..."

"Mmmm," says Jo, but her voice is thick with uncertainty.

"What if he is married? Christ, I could have a wicked stepmother." Different possibilities start to seep into Lily's brain, but before Lily can voice any of them, a smaller, wrought iron side gate that neither of them has noticed opens, and a teenage girl steps out. The girl closes the gate behind her, locks it and puts the key into a purse and the purse into her bag. She's dressed in a school uniform, with royal blue knee socks, and her long brown hair is in pigtails. She adjusts the bag hanging over her shoulder, bends down and pulls at a knee sock before ambling down the street. Lily and Jo shrink into their seats. Jo buries her head in the street map, but Lily can't take her eyes off the girl. She watches her fiddle with a Walkman and guesses she's about fifteen.

"If that's his girlfriend, he's more than a complete arse." Jo says.

"That's not his girlfriend. That's his kid. She even looks like him. But..." Lily struggles to get the words out. "You wouldn't leave a baby and then have another would you? Not without... I mean... I've always thought that must have been what made him leave. He

47

thought he wanted kids, but when it came down to it, he realised he couldn't go through with it."

"Oh, Lily." Jo turns her head, so Lily doesn't notice the tears that threaten her eyes. Lily reaches for another cigarette, her heart thudding against her chest. The cigarette packet is empty. She crunches it up in her hand and throws it against the windscreen. She throws opens the car door. "Come on."

Jo grabs her arm. "What are you doing?"

"I'm going to take a look. There's no one inside. She locked the gate."

"But what if someone comes back?"

"We'll say we're looking for our dog, or something. I don't know. Come on." Lily takes a hair band from round her wrist, pulls her dreads back off her face and ties them back in a loose ponytail at the base of her neck. She slams the car door, glances up and down the street and then strides up to the front gates. A number pad on the right hand side blinks at her, waiting for a code. She starts to climb the gates, pulling her small wiry frame up with ease as Jo, realising Lily is actually going to do it, struggles from the car. Lily marches up the drive as Jo reaches the gates.

"Lily, wait for me."

The house has three bay windows and a stone built porch. Lily peers through one of the windows, cupping her face with her hands to stop the light reflecting. Inside is the largest front room Lily has ever seen. The polished wooden floor reminds her of a ballroom, the settees are square and leather, like the ones in Agatha Christie murders, set in country mansions. Lily tries the gate at the side of the house. It clicks open and leads her into the back garden, where a tree swing hangs centre stage from the branches of an oak tree. A greenhouse with white wooden sides stretches along one wall, with what looks suspiciously like grapes growing inside. Lily marches up to the house and stares through the glass doors that lead from the patio. In the dining room, school books lay open on a long wooden table, next to a half empty glass of blackcurrant juice. Lily counts eight chairs set around the dining table. She moves to the kitchen window. The schoolgirl smiles from a picture on the wall, despite the braces on her teeth.

Lily puts her forehead against the pane of glass to cool her thoughts, but the rage leaps in her like a fire. She turns from the window. The garden spreads itself before her. She notices a fish pond, has the sudden urge to urinate in it. Her father takes better care of fish than he ever has of her. He thinks more about them, thinks more often of them, than he does of her. She's about to undo the button on her trousers when Jo comes round the corner, out of breath. Lily slams her hand so hard against the side of the shed, the walls shake and the pain in her palm focuses her.

Lily kicks a flowerpot, standing on a low wall next to the patio. The pot topples over and smashes, its contents sprawling over the lawn. "It's like Neverland. All we need is Bubbles the chimp." Lily looks wildly around, as if actually expecting to see a monkey come bounding over the lawn.

"He probably thinks you're after his cash. He's an arse, Lily. Let's get out of here." Jo takes Lily by the arm. "We need to think what to do."

Chapter 10

The next morning, the sound of Lily roaring wakes Jo. It's a primitive, physical expression of pain. By the time Lily comes out of the bathroom, Jo is dressed. "I thought I'd go and get us some food, supermarket, you know." Jo drops her keys and bends to pick them up. "Do you want to come? Will you be ok, Lily?"

Lily stands in the doorway staring at the floor. "I need to be alone," she says quietly.

As soon as Jo steps out of the door, Lily goes back into the bathroom and opens the small cabinet on the wall. Hidden behind an old toothbrush mug is a packet of razor blades. Why they are hidden is anybody's guess, as Lily can't remember how old she was the last time her mother made it upstairs. Must have been at least six years ago, but old habits die hardest. Lily takes them out and closes the cabinet door, catching sight of her reflection in the mirror as she does so. She stares at herself for several minutes. Her father's eyes stare back at her. Her reflection shakes its head slowly at her.

Lily drops the packet of razors in the overflowing bin and runs down the stairs two at a time, to the kitchen. She throws open a cupboard door and grabs a pile of plates. Taking them into the front room, she then hurls each one like a Frisbee across the room, watching it smash against the back wall. When every plate is destroyed, she goes back into the kitchen and grabs another pile. Once the kitchen cupboards are bare, she turns her attention to the cheap ornaments, picture frames, anything she can find. Only when everything is broken (except for two mugs – she's not that crazy, yet) she stops.

Jo returns to find Lily asleep on the settee mattress, surrounded by a mound of broken glass and china. She closes the front room door quietly and starts emptying the shopping bags into the kitchen cupboard. A few minutes later Lily appears in the doorway, rubbing her eyes. Jo glances sideways at her. "Well, at least there's plenty of space for the food."

Lily's smile is brief, just the faintest glimpse of an upturned mouth, but it was a smile. "There's another box in the loft," she says. "I couldn't, I didn't open it before. It's full of letters. I looked but I couldn't. I'm going to get it."

"Do you want me to come up?"

Lily shakes her head. "No, I'll bring it down."

Jo puts a frozen pizza in the oven and sweeps up the broken crockery, while Lily fetches the box. Once they've eaten, using torn up pieces of the cardboard packaging as plates, Lily opens the small wooden box, which despite the layers of dust is highly polished and inlaid with an intricate design. She shudders at the mound of letters inside. Jo picks up the top envelope and glances at Lily. Lily nods. Jo pulls out a small sheet of paper and clears her throat.

"'My dear darling wife...'" She reads. "By the way, this is dated April '66:

> *'Being away from you does not get any easier, even though we can now count ourselves an old married couple. I'm stuck in the middle of nowhere and it's beautiful and utterly pointless without you.'*

"Such romance." Jo holds her hand to her heart for a brief moment. "Shame he's a complete knob."

She turns the piece of paper over and reads from the other side:

> *"'I am counting the moments until we are reunited (forty-seven hours and thirty-five minutes). I have plans to take you straight to bed and keep you there the entire weekend.*
>
> *All my love for ever, David.'"*

Lily puts her hands over her ears. "Too much information."

Jo pulls a face. "I wonder what he does, your dad? I mean he clearly earns a fortune."

Lily reaches for a letter. "I don't know. But if he was that rich when he was married to my mum, it's no wonder she was pissed off."

"And why hasn't he paid any to you? I mean when your mum got divorced she should have got half, shouldn't she?"

"I don't even know if they got divorced."

Jo opens another envelope. "What about this?

> *'You are the woman of my dreams.*
> *Thank you so much for last night.*
> *I will remember it forever.'"*

Lily isn't listening. Her eyes scan the letter in her hand. "God, this one's from my mum:

> *'I love you so much I can hardly breathe.*
> *I yearn to be with you.'"*

Lily drops the letter like it's contagious. "Yeah well, that's what killed her. I don't know if I can read any more of these." She spots an envelope addressed to her mother in a different, loopy handwriting. Lily squats on her haunches, elbows over her knees, rocking slightly as she opens it. "This one's from my Gran:

> *'Dear Pamela. I'm sorry about today. I thought*
> *I'd try writing instead, in the hope that maybe*
> *you'll try to understand, what I'm saying isn't a*
> *criticism of you. I'm trying to help. I can't bear to*
> *think of you in this state when I'm gone. I'm not*
> *blaming you. I will never forgive that man for what*
> *he's done. After all I did for him; he's broken my*
> *heart too. And I haven't the time to recover. But*
> *you do. You have to carry on, Pamela, if only for*
> *Lily's sake. You're still young. Please don't let life*
> *pass you by. It doesn't last forever. I don't want to*
> *fight. Please don't let it end like this. Mum.'"*

Lily sits back with a thump on the floor. The silence broken only by the faint hiss of the gas fire. "God, he really screwed my family

52

didn't he?" She looks at the postmark on the envelope. "1972, that's the year she died."

Jo lets the letter she's holding fall onto the mattress. "It's so sad. No one recovered."

Lily's eyes are bright. "It's like he stole everyone from me. He didn't just leave me, he took everyone with him. He left me nothing. Where are all his relatives? Not one of them kept in touch with me. Where are my grandparents? Why didn't they send me the odd birthday card? Cousins, aunts, uncles; I had no one." Lily draws breath and allows her anger to rise like fire. "I have no one. Who am I going to spend Christmas with? I'll end up with bloody Bert next door."

"You can come to ours," says Jo.

Lily remembers Jo's spluttering indignation when she had come back to Leeds after spending three days with her family last Christmas. It had taken her almost a week to stop regaling tales of how her brother had nicked her Billy Bragg album, and how her father had insisted on them going to church on Christmas Eve, despite the fact he wasn't religious, because his young wife wanted them to sing carols. Jo had had some great argument with… was it an aunt or a cousin, about politics or racism or something. She had come back to Leeds a ball of anger and frustration.

Jo stands up. "At least we're friends. I know it's not exactly family."

Lily pours them another drink. She stands up to hand Jo the mug. They dwarf the dingy room, with its nicotine striped wallpaper.

"Do you know what I want? I want him to get some idea of consequence. That he can't do what he did and it not to have any consequence." Lily's words are slurred. "When I was eight years old, I came home from school to find my mum lying on the kitchen floor with her head in the oven. Afterwards, this doctor pressed a bottle of tablets into my hand and said, 'make sure your mummy takes two every morning when she gets up and two before she goes to bed.' And I was too embarrassed to tell him my mum never went to bed. She lived on the sofa; so I didn't know when to give her the pills."

"You can't let him get away with it, Lil. He can't be allowed to say he has no wish for contact. No way. Let's go back again," says Jo. "Take another look. Hey, we might have got the wrong David Winterbottom for all we know."

Lily shakes her head. Unusually for her, inside her is a sense of deep certainty. She knows they were at the right house.

"Well then, Lil," says Jo, when it becomes clear Lily isn't going to speak. "Let's pay him another visit. It's not like we've got anything better to do."

Chapter 11

Jo parks the Mini a few hundred yards away from Newlands and looks at the clock on the dashboard, three twenty. "Hope we're not too late."

Twenty minutes pass before the schoolgirl appears around the corner, hands in pockets, sucking on a lollipop. "God, what a stiff," mutters Lily, as the girl stops outside the side gate, gets her purse from her bag and her key from her purse and lets herself in.

Less than half an hour later a dark green Volvo estate pulls up outside the front gates. The driver taps in a code and the wrought iron sweeps aside. Jo watches through the rear view mirror, while Lily cranes her neck to watch through the passenger's wing mirror, but they see no more than a flash of the side of a face. "I think it was a man," says Jo.

Lily bangs her arm against the door. "This is no good."

"What we need is equipment," says Jo. They wait in silence as the light gradually fades from the day. "And a proper plan."

Three days later they are back, sitting in the red and white Mini, in the small, cobbled side street across the road from Newlands. The side street is only a few hundred yards long. It ends in a pair of large wooden gates. The back entrance to the large detached house is on their right. Each house is shielded from the road by a combination of tall fence and high hedge. Not the privet kind; more the well established beech or laurel. They are both wearing black combat trousers and black sweatshirts. Lily's dreads are tied back in a ponytail and pulled through a baseball cap, which she wears with the peak pulled down over her eyes. Jo is wearing sunglasses and a black beanie hat. She pulls out a pen and their specially purchased notebook from her bag, and begins to write.

"Do you think anyone can see us here?" asks Lily.

Jo underlines her heading with two thick black lines, before twisting and turning in her seat. "Don't think so. I can't see any windows from here."

Lily pours them a cup of black coffee from the new thermos flask, and unwraps the toast they didn't have time to eat before they set off that morning.

Moments later, Jo nudges Lily's elbow. The coffee that Lily has just poured spills over the top of the mug and onto Lily's inner thighs. Lily leaps up in pain, trying to hold the material of her trousers away from her flesh. Jo, her mouth full of toast, nods towards the house. The gates are opening. With one hand, Lily raises the binoculars to her eyes. A sleek, black sports car pulls out, pausing momentarily to check for traffic. Lily watches it roar off down Primrose Glen. She doesn't remove the binoculars until the car is out of sight.

"It was a woman, I'm pretty sure."

"And?" asks Jo. "Hair colour? Age? Was she white? Black? Purple? Come on, Lil, you must have seen something."

"White, I guess," says Lily, rubbing at the warm wet patch on her trousers.

DAY ONE (Monday)
07:30 Newlands. All quiet.
07:40 Adult Female (AF) leaves. White.
Black nifty sports car (expensive).
07:55 Postman drops letters into box on outside of gate.
08:25 Green Volvo leaves. Adult Male (AM).
No description available at this time.

Lily puts the binoculars down. "I can't tell. It's a man. It could be your dad for all I know."

Jo creates a new column, Adult Male. "Did you get its registration?"

Lily doesn't answer. Ten minutes later the schoolgirl steps out of the side gate. They watch as she almost skips down the street.

Lily nods towards a tree spreading its branches above them. "We need a better view. We need to be higher up. Drive under that tree there."

Jo moves the car a few feet forwards and Lily winds down the passenger window. Lily bends her body out of the window and climbs onto the roof. From here she can reach the lowest branch. She pulls herself up and stands in the tree. Its last few leaves are clinging on, but for the moment its canopy is enough to obscure her from view. Lily wedges herself between two branches and trains the binoculars on the house across the road. She can see the dark leather of the settees through the front room window. Satisfied, she drops back into the car. "It's perfect."

It's another two hours before the window cleaner shows up, just before lunchtime, and keys the number into the security pad. Lily stays in the car, training the binoculars on him, but she can't make out which numbers he pressed. The last one may have been an eight.

An elderly woman walks past the entrance to the side street at 11:00 hours. She glances up the side street and frowns at them. Lily holds up the Skipton A-Z in front of her face. The old woman pauses for a moment, as if deciding whether to approach them or not. Jo smiles at her and the woman nods and walks on. "Shit," says Jo. "We don't look like we fit in. Let's go somewhere else for a bit."

They park up a couple of streets away, opposite a petrol station. Jo drums her fingers on the steering wheel. After a couple of minutes she asks, "Did you ever want to learn to drive, Lil?"

"No."

"Want to give it a go now?"

"What?"

"It'd be a cool disguise. All we'd need is L plates." Jo climbs out of the car and hurries across to the shop inside the petrol station. A few moments later, she sashays back across the forecourt, holding a red letter L above her head.

Lily winds down the passenger window as Jo starts to peel the backing of the red and white squares. "Are you crazy?" asks Lily, as Jo sticks the first one onto the bonnet.

"It'll give us something to do. And stop people getting suspicious. Think about it. We've seen at least three learners since we've been here." Jo sticks another one on the right hand side of the bonnet before walking around to the rear of the car. She sticks another two above the back bumper before getting back into the driving seat.

That afternoon, Lily has her first driving lesson. She manages to get up to second gear and turns a corner. Her cheeks are flushed pink by the time they are back in the side street, to witness 'Teenage Female' returning home. Jo logs the time in the notebook; 15:35

hours. It's not much later before the dark green four-by-four swings into the drive. The house lights up against the encroaching gloom. Through her binoculars Lily watches 'Teenage Female' close the front room curtains. Jealousy as strong as acid burns in her stomach.

DAY TWO (Tuesday)
07:20 Knackered. All quiet. Coffee.
07:25 LA in tree.
07:39 AF leaves Newlands.

From her vantage point in the tree, Lily watches the older woman, 'Adult Female', stride around to the rear of the sleek, black car and toss her briefcase in the boot. She slams the boot lid shut with one hand, before ducking into the driver's seat and adjusting the rear-view mirror. Fumes start to billow from the exhaust as the iron gates sweep open. Once the car has disappeared from view, Lily drops back down onto the roof of the Mini, and jumps in the car again. "She's not even good looking," says Lily to Jo. "And she's fat. Well, overweight."

Jo picks up the pen and writes 'AF-fat'. She turns to face Lily. "Are we talking specialist dress shops?"

"Well, no, but she's short."

"How short?"

Lily reaches for the tobacco tin, disgruntled that her father had left her for an unattractive woman. "Dunno, smaller than me."

"About my height then?" Jo asks, her pen poised and her eyebrow raised.

"Yeah, but she's fatter, well..." Lily senses a change of conversation is called for. "She's got dark hair in a kind of bob."

"How long?" asks Jo.

"Shoulder length."

"What's she wearing?"

"Trouser suit, a dark one. Black or dark blue maybe. She looks old too. Maybe we haven't got the right house after all." Lily scratches her cheek.

"How old?" asks Jo as she adds 'butch' and 'bob' to the description in the notebook.

"Dunno. Fifty-five? Maybe even older. What time did 'AM' come out yesterday?"

58

Jo flicks back through the notebook, "08:25 hours."

"Ok, I'll wait ten minutes and then I'll go back up." Lily lights a cigarette and smokes it in silence, absent-mindedly pulling on the skin of her lower lip. At 8 o'clock she climbs back into the tree and settles on a branch to wait.

Twenty minutes later, 'Adult Male' steps out of the front door, wearing a dark brown suit. His hair is flecked with grey. Lily leans forward through the tree, binoculars in one hand, the other hand gripping hold of a branch to anchor herself. He squints in the sunshine, before opening the door of the four-by-four and throwing what looks like a sports bag onto the seat. 'Teenage Female' is standing in the porch eating a slice of toast, her school tie unfastened around her neck. He stoops slightly to kiss her on the cheek as she says something to him. He shakes his head and smiles, then turns back to the car and ducks inside it. Lily leans a little further forward, desperate not to lose sight of him, but he's gone in less than a minute; the gates automatically opening to allow him to escape. Several minutes later Lily gets back into the car.

"Well?" asks Jo.

Lily sits up straight in the passenger seat, her gaze focussed on some distant spot beyond the windscreen. She speaks so quietly it's difficult for Jo to hear her. "It's him."

Chapter 12

DAY THREE (Wednesday)
07:25 Fucking knackered.
07:40 AF left house (Routine?).
08:25 AM left house.
08:50 No sign of Teenage Female (TF).
Number of spliffs smoked: 3.

"TF must have a free period on a Wednesday," says Jo. "It was lunchtime the first time we came, remember? She was just leaving the house then."

Lily smiles at the biro mark Jo has above her lip, giving the appearance of a moustache, and hands her a cup of coffee, "your deal." She nods towards the two packs of cards balanced on the centre of the dented tea tray Jo found yesterday, in a skip near Lily's house, which is now propped against the handbrake.

It is quarter to one before the schoolgirl emerges from the side gate, her royal blue knee socks protruding from under her duffle coat. She is carrying a covered wicker basket, which she rests on the floor while she puts the key into her purse. "What's with the basket?" Lily asks. "Is she going to pick wild flowers on her way to school?"

Jo shakes her head. "TIFF's got cookery classes today. I wonder what's on the menu?"

"Something posh," says Lily. "Like homemade apple pie."

"What school do you reckon she goes to? Pass us the A to Z." Lily picks up the crumpled book off the floor of the Mini and hands it to Jo. Jo finds three schools in the vicinity and makes a note of all them. "Socks that bright can't be that hard to find." She waves the notebook at Lily. "Let's check out the neighbourhood."

St Michael's Catholic School is the nearest. A crucifix bearing a bleeding Jesus Christ stands to the right of the main entrance. Jo pulls up on the yellow zigzags outside the main entrance, and Lily shudders as she sees the anguish on Christ's face. The school playground is full; hundreds of children in grey trousers and sage green sweatshirts mill around, trying to keep warm. Lily draws a line through it in the notebook as Jo drives to the next school on the list.

After several wrong turns, they eventually find the street they're looking for. Skipton Grammar School for Girls is housed in an imposing Victorian building, with expansive lawned playing fields, keeping the neighbours at bay. The car park is filled with cars. It is quarter past one and there is no one in sight. Jo pulls up the handbrake. "Shall we go and look through a window?"

"Let's just wait for break."

Radio 1 is playing 'I Should Be So Lucky' by Kylie Minogue. "Did you know they wrote this song in forty minutes?" asks Jo. "I read it somewhere," she says, before switching the radio off. "I'm surprised it took them that long."

They sit in silence, until a knock on the glass makes them both jump in their seats. They turn to see a man's face pressed up against the glass of Jo's window. He gestures at them to wind the window down. Jo does so slowly, dropping the glass down five or six centimetres. The man speaks through the gap. "What are you girls up to?"

"Nothing, just talking. What's it to do with you?"

"You're on school property." He points to the yellow lines on the road. "I'm the caretaker. You'd better be on your way."

"Well, excuse me," says Jo. "My friend here is very upset. We just stopped because she's very, very upset."

The man peers past Jo, trying to get a look at Lily. Lily immediately ducks her head, and sniffs.

"Well, sorry, but you can't be too careful these days. You're on CCTV." He points to a white camera attached to a lamp post.

Jo starts up the engine. "Honestly, you can't even have a chat these days, Big Brother is watching. Talk about paranoid. Her mother's just died, you know. But what do you care?"

"Sorry, love. Just doing my job."

"That's what the Gestapo said," yells Jo through the window as she pulls away from the kerb.

An hour later, they are back outside the school, this time on foot. As soon as the first children start to spill from the building, shortly after two fifteen, they know they are in the right place. Every child sports a pair of royal blue knee socks. "I didn't realise stalking could be so easy," Jo says with satisfaction, as she adds this latest piece of information to the notebook.

Lily stares at the girls, each dressed in pleated skirts and gold and blue striped ties. Some girls even sport berets. She watches one group playing elastics, while others huddle together around picnic benches, plaiting each other's hair, and tries to imagine herself at such a school. The one she went to had broken shards of glass embedded into concrete running all around the top of the brick walled playground.

DAY FOUR (Thursday)
07:40 AF leaves house.
08:25 AM leaves house.
08:40 TF leaves house.
09:35 Finished toast.
11:35 LA driving lesson. Highest gear reached: 2nd
11:45 Bum numb.
Number of spliffs smoked: 4

"Come on Lil. Let's go for a walk." Jo parks the mini up the side street and they traipse for twenty minutes around the tree-lined avenues without seeing another person.

"Where is everyone? It's like a ghost town."

"They're all at work, trying to earn enough to pay off the mortgage on a house they hardly ever see in daylight, morons." says Jo as Lily kicks at the piles of scrunched up leaves and watches a cat chase a squirrel up a tree. "I think we should follow her tomorrow."

"Who?"

"AF, Afghan. Let's see what she gets up to."

"What's the point?" asks Lily.

"Come on, aren't you curious? Maybe there's a reason why he doesn't want to meet you."

"Like what?"

"Dunno. Maybe he's a Tory MP or something. One of those that's always spouting on about family values. Or maybe she is."

"Look, there's a newsagents. We need food and fags."

"Haven't seen you two before." The elderly shopkeeper smiles at Jo. "I would have remembered that hair. How do you get it so white? I can never get any of those hair colours to work."

"It's bleached," says Jo, while Lily pretends to be involved in a difficult 'which flavour crisps' decision. "But that's the best way to get a colour to stay in, bleach it first. I dyed mine fluorescent pink last year."

"Ah, that's the secret is it? I might have another try then. I'm not sure pink's my colour but I'd like something a bit brighter." She pats at her grey locks.

"Twenty Marlborough Reds," says Lily.

The woman turns to the shelf behind the till and reaches for a packet. She places it on the counter. "What are you girls up to?"

Jo and Lily turn to stare at each other, pupils wide. "We're visiting our… Uncle," says Jo, when she realises Lily isn't going to answer the question.

"Nice. Does he live around here?"

"Primrose Glen."

"Very nice. Well, you've picked a lovely day for it."

"And a packet of king size Rizlas," Lily re-enters the conversation. "Please."

Jo selects two packets of prawn cocktail skips and a Curly Wurly. She brings them to the counter. "Do you deliver his newspapers? He's called Winterbottom. David Winterbottom."

"Probably, we do everyone round here."

"Ooh, what does he read? I bet it's the Telegraph. Go on; tell us he orders a secret copy of the Daily Star." Jo starts to giggle.

"You'll have to ask him, I'm afraid." The shop assistant pulls her peach cardigan tightly around her bust. "I can't divulge information about customers; although I can tell you no one reads the Daily Star round here. We don't even stock it," she says with some pride.

Lily looks at the pile of Daily Mails and Daily Expresses jostling for position on the bottom shelf, and then looks at Jo. Jo grins. "No, I can see; nothing but quality press here."

The shop keeper doesn't get the joke. As she turns to the till Jo pulls a face at Lily, which pushes Lily over the edge. She explodes in a giggling fit. By the time the woman turns back from the till to say, "Two pounds fifty seven please," Lily has had to leave the shop while Jo pays.

DAY FIVE (Friday)
07:40 AF leaves Newlands.
LA and JB follow.

On Friday morning, they park the Mini right at the T junction at the top end of Primrose Glen, so that they can set off as soon as 'Afghan' passes.

'Afghan' passes by at exactly 07:40 hours and Jo follows a few hundred yards behind. It takes twenty minutes to drive into Skipton, even though it's only two miles away. It's an easy journey on which to tail somebody, as the early morning rush hour traffic inches along into the town centre. They are still close enough behind to see her turn into a private car park. They find a pay and display car park a few blocks away, but by the time they've sorted out enough change for the meter there is no sign of 'Afghan'. "Ok," says Jo. "We'll meet her here on Monday."

On Saturday morning, Lily wakes up at half past four and can't get back to sleep. She smokes three cigarettes, one straight after the other, while waiting for Jo to gel her hair. As Lily stubs the last one out, she bangs on the bathroom door. "Come on, we don't want to miss them."

"Hold your horses. They're probably having a lie in," mutters Jo from inside the bathroom. "Lucky for some."

DAY SIX (Saturday)
08:00 All quiet.
08:30 Curtains open, top right window.
09:02 Milkman arrives (2 pts milk, 2 pts fresh orange. Eggs).
09:38 TF and AM. Side gate. Walking.
Spliffs smoked: 7 (well it is the weekend).

Lily watches the two of them walk down the street together; her father's arm draped loosely across his teenage daughter's back. Lily pulls at a dreadlock until her eyes water. "Where do you think they're going?"

"Well, the jodhpurs give it away. Darling 'TIFF' is going to the local pony club. Either that or she's got a pony of her very own."

Lily bangs her hand against the steering wheel in frustration. "I want to know where they're going."

"Patience my dear, the best things come to those who wait."

DAY SEVEN (Sunday)
Cancelled.
Spliffs smoked: 9

DAY EIGHT (Monday)
07:55 Bench. Skipton town centre.
Weather: pissing down
Hangover: severe.

Jo holds the umbrella over both of them, while Lily tries to warm her hands on the plastic cup of coffee they bought down by the bus station. Lily's eyes have deep black rings underneath them.

By the time the black BMW slides around the corner and into the car park, the rain has stopped. Lily watches out of the corner of her eye, as 'Afghan' steps across the paved courtyard at the rear of the car park, and enters the third building on the right. They wait a few minutes and then run over to see a plaque engraved with the words, 'Totten, Hurst and Ingham Solicitors'. Jo counts to ten and then pushes through the revolving door.

The door opens onto a reception area, with grey slate tiles and a huge, circular reception desk in the centre of the room. A young receptionist sitting behind it looks up at Jo and smiles. "Can I help you?"

"Does Mrs Winterbottom work here?"

"You mean Ms Hurst? I believe she is called Winterbottom, but she uses her maiden name here. Would you like an appointment to see her?" The receptionist picks up a pen.

65

"Erm no, not just now thanks. Do you know what her first name is?"

"It's Ruth."

Jo nods sagely, wondering how much further she can push it. "And is she, what does she do here?

"She's a solicitor. Why do you want know?"

"Has she worked here long?"

"It's her firm. She set it up. Why do you want to know?"

"Oh, just curious. Thank you." Jo pushes the revolving doors so quickly she nearly does a three hundred and sixty degree spin, but she manages to jump out in time. She shouts over to Lily when she's halfway across the courtyard. "She's called Ruth Hurst. She's a lawyer. Lawyer, lawyer, pants on fire."

That afternoon Lily has another driving lesson. Primrose Glen and the streets around are deserted in the early afternoons; perfect for the learner driver, without the hazards of parked or moving cars and pedestrians. The only traffic consists of other learner drivers, sometimes queuing to perform three-point turns in a particularly wide avenue. Lily takes three attempts to pull the car away from the side of the kerb, hopping kangaroo style down the road at three miles an hour, until finally stalling. The girls both roar with laughter.

"I think you need another spliff, Lil. You're not relaxed enough."

DAY NINE (Tuesday)
07:30 AF leaves Newlands.
08:25 AM leaves. LA and JB follow.

'Adult Male' leaves the house every morning at exactly the same time. On Tuesday morning, emboldened by their success the previous day, Jo and Lily follow him at a safe distance, Lily wearing her baseball cap, sunglasses and having added a scarf wound around the lower half of her face. The journey doesn't last long. Five minutes later he pulls into the car park of St Andrews, the third school on their list; the one they didn't visit on day three. They watch as 'AM' pulls his briefcase from the car and heads through the double doors into the school.

"He's a teacher?" For some reason this news doesn't please Lily. Whether it's jealousy that he spends all his days working with

66

children, or whether it's a certain snobbery that he's not a rock star or a peace protestor, is not something Lily wants to think about. Instead she scowls at a schoolboy who passes in front of the windscreen. He looks alarmed and scurries through the school gates. "A teacher."

"Obviously Afghan is the chief breadwinner," says Jo. "Tres modern."

They are back outside Newlands in time to see 'Teenage Female' return to the house, this time carrying a black leather case.

"Clarinet," says Jo with authority.

"Fuck me. Is there anything the girl doesn't do?" says Lily.

Ten minutes after 'Adult Male' arrives home, Lily watches her father and his daughter wheel out their bicycles. As they pass through the gates, 'Adult Male' pulls alongside 'TIFF' and checks the chinstrap on her helmet. Lily sinks lower in her seat and mutters under her breath, "I'd love to show him how it feels to not have any family."

Jo crumbles some warm resin onto the line of tobacco in front of her. "I've got an idea," she says.

Chapter 13

Lily tugs at her black woollen hat but it's no use; it springs back up so that it is merely perched on the top of her head, barely skirting her forehead. Her dreads are piled up on the top of her head, and the hat has used all its capacity trying to contain them. She nestles her nose into her scarf instead. The November day is so cold her breath is crystallising.

"Right, I'm guessing she's going to take this road here, and then walk down Princess Street here," says Jo, bending the pages of the A-Z so that Lily can see the route. "So, if you wait on North Avenue, I'll wait here," she points to a spot on the map, across the road from the grammar school, "and we'll see what happens."

Lily thrusts her hands deep into her pockets. "I don't know about this."

"We're only watching, we're not breaking any laws. You'd better get going," says Jo. "Good luck. And remember, if you think she's spotted you, just turn round the next corner, or cross the road."

Lily walks to her designated waiting post on North Avenue, which meets Primrose Glen at a T-junction. She yawns; they'd stayed up late last night. Jo had insisted on them wandering the streets around the house in Accrington, taking it in turns to follow

68

each other. She had managed to follow Lily for a good five minutes, without Lily realising she was there.

Her canvas bag is heavy on her shoulder, so Lily swaps it to the other side. In it is a book to read, a letter to post, a brightly coloured scarf, a red bobble hat which last fitted Lily about eight years ago, and some money if she needs to duck into a shop. Ten minutes after Lily has found a garden wall to sit on, 'TIFF' appears round the corner from Primrose Glen, Walkman on. She's wearing a duffle coat, which is so big it makes her legs look like a couple of matchsticks sticking out of the bottom. Lily remembers the days of walking to school, so cold her fingers would sting with pain, a winter coat being one of those luxuries that her mother's sickness benefit just didn't stretch to. Lily slips her book into her bag and counts to ten, before setting off after the schoolgirl.

Five minutes later, instead of crossing the road to turn into Princess Avenue, as Jo had anticipated, 'TIFF' takes a sharp left. By the time Lily reaches the spot where 'TIFF' disappeared, 'TIFF's royal blue socks are disappearing down a narrow ginnel. Lily waits a moment, looking anxiously up and down the street. Should she carry on the way Jo had told her to go? She hesitates for a moment, trying to imagine what Jo would say, and then follows after 'TIFF'.

The ginnel leads to an eight foot high red brick wall, with a dirt track next to it. Lily wonders which way to turn and then decides the path to the left looks more well trodden. She follows the outskirts of the wall for a few yards, until she sees an open gate. Lily peers through the gap in the wall and sees the lawned playing fields at the rear of the school, and tennis courts. She forms one hand into a fist and blows warm air into it, before turning back the way she came, to find Jo.

Jo is pacing up and down, pulling heavily on a cigarette as Lily turns the corner into the road where she'd arranged to meet Jo. Further up the street, cars are queued, dropping off identical children in royal blue socks. "What the fuck happened?" she says, as soon as Lily approaches.

"There's a short cut, down a ginnel. Leads right up to the school."

"A ginnel?" says Jo, stamping on her cigarette butt with a deep red Doc Marten boot. "That could be interesting, show me."

Lily pulls her coat around her, as they cross the road and retrace Lily's steps. The ginnel isn't wide enough for them to walk shoulder to shoulder, so Lily goes ahead, both of them looking up, above the privet walls. "No one would see us here," Jo says.

"Come off it Jo, stop fucking around. We can't kidnap a schoolgirl." Lily turns and storms off down the ginnel, back to the road. Jo takes one last look around before following after her.

DAY ELEVEN (Thursday)
Driving lesson: Number of points in three-point turn: 7
Spite and malice: Jo: 8 Lily: 3
Spliffs: 6

"He'd know it was me anyway," says Lily as Jo deals the cards. "A daughter he's never met tries to get in touch, and then a month later his other daughter is kidnapped. It hardly needs Miss Marple to work it out."

Jo starts dealing the cards with more urgency, slapping each one down on the tray and counting them out loud as she does, like she can't reply in case she loses track. When she's dealt forty cards into two equal piles, she deals a further five each. Then she places the remaining pile of cards in the centre of the tray and looks up at Lily. "Does he know where you live?"

Lily picks up her five cards. "Doubt it. I once said to my mum that I wanted to go and live with my dad. We were having this huge fight, she spat at me. Said not to get any stupid ideas. And I remember her saying, 'he has no idea where you are.' And I thought it was odd, because I'd always thought up 'til then, that he'd left us, so why didn't she say, 'I have no idea where he is?' We were always ex-directory too. And she changed our name. I don't even know where she got Appleyard from."

"Well then, does it matter if he does think it's you? He won't know for certain, and it still means he has no idea where his daughter is."

Lily considers this for a moment while toying with a dreadlock. "Guess not."

DAY TWELVE (Friday)
Suggestions for the I in TIFF: Imbecile, Ignorant,
Incredibly Boring, Indescribably posh
Spliffs: 6

"You know Lily, if we are going to do anything it's going to have to be next Wednesday. It's already December, Wednesday will be..." Jo turns a couple of pages, "the 12th. If we don't do it next week, it's going to be too close to Christmas. She might not even be at school the Wednesday after. And families like theirs usually go away for Christmas."

Lily stalls the car half way through what had, up to that point, been a perfect reverse around the corner. She tries to start the car again, forgetting to put the gears into neutral, so that the car jumps a foot backwards and the contents of the spliff Jo had been rolling, land down the side of the handbrake. Jo sighs as Lily sinks her head against the backs of her hands on the steering wheel.

Last Christmas had been awful, watching her mother eat four boxes of mince pies for breakfast. Bert had come round in the evening and they had all got quietly pissed, watching some soft porn he had pretended was an actual film. Her mother had been too comatose to notice. Lily peels a piece of skin from the side of her thumbnail, watches the skin underneath flush up pink.

"What would we do? Grab her?" Lily tries to imagine herself with a large potato sack, one of those brown hessian ones.

"We could tell her we work with her mum; her mum's been taken ill. We've come to take her to the hospital."

"What if she doesn't come?"

Jo shrugs. "Then we'd grab her."

DAY THIRTEEN (Saturday)
TIFF – Teenage Incompetent Fresh-faced Female,
Teenage Inept Frigid Female,
Teenage Immaturely Farting Female
Spliffs: 5 (Need to score soon)

Lily brings Jo a cup of tea and opens the front room curtains. Jo tries to raise her head from the pillow, but the vodka they drank last night has formed a leaden pool at the back of her brain. "Fancy a day off?" says Jo.

Lily shakes her head; she's already dressed. "I want to see if they go horse riding again. You don't have to come."

The curtains are still drawn when they arrive at Newlands. "What are we going to do if we don't do it? We can't spend the rest of our lives watching them play happy families. We might as well be watching Coronation Street with all the rest of the great unwashed," says Jo, as she pushes back the driver's seat of the Mini.

Lily trains her binoculars on the top right bedroom window and doesn't say anything.

DAY FOURTEEN (Sunday)
No rest for the wicked
09:50 AM, AF and TIFF all leave Together (1st time) in Volvo. Follow them to church. (C. of E.)

The vicar shakes 'AM's hand and smiles. 'AM' puts his arm around his wife and daughter's back and leads them down the path in the weak December sunshine.

Lily and Jo watch from their hiding place amongst the headstones.

"It's not like I want to hurt her. It's not kidnapping, more like..." Lily searches for the right word, "borrowing."

Jo finishes chewing her mouthful of cold pizza. A smile appears slowly across her face. Then she puts her head back and laughs. "We're doing it! We're actually fucking doing it."

On their way home, they stop off at Passage to India. "Lily. You not been in for ages. How you doing, girl?" Mr Khan comes out from behind the counter. "You not eating enough. No man likes a skinny girl. I fix you a feast." He points to one of the tables, indicating that they should sit.

Lily shakes her head. "We want take away, please. We've got stuff to do."

"Is this your friend from university?"

"Poly, yeah."

"This what men like," he says, laying a casual arm around Jo's shoulders. "Meat on bones."

Jo looks like she's about to say something, but she doesn't. Lily tries to smile apologetically.

If Mr Khan notices he's upsetting Jo's feminist sensibilities, he doesn't mention it. "Your mum was proud, Lily. University, very, very clever. What you study?"

"Politics."

"Prime Minister." Mr Khan nods like it's all decided. "I vote for you."

He won't hear of them paying. "On the house. Don't forget where you came from, Lily girl."

Back at the house, Jo takes the lids off the silver trays while Lily rolls a spliff. "Wow, there's enough here for the week. Nice that he gave it to us, you."

"He kept my mum in Kormas," says Lily. "He just lost his best customer." Lily lights up the spliff, inhales and leans back against the pillows on the mattress, her eyes closed. "I'm surprised he's still in business."

"Once we've eaten, we need to think about accommodation for our overnight guest." Lily opens one eye. "She'll have to sleep somewhere," Jo says.

Lily's old bedroom looks like it's been burgled. One of the doors is hanging off the single wardrobe in the corner of the room, and clothes spill from a set of drawers. The desk has been extensively grafittied, and the curtains are missing about half of their hooks. "Did you never put up posters?" Jo asks.

Lily shrugs and pushes a plate under the bed with her foot. It stinks in here.

"Can you lock the windows?"

"No."

Jo claps her hands together. "Right, we'd better get cracking."

"What, now?"

"Strike while the iron is hot," says Jo.

73

Chapter 14

DAY FIFTEEN (Monday) D-DAY– 2
Dress Rehearsal starring Jo Battersby as
Teenage Inconsiderate Fainting Female and
Lily Appleyard as evil kidnapper.

Jo checks her watch, twenty to nine. She trains the binoculars on the side gate and holds her breath. A minute or so later it opens, and 'TIFF' emerges. Jo presses a button on the stopwatch they bought yesterday afternoon. When 'TIFF' is out of eyesight Jo starts the engine.

Lily is waiting at the bottom of the ginnel, outside the school wall. The ginnel meets the school wall at a T-junction and Lily turned right and found a place to crouch out of sight. 'TIFF' will turn left to enter the school gates. Sure enough, at seven minutes before nine, Lily sees 'TIFF' turn the corner and watches her shiny, dark hair disappear down the left side of the wall and through the gates at the bottom.

Five minutes later Jo appears. "Ready?"

Lily nods, and Jo turns around and walks back the way she came. Two minutes later she reappears, skipping along like she's nine years old. Lily has moved position so that it appears she's entering the bottom of the ginnel from the direction of the school gates. She breaks into a kind of run. "Hello," she calls to Jo. "Is your name Winterbottom?"

"Yes, yes it is. Why?"

Lily bends over, pretending to catch her breath from the exertion of running. "Your mum's been taken ill, she sent me to fetch you…"

She looks up at Jo. "You know, I think we need to know her name. Don't you? I mean her mum wouldn't ask us to call her daughter without telling us her name, even if she is bent over double with a heart attack."

"Winterbottom isn't her name either, is it?" Jo pulls the notebook out of her pocket and starts flicking through the pages. "She's called Hurst at work. What if 'TIFF's got her name?"

Lily paces up and down the ginnel, shaking her head. "And why didn't we just ring the school?"

"We tried and it was engaged. Then the ambulance arrived, so we decided to jump in the car."

"We still need to know her name."

"Ok, then we need to go shopping."

In the Skipton branch of Scope they find a charcoal grey trouser suit and a white blouse for £3.75. Jo holds the suit against Lily. "I think it says wannabe lawyer, don't you?"

Across the road at Oxfam, Jo pulls a pair of slim black shoes with a small heel from a wire basket and shows them to Lily. "Man, can't I just wear my docs? They're not going to look at my feet."

"It's about feeling the part," says Jo, taking them over to the counter.

In the toilets in McDonald's, Lily puts on the trouser suit and ties her dreads back as neatly as possible. Jo parks up in a car park in Skipton town centre, and watches Lily sway in the second hand heels, into the law offices of Totten, Hurst and Ingham. Lily turns around to glance at Jo before she pushes through the revolving doors. Jo nods at her and holds her thumb up.

The receptionist isn't much older than Lily. She looks up as Lily's heels clip clop across the smooth wooden floor and tries to hide a smile at the sight of Lily swaying. "May I help you?"

Lily holds on to the chest high reception desk for support and tries to remember her first line. "I was just wondering whether you do any work placement schemes here."

"I don't think so, I mean I've never seen any. Do you want to leave your phone number and I'll ask?"

She hands Lily a pen and piece of paper. Lily's hands shake as she begins to write. She clears her throat. "What kind of work do you do here?"

Her speech sounds too rehearsed, even to her own ears. She starts to adlib. "Do you do much criminal stuff? I've always wanted to defend."

"No," says the receptionist. "Nothing exciting like that. It's mainly divorces, family law." She drops her voice. "It's pretty boring to tell you the truth."

Lily takes a deep breath and asks in the most casual voice she can muster, "You know the woman who set this place up, Ruth Hurst?"

The secretary glances over her shoulder, "Yeah."

"I think I was at school with her daughter."

The receptionist looks puzzled. "Fiona? She goes to the grammar school, same school I went to. How old are you?"

Lily's cheeks redden, but she is saved from replying by a door behind her opening. The receptionist jumps and immediately starts talking to Lily in an overloud voice. "So, yes thank you, Miss," she looks at the piece of paper that Lily has scribbled across, "Miss McDonald. We'll be in touch if anything comes up."

Lily turns and sees a middle-aged man clutching a bunch of files, emerging from a room behind her. She also sees the exit. Her legs weaken, but she manages to make them carry her towards it. She hits the revolving doors running and is spewed out of the exit, sweating. Jo grabs her hand and pulls her round the corner. Lily bends over, her hands on her knees, out of breath. "I did it, she's called Fiona. Fiona. What a poncy name."

Chapter 15

Lily sits with her feet on the dashboard, staring at the house through the binoculars.

"If she kicks off big time, we can always let her go," Jo says. "It's not like we can't get out of it. She's not going to know who we are. And even if she tells him two girls tried to kidnap her, and he guesses it was you, he's not going to tell anyone."

Lily doesn't answer. She's watching a dry-cleaning van pull up at the gates.

"We've got to do it, Lily. This is direct action. It's our chance to really do something."

"Jesus, even the dry-cleaners have the code," Lily murmurs as the gates part.

Jo pours a cup of black coffee from the thermos. She takes a mouthful and then passes the cup to Lily. "We can't sit here forever, just watching. We have to do it." She picks up the packet of Marlboro from the dashboard but it's empty. She crumples it up in one hand and passes Lily the notebook. "I'm going to get some fags."

Jo heaves herself out of the car. She shuts the door on Lily, who still has her binoculars fixed on the house. She's watching a small Asian woman unload bags and bags of dry-cleaning from the rear of the van. 'AM' opens the door and stands aside to allow the woman to carry them in.

When Jo gets back to the car Lily asks, "What time is it?"

"Almost nine."

"Why haven't they left?"

"Who?"

"'AM' and 'TIFF'. They're still inside."

Jo takes the binoculars from Lily. "Maybe they're sorting out the dry-cleaning?"

They wait a few more minutes in worried silence. "Shit," says Jo. "What's going on?"

Half an hour passes. "There's only one thing for it." Jo starts rummaging in her canvas bag and pulls out a sheet of folded paper. "Here it is." She smoothes out the creases from the page she stole from Accrington Library's copy of the Skipton telephone directory. "Right, I need a phone box."

"What you going to say?"

"I have no idea." Jo checks the time again. It's almost ten. "Stay here, keep watch."

Twenty minutes later Jo is back. "'TIFF's ill."

Lily's mouth drops open. "How…?"

"I pretended to be from a double glazing company. You know those, 'we're in your area…' 'TIFF' answered the phone, ever so polite. 'I'm terribly sorry but I don't think we'd be interested.' I said, 'shouldn't you be at school?' And she said she'd had a migraine this morning. I said, 'oh that's a shame. Migraines can be terrible.'"

"Why do posh people get migraines? Normal people get headaches."

"I said, how many days do you get off school with a migraine?' and she giggled and said, 'only one'.

"Then I asked if I could speak to her mum and she said, 'she's at work' so I asked to speak to her dad."

"You didn't."

"I could hear them talking in the background. Then she came back all embarrassed. "I'm sorry he's really busy at the moment. Shall I take your number and maybe he could call you back?"

"Maybe he could call us back," Lily repeats, imitating the upper class accent Jo is using. "Or maybe he has no wish to communicate. Capital letters. Underlined."

They sit and stare at the house in silence for another twenty minutes until Jo says, "Come on. Nothing's happening here today. Let's go home. We need to go over everything one last time. Why don't you drive?"

"Drive us home? Are you crazy?"

Jo climbs out of the driver's seat and walks round the front of the car to the passenger door. She opens it and nods at Lily to move across behind the steering wheel. "You can do it, Lil."

Lily hesitates and then swings her skinny legs over the handbrake and shifts across to the driver's seat. "You'll have to tell me the way."

They stop at Morton's sandwich shop on their way home; Lily's knuckles white and stuck with sweat to the steering wheel. "That was great driving," says Jo as they pull up outside Lily's house.

"Apart from when I nearly hit that motorbike."

"Yeah, apart from that."

"And that fucking roundabout."

"I'm going to get a bath," says Jo. "Roll us a spliff for afters."

When Jo pads down to the front room, a towel tucked around her breasts and another twisted up on her head, Lily is pacing in front of the gas fire. She looks almost shocked to see Jo. "It's like, there's no way back for me. I can't go back to poly and pretend like nothing's happened. I have to do something or my life is over. I'll end up like my mother, dying by degrees. Do you know what I mean?"

"Yeah, I know what you mean."

"The only thing I'm worried about is you." Jo opens her mouth to speak but Lily carries on, rushing to get the words out. "You're the only friend I've ever had. It would be shit if you regretted something because of me. That's the only thing stopping me."

"This isn't just about you, Lil. This is about men and the way they treat women. Honestly, I'm grateful for the chance to be involved. To do something meaningful, instead of watching 'Corrie' with all the other zombies out there."

"But, what if…"

"Fuck it, we're doing it. We're bloody doing it." Jo holds up her right arm, her fist clenched in a comrade salute, like at the Socialist Workers' Party meetings she's dragged Lily to on a few occasions.

A strange sensation fills up in Lily. It starts in her stomach and pushes up through her chest into her head. Her eyes hurt, and for a moment she worries she might be sick. Jo hits her on the arm. "Where's the spliff you were meant to be rolling?"

"Oh sorry, I forgot."

Jo picks up the dope tin from the top of the gas fire and hands it to Lily.

"Jo?"

"Yeah?"

"I don't know what I'd have done, you know, if you hadn't shown up..." Lily's voice falters.

"Shut up and skin up. And then we need to rehearse your lines again."

"I need a drink too."

"I'll sort those out. Let me get my PJs on."

"It's only half three."

"I know but I'm shagged. It's all these fucking early mornings. But you know what they say, early bird catches the worm. I want to be asleep by ten."

It's half past ten by the time Lily has rehearsed her lines enough to know she knows them backwards. While Jo is cleaning her teeth, Lily knocks back one last nightcap, anything to try and extinguish the flames of fear in her stomach. When Jo comes back down the stairs, Lily is under the duvet. Jo climbs in next to her and turns out the light.

Lily switches it back on again at quarter to eleven. "I can't do it."

"What?"

"What if she recognises me? I mean, what if I look like him? What if she won't come into the car? I can't drag her, what if she's stronger than me? I can't do it." Lily sits bolt upright on the mattress and reaches for a cigarette.

"Calm down, Lily. Breathe."

"What if her dad's told her that I tried to contact him? What if she's been told to watch out for me?"

Jo puts an arm around Lily's shoulder. Lily shakes it off. "I can't do it, Jo. I'm sorry."

"I'll do it. I'll get her into the car. You drive."

"I can't drive."

"Yes, you can. You've had loads of lessons. You're a great driver," she lies. "Come on, Lily. We can't back out now."

It takes Jo another twenty minutes to calm Lily down, to the stage where she can switch the light off again, but the fear and excitement in their stomachs means they are still awake when the dawn creeps across the sky.

Chapter 16

DAY SEVENTEEN (Wednesday 12th December 1989)
D-DAY
Weather: bright sunshine. Ice cold.
Spliffs smoked: 1
07:30 AF leaves.
08:25 AM leaves.
12:20 Move to positions

At half past twelve Jo parks the Mini at the kerbside a few hundred yards past the entrance to the ginnel. She climbs out of the car and blows a kiss to Lily. She crosses over the road and stands at the bus stop, the hood of her parka up. Lily moves into the front seat and chain-smokes as she watches for 'TIFF' in the rear view mirror. Exactly on schedule, she turns the corner into the street. As soon as she enters the ginnel, Lily switches on the engine and reverses the car up to the mouth of the ginnel, as Jo pulls off her hood, crosses the road in front of her, and starts to run after Fiona. Lily holds onto the steering wheel as tight as she can, trying to stop her whole body shaking.

Jo enters the ginnel fifteen seconds after 'TIFF'. She shouts out after her, "Fiona!"

Fiona turns round to see Jo. Jo waves her arms in the air. "Wait, stop. I've been sent from your mum's office." She catches up with the schoolgirl and then stops and pretends to breathe great lungfuls of air. "She's been taken to hospital. We've come to take you to her." She gesticulates to Lily at the far end of the passageway, waiting in the car with the front passenger door open and the engine running.

To give Fiona credit, she doesn't hang around; she starts running immediately towards the car "What happened?"

"I don't know," says Jo as she runs alongside her. "One minute she was just standing there and the next thing she just went really pale and clutched her chest." They reach the car and Jo opens the back door for Fiona. Then she slams the front door shut and climbs into the back seat, next to Fiona. Lily stares at Jo via the rear view mirror. Jo was supposed to get into the front passenger seat. Jo nods at Lily. Lily turns to face the road and takes a deep breath; she can do this. She releases the handbrake and stalls the Mini as she tries to pull away from the kerb. Then she almost floods the engine trying to get it to start. As the sweat starts to form on Lily's palms, and she's just about to scream she can't do it, the car roars into life. She yanks it away from the kerb and they are off.

"Does Daddy know?"

"Yeah, I think someone rang him. I don't know, I just set off for you as soon as the ambulance got there."

"Ambulance, oh goodness."

Lily and Jo catch each other's eyes in the rear view mirror, "Goodness?" mouths Lily.

No one speaks for five minutes. Jo draws flowers in the condensation on the windows. Then Lily hits the road out of Skipton.

Fiona is in such a state of anxiety, she doesn't notice at first. "How did you know where to find me?"

"Your mum said you'd be at school, so we went there first and they said you had a free period, so you wouldn't be in until one, so we went to your house and guessed you must have left, so I ran after you." Jo smiles self-deprecatingly.

It takes another two minutes for Fiona to realise they've left Skipton behind. "Where are you going? This isn't the way to the hospital?"

Jo takes a deep breath. "Skipton hospital's full, bed shortage, she's being taken to the next nearest, which is Accrington."

"Accrington?" Fiona is incredulous. Lily raises an eyebrow. Hardly known for its provision of health care services, Accrington is so small it doesn't even have a McDonald's.

"Well not actually Accrington it's-"

"Blackburn she means," says Lily. "There's a big heart unit there. We're just going via Accrington. Don't worry I know the way."

Fiona shrinks back against her seat. "I wish Daddy was here."

"I'm sure he's on his way by now. In fact I bet he's there already, holding her hand," says Jo.

"Why didn't he pick me up?"

"I'm sure he thought it was best to get straight over there."

"But how will he find it on his own?"

"Perhaps one of the teachers will go with him."

"How do you know Daddy's a teacher?"

"Aren't you a bit old to be calling your dad, daddy?" Jo asks.

"Do you work with my mum?" Fiona looks at Jo's bleached white flat-top.

"I'm a work placement student."

"And she told you Daddy's a teacher?"

A sign at the side of the road welcomes them to Lancashire. Lily exhales and her shoulders drop half an inch.

Jo brazens it out. "She must have done."

"And what about you? Are you on placement too?" Fiona addresses Lily directly for the first time. Their eyes meet in the rear view mirror and Lily flinches under her gaze. "Do I know you?"

Lily can feel the sweat running down her back. She wishes the clapped out Mini would drive quicker, as she wants to be back home. She's finding driving much easier at forty miles an hour. Her hands are feeling clammy on the steering wheel and she's gagging for a drink. "You don't know me."

"What's going on?"

At last there is Accrington, a jewel in the crown. Lily has never been happier to see her home town in her whole life.

"Stop the car, I want to get out."

"Ok Fiona, we've not been exactly straight with you," Jo begins. "But the good news is your mum's fine. She's not in hospital; she's not been taken ill. We just wanted to have a chat with you about a few things. When we have, we'll take you straight home again I promise."

"I want Daddy."

"Will you stop calling him Daddy," Lily snaps. "For God's sake. How old are you?"

"Sixteen, nearly."

Lily turns their car into her mother's council estate and feels a huge wave of relief sweep her body. She pulls up at the kerb outside the house, mounting it slightly and nudging a lamp post as she does so.

Fiona's face pales. She twiddles a pigtail round and round her forefinger and thumb. "Where are we? What are we doing here? Who lives here? What's going on?"

"I've told you we just want to chat to you for a bit." Jo leans across her and pulls the door handle. The back door opens a couple of inches.

Fiona shrinks back against her seat, bracing herself with her hands on the back seat. "I don't want to. I don't want to go in that house." Her voice has risen an octave.

"Don't be so rude," says Jo. "That's Lily's home."

"I'm sorry. I didn't mean... I just want to go home."

Lily turns off the engine and speaks to Fiona via the rear view mirror. "I will take you home in a short while, but first I want to show you something. This is my house. I want you to come inside with me and see what it is I want to show you, and then you can go home."

"Daddy will be very worried if I'm not home by four o'clock."

Lily's never met anyone who speaks like this. Contrast this with, 'daddy has no wish to communicate', capital letters, underlined. She takes a very deep breath. "Then we must make sure you are home by four o'clock. It's twenty past two. So long as we set off by twenty past three we'll be fine."

"An hour? What do you want to show me that's going to take an hour?"

"Look." Lily pulls the keys out of the ignition and swivels round in her chair to face her. "Just get in the house, Ok?" The adrenaline of the day has now collected in a queasy mass in her stomach, and she needs to stand up, to get out of this car, to get home. Funny how today is the first time this house feels like home.

Lily gets out of the car and yanks the back door open wide. She stands and waits for a few moments, but Fiona doesn't move. Lily puts one hand on the roof of the Mini and ducks her head down so she is at the same level as Fiona. She speaks quietly but firmly. "You can either step inside or I will drag you in by your hair. It's your choice."

Fiona turns to Jo, beseeching her with her eyes. Jo tries to smile a reassuring smile at her. Fiona's bottom lip starts to wobble.

"We're not going to hurt you," Jo adopts the voice of a mother talking to a small child, "honestly."

Fiona glances from Jo to Lily and then pulls herself out of the car. She stands in front of Lily. Fiona's dark brown eyes stare into Lily's for a moment, challenging, defiant. Lily doesn't look away. Fiona tuts loudly and then turns towards the house, flicking her dark brown fringe across her face, her head held high. Jo scrambles out of the car after her, pausing only to grin at Lily before chasing after the schoolgirl. Lily bangs the car door closed, closes her eyes and takes a deep breath, before following the two of them up the path.

Chapter 17

Lily's hands are shaking so much she has trouble getting the key in the lock. When she finally manages to push the door open, Jo propels Fiona across the threshold first. Fiona looks like she's going to go willingly, until the smell hits their nostrils and her hands grab onto the doorframe. Jo gives her an extra shove - two firm hands in the centre of the girl's back and she's through. Lily steps into the hallway quickly behind them and shuts the front door. She locks it and gives the key to Jo. Jo pockets it.

"Upstairs?" asks Jo.

Lily's eyebrows meet in the centre of her face. They hadn't got this far in the plan. She nods. Fiona sees the nod and grips onto the banister with both hands. Her schoolbag drops to the floor. "I'm not going upstairs."

"Oh yes you are," says Jo.

"Why does it stink?" asks Fiona, her voice high.

"Don't be so bloody rude," says Jo, trying to loosen Fiona's grip on the banister. "Get her other hand, Lily."

As Lily prises Fiona's left fingers from the stair-rail, Fiona opens her mouth and emits a scream that cuts through Lily's central nervous system. Lily lets go of the one finger she's managed to prise from its grip and puts her hands to her ears. "Alright, alright."

Fiona continues screaming.

"Shut up." Lily shouts the last two words at the top of her lungs. Fiona stops screaming, her cheeks are flushed red. Lily savours a second of silence, before saying, "We can do it in the front room."

Lily steps into the front room, stooping to pick up a polystyrene box, half full of cold chips and curry sauce, and drops it in the bin-liner that is propped up against the wall. Then she pulls back the curtains and is about to open the window, but stops herself. Textbook stuff; keep the windows closed.

Fiona looks around the dim room, with the wallpaper peeling off above the gas fire which is lit. She swallows audibly. "What do you want? I haven't got any money with me."

"I don't want your stupid money." Lily leaves the room and returns moments later with two tumblers and the vodka bottle. She pours Jo and herself a drink, and then, as an afterthought, says to Fiona, "Do you want one?"

Fiona shakes her head.

Lily drinks more than half of her vodka without pausing for breath. She wipes her lips on the back of her sleeve and watches Fiona take in the contents of the room. "I'm sorry there's no settee. I've, er, I've just bought a new one, waiting for it to be delivered. It was supposed to be here last week." Lily raises her eyebrows and tut-tuts in a way she hopes will portray her general dismay at the furniture delivery industry. She smoothes out a corner of the quilt on their bed-cum-settee in the corner of the room, swatting off broken crisps. "Do you want to sit on here?"

"No."

"Sit," says Jo.

Fiona stares at Jo for a moment and then folds her long colt-like legs beneath her, and perches on the edge of the mattress, barely making contact with the fabric. Jo sits on the floor by the window. They all look at each other expectantly as silence fills the room. When her mother was alive, Bert was a constant presence, always here when Lily got home from school, sprawled on the sofa with his Special Brew, as her mother grazed her way through a box of Family Circle biscuits. But now the house feels too small for three people. Lily paces in front of the fire, fighting the urge to run. Jo and Fiona both look up at her, Jo nodding encouragingly. Lily drains the rest of her glass.. "So," she says, "I'm sorry we lied. We tried to think of a lie that wouldn't worry you so much, but we couldn't think of a good one. Anyway, your mum's fine, which is more than my mum is, so that's good. Good for you. So, so we wanted to talk to you because... because."

Fiona is staring at Lily, her eyes wide. Lily focuses on the badge on the breast pocket of Fiona's blazer. It looks like two unicorns carrying a shield between them. Lily tries to make out the letters, 'Fortis est Veritas. She wonders what it means, almost asks but then Jo stands up and starts talking. "We're pissed off with your dad."

87

Fiona's face crumples into a frown. "My dad?"

She says it in a tone of utter disbelief; like it was the last thing on earth she expected Jo to say. "Did he used to teach you?"

"No," says Lily, pouring another vodka. "He hasn't taught me anything."

"Then..."

"Your dad is a lying, cheating coward and we think he needs to be taught a lesson."

"What?" asks Fiona, the confusion evident in every inch of her body.

"Your dad," Jo pauses and shifts her gaze from Fiona to a stain on the wall behind her, "your father is actually Lily's father and Lily wanted to meet him, because she's never met him. Which is fair enough, I think. Don't you?"

Fiona's mouth opens like she may be about to say something, but no words come out.

"And Lily asked nicely and he said no, no way. He refused to meet his own flesh and blood. Which makes him a lying, cheating coward." Jo turns to Lily. "And he has to pay for that."

Fiona doesn't move. She sits on the edge of the mattress, as if waiting for a punch line. Lily watches Fiona's cheeks turn red as she shakes her head. She licks her lips before speaking. "No way. I'm really sorry but you've got the wrong person."

Jo copies Fiona's head shake. "I'm really sorry but we haven't."

"You have, there's been a terrible mix up. There's no way Daddy would... I mean there's just no way." Fiona smiles with the absolute confidence of someone who has never been lied to, disappointed, betrayed. Her whole body relaxes, like someone has pulled out the plug. Her shoulders sink half an inch. Lily slips quietly from the room as she hears Jo start to explain about how the Salvation Army tracked him down. Jo shows Fiona the letter from the Salvation Army as Lily re-enters the lounge.

"That doesn't prove anything." Fiona says. She turns to Lily. "You must have a father with the same name or something. This is a case of mistaken identity. I'm an only child. Daddy always says, before he had me he wanted six children, and then when I was born, he realised he had everything he wanted."

Lily stands in the corner of the room, leaning against the door, clutching the wedding album to her chest, waiting to hear more; in fact, willing Fiona to continue, to share more happy vignettes of nuclear family life, but Fiona sees her expression and falls silent. Lily waits a few moments and then hands her the wedding album.

Fiona sits back down on the bed-settee, shaking her head as she opens the first page. She smiles when she sees the first picture, the one of Pamela rushing in through the rain. "That's not my mum."

"No. She's mine, was mine. Keep going."

Fiona turns the next page and her eyes widen as she takes in the picture of Lily's parents happily entwined. She turns another page, and another. Her cheeks are flaming red. "God, there's Granny."

Lily cranes her neck to see which photo Fiona was looking at. It's a group photograph with several elderly people in the frame. "Which?"

Fiona points her out with the thumb on her left hand, while the right index finger traces over the rest of the people in the photograph. "I can't believe it. Nobody has ever, ever, ever said a word to me, I swear."

"Is Granny still..." Lily's voice falters.

Fiona looks up at her. "What, alive? Oh God, yes. She was bungee jumping in Australia last year. Daddy... Dad, always says she'll outlive everybody, even me. I can't believe he's lied to me. There's Auntie Sue, Uncle Norman." Fiona's eyes are bright with tears.

"All I wanted was a chance to meet him; to find out something of where I'm from."

Fiona takes in a deep breath. "Just because they were married, doesn't mean, I mean, he might not be your dad. Maybe that's why he left. Maybe your mum had an affair."

"My mum did not have an affair," Lily shouts, almost blown off her feet by the wave of anger that surges up inside her. Without a moment's hesitation she launches herself at Fiona, knocking the schoolgirl backwards. There's a loud thwack as Fiona's head hits the wall behind the mattress. Lily grabs one of Fiona's plaits and pulls her head up off the bed, so that Fiona's face is only centimetres from her own. "Don't you dare... She loved him all her life. He was the only man she ever loved. And when he left her, it killed her. Do you understand?"

Fiona's face is pale and when Lily lets go of the clump of hair, Fiona falls backwards again, banging her head a second time, but with less force. Her eyes close. "Steady on there, Lil" says Jo, coming over from the other side of the room. She hauls Lily up off Fiona and the mattress. Lily sways as she tries to find her feet.

"Is she ok?" asks Jo. Fiona is lying, pale and lifeless on the mattress, her head slumped at an odd angle.

The gas fire hisses quietly as Lily observes Fiona's form. After a few seconds, Lily turns to the bottle of vodka sitting on top of the gas fire and pours herself another shot. She fills the glass to the brim from the carton of almost fresh orange and takes a mouthful.

"Course, she is," she says as she flings the contents of the glass over Fiona's face. Fiona's eyes open immediately and she sits up, spluttering and trying to wipe the juice from her eyes. "See?"

Jo exhales deeply. She feels in her pocket for her packet of Marlboro's and lights one, running her left hand through her spiked hair as she smokes with her right.

"You shouldn't have done that," says Fiona, her eyes filling with tears, or vodka and orange. Lily isn't sure which.

Lily runs from the room and up the stairs. She comes back a moment later and throws a folded piece of paper at Fiona. It lands on the mattress next to her but she doesn't reach for it. Instead she asks, "Is your mum…"

"Dead." Lily finishes the sentence for her and reaches across to take the lit fag Jo is handing to her.

"I am so sorry," says Fiona, and from her tone of voice, Lily believes her. "When, how old were you… when she...?"

"She died two months ago."

Fiona looks at her. "I don't understand."

Lily takes a deep drag of the fag before speaking. "The life went out of her when he went. He might as well have shot her on his way out of the door. She never recovered. It just took nineteen years for her body to die."

Jo sits back down on the floor and takes her tobacco tin out as Fiona studies the picture of Lily's mum in the album.

"That's not the mum I knew," says Lily. "In fact, I didn't even recognise her at first." Lily goes to a drawer in the dresser and rummages through the over-spilling mishmash of pools coupons and take away menus. She pulls out a dog-eared photo, a picture she'd taken on one of the rare occasions she'd managed to get her mother out of the house and into the garden. She's sat on a low wall, wearing a grey dress that could double up as a scout tent. The photo is seven or eight years old, and her mother is half the size she was when she died, but still immense. Her face is almost lost, drowned in a sea of fat. Fiona recoils.

The doorbell rings, causing all three of them to jump. Lily hisses. "Get down."

Jo jumps across the room and pushes Fiona so that's she horizontal on the mattress. "Ow," says Fiona, rubbing her head.

Lily runs to the window, puts her back against the wall and peers round the curtains. "Oh bloody hell. It's Bert. Hang on I'll get rid of him." She turns to Fiona. "Be quiet."

Lily opens the front door, "What's up?"

"Just wondered if you wanted to come round, watch the snooker, have a drink."

"Ah thanks, Bert, can't right now. Maybe tomorrow."

"What are you up to?" He tries to look over her shoulder.

Lily adjusts her position to block his view.

"Who've you got in there? Come on out, whoever you are," he shouts over Lily's shoulder.

"Hel-", Fiona starts to shout, but Jo is on her straight away, pushing her into the mattress and lying her short but weighty body over the top of Fiona's. She clasps her hand across Fiona's mouth.

Fiona stares at Jo as Jo holds up the piece of paper Lily threw at Fiona earlier. Jo opens it out with her left hand, her right still clasped over Fiona's mouth, as she sits straddling Fiona's body. It's Lily's birth certificate, blue round the edges from spending so many years hidden in her school bag. There's a column entitled 'Father', and Fiona sees 'David Winterbottom' typed in it. Jo releases her hand from Fiona's face, just a centimetre at first. Fiona holds her breath as they both listen to Lily.

"It's just a friend from college," Lily is saying to Bert. "She's come to visit."

"Bring her round too. What's with all the secrets? I've got Hula Hoops."

"Tempting, Bert, but not today. I've got to go. I'm making tea. I'll see you." She closes the door in his face and goes back to the front room. Fiona is sitting mutely on the bed. Jo smiles at Lily.

"I can't believe it," Fiona says again, as she takes off her blazer. She glances around for a place to hang it, before folding it neatly in half lengthways, and laying it flat on the edge of the mattress.

"Yeah, well. I had to believe it," says Lily, pouring herself another drink. "I didn't get the choice.".".

"He can't have known she was pregnant. Daddy... Dad, would never leave his own child, I'm absolutely sure of that," although her voice doesn't give the impression of someone secure in her facts.

"He was having an affair the whole time she was pregnant. My Aunt Edie told me. Everyone knew about it."

"Probably wasn't getting enough sex once he'd got his wife up the duff," says Jo.

"But-" says Fiona.

Lily interrupts. "What about the letter he wrote to the Salvation Army? I asked them to help me trace him. He wrote back to them. The guy read me his letter down the phone. It didn't say, 'what are you talking about? I don't have another daughter'."

"Did he say-"

"He said, 'I have no wish to communicate'. The 'no' was in capital letters and underlined. Did I mention that?" A gob of spit flies out of Lily's lips and lands on the floor in front of Fiona. "He didn't even send note for them to pass on to me to explain. That's what makes me so mad."

A solitary tear runs down Fiona's right cheek. "I saw him get the letter. He opened it in front of me. I saw the Salvation Army written across the top. I thought..." She doesn't finish the sentence. Two more tears spill down her face. She doesn't wipe them. Instead she picks up the photo album and turns to another page "My whole family's here. Mum's going to kill him when she finds out."

"Fiona, you're nearly sixteen years old. I'm nineteen. It was probably your mum he was having the affair with."

Fiona shakes her head firmly. "You don't understand. Mum's a lawyer, a really good one. She represents women who've been abandoned by their husbands. There's no way she'd marry someone who hasn't taken responsibility for his... no way."

Jo starts to roll a spliff. Lily sits on the floor at the edge of the mattress and scratches her arms.

Fiona continues to turn the pages in the wedding album. "They didn't get married in church. I always thought that was odd; we go to church every Sunday." Jo and Lily both nod but Fiona doesn't notice. "They got married in the Registry Office; Mum said she didn't want a big fuss."

Jo raises a single eyebrow.

"But you're not allowed to get married in church if you're divorced are you?" Fiona looks to them for answers. Lily, having only set foot in a church on two occasions; her Aunt Edie's fake funeral and her mother's, shrugs her shoulders.

"When did your parents get divorced?" asks Fiona.

"I don't even know that they did."

92

"My parents got married in 1971, three years before I was born."

"I was born in 1970, August."

"But Daddy said they were going out with each other for two years before they got married. Daddy always says you should spend as long as possible getting to know someone, before making any kind of commitment."

"Daddy tells lies," says Jo. She licks the Rizla to seal the spliff. "I think that's clear."

Fiona stands up in front of Lily, her bright eyes begging for a different explanation; one that doesn't involve her father having lied to her, her whole life. Lily looks away. Jo lights the spliff and goes over to the window.

"I'm not even allowed to go friends' houses unless their parents are at home. He's so worried that boys might be there. And when I tell him he should trust me, he says he does trust me, he just doesn't trust teenage boys." Fiona sits back down on the bed and looks at the photo album again.

"He knows what boys are capable of. He knows what bastards men are. How does he know?" Jo asks the room as she exhales a plume of smoke. "Because he is one."

"He absolutely hates the fact I've got a boyfriend," Fiona murmurs, as she turns another page. "He can hardly bring himself to mention his name. We've been having the most dreadful rows about it. And all the time he knows he cheated on his pregnant wife, and then abandoned his own baby?" Her voice rises an octave. "I just cannot, cannot believe it."

Jo glances at the clock. It's almost four. Already they won't get Fiona home on time. Not that that was ever the intention, but now they are committed. People will start worrying soon. "What are we going to do? I mean, it's getting late."

"What are you planning to do? I mean, you wanted to bring me here and show me this why? What did you think I would do? Have it out with my dad?"

Lily looks first at Jo and then at Fiona. "I wanted you to stay here for a night, without your dad knowing where you were, because I wanted him to feel what it's like to go to sleep for a night and not know where your family is."

"What if I go home and talk to him about it?"

"That doesn't really help me," says Lily. "I'm sick of wondering what he's thinking, or how he's justifying it, or who knows what. This is the first time in my life where I'm the one that knows what's happening." She grins at Jo, the alcohol content in her stomach finally overcoming the adrenalin. "I kinda like it."

Jo brushes cigarette ash from her leggings. "Fiona, try to see Lily's point of view. Her mum's dead. She grew up in this house," she stresses the 'this' and gives Fiona a moment to fully take in the conditions before continuing, "and her dad won't even do her the courtesy of meeting her one time. It's a bit insulting really. And all we're asking is that you give up one night of your privileged existence. It's not exactly much to ask, is it?"

Fiona loosens her tie and looks down at the photograph of her father on her lap. His arms circle his new bride's waist, his head is tilted, their lips only millimetres apart as he bends to kiss his wife. . She lifts her head, meets Lily's gaze. She doesn't speak for a few moments, but when she does her voice is steady. "No, it's not a lot to ask."

Lily closes her eyes.

"And," says Fiona, in a quiet voice as Lily reopens her eyes, "it might do us all good to have some time to think."

Chapter 18

Time suspends for a moment, until Jo claps her hands together. "Ok," she says "O – K."

No one else says anything. Lily is looking at the schoolgirl and for the first time thinking she looks older than fifteen.

"What we need is food," says Jo. "I don't know about you guys but I'm starving. I'll go to the chippy. What do you fancy?"

Lily speaks directly to Fiona. "Are you sure?"

Fiona nods, a 'blink and you'd miss it' nod. "May I have fish and chips please? And mushy peas? I haven't had any lunch." Fiona reaches across the mattress for her blazer. "Here," she says, handing Jo a handful of coins, "take my dinner money."

Jo tots up the change in her hand. "You get three pound fifty dinner money?"

"It's for drinks as well," Fiona says defensively.

The phone rings. Lily jumps so much she spills her vodka down her jumper. She looks over to Jo.

Jo nods at her to answer it.

The phone is in the hallway, but the flex is long enough for Lily to bring it into the doorway of the front room. "'Lo?" Lily mumbles into the receiver.

"Lily, is that you? Where have you been? I've been worried sick."

"Aunt Edie?"

"You were supposed to come for tea a fortnight since."

"Oh. Sorry. I've been a bit… busy."

"Well, so long as you're alright," Aunt Edie grumbles. "What about tomorrow? I could get us a nice bit of tongue from the market."

95

"I, I've got a friend staying from college. We've been, er exploring together."

"A friend?" Aunt Edie asks suspiciously. "A man friend?"

"No, no, a girlfriend. I mean, a friend who's a girl."

"Ah well, bring her with you," Aunt Edie says. "I'd like to meet your friend. I bet you have a great time together."

Lily looks at Jo helplessly. "That's kind but we can't come tomorrow." Her eyes plead with Jo for help. Fiona is engrossed in the wedding album. She's pulling out the telegrams and messages of congratulations from an envelope fixed to the back cover and reading each one. Lily wonders whether she should grab the album off her. She hasn't read them all herself yet. "We're…"

"Going away for a few days," Jo mouths.

"We're going away for a few days," Lily parrots into the receiver.

"Are you now?" says Aunt Edie in a tone that suggests going away for a few days is akin to running naked through Morrisons. "Where?"

"What?"

"Where are you going?"

"Can I ring you back, Aunt Edie? I've got something in the oven. I think it might be burning." Lily watches Fiona shaking her head at one telegram before stuffing it back inside the envelope.

"Bit early for tea, isn't it?" Aunt Edie asks suspiciously.

"I'll ring you when we get back."

"I've got some information for you, I didn't want to tell you over the phone."

"Information?"

"About your dad. I've been asking about. Turns out he had a baby with his fancy woman."

Aunt Edie pauses, like she's waiting for a reaction. A gasp or some kind of acknowledgement. Lily stares at Fiona. "A baby? No way."

"No wonder you mother went like she did. Nora Jenkins'; her daughter Flora, was in the same delivery ward when she had their Bernadette. You remember her, Bernadette Briggs they called her; with those funny things on her teeth? Made her look like that one from the James Bond film. Although Nora told me she's found herself a husband, Lord alone knows how."

"Well, thanks for letting me know. I've got to go Aunt Edie. But I'll come and see you next week." Lily puts the phone down and wipes her forehead with the back of hand. Her forehead is moist.

"Right," says Jo, pulling on her man sized donkey jacket. "Will you two be ok without me?"

Lily leans against the wall. The adrenalin seems to be gaining the upper hand.

"I'm sure we'll be fine," says Fiona. She puts the wedding album down on the bed and pulls at her school tie until it forms a loop big enough to go over her head. She throws it down on the bed next to her wedding album. "We are sisters after all."

She says the words calmly, almost as an aside, but they hit Lily's ears like they'd been blazed through a megaphone. The hairs on her arms rise and her throat is so dry she panics she won't be able to breathe. Sisters. It never occurred to her. Several thoughts erupt in her mind at the same time, each obscuring the other. A sudden flash of memory, of pretending; an imaginary sister called Emily.

Fiona stands in front of Lily "I always wanted a sister. I hate being an only child."

Lily wants to shout, "Me too!" but she can't speak. What little colour her skin contains drains from her face and she feels like she might faint. Fiona seems to sense what's happening and puts her arms around Lily's shoulders like she's the big sister, keeping Lily safe. Lily's ears pound and she feels like there's too much blood inside her. Her veins are throbbing, like they do just before she cuts herself. It's never about pain; only release.

Jo watches for a moment and then slips out the front door.

"I'm sorry. I'm sorry," Lily keeps saying over and over, into Fiona's ribcage. "God, what am I like? I've kidnapped my own sister."

Fiona does her best to stroke Lily's dreadlocks. "You haven't kidnapped me."

"I did, I did. If you hadn't have got out of the car I would have dragged you in here by your hair."

"I don't want to go home. That's the truth. I want to stay here with you."

"I was so angry with him. It's like, I didn't get that you're my sister. My sister." Lily breaks away from Fiona and gulps some air. She lets out a long yell. It rings out for what feels like minutes. Once it's over she feels a little calmer, a little steadier. She reaches for her glass. "I need another drink. Please, have a drink."

"Ok," says Fiona. "But don't make it too strong."

Fiona follows Lily into the kitchen. Lily's hands are shaking as she opens the vodka bottle. She looks around for a glass for Fiona but then remembers she's smashed them all. They will have to buy another cup. Then a thought occurs to her and she rushes upstairs to the bathroom. In the cupboard is an old mug, which used to house toothbrushes. She returns to the kitchen with a look of triumph, holding the mug aloft, before washing it in the sink.

Lily hands Fiona a vodka and orange and the girls chink mugs. "To sisters," says Lily, her hands shaking.

"And truth and justice," adds Fiona, as she raises the mug to her lips.

They drink in silence, Fiona recoiling slightly from the heat of the vodka. Lily leans back against the kitchen worktop and stares at her feet.

"Shall we go into the front room?" says Fiona. "I want to see the photos again."

"So, who is everyone? Will you tell me?" asks Lily, as they sit side by side on the mattress settee.

"That's Uncle Norman." Fiona points to one of the groomsmen, the one holding the umbrella above Lily's mother's head, as she runs in through the rain. "He's Dad's brother. Our dad's brother. 'Our dad.' Doesn't that sound weird?" Fiona practices the words, feeling their unfamiliar shape on her tongue. "Our dad. Uncle Norman lives in Hebden Bridge. Dad calls him the black sheep of the family because he lives with Aunt Becky and they're not married." She lowers her voice, "And they've got children two, Nat and Ellie."

"How old are they?"

"Nat's seventeen and Ellie's the same age as me. And that's Auntie Sue, Daddy's sister." She points to a slim woman with a beehive haircut, wearing a bridesmaid dress. "She's married to Uncle Freddie, they live in Edinburgh. They've got three children. That's who you remind me of," she exclaims, clicking her fingers. "You look like Hannah, their daughter."

Lily is adding up in her head; five cousins, an aunt and two uncles, grandparents and a sister. A sister with pigtails, for crying out loud. Lily sits back on the bed. "Why did no one stay in touch? On my 18th birthday I spent the whole day waiting for the postman. I thought a load of cards would pour through the letterbox," her voice breaks.

"I can't believe no one told me," says Fiona. "I wonder if my cousins know." She glances at her older sister, "If they do…" The sentence hangs uncompleted in the air.

"Tell me about the people I don't know," says Fiona, changing the subject. "Who's that?"

"That's my granny, my mum's mum," Lily touches the picture with her finger. "She died when I was little. And that's her husband, Granddad. He died when I was five. Apparently he was lost without her." Lily tries to remember something about him; to a five year old child he just seemed tall and rigid. "That's my Aunt Edie. She's still alive, although she was dead for a while."

Fiona's pretty face wrinkles in a frown. "What?"

"I thought she was dead, it's a long story. I'll tell you another time. And that's the only people I know," she says staring at the group photo. "I didn't even recognise my mum at first." Lily lays the photo album down and lights a cigarette. "I can hardly remember seeing her stood up for one thing."

"Where did you get this?" Fiona rubs her palm across the cover of the wedding album.

"Aunt Edie gave it to me, after my mum's funeral. My granddad gave it to her to give to me, but she didn't dare while my mum was still alive. I'd never seen a photo of my dad. That was the weird thing; I was expecting to be shocked to see a picture of him, but actually I was more shocked to see my mum. It's like I never really met her either. Do you know what I mean?" Lily takes another slurp of vodka. "I hadn't seen her for three months before she died. I feel bad about that, but it was horrible coming home. It was just easier not to."

Lily turns to face Fiona. The similarities between them are impossible to ignore. How could she not have realised this girl was her sister? Looking at her face is like looking into a mirror; a rose tinted mirror. The same dark eyes, the same dimple on their left cheek. Fiona's skin is clearer, the whites of her eyes brighter, her teeth straighter, but essentially they are the same stock.

Fiona lies back on the mattress, staring up at the ceiling. "It's not fair, I can't believe Dad did this."

"What's he like?"

"Dad?" Fiona sighs heavily. "You know if you'd have asked me that six months ago I'd have said he was the best dad ever. Mum works all the time, she's never there, so it's always been Dad and me. He didn't work at all when I was little but now he's a teacher. Oh but you knew that already." Fiona watches Lily's hands tremble as she tries to stick three Rizla papers together to make a spliff. "What's he like?" She thinks for a moment. "He makes the best jacket potatoes stuffed with cheese and onion and butter, he's great at helping with my homework, except for physics, which he's rubbish at. He's always got time to talk. He read me a bedtime story every night until I was about fourteen and I had to tell him to stop."

"Sounds..." Lily's voice trails off as she fails to come up with a suitable adjective. She gives up on the spliff, crumples the papers into a little ball and flicks it across the front room. "Sounds like a fairy tale."

"That's the thing. But lately-"

The front door opens and Jo bursts into the room with two carrier bags. The smell of warm newspaper fills the air. "Food."

Lily is relieved to see her, to breathe the late afternoon air that comes in with her. "So," says Jo. "How are you two getting on?"

Fiona glances across at Lily and smiles, a tentative ghost of a smile. "Good." Silence falls over the three of them, while they devour their fish and chips. Lily eats hardly anything, before folding up the papers and lighting a cigarette. "What are we going to do?"

"Do you know what I think?" asks Fiona, her cheeks flushed by the vodka. "I think you should tell him I've been kidnapped and get him to pay."

"I meant, what shall we do tonight?" says Lily in alarm.

"Pay?" asks Jo, licking curry sauce off her fingers.

"A ransom, that's usually the point of kidnapping. I know it won't make up for what's happened, but look at this place." Fiona stares at the peeling wallpaper and the nicotine stained net curtains. "We have so much more than you, so much more. You should be compensated. What's it called? Child Support, backdated nineteen years."

Jo scrunches up her chip papers and laughs. "I agree, I think we should work this out. Let's see, what do you think is reasonable for one child? I mean babies don't come cheap – there's cots, prams, all that kind of stuff. But we could average it out? Forty quid a week? That's what a grant cheque boils down to, and it's not exactly the high life."

"A hundred," Fiona suggests.

"Don't be crazy," says Lily.

"I get twenty pounds a week pocket money. That's on top of my dinner money."

"Really?" Lily and Jo both ask at the same time.

"I have to pay for my clothes and everything out of it, and my horse riding lessons."

"Let's split the difference, seventy-five quid," Jo mediates. "So, give me that pen... seventy-five quid, times fifty-two weeks, times nineteen years equals..." Jo starts scribbling across the back of an envelope. She crosses out several times before finally underlining a final figure. "£74,100. Call it a nice, round seventy-five grand. Like Fiona says, it doesn't redress the balance, but it's a start. And you've got to start somewhere."

"I can't blackmail my own father."

"You don't have a father, Lily. That's the point." Jo underlines the figure of £75,000 a second time. "I don't think you've got anything to lose."

Lily looks at Fiona, who shrugs her shoulders. "They can easily afford it. We're loaded. You should see our house. And the money would give you a start. I don't mean to be rude, but did your mum leave you much?"

Lily buries her face in her hands. It's starting to feel like the longest day of her life.

"Ok, what's the alternative?" Jo sits back and lights a cigarette. "Fiona goes home and we pretend nothing's happened? You let him off the hook, like every other downtrodden woman in history? Fiona's right, you're owed, Lily. This might be your only chance of getting ahead of the game. You can't back out now. Otherwise you're an orphan with an overdraft."

"We could make a ransom note," says Fiona, her eyes resting on the pile of newspapers Lily never got round to taking to the tip. "Cut the letters out like they do on the telly." She giggles.

Jo leans over, picks up the top few copies, and throws them into the centre of the room; a gauntlet at Lily's feet. Lily picks up the top copy. The headline reads 'Teenagers getting Pregnant to get Free Council Houses'. Alongside it is a sneak preview of Sarah, the page 3 girl, covering both nipples with her fingertips.

"Come on, Lil. Just for the laugh."

"Alright," says Lily, "but don't blame me if we all end up in prison."

Jo runs down to the SPAR for a Pritt Stick and the three of them huddle around the gas fire, while the wind blows a gale around the house. Jo keeps them laughing by cutting out words like 'helicopter' and 'luxury holiday in Mauritius' to add to their demands. Finally they settle on:

We have your daughter

Do not contact the police.

"I thought we said seventy five?" Lily says as she reads the final version.

"I couldn't find a big seven. Thank God for 0800 numbers."

"Oh."

"How shall I end it? Yours sincerely, the kidnappers? With best wishes? A drop of Fiona's blood?" Jo turns to Fiona, "Joke."

"Leave it blank," says Fiona.

Jo picks up the car keys. "I'll drive it round for a bit so it can't be traced here."

Jo is halfway out of the door when Fiona calls, "Wait."

As Jo turns back round to her, Fiona picks up the big paper scissors, and holds one of her pigtails out at a right angle. Lily realises what she's about to do and shouts "no," but it's too late. Fiona lops off the long brown plaited pigtail in one smooth cut. "Put that in the envelope. That should shake him up a bit."

Jo gingerly accepts the pigtail, the bobble still intact, and stuffs it into the envelope. "I hope he hasn't seen *Fatal Attraction*. This'll scare the shit out of him. You haven't got a bunny rabbit have you?"

"No but we do have Treacle the guinea pig." Fiona can hardly speak for laughing.

"I'll try and find a sorting office, so that he'll get it in the morning. See you in a bit."

"I can't believe you just did that," says Lily.

"I've wanted to get my hair cut short for ages but Dad wouldn't let me. It serves him right."

It's the early hours of the morning when they take Fiona up to Lily's old bedroom. Jo opens the door and Fiona's mouth falls open. The room is bare, apart from a single mattress on the floor, and a sleeping bag. The light bulb hanging from the centre of the ceiling doesn't have a shade and the light it casts is too bright. Jo and Lily have nailed wooden planks they found in a skip, across the inside of the window.

Lily turns to Fiona. "Shit, what were we thinking? I'm sorry."

"We didn't know what to expect," Jo says, as Fiona nods slightly, but doesn't speak.

"You can't sleep here," says Lily. "Let's drag the mattress downstairs. We can all sleep in the front room."

Chapter 19

During the night, Lily has crept so close to the edge of the mattress, when she wakes up her head is on the floor and her neck is so badly cricked she can't move it. Whether she was unconsciously creeping closer to her sister or distancing herself from Jo's gentle snores, only a psychiatrist could answer. As Lily tries to twist her head to look across to the single mattress, a slicing pain shoots down the right hand side of her neck. She holds her face in both hands as the realisation hits her. The single mattress is empty; the sleeping bag forms a heap on the centre of the bed.

"She's gone," says Lily, turning her body over onto her stomach and hauling herself up by her elbows. "Jo, she's gone."

Jo sits bolt upright, like she's been switched on by a jolt of electricity. Her frown is deep, yet uncomprehending. Lily has often been unnerved by the vacant expression on Jo's face in a morning; without her make-up, in those first few moments of the day, she looks childlike, bewildered, afraid. Not the Jo Lily knows and depends upon. "Shit," says Jo.

"I'm here." Fiona appears through the door carrying a tray. She's wearing Jo's Billy Bragg T-shirt, the one that says, 'Capitalism is Killing Music'. It's about four sizes too big for her and hangs off one of her slender shoulders. "I woke up early and couldn't get back to sleep. So I hope you don't mind, but I've had my breakfast. I've made you some toast."

Fiona sets down the tray. Once it's on the floor, Lily can see a plate of toast smeared with Marmite. The smell makes her gag. She flops back down onto the mattress, burying her face in the pillow, and offers up a small thank you to a God she doesn't believe in. When she sits up, Fiona is sitting on the single mattress, her legs crossed in a yoga position, her knees flat against the bed. Her eyes look red-rimmed, the eyelids puffed and swollen, but she smiles at them both. The smile stays on her lips though, doesn't make its way up her face to her eyes.

"Do you want to go home?" says Lily. "You know you only have to say and we'll take you."

Fiona reaches for the plate of toast. The shake of her head is so slight, Lily's not sure whether she imagined it or not. "I think you should ring him," says Fiona. "I want to know what he's thinking."

"He'll have got the ransom note this morning," says Jo.

"We need to see if he's taking it seriously; whether he suspects Lily."

Jo pulls a face at the plate of toast Fiona offers to her, but reaches across Lily to take a cup of tea from the tray. She rolls a cigarette and inhales before speaking. "It doesn't matter if he does. He still won't know where you are."

"Doesn't the Salvation Army have your address?" Fiona asks, reaching for a piece of toast once she realises no one else is going to eat it. "What if Dad rings them and tells them what's happened?"

There's a moment of silence, punctuated only by the sounds of Fiona crunching toast.

"Fuck." Lily turns her upper body to look across at Jo, hoping for some quick reassurance. From the expression on Jo's face, it's clear it's a possibility she hasn't previously considered. Lily's voice gets higher, more frantic. "What if he rings that old buffer at the Salvation Army? Shit." She swings her legs from under the covers and stands up. "He's probably on his way here now."

Fiona takes another bite of her toast as Jo crushes her cigarette in the ashtray, and throws back the duvet on the other side of the double mattress. She stands up, revealing a pair of startlingly white, dumpling-like thighs under her T-shirt, as she leaps across the room. The pile of newspapers they spent the previous afternoon cutting up catches her unawares, and she catapults forward, almost head butting the window. Lily appears frozen to the spot, her eyes fixed on Jo, waiting for her to say something. Jo recovers her balance and peers out behind the still drawn curtains, checking up and down the street. She turns back to Lily and shakes her head.

"What are we going to do?" asks Lily, hysteria creeping into her voice.

When Jo doesn't answer, Fiona, still sitting on the single mattress, swallows her toast and clears her throat. "I've got an idea." She pauses, long enough for Lily to feel she might try to shake the idea from her, if she doesn't start speaking soon. Fiona looks first at Lily, then at Jo, then back to Lily again.

"What?" shouts Lily, unable to stand the suspense.

"We could," says Fiona slowly, "go to Lancaster."

There's a moment's silence. "Lancaster? Why the fuck would we go to Lancaster?" says Jo as she pulls on a pair of black Lycra leggings.

"My boyfriend's at uni there. His name's Stuart and he's got a job in a pub, so he's staying there over Christmas."

Jo pulls a long, shapeless jumper over her crumpled, black T-shirt. It hangs like a dress over the top of her leggings. "That's going to be the first place your dad will look."

Fiona continues as if she hasn't heard Jo. "He shares a flat with this guy, Andre, but he went back to France on Sunday and he won't be back for ages, so there's a spare room."

"Jo's right," says Lily. "Your dad will have thought of that."

"I know, but he'll have rung him yesterday when I didn't come home from school. And Stuart would have said he honestly didn't know where I was. Then Dad will have got the kidnap note this morning, which will completely put Stuart in the clear. He's hardly likely to ransom me is he?"

"How do you know the French guy won't come back?" asks Lily.

"He's gone home for Christmas, he's been really homesick. Stuart and I were trying to think of a way I could visit him in the hols, you know, without Dad knowing. But..." she sighs heavily, "it's impossible trying to get anything past Dad."

Jo smirks at Fiona, causing Fiona's cheeks to redden. "All we wanted was to spend a bit of time together, not for, you know, just to spend some time together without Daddy breathing down our necks."

Jo screws up her face. "I think the lady doth protest too much. I don't think..."

"It's the perfect place. And if you really want to get one over on Dad, he hates the fact I've got a boyfriend, especially one who's eighteen."

"We can go to Leeds," says Jo.

"Tim and what's-his-face will be in Leeds," says Lily.

"Do you know on our third date, Stuart and I went to the pictures together, and half way through the film I saw Dad sitting there on his own, right at the back. He made up some stupid story about how he'd always wanted to see the film, and he hadn't realised it was the one we were going to. Stuart says he's obsessed."

Lily is fully dressed and lacing up her Doctor Martens. She looks first at Fiona and then at Jo. "There's no harm in ringing him. He might be able to tell us what Fiona's dad's thinking."

Jo weighs this up, her bottom lip protruding. "Ok, but if you get any sense your dad is there, hang up the phone."

Fiona dials the number sitting on the bottom step in the hall while Lily and Jo try to squeeze next to each other on the stair above. Fiona stops dialling and turns to them. "You're as bad as my father."

"Sorry, we'll wait in the front room." Lily steps over Fiona and beckons to Jo to follow her. Jo pulls a face at Lily, but follows her all the same. They close the door behind them, standing pressed against it, straining to hear the conversation.

Fifteen minutes later, Fiona opens the door as Lily and Jo try to fling themselves across the room and onto the bed. "What did he say?"

"Crikey." Fiona sits down on the single mattress. Her cheeks are pink. "Daddy drove up to Lancaster last night. Stuart said he thought he was going to hit him. Stuart told him he hadn't any idea where I was. Then…" she pauses to check she has the full attention of her audience, "the police turned up."

"Shit," says Lily.

"Stuart said he thought they were going to start lifting the floorboards. You know, looking for my body."

"Your dad must be going crazy." Jo makes a clenched fist and punches the air. Fiona nods, and Lily can't decide whether she's appalled or at excited at being the centre of a police investigation.

"He'll be out of his mind with worry," she says with confidence. "But I don't think the police are. Stuart says they started asking if he thought I could have fallen out with mum and daddy, and Stuart said he thought it was a possibility. Stuart thinks Dad is far too protective. He told the police we'd been trying to work out a way for me to go up there, for a couple of days over Christmas." She pauses for a moment as the consequences of what she's just said weigh upon her mind. "I hope they don't tell Dad that."

Lily feels a surge of irritation. She's looking at prison time for kidnapping a minor, but God forbid 'daddy' should find out his little darling was planning on visiting her boyfriend. She squashes the feeling down and reaches for a cigarette.

106

"Anyway," Fiona wrests her mind back to the present. "Stuart said that the police didn't appear too concerned. They said to give me forty-eight hours to show up. Stuart said he was expecting me to ring. I told him I was coming to stay with him, and I was bringing my sister and my sister's best friend, and he didn't even ask what sister?" She giggles, her face having returned to its normal colour. "He said 'Really? You're going to stay overnight?'"

Jo and Lily exchange a look, each trying to work out what the other is thinking. Lily's neck is aching.

Fiona fingers the ends of her short hair at one side of the base of her skull. The right plait is still in place. "Has anyone got any mousse?"

"What do you think we should do?" asks Jo to Lily.

"Dad's already been to the police," Fiona reminds them. "If he tells them he's got a ransom note this morning, and he suspects it's something to do with you, the Salvation Army will have to give them your address."

"Let's go," says Lily. "I've never been to Lancaster."

Fiona leaves her school uniform in a heap at the end of the single mattress. Jo lends her some of the clothes they brought back from Kirby. They are all in the Mini less than ten minutes later, Jo driving, Lily in the front with a scarf round her neck trying to keep the icy December air off her stiffened skin. Her neck and shoulders feel like a cage inside which her body is trapped. "We could do with some cash," says Jo. "I'm nearly at my overdraft limit."

"I can get us some cash," says Fiona, picking up her school bag and rummaging through it. A moment later she holds up a cash card triumphantly. "It's for emergencies, but hey, I've been kidnapped. If that isn't an emergency what is, for heaven's sake?"

Jo regards her through the rear view mirror. "You mean that's a card to your parents' account?"

Fiona nods.

Jo lets out a low whistle. "I'm impressed. Jeez, there's no way my dad would ever have trusted me with a card to his account. How long have you had it?"

"Not that long. A year."

"Any you've never used it?"

Fiona shakes her head, "He made me promise, emergencies only."

"God, I would have cleaned it out within days. Which is probably why my dad never gave me one," she concedes as an afterthought.

107

They stop at a motorway service station and cross over the footbridge, so it appears they are heading to Burnley, rather than Preston to join the M6. Fiona withdraws five hundred pounds from her father's account.

Jo claps when she sees the wad of notes Fiona has in her hand. "I like your style."

"Well I thought, I'll need to buy some clothes. I can't keep borrowing yours."

Lily wonders how long Fiona is imagining her kidnap will last, but Jo is leading them all into the general store to stock up on essentials, and the question never makes it to her lips.

Fiona has only visited Stuart once since he started university, in the October half-term, when her father drove her up for the day and spent his time wandering round bookstores, while Stuart showed her around the Students' Union and they spent ages kissing round the back of the duck pond. "You have to park the car first. There's a car park round the back."

The three of them walk from the car onto the main street through town, where Stuart lives in a flat above an antiques shop. As they near the shop, Fiona shouts out, "There he is," and Lily notices a tall, thin man, with a mop of black, curly hair, pacing the street. Stuart looks up as he hears Fiona shout, and starts running towards them. He embraces Fiona, throwing his arms around her shoulders and pulling her tightly against him, bending his head to say something to her, which Lily can't hear. Fiona reaches up towards him and the pair kiss, as Jo and Lily stand like two lemons on either side of the them. Stuart breaks off the kiss as Lily starts to feel like a voyeur. She notices the veins on his hands as he cups Fiona's face and stares at her. "God, I hardly recognised you. Are you ok? And what did you say on the phone? You're an only child."

The black canvas trousers she borrowed from Lily cling to every centimetre of Fiona's long legs, emphasizing the swell of her hips. Jo's oversized jumper hangs off one of her shoulders, exposing a lacy bra strap. "Not any more, I'm not. I want you to meet my sister. This is Lily, and her friend Jo."

Stuart looks suspiciously at Lily. "Pleased to meet you," he says, but Lily's not sure he means it. "I think we better go inside."

He unlocks a chocolate brown door by the side of the antiques shop, and the four of them enter a dark stairwell. Fiona goes first and leads them up the stairs and into the first floor hallway of

Stuart's flat. A tailor's dummy stands in one corner, wearing a hat and a with a couple of coats draped over it. Lily looks at a framed photograph of a woman talking into a microphone, obviously some kind of reporter, with a flock of hungry Africans in the background. Stuart leads them past a second flight of stairs going up to the second floor, and into the kitchen, where there's a coffee percolator dripping hot coffee into a jug. He sits them down at a red, Formica topped table. "What happened to your hair?"

"Long story."

"Would you like a drink?"

Lily's first thought is of the bottle of vodka they bought from the service station, but she accepts the cup of coffee Stuart hands to her. Fiona skips round the kitchen, opening cupboard doors. "Any chance of some food? We haven't eaten since breakfast."

Stuart laughs and catches Fiona, using his arm like a crook around her neck, pulling her in for a kiss. Lily can't help staring. "You are always hungry," he says. "How about a Spanish omelette? You probably should have a decent last meal, coz your dad is going to kill you when he gets his hands on you."

While Stuart chops up onions and whisks eggs, Jo and Fiona compete to fill Stuart in on the past twenty-four hours. Lily marvels at the rack of herbs and spices that hangs on one wall. There must be thirty or forty different types, and Stuart seems to know which ones to use. When he puts down a triangle of perfectly fluffy omelette in front of Lily, fifteen minutes later, she worries she might be sick over it. Luckily no one seems to notice, because the other two barely pause for breath, as they eat and fill Stuart in on the details of the kidnap at the same time. "I didn't realise you were snatched," he says.

"Do you mind if we smoke," asks Jo, after she's finished the last mouthful. "That was delicious by the way."

"Good, you can smoke in the front room," he says, taking Jo's empty plate. "Are you not hungry?" he asks Lily.

She tries to shrug her shoulders, but the upper half of her body seems almost totally rigid. "I, I'm not feeling very well, but it was nice, thank you." She jumps up after Jo and follows her into the front room.

As soon as they leave the room, Stuart turns to Fiona. "How do you know this is true, Fi? I mean, I'm not your father's greatest fan, but I can't believe he'd abandon his own child."

"I know. I couldn't believe it either at first, but look." She unhooks her school bag from the back of her chair, and pulls out Lily's birth certificate and the letter from the Salvation Army. "And I've seen photos of their wedding day; dad's and Lily's mum's wedding. Did I tell you, when Lily tried to contact him, he didn't give any explanation as to why he didn't want to see her? He didn't even ask how she was. What if it had been the other way round? What if I'd been the daughter he'd left behind? Would he have said the same to me?"

Stuart glances at the birth certificate before starting to read the letter from the Salvation Army.

"I was there when he got that letter," says Fiona. She stands up and goes to lean against the worktop. "He opened it in front of me. He looked like he'd seen a ghost. And do you know what he said when I asked him what it was?"

"What?"

"He said, "It's just another begging letter from some bleeding heart charity concerned about waifs and strays." They were almost his exact words."

"What are you going to do?" asks Stuart, the birth certificate still in his hand.

"Whatever Lily wants."

Stuart wrinkles his nose. He's about to speak but Fiona doesn't let him. "I like being with her."

"But…"

"She's had nothing her whole life. Her mum just died two months ago. And you should see their house, where she grew up. It's a complete hovel."

"What if your dad comes here again?"

"No one's ever looked after her. You can tell. But she's been really sweet to me…"

"You mean after she kidnapped you?"

"By rights she should hate me because I've got everything she's never had." Fiona draws breath.

"She's…"

"I've been an only child for sixteen years, and now I've got a big sister."

"Don't you think you should at least let your dad know you're safe?"

"I'm so mad with him. All that stuff about truth. You know what he's like. He doesn't trust me at all and I've never lied to him."

"Everyone deserves a chance to give their side of the story."

"I know. But whatever he says, he's lied to me. My whole life he's lied to me. I can't talk to him about it yet. Later maybe, but just not yet. I want to hang out with Lily while I have the chance. You know what'll happen when Mum finds out; all hell'll break loose. I want to spend some time with Lily while I can."

Stuart leans back against the worktop and folds his arms. "You've got it all figured out."

"Did I mention we've ransomed me for eighty-five thousand pounds?"

Stuart's eyes widen. His mouth is still open. He closes it and reaches for the vodka bottle.

"Try it with cream soda, it's lovely," says Fiona.

Lily comes back to ask for an ashtray, just in time to hear Fiona saying, "I can't go back. I can't face any of them."

Chapter 20

The pub where Stuart works is twenty minutes walk from his flat on the outskirts of town. A banner hangs over the door advertising its farmhouse grill. Inside, the polished brasses are almost obliterated by a profusion of garish Christmas decorations. It looks like someone has stood in the centre of the room and hurled tinsel around, until enough of it stuck. Lily ducks to avoid a golden ball that hangs over the doorway.

Fiona pauses before crossing the threshold. "Wait, how do I look?"

Lily turns and examines Fiona's new outfit; skin tight black jeans, that they'd helped her choose from Lancaster market that afternoon, and a pair of ankle boots with a heel, combine to make her legs look even longer. Underneath Stuart's thick, black donkey jacket, she's wearing a T-shirt that says 'Cocaine' in the Coca Cola logo. Her cheeks are flushed from the cold, and the twenty minutes she spent with the contents of Jo's make-up bag, have made her eyes seem bigger than ever, emphasized with thick smudged kohl pencil. She's tied the half a plait into a pony tail at the crown of her head so it doesn't look too odd. "You look great," says Lily. Then when she notices Fiona waiting for something more, she adds, "And old."

"Easily eighteen," says Jo, walking past her on her way into the pub. "Just walk like you rule the school."

Fiona and Lily follow Jo through the doors. Lily steers Fiona to a corner table by a roaring log fire, while Jo marches up to the bar. Stuart appears almost immediately, in a pair of checked blue trousers and a white jacket. "It's pretty quiet. I'll make you the house speciality in a bit," he says, as he takes a seat next to Fiona on the padded burgundy velvet bench. She reaches for his hand.

The landlord looks like he's about to give birth; his hard, round belly protruding under his jumper. "Ah, so this is the girlfriend? I was beginning to think you were a figment of his overactive imagination. How've you managed to give your dad the slip?"

"It's a long story," says Fiona.

"Your secret's safe with me," he says tapping the side of his bulbous red nose. He turns to Stuart. "Don't suppose I'm going to get much work out of you tonight."

"It's all in hand. Just waiting for some orders," says Stuart pointedly, looking around the empty pub.

Jo returns from the bar, with four double vodka and cokes, and a pint of lager shandy on a small, circular tin tray. She hands the shandy to Fiona. "Sorry, do you want a drink?" she asks Stuart.

"No thanks. I've got one in the kitchen."

"Well, cheers," says Jo, raising one of her vodkas. Lily and Fiona chink glasses.

"I'd better look like I'm doing something," says Stuart. "Is anyone hungry?"

Jo and Fiona both nod.

Half an hour later, three plates of home-made steak and kidney pie, with mushy peas and chips that are fatter than the landlord's fingers, sit in front of them. Gravy oozes from under the crisp, golden pastry.

"Wow," says Jo.

Silence descends on the group while everyone eats. Lily dunks a chip in her gravy and sucks it. Jo is the first to finish.

"So," says Jo, wiping her finger around the edge of her plate, licking up the last remnants of gravy. "What happens next?"

Fiona makes a gesture that says she can't speak because she's still chewing. Lily shrugs her shoulders.

"I think we should ring him tomorrow, and give him the arrangements for dropping the cash," says Jo.

"Who's going to ring him?" asks Lily.

"Well, it can't be Stuart, so it's me or you, Lil." Jo holds a coin in her fingers. "Want to flip me for it?"

"I can't," says Lily.

"I can," says Fiona. The other two stare at her. "If either of you two ring he's going to guess it's Lily. There can't be that many female kidnappers around."

"What's up?" says Stuart, slipping into the seat next to Fiona. He looks at Lily's untouched plate. "Not your thing?"

113

"Not hungry, sorry."

"We were just saying who should ring Dad," says Fiona.

"I should ring your dad," Stuart says.

"You?" says Fiona, at the same time as Jo shakes her head.

Stuart kisses Fiona's hair. "I should ring him, because if I hadn't heard from you, I'd be really worrying by now. I don't want him getting suspicious I'm involved, and turning up here again. Not after last night."

"I didn't think of that." Fiona looks to the other two.

"I'll come with you," Jo says. She stands up.

"What, now?" asks Stuart.

The three girls all nod simultaneously.

"What do I say?"

"Ask him whether he's heard from me," says Fiona. "When he says no, worry a bit. 'Oh no, I wonder where she could be?' Ask him what the police are doing. Hey, you could offer to go on 'Crimewatch'. And say you'll ring him if you hear anything."

"What if he tells me about the ransom demand?"

"Tell him to do exactly what the note says." Fiona finishes her lager shandy. "Will you get me another drink while you're up?"

Stuart shakes his head at her in disbelief, and heads to the payphone outside the men's toilets. Jo follows him. He turns to her and creases his brow. "Come on," she says. "Look at it from my point of view. We can't have you telling him where we are."

"Maybe he has the right to know his daughter's safe."

"Maybe you should ask his daughter what she thinks about that."

Jo lights a cigarette while Stuart dials the number from memory. Stuart turns his back to Jo as he speaks, but she can hear his every word. "Mr Winterbottom? It's Stuart, Fiona's boyfriend."

There's a moment's pause and then Stuart says, "I was just wondering whether you'd heard anything? I haven't heard from her."

Another pause, a longer one this time. Stuart turns round to face Jo and raises his eyebrows. He speaks into the receiver as he stares at Jo. "She's back home?" he repeats.

Jo blows a string of smoke rings and pulls a face.

"Why hasn't she rung me?" says Stuart, still looking at Jo.

He listens to the answer and then says, "Why doesn't she want to speak to me?"

Stuart turns back round again to face the wall, his back to Jo, and takes a few steps forward. "I want her to tell me that, please will you put her on?"

There's a much longer pause and then Jo can hear the low hum of the dial tone coming through the receiver. Stuart hangs up and turns round to Jo. "That man has it coming."

"What?" Fiona shrieks.

"That's what he said."

"How dare he?"

"He's never liked me," says Stuart.

"Who does he think he is?" says Fiona.

"Ok," says Jo, returning from the bar and setting another round of drinks down on the table. "Either he knows it's us and he doesn't want anyone else to know, or he doesn't know it's us but he's following the spirit of the ransom note and not telling anyone. Both of which are good for us." She takes her seat between Lily and Stuart. Excitement wells up in her voice. "I think he's going to pay."

"How dare he tell you I don't want to go out with you anymore."

Jo pulls the notebook and pen from her outsize bag and starts scribbling. "How long do you think it would take him to get that kind of money together? What's reasonable, a week?"

"Do you really think we can go through with this?" Lily asks. "What if we all end up in prison?"

"So what?" says Jo. When she sees the look on Lily's face, she adopts a calmer tone. "He's not going to press charges. He's not even going to tell the police about the note. Otherwise why would he tell Stuart she's at home? Even if he doesn't want to tell Stuart she's been kidnapped, he would have said, 'no I haven't any idea where she is, it's all very worrying, blah, blah'. This is going to work."

Fiona takes a sip from Lily's vodka and orange. She nods slowly, "He can't have told anyone about this other life. I mean people like my headmistress, or the vicar. We go to church together every Sunday. None of those people know he's a compulsive liar, I didn't."

"What about your mum?"

"I don't know. I still can't believe she knows. How could she live with a man who hasn't paid any child support? The tabloids would make mincemeat of her if this was to get out."

Jo puts down her drink. "I don't think the *Sun* is going to be taking up the cause, not unless we agree to go topless."

"Honestly, she's that high profile. You've heard of Helena Kennedy?" asks Fiona, her eyebrows raised.

Lily looks blank as Jo nods. Jo turns to Lily, "You have Lil. She's that feminist barrister bird."

"Well, there's her, and then there's mum. I don't get it. If she does know, she certainly won't want it getting out and if she doesn't know, dad won't want it getting out. She'd kill him. Either way, it works in our favour for getting the money."

"So," Jo presses on, "how long do we give him to get the money together?"

"Why don't you ring him and see if he's got it? That's the next step," suggests Stuart. "He might say he knows who you are and he's not going to pay." He pauses, then nudges her. "Hey, he might not want you back."

"I'll ring him," Fiona says. "If he thinks I don't know who you are, he's more likely to pay up. If he knows I know about you, it's game over. He knows I'd never forgive him for lying to me."

Lily tears the beer mat in front of her into a hundred little pieces.

Chapter 21

"Daddy? Daddy, please help me. Please do as they say. Give them the money or they are going to really hurt me."

"I've got the money here," says a deep voice, with a soft Liverpudlian accent. "Just tell me where to drop it."

"They've already cut my little finger off," Fiona gasps into the Sellotape dispenser.

"Tell those bastards I'll pay a hundred and eighty five thousand, whatever it takes to get my little girl back," says Jo, wheezing like an old man.

Lily laughs out loud. Stuart had gone to work by the time Lily and Jo woke up, and they've spent the whole morning rehearsing Fiona and Jo's lines and getting stoned. Lily feels an unaccustomed lightness. Maybe it's the fact she can turn her head again.

Jo sits down on the settee and flicks through the notebook. "He gets home early on a Friday. We should ring him at four o'clock at the latest, before your mum gets in."

"How do you know he's home early? Let me see that." Fiona grabs the notebook from Jo's hands. She glances at a few pages as Jo flashes Lily a worried look. "You were following us. I had no idea. What's 'TIFF' mean?"

"That was our, er nickname for you." Jo tries to grab the book back but Fiona runs behind the settee.

"What does it stand for?"

"Er, Teenage Female."

"What's the I for?" Fiona turns another page.

"What time is it now?" Lily quickly asks.

Fiona turns another page. "Hey. You've got dad down as a headmaster. He's not the headmaster, he's only a maths teacher. He isn't career focussed. Well, that's what he says. Mum says he lacks ambition and he's just lazy."

Jo stands on the settee and snatches the notebook out of Fiona's hands. "Right, we've only got an hour. Let's go through it one more time."

Fiona groans and resumes pacing.

They don't know it but Fiona's father hasn't been to work since he got the ransom note yesterday morning. When the note came, he had rung both his school and Fiona's and told them his daughter was ill and neither of them would be in for the rest of the week. His third phone call had been to the police. He'd told them that a friend of Fiona's had been in touch and Fiona was with her. He told them he was certain Fiona would come home of her own accord in the next day or so. They had asked him if he wanted them to go and have a word with this friend and he had said no and apologised for troubling them. He figured that even if this wasn't what he thought it was, he could tell the police he'd been obeying the kidnappers' orders.

Ruth, his wife, had stayed at the office the night Fiona went missing; something she often did in the lead up to a big trial. He hadn't troubled her with the news that her daughter hadn't come home from school; just as he hadn't bothered her with the news that the Salvation Army had contacted him a few weeks ago. Nor had he mentioned that over the last couple of weeks, on three separate occasions, he had thought he was being followed by two young women; one with dreadlocks.

On Thursday morning, yesterday, his fourth phone call had been to his wife. "I just thought you should know Fiona and I have had words and she's gone to stay with Caroline for a few days." Caroline was Fiona's best friend. All Ruth had said, before asking whether the dry cleaning had been delivered, was "Well, that's been brewing for some time."

As he makes himself a cup of tea, he calms himself with the idea that if Fiona has been kidnapped by real kidnappers, he can always claim he didn't want her to worry. But what real kidnappers demand eighty five thousand pounds?

David is the one that takes care of Fiona. That's his job. Ruth hadn't said anything, but David was pretty sure their marriage had been heading for the divorce courts, until Ruth had found out she was pregnant with Fiona. It had been a difficult two years, just the two of them. Fiona had saved his marriage. Given him a purpose in Ruth's eyes. He had taken such great care of his wife when she was pregnant, cooking for her, massaging her feet when she got in from work. Ruth was 40 years old when Fiona was born. He had given up his job so that Ruth could return to work less than six weeks after the birth. Admittedly it hadn't been much of a sacrifice, he was working as a bank clerk at the time, but Ruth had been grateful that there was no impediment to her returning to work.

He had made himself essential to Ruth's life. Making sure there was always a warm meal to come home to, no matter what time she finished work, running her warm baths, fetching her drinks, anything so that he could be with his daughter.

If it had been up to David, he would have spent the next ten years listening to Woman's Hour and baking bread, but once Fiona had started at school, expectations had been raised. So he had convinced Ruth that he should take a teacher training course, so that they wouldn't have the problem of what to do with Fiona in the school holidays and after school.

He sits at his desk in his study and takes out the letter he's hidden in a pile of school-books. His hand hovers over the receiver for a few seconds before he snatches it up. "Hello. May I please speak to Major Farley-Greystone?"

The phone goes quiet while the voice at the end goes off in search of the Major. David tries to frame the questions in his mind. 'Did you speak to (he still doesn't really know what to call her) a Miss Lily Appleyard? My daughter?'

'How did she take my hurried, unthinking, panic-stricken rejection?'

'Did she sound cross? Cross enough to kidnap my other daughter?' He replaces the receiver before anyone returns to the phone.

He opens the suitcase and looks at the neat bundles of money all lined up. It was absurdly easy to get hold of it. He had made one telephone call to their financial advisor and asked if he had any policy that could be cashed in without Ruth knowing. He'd told him he wanted to organise a surprise for Christmas. The financial advisor didn't even question what on earth he would buy his wife that cost eighty five thousand pounds. Instead he had rung him back five minutes later to tell him they had a couple of bonds that Ruth had bought when they were first married that required only one signature.

"So, what I just go to the bank and pick it up?"

"I'll ring them. They'll want 24 hours. It should be ready first thing tomorrow morning."

So, this morning he had left for work as normal, but gone straight to the main branch of the Nat West, which they'd opened specially for him at 8.30, and picked up the suitcase. Just like that. He'd thought he'd got used to their wealth but when the cashier had handed it to him, he had to fight the urge to say, "It's not mine you know. This is more than I earn in five years."

David looks at the money again. Will this make it all go away? That is the question. If he does as they ask, will she return his beloved daughter, the one he didn't screw up on, undamaged, unknowing to him and leave his family alone? Ruth won't be back until late tonight and she's leaving for London on Sunday morning so if he can just get her through another day, then he has some breathing space. He knows his wife is pleased at this perceived falling out, between father and daughter. She's been telling him for years that their relationship is too intense.

At three o'clock Jo, Fiona and Lily climb into the Mini and start to drive; their sole mission to find a phone box somewhere that isn't Lancaster. They arrive in Morecambe by chance; no one really concentrating on where they are headed. Jo parks the car round the corner from a telephone box and they all take a moment to hold hands.

At seven minutes past four, Fiona's trembling fingers dial the number she knows so well. Her father answers it on the second ring. "Daddy, is that you? Oh, Daddy."

Fiona's sobs are loud and noisy, real tears surprising her at the sound of his voice. They fall down her face and into the receiver, making the sound of her voice distort. "I miss you, I want to come home, Ouch..." Fiona screams, as Jo pulls a handful of her hair as rehearsed; to add some realism to the occasion. "They've told me to tell you they won't let me go until you've paid them the money. No wait," Lily pulls her roughly away from the receiver, as she shouts, "I love you, Daddy."

Jo holds one of Stuart's socks over the mouthpiece and growls down the phone. "Have you got the money?"

"What are you doing to my daughter?"

"I said have you got the money?"

"Yes, but it hasn't been easy. Don't think that I can just keep..."

120

"We'll ring tomorrow. No police."
She bangs down the phone.

Chapter 22

Jo looks at the stopwatch: 1 minute 50 seconds. She locks eyes with Fiona and a great snort of laughter erupts from them both.

"No police, Slam. It was like 'Hill Street Blues'," says Fiona eventually. She wipes her eyes and starts to laugh.

"He's got the money!" Jo screams.

"Can you believe they turned me down for Sandy in *Grease*?" Fiona asks. "Blummin' Janet Jeffries got the part. They only gave it to her because she's blonde... and utterly gorgeous," she adds as an afterthought. Tears begin to stream down her face again, as she tries to stop laughing long enough to get out her final sentence, "Shame she's stupid."

"You were great," says Jo, her legs crossed to stop herself wetting herself with laughter. "'I love you, Daddy' Fan-fucking-tastic."

Lily wishes she could share the funny side. She doesn't want to admit it, but she's starting to feel something like sympathy for Fiona's dad. She's not sure why. Squashed between the metal box of the telephone and the door, she pulls a face, which Jo mistakenly interprets as a request for a spliff. Jo pulls a ready rolled one out of her bag.

"Do you know what he said to me? 'Don't worry baby, Daddy will sort it all out.' It's like I'm twelve."

Lily frowns as Jo lights the spliff.

"We should have asked for more money. I wonder what the average kidnap demand is these days. Shall I ring the police and ask?" Fiona picks up the receiver and pretends to dial. "Yeah hi, can you tell me... what's a white, middle-class schoolgirl go for these days?"

"He's got the money." Jo blows a cloud of smoke at the ceiling. "Can you believe it? We might actually get eighty-five grand out of this. I might actually be able to pay off my debts." She looks over to Lily, her eyes dancing with excitement. "We could go on holiday."

Lily tries to smile. "Holiday?" Now there's something she hasn't considered. "Where?"

"I don't know, anywhere. We could travel the world."

"Can I come too? I've always wanted to go travelling," says Fiona. "I was hoping to go to San Francisco in my gap year."

"You've got your exams. Once you've passed them and done your 'A' levels maybe." Lily pushes the phone box door open a few inches with her bottom. The cold fresh air wraps around her waist, making her stomach ache worse.

Fiona cocks her head to one side. "I'm not going back, you do realise that don't you? I mean even if we get the money."

"Don't be stupid." Lily shakes her head as Jo offers her the spliff.

"Don't you be stupid. What did you think was going to happen? You kidnap me, tell me my whole family has lied to me all my life, collect eighty-five thousand pounds and then I just go back and live there like nothing's happened? Everything has changed; I've grown up."

Jo winks at her. "We know you have."

"I don't mean like that. For your information, we didn't even do it. We just stayed up all night talking. We talked about me moving here, getting a job. What am I doing at school anyway? All the subjects I'm doing: biology, chemistry, physics, Mum chose for me. She thinks there should be more women scientists." Fiona hesitates before adding, "Women are terribly under-represented in the field." The telephone box is filling with smoke. "But it's not me."

Lily feels like the walls are closing in.

"I want to drop out and go to beauty school... joke." Fiona adds, when she sees the expression on Lily's face. "But drama school maybe. Come on, you didn't think you could just pluck me out of my life for a couple of days and then send me straight back to it, untouched."

Lily starts picking at the scab on her arm.

"Did you?"

"Is it foggy out?" asks Jo.

Lily wrests the spliff from Jo's lips, hitting her elbow on the metal shelf as she does so; catching herself right on her funny bone. She rubs her arm and pushes at the door of the phone box. "Let's get out of here."

123

"I feel like Superman. Where are my tights?" Fiona starts to giggle. She tries to speak, but whatever she wants to say gets lost. She crosses her legs and bends double, screeching with laughter. Lily pushes her out of the telephone kiosk. Fiona gulps some fresh air and tries to stand up. "I think I've just become a dope smoker. Will you make one for me? I feel fabulous."

Jo sits down on the bench outside the kiosk and starts unloading the tobacco packet, her dope tin and cigarette papers out of her bag.

"Stop it," says Lily.

"What? She wants a spliff. 'TIFF' wants a spliff."

"She's only fifteen."

"I'm nearly sixteen."

"Oh I am sorry," says Jo. "And how old were you when you had your first one?"

Lily thinks for a moment. Her automatic response is that she was older than Fiona, but thinking about it, she'd been eleven. Dave Marsh had given it to her, telling her it was a roll up. It was the same evening she'd got pissed for the first time, up at the ramshackle garages, where cars weren't so much parked as abandoned. Most of the estate's young teenagers hung out there, before graduating to the Dog and Duck. "That's not the point, its illegal."

"It's illegal for you to do it too," says Jo, not unreasonably. "And I'm not sure kidnapping, or demanding money with menaces is exactly law abiding either. What's up with you?"

"Let's just get back to the flat. You can't skin up here anyway. Someone might come."

Jo looks up the deserted back alleyway. The Mini is parked at the top of the street. They haven't seen a soul since they arrived.

"Come on." Lily marches on ahead, to the car.

Jo shrugs her shoulders and puts the tobacco packet back into her bag. Fiona holds out a hand and helps Jo to her feet. They follow Lily up the cobbled back street, Fiona's giggles periodically erupting, like snorts, punctuating the silence.

Lily doesn't speak all the way back to the flat. As Fiona lets them in with the spare key Stuart gave her, Lily realises how tired she is. She starts to say that she's going to go straight to bed, when Stuart appears at the top of the stairs. "I was expecting you ages ago. What happened?"

"He's got the money," says Fiona as she takes off her boots. "Mmmm, that smells delicious, what is it?"

"Really, he actually said he's going to pay?"

"I was so nervous, but I did it. You should have heard me, 'Daddy, Daddy, please rescue me.' I was great." Fiona leads the way up the narrow staircase into the hallway where Stuart stands, his bare feet poking out from the bottom of his soft blue jeans. She stands on tiptoe to kiss him.

"Modest too," says Jo, pushing open the kitchen door, her nose following the smell like the 'Bisto' kid. The others follow.

Fiona takes a seat at the kitchen table. "We said, well Jo said, we'd ring him tomorrow. We need a plan. I'm starving. Have you got a map?"

Stuart puts a plate in front of her and smiles as she grabs a knife and fork. He gestures at Lily and Jo to do the same. Jo doesn't need asking twice. Lily sits down next to Jo and watches Jo remove a piece of chewing gum, before picking up a fork. Lily looks up at Stuart. "What is it?"

"Toad in the hole. Haven't you had it before?"

As Fiona fills Stuart in on the details of their telephone conversation with her father, Lily cuts up the pork sausages into small slices. She pushes the pieces around in the gravy for a while, stacking them up like pennies.

"I can't believe he's going to pay," says Stuart.

The red, Formica topped table is only just big enough to seat four. Stuart sits at the top of the table, Jo facing him at the opposite end. "I need a beer," says Jo. "Anyone else?" Lily nods. The table falls silent as the others eat. Lily drinks her beer silently, head bowed. "Delicious," says Jo eventually, pushing her plate away. "Respect."

"You not hungry again, Lily?" Stuart asks. She shakes her head and mouths 'sorry' and pushes herself up from the table. Once the others have cleared their plates, they join her in the front room. Fiona has Stuart's road atlas clutched under one arm. Lily is sat, Buddha-like, rolling a spliff. The others spread the road atlas across the coffee table and kneel around it, their heads touching.

"So, do we go for somewhere small and quiet, so there's less chance of the money getting nicked?" asks Jo. "Or somewhere busy, less chance of attracting attention?"

"You need loads of people," says Stuart. "You can always disappear in a crowd; a train station or something."

Fiona shakes her head. "But then the police could be watching you and you'd have no idea. It needs to be dark."

Lily lights the spliff and lies back on the floor. Small, smouldering specks of dope keep falling from her spliff, burning her face. She flinches but perseveres, allowing herself to drift away from the conversation.

"That's no good," she hears Fiona arguing when she drifts back. "What if the police are watching and arrest her? It has to be dropped somewhere and collected later." Lily raises her head slightly so that she can see Fiona's inflamed cheeks, her pouty lips. She watches as Fiona reaches across the table to take a cigarette from Jo. Lily collapses back on the floor, frowning as another shower of sparks hits her chest.

As the conversation grows more heated around her, Lily sits up, using her stomach muscles alone to pull her up from her prostrate position on the floor. She pats out the embers that have fallen down the front of her shirt. "I've just thought of something."

"What?"

"Remember when Aunt Edie rang? You know, that first night. She said she knew my dad had another baby because one of her friend's daughter's was having a baby at the same time. They were in hospital together."

"So?"

"Well, her friend's daughter's baby was called Bernadette Briggs. She was at the same school as me, but a year below."

"So?"

"So, if she was born at the same time as my dad's other child, that child will also be a year younger than me." She looks at Fiona. "Not three and a half years younger."

Fiona stares at her elder half-sister. "You mean he's got another child?"

"What else can it mean?"

No one speaks. Lily crushes the spliff out in the ashtray. "Maybe Aunt Edie got mixed up," says Jo. "You know how old people get."

"I'm going to do it," says Lily, feeling her resolve set like concrete.

"Do what?" asks Jo.

"I'm going to take the money from him."

"That's way too risky," says Stuart.

"What if he recognises you?" asks Jo.

"How's he going to recognise me? He's never even seen me. And I don't look like him." Jo opens her mouth, and then considers whether she's brave enough to tell Lily she looks like her mother.

She closes her mouth again. "And besides," says Lily, "even if he does know it's me, he's still going to go along with it, because all he cares about is whether Fiona knows his secret."

"What if he refuses to hand over the money until Fiona's back with him?" Stuart's cheeks are flushed and his voice seems louder than usual.

"I don't care about the money."

"There's too much that can go wrong." Stuart gets up off his knees and sits back on the settee behind him. "It's hardly the right environment for your first meeting with your father."

"I have to do it, Stuart."

"What if the police are there and you get arrested?"

"I've kidnapped a minor, got her drunk and stoned. I've demanded money with menaces. I've driven a car without a licence or insurance. Don't you think I've already considered the 'I might go to prison' angle? At least I wouldn't have to worry about how I'm going to pay the rent next month." Lily tries out a smile; it convinces no one. She stands up. "You're all always telling me I have nothing to lose. I don't care about prison. It's like, my mum died and my first thought was great, I get to meet my dad. So, I'm fucking going to meet him."

Stuart storms out of the front room and slams the door behind him.

"What's up with him?" Lily turns to Fiona.

Fiona shrugs. "He worries too much."

"Ok," says Jo. "If you're going to do it, where's the place?"

"Somewhere quiet, just me and him. I'll say I'm the messenger for the bad guys. I'll say these blokes have paid me to come and collect a suitcase, I don't know why and I don't want to know why. I'm just in it for the money. And he may suspect it's me, but he won't know. He'll still have to consider the possibility that it could be someone else."

"Do you think we asked for enough money?" Fiona wonders out loud.

"I was thinking that," says Jo, doodling a swag bag on the side of the map. She draws a dollar sign on the front. "He didn't have much trouble getting it together, did he? Maybe we should ask for more?"

Lily shakes her head. "All my life I've wanted to meet my dad. Other kids wrote to Father Christmas asking for Barbie dolls and Girl's Worlds. I wrote asking for a dad," she looks over at Fiona and her voice falters, "and it's great to have met you, but still, I started this madness, I have to finish it."

Chapter 23

Stuart trips over a pair of boots that have been left on the top step, and falls flat on his face in the hallway. Fiona steps out of the front room as he crashes to the floor. "Where have you been?"

"I needed some air." He rolls over and lies on his back, his face red from the cold night. "Where is everyone?"

"Jo's gone to bed; Lily fell asleep on the sofa." Fiona kneels on the floor next to him and strokes his face; the beer fumes rising from him, stronger than scent. "You're freezing, wait here."

She steps over him and into the kitchen. Ten minutes later she's back carrying a tea tray. His eyes are closed and he doesn't stir as she steps over him again to take the tray up the attic stairs and into his bedroom. Moments later she returns and pulls him by the arm, half leading him, half dragging him up the stairs.

In the bedroom, Fiona sits Stuart down on the bed and feeds him toast and Marmite. She puts a large mug of hot chocolate by his side. When he's swallowed his last mouthful of toast he says, "Do you think we should let her…"

"I don't think we can stop her."

"But she's so fragile. What if he has rung the police and she gets arrested?"

Fiona shakes her head. "It's what they both need. As soon as Dad sees her he'll come round, I know he will." She kneels by his feet and begins to unlace Stuart's trainers.

"God, I wish I had your faith, Fiona. What if he has her arrested?"

"He's not going to have his own daughter arrested." She pulls off both his trainers. She can feel the coldness of his toes through his socks. "It's weird that he won't just be my dad anymore."

Stuart drains his hot chocolate and shivers. "It's freezing out there."

"I could warm you up." She kneels up, her eyes dark beneath her fringe. She stands and leans the weight of her body against him, tipping him backwards onto the bed, as she brings her lips down on his, soft and tentative.

A few minutes later he tries to sit up. "I don't think we should be doing this, Fiona."

"Shh." She puts her finger to his lips. "I really, really want to." Her lips press down on his again and she runs a hand up under his shirt, feeling the smooth skin of his chest. As her fingers brush past his nipples, a moan escapes his lips. She pushes harder against him, using all of her strength, until he's flat on his back on the bed. Her hands tremble as she sits astride him and undoes the buttons on her shirt.

Afterwards, Fiona curls up in his armpit, breathing in the smell of sweat and Right Guard. Her fingers toy with his underarm hair and her legs entwine with his own. She waits until he's fallen asleep before she whispers to him, "I'm never going home."

The sound of the delivery van, unloading the day's produce at the bakery across the street, wakes Fiona. It's still dark outside. She wraps a sheet around her and floats downstairs to the kitchen. Sitting on the worktop, smoking a cigarette while she waits for the kettle to boil, is Lily. She looks miles away.

"You're up early," says Fiona from the doorway.

"I woke up on the settee at two. Couldn't get back to sleep," says Lily, as Fiona steps into the kitchen. Lily takes one look at Fiona's mussed up hair, the smudged eyeliner around her eyes and the smile on her face, and jumps down. "Oh. My. God."

Fiona giggles. Lily pulls her younger sister into her arms. "Oh Fi, I hope you know what you're doing."

Fiona stands back from Lily and takes the cigarette from Lily's hand. She puts it to her lips and inhales, her eyes screwed up against the smoke. "I do now."

They both start to laugh, and the smoke Fiona's inhaled makes her cough so much she can hardly breathe.

An hour later the four of them are eating breakfast together at the red topped table in the kitchen. Jo says, "So we've still got to think of a place for Lily to meet him."

130

"Why don't we do something different today?" says Fiona. "Let's go to the seaside."

"The seaside?" says Jo. "Don't be ridicul-"

"Why not?" asks Lily. "It's a great idea. Come on Jo, let's have a break."

Fiona licks Marmite off her fingers. "I'm sure the biggest criminal masterminds give themselves the odd day off. Stu?"

Stuart clasps his forehead, as if feeling for his own temperature. "Now you mention it, I'm not feeling so good. I think I feel a sick day coming on. I haven't had one since I started this job."

Fiona claps her hands and jumps up from the table. "I'll get ready."

The journey to Blackpool takes less than an hour. Lily sits in the front, with Stuart's road map taking up most of the space, twisting it through angles of 360 degrees, trying to follow their route. She looks up. "I don't know," she says, beaten.

"We're here," says Jo. "This is Blackpool."

"Where's the sea?" asks Lily.

Fiona has her head out of the rear window. "There's the tower." She pulls her head back inside the car. "Head for that." Jo makes a last minute right hand turn and they are on the front, heading north. Lily looks out of her window. "Oh my God, it's the sea. Stop the car," she shouts at Jo.

Jo finds a space on the front and pulls the car into it. She turns to Lily. "Tell me you've seen the sea before."

Lily is already half way out the door. "Duh, of course," she stands up, feeling the sea air catch her dreadlocks and send them flying. The wind is so strong it whips the rest of her sentence away, so Jo doesn't hear the last two words, "on TV."

Stuart and Fiona climb out of the back seat and join Lily at the railings by the beach. Stuart takes in the endless strip of tacky rock shops, nightclubs, pubs and amusement arcades. "This is the ugliest place I've ever seen. I've been to Third World countries that look way better than this."

Lily stares out to sea, holding onto the railings. A few hardy souls are down on the beach, wrapped up against the freezing cold wind. The sea stretches to the horizon, the grey water blending with the low, heavy clouds. "It's so massive," she whispers.

"Ok," says Jo, having locked the Mini. "Pleasure Beach." She nods down the front. "It's opposite the south pier."

"Oh, look," says Lily, as a horse and cart trots past them. "Can we have a ride in one of those?"

Jo looks at Lily like she doesn't quite recognise her. "Seriously?" She shrugs her shoulders at Stuart and Fiona. "Why not?"

Lily strokes the nose of a white and tan pony wearing blinkers, before climbing up into the trap. She laughs as the driver flicks his reins and the cart lurches forwards.

The white arch bears the sign 'Pleasure Beach'. They walk through, Fiona and Stuart holding hands, leading the way. Fiona hears the screams from the riders of the Wild Mouse ride. "Look at that," she says pointing to the wooden roller coaster. The bolts are rusted, so that long lines of rust stain run down the woodwork. "Who's coming?"

"I will." Jo digs in her bag for her purse.

Fiona holds up her hand. In it is her purse, which contains the remainder of the £500 she withdrew from her father's account. "This is on me," she says grandly. She looks to Lily and Stuart. "Coming?"

"No chance," says Lily.

"I'll, er, wait with Lily," says Stuart. "Keep her company."

"Chicken." Fiona grins. "Meet you back here." She kisses him on the lips and then runs off after Jo, who's already joined the queue.

Lily and Stuart watch Jo and Fiona inch up the line, and climb into the car. Lily starts to chew on a nail. "Do you want to hook a duck or something?" asks Stuart.

"Yeah, ok." Anything not to have to watch her little sister and only friend cheat death a moment longer. "Oh look, there's a carousel. I've always wanted to go on one of those."

"Come on then," says Stuart. "What are you waiting for?" He helps her onto a horse called Jean Michel and hands the dark attendant some cash. Then Stuart climbs up onto the horse next to her as a waltz starts to play. Lily grips on tightly as the carousel speeds up. "Are you ok?" Stuart reaches out and touches her hand.

"I didn't realise they go so fast." Lily opens her eyes and shouts to him, but her words get lost in the music. Stuart smiles at her.

When the ride ends he helps her down. "Let's go meet the others."

Fiona shouts over to them, "That was fantastic. I want another go. We nearly died. It's so fast."

Stuart nods towards Jo as Fiona puts her arm around him; Jo's bleached hair is standing upright on her head like its frightened, and her face seems to have lost some of its colour. "I think you'll be going it alone next time."

"Oh look, there's a cash point. Hang on," says Fiona already running off towards the machine. "It's the least he can do," she says as she walks back to them, stuffing another wad of notes into her purse. "This is our first family day out. Hey, maybe we should go to the zoo tomorrow."

They all laugh as Fiona starts singing, "Daddy's taking us to the zoo tomorrow, the zoo tomorrow, the zoo tomorrow," as she skips up the concrete path towards the ghost train. Lily starts to pray that Fiona won't want her to ride that. She's had a phobia about ghost trains ever since she went on one with Gail Foley at Burnley fair. Her parents had taken them over for the trip, now she comes to think of it, her last family day out, albeit with someone else's family. How old had she been? About ten probably. Something, someone had jumped out at her half way round and fondled her non-existent left breast in the pitch black.

"Hey look, the log flume." Fiona turns back to the others and points across to the left. "Come on Lily, you can't say no to that."

Lily smiles with relief and follows her younger sister up the ramp. Fiona and Lily share a log. It wobbles furiously as Lily steps inside. She feels excitement welling up inside her, making her feel like a kid. As the ride starts its climb, she feels the adrenaline rush into her stomach.

As they career down the last water chute a flash goes off, and by the time they disembark there's an image of them on the screen above the pay desk. It shows Lily in the front of the car, her body rigid and the smile on her face tense, while Fiona sits behind her, her arms wrapped around Lily's neck, her head lent against her elder sister, mouth open with shouts of laughter. Lily orders a print to be sent to Stuart's flat.

It's almost dusk when Jo and Fiona race against each other on the Grand National steeplechaser. Stuart persuades Lily to ride the Derby Racer, which is like the carousel only faster, but by now Lily feels like a seasoned thrill seeker. Her cheeks are bright pink and her pupils wide, when the ride ends and she steps off. Stuart pushes a dreadlock off her face and tucks it behind her ear.

"Come on," says Jo, coming up behind them. "Let's go and get something to eat."

133

They buy bags of warm potatoes in their skins, doused in vinegar, and wander out, back on to the front. "I want to go on the beach," says Lily.

"Are you crazy? It's freezing," says Jo, but Lily is already crossing the road.

"Watch out for the tram," shouts Stuart.

Lily runs across the tram line and down the steps to the beach. As soon as she is on the sand, she sits down and unlaces her boots. By the time the other three have joined her, she's running barefoot towards the sea, the legs of her tight black trousers scrunched up over her calves. She screams as she feels the cold sea water on her toes.

They make their way along the edge of the beach, back to the car, pushing each other into the freezing surf, and screaming with laughter. Lily yells as Stuart tries to trip her up in the sand, her hair is flying around her shoulders, whipping her face like wet rope; the stinging sensation a mixture of pleasure and pain.

"Come on," says Jo, pulling herself out of the sand. "We'd better get back on the front or we'll miss last orders."

"We can't go in a pub looking like this, look at us." Stuart points to his jeans that are wet to the knees. His turn-ups are filled with sand.

"But we haven't had a drink today."

"We've got vodka back at the flat," says Lily. "We can have a drink when we get home. I'm freezing."

Lily slumps across the back seat on the journey home, with her head in Fiona's lap. Fiona does her best to stroke Lily's hair, but it's almost solidified; full of sand and sea salt. "I could have a go at sorting out your hair you know," Fiona speaks quietly, so that only Lily can hear her. "If you wanted. It's a bit, sticky."

Lily tries to open her eyes, but her lids are too heavy. "I'd like that."

Stuart and Jo carry Lily from the car when they get back to Lancaster. She barely moves; and the two of them lift her easily. As Fiona unlocks the front door, Stuart puts his arm under Lily's legs. "I can manage," he tells Jo, and Jo lets go of Lily's feet, so that Stuart carries Lily like a child up the stairs and into her bedroom. Jo follows behind them. Stuart lays Lily down on the bed. "I think you'd better get her pyjamas on."

Jo pulls a face at him, as she falls like a log onto the bed next to Lily. Her eyes close as soon as she hits the pillow. Stuart pulls the duvet over Lily's legs and leaves the room.

Fiona is waiting for him outside his bedroom door. She takes his hand and pulls him inside. "Fiona, I'm knackered."

Fiona leads him over to the bed. "Then lie down and close your eyes."

Chapter 24

Lily doesn't know why she is awake, as it's not even light outside. She tries to remember how she got to bed, but no matter how hard she tries, nothing comes to her. Ironic that the first night she goes to bed sober in years, she can't remember the first thing about it. She spends ten minutes trying to work out what day it is. Sunday. She scratches her head and her hair moves in one solid lump, like a piece of cardboard. Lily swings her legs out of the bed, glances over at Jo who is still fast asleep, and creeps across the bedroom and down the stairs. She grabs the scissors from the kitchen and locks herself in the bathroom. One by one she holds each dreadlock up in front of the mirror and then chops it off.

Afterwards, she's startled by what she's done. Her hair springs from the top of her head like the cork has been pulled from a bottle of champagne. She can't remember ever having curls; it's like her hair is jumping for joy at being freed from the weight it's carried for so long. She tugs at it with her fingers, trying to uncurl it and make it longer at the same time. She wants a cigarette but she's too scared to leave the bathroom, in case the others are up. Footsteps sound in the hall outside and then someone tries the door handle.

"Who's in there? I need to wee."

Lily opens the door and Fiona dashes past her, bleary eyed. It's only after she has sat down on the toilet and started emptying her bladder, that Fiona looks up at Lily.

"Oh my God."

"I look ridiculous."

"No." Fiona tries to form her lips into a reassuring smile. "Don't worry. We can sort it out. Wait here." Moments later, Fiona returns with a pair of smaller scissors and locks the bathroom door again.

Fiona wraps a towel around Lily's shoulders and leads her over to the sink. She pours jug after jug of warm water over Lily's head, shampooing and conditioning what little hair remains. When she's finished, she puts the toilet seat down, and sits Lily down as she gently massages her hair dry. Fiona's tongue protrudes between her lips as she combs and cuts Lily's hair into something resembling a style. Half an hour later, Fiona stands back and sighs. "There."

They stand side by side in the mirror, and four identical brown eyes stare back at them. "I think you need a bit of make-up to carry off such a short cut."

Fiona shows Lily how to apply a bit of mascara. "Don't go mad now," says Lily. "I don't want to look stupid."

But she doesn't, Lily realises, when she looks back in the mirror. She looks cleaner, sharper, like the camera's lens has been focussed.

Stuart and Jo are both in the kitchen when Fiona and Lily finally leave the bathroom, satisfied with the new look Lily. "God, Lily," says Jo. "You're much better looking than I thought you were."

Stuart puts the milk back in the fridge and hands Jo a mug of tea. He doesn't look at Lily.

After breakfast, they convene in the front room. Fiona sits on Stuart's lap and says, "Stuart's had a great idea for where to meet Dad."

Jo and Lily look at Stuart, waiting for him to speak. He shifts the weight of Fiona onto one leg so that he can lean forward slightly in the armchair. "There's this churchyard," he says. "It's in a village, not far from Skipton. I used to cycle up there a lot, and it was always deserted. It is at the top of a very steep hill, overlooking the valley. I thought it would be good because you can see for miles around, and there's only one road up to it."

"Show us where it is." Jo passes him the map and Stuart points out a road to the west of Skipton.

"It's where that cross is, that's the church."

"Fine," says Lily. "Tell him I'll meet him there. Once he gives me the money, I'll go back to 'the kidnappers' and Fiona will be released."

"I can hide my bike somewhere nearby," says Stuart, "and then once you've got the cash, just jump on the bike; it's downhill all the way. If he tries to follow you, there's loads of bridle paths; he won't be able to keep up with you. We can meet you somewhere at the bottom of the hill."

"And what then?" asks Fiona. She reaches across the table and takes the cigarette from between Jo's lips. "I'm not going home."

"You've got to finish school, Fiona," Lily says, "please. I couldn't live with what I've done if your life messes up because of me. Can't you just go back for six months, finish your GCSEs and then, maybe you could go to college or something? But you've got to do your exams."

Jo lights another cigarette and shakes out the match. Smoke billows from her mouth as she speaks, "Listen, if you don't go home after we collect the money, Lily will go to prison."

"But what will I say to him?"

"Whatever you want," says Lily. "You can tell him it was me; I don't give a shit. He can have the cash back. But you have to give him a chance, Fi. You can't just disappear. You love him."

"No I don't. I hate him."

Lily holds her arms out. "You loved him before all this."

"Before I found out he was a complete liar, you mean? You don't know what he's like. When I was eight he made me go back into Woolworths because I'd pinched a white chocolate mouse out of the pick and mix. I couldn't resist it. He made me tell the security guard and all three of the women on the checkouts what I'd done. 'Honesty is the best policy' he said."

"You haven't given him the chance to explain. Everyone deserves that."

"He didn't give you the chance. Why are you defending him now?" Fiona stands up and walks over to the fireplace. "I get it. You want to ditch me now you think you might get your hands on the cash?"

"Shut up." Stuart stands up and grabs one of Fiona's arms. "That's really not fair, Fiona."

Tears start to fall down Fiona's face. She turns to Lily. "What about me and you?"

Stuart lets Fiona's arm fall and Lily takes his place. She puts her arms around her younger sister. "We can see each other as often as you want. You can come to..." Lily pauses, realising she doesn't know where she lives anymore, "me."

"What if he doesn't let me?" Fiona wails. She hesitates as the realisation dawns. "He can't stop me now."

"Exactly, you're almost sixteen. I want to be sisters forever. If it means waiting a few months, or even a couple of years, til you're eighteen, so what? I've been waiting my whole life. And at least I know you now."

As Fiona and Lily hug, Jo looks at the clock and glances over to Stuart. He nods.

"Ok, I'm going to chance one of the phone boxes in town." Jo pulls on her donkey jacket. "Give me the map. You'd better come too, Fiona. Just in case he wants some proof you're still alive."

Jo presses fifty pence into the slot as the phone is answered. She gives him the time, the instructions, the place. "If the police are there, you won't see her again."

"I want to speak to her."

Jo passes the receiver to Fiona. Fiona turns her back to Jo, her voice instantly breathless again, "Daddy?"

Jo snatches the phone back. "Two o'clock tomorrow. Alone. Don't make me hurt her."

Chapter 25

Stuart lies on his back, his right arm bent behind his head, Fiona asleep next to him. She's sprawled across the bed, taking up way more than her fair share, but he hasn't the heart to move her. Her left arm is draped over his chest. He picks it up gingerly and slides his body out from underneath, replacing it on the bed when his feet are on the floor. He pulls his dressing gown from the hook on the back of the bedroom door and goes downstairs. Lily is sitting at the kitchen table, smoking a spliff. Stuart smiles at her, "Can't sleep either?"

Lily doesn't answer, but glances up at the clock on the kitchen wall, it's quarter to five. Stuart flicks the switch on the side of the kettle and it starts to boil immediately. He looks across at Lily. "Are you having second thoughts?"

"When I was a kid I thought everything would be alright once I left home. You know, once I was away from my mum."

Stuart comes to sit at the table with her. Lily moves her chair so that they're not directly opposite each other, so that she isn't face to face with him.

"From what Fiona's said, I think I'd have thought the same too."

"Every other kid on my estate left school at sixteen. They used to rip the piss out of me for doing 'A' levels."

"Yeah, well I bet they're not laughing so much now."

"I had this teacher, Miss Lewis; she kept on at me to go to college. She knew things weren't great at home. She said I'd have the world at my feet if I got to college. She said I'd meet all these interesting people, my life would change. She was so passionate about it. I didn't want to let her down, although it freaked me out, her passion. I'm not used to passion."

Stuart doesn't speak, but he nods at her, encouraging her to go on.

140

"But life didn't change. I met Jo. That's the one good thing, but the rest is just the same. Accrington, Leeds. It's just the same. School, poly. It's still a bunch of people telling you what to think."

"Do you miss your mum?"

"I never had a mum. She left me. Just like my dad. He left for another woman; my mum left for a doner kebab and a crate of Special Brew."

"It's hardly free choice though, is it? No one chooses to be an addict."

"That's bullshit. She chose alright. Every morning she chose to start the day with a two litre bottle of coke and a couple of cold pizzas. I was getting myself ready for school aged seven, because she chose to drink herself unconscious every night. She could have stopped anytime she wanted to; she just didn't want to."

"Maybe she felt she couldn't stop."

"She knew she was killing herself. It's not ok to eat a whole loaf of bread and three packets of bacon for breakfast."

"Whereas a spliff and a cup of tea is a nutritious way to start the day?"

Through the fug of smoke, Lily stares at Stuart for the first time since he sat down. "What do you mean?"

Stuart swallows before speaking. "I mean, I don't think your mum decided to leave you," he stresses the word 'decided'. "Not in a conscious way. For some people, addiction is an illness. A friend of mine, his dad died when he was a kid. He felt the same way you did. He really believed that his dad chose to leave him and he was so angry with him. But no one chooses to get cancer. Just like no one chooses to be an addict."

Lily stubs out the spliff in the ashtray. "Are you saying you think I'm an addict?"

"When was the last time you woke up and didn't smoke a spliff?"

"It's spliff, it's hardly chasing the dragon."

"Well, neither is eating a plate of chips."

"Five plates of chips." Stuart shrugs. "That's what she'd order from the chippy," Lily pushes back her chair and stands up. She holds up five fingers, like a starfish. "Five portions of chips. They used to order special polystyrene trays in, just for her."

"I didn't mean to make you mad."

Lily storms out of the room. Stuart listens to her feet clatter down the stairs and hears the front door slam.

He's still sitting in the same chair in the kitchen when Lily returns over an hour later, although even Lily notices it's much cleaner than it was when she left. All the washing up has been done and put away, and the worktops are clear. Lily's shoulders are hunched from the cold. Stuart stands up as soon as she enters the room. "I'm sorry. I shouldn't have said what I said; open mouth, insert foot, that's me. I'm always being pulled about it. Look, I made you a spliff."

He holds up the fattest, most badly rolled spliff Lily has ever seen. A small dusting of tobacco falls out of one end as he holds it aloft. Lily allows herself a small smile. She'd rather die than admit it, but one of the reasons she came back was because when she'd stormed out, she'd left her tobacco on the kitchen table and she didn't take her wallet. "Ok," she says, ignoring the spliff, but reaching for the tobacco packet. "Thank you for saying sorry."

"I'll make you a cup of tea."

The sound of an alarm clock reverberates around the flat. Lily hears Jo swearing. Minutes later Fiona jumps through the doorway, wearing a black jumper, black leggings and a black balaclava. "Freeze!"

Lily almost drops the cup of tea she's holding. "Fiona, you scared the shit out of me."

"Do you like it? I got four of them from the market."

Jo stumbles down the stairs rubbing her eyes, and sits next to Lily at the kitchen table. Jo reaches for the cigarette packet as she looks up at Fiona, "Cool. You look like Batman."

"I got one for everybody."

"Why?" asks Stuart.

"To disguise ourselves."

"You don't think maybe people will notice a group of four people wearing balaclavas?"

"They were only a pound each."

"Fiona, you'll have to stay here," says Stuart. "If your dad has called the police, they will all have seen a photo of you."

"That's why I bought the balaclavas. I'm not staying here on my own, no way."

With Stuart's bicycle strapped to the roof of the car, Jo drives to the graveyard, Fiona in the back seat wearing one of Stuart's large, hooded tops. They park the car in a small lay-by, and walk up to the huge wrought iron gates. A big rusty padlock is attached to a chain, but the gate isn't locked. Stuart pushes it open, wheeling his bicycle up the overgrown, cobbled path. Thick bushes line either side and he pushes his bike purposefully towards one. "I'll stash this in here. No one will see it."

The path leads further up the hill into the ramshackle graveyard. Lopsided gravestones compete for space, amongst the weeds and the brambles. The sun streaks through the valley, making the morning frost glisten. Lily and Stuart weigh up the site, walking down each of the overgrown paths while Fiona and Jo hide among the tombstones, jumping out on each other with their balaclavas on, pretending to be hit men.

"Ok?" asks Stuart.

Lily takes one last look around. She likes it here, up above the town. There are a million places to hide, and it feels safe; a good place to keep secrets. She nods.

"Come on then, let's go and find some food. We should get back here no later than one."

They buy fish and chips in the town centre, and eat them down by the river. The warmth and smell of the chips wrapped in newspaper makes Lily feel safe.

At one o'clock, Stuart walks Lily back up the hill, while Fiona and Jo stay out of sight in the car. Lily lights a cigarette, but the hill is so steep she can't waste the lung space on smoking. She's already sweating. As they turn the last bend in the lane, they see three cars parked up by the gates and one more further on, blocking the lane. "Shit, is that the police?"

They both flatten themselves against the wall at the side of the road. "It's a funeral," says Stuart. "Look, there's the hearse."

They squeeze past the cars and look through the gates. A black swarm of people hover at the far end of the graveyard. Lily sees the bald head of a vicar in the centre of the throng. She turns to Stuart, sees the expression on his face, a mix of horror and bewilderment. He tries to say something, but the words don't seem to want to come out. Lily starts to laugh, really laugh, and before she knows it tears are running down her cheeks. Stuart takes hold of her by the elbows. "It's ok, Lily." He stares into her eyes until she stops laughing and remembers to breathe.

"It's good; you can hide out a bit, mingle. Look for the guy carrying a bag or briefcase and looking uncomfortable. If you lose your nerve you don't have to go through with it, just blend in the crowd. Lucky you wore black."

Lily relights her half-smoked cigarette and tries to smile. She's never worn anything else.

143

"You're going to be fine," says Stuart. Lily takes three drags on her fag before flicking it high up into the air. What the fuck. She kisses his cheek. Then she straightens her shoulders and strides into the graveyard without looking back.

No one asks Lily any questions. She's good at blending, avoiding conversation. She makes no eye contact and threads her way through until she's at the far end of the graveyard, a few yards back from the rest of the mourners. Lily turns and watches the widow, a small yet statuesque woman, wearing a black hat and shocking pink lipstick, framed at each side by two tall men. Children as young as four or five years old mingle with the crowd, to remind people that in the midst of death, life keeps on.

Lily cranes her neck to see the watch on a mourner's wrist. It's twenty past one; forty minutes to go. She decides to have a cigarette to calm her nerves and finds a table type gravestone, tucked away amongst the brambles. She can see for miles across the valley. The world seems frozen, crystallized. No one can see her as she sits down, enjoying watching the mourners in their moment of goodbye.

And then she turns her head and sees him. A lone man carrying a small suitcase, his hand shielding his face from the bright sun. A woman turns to speak to him, and Lily watches him say something and shake his head. Then the vicar speaks up and everyone falls silent, heads bowed. Lily can't hear the words, but she knows the sentiment, as the vicar invokes God's blessing on the newly departed. Then everything goes quiet and Lily feels suddenly closer to it, whatever it is, then ever before in her life. She has this sense that everything, every moment of her life, has been constructed to bring her to his place. Euphoria sweeps up inside her and threatens to make her shout out. She puts a hand on the tombstone to steady herself and closes her eyes. When she opens them again, she sees the widow throw a flower into the grave, before turning to look up at her family and smile. Suddenly it's like someone has pressed play on the video recorder. People start to move, to chat, to embrace. And as the people start to melt away, to the fleet of black cars blocking the small country lane, only Lily and her father remain. He hasn't seen her - won't until she stands up - so she takes the opportunity to study him further. He looks older than he did in the school playground, the day they followed him to work. Fiona has told her he's forty-four years old, three years younger than Lily's mum. He looks at his watch and frowns.

144

Lily puts out her third cigarette, takes a deep breath and stands up. As she begins to pick her way through the overgrown paths, he takes a seat on a bench that faces away from the gravestones, out across the valley, still unaware of her presence. She creeps up behind him and only when she is standing a few inches behind him does she speak, "Hello."

He startles but doesn't turn round. She clambers over the rough ground and sits down next to him, staring straight ahead. He turns to look at her. "Are you here to…"

"Before you ask, I don't know anything about your daughter. I've just been told to come here, collect the money and then take it to the guys. I was told to tell you that if I don't meet them at the time I'm supposed to, you will never see her again." Her heart is thudding against her chest. She takes a breath and turns to face him. "Sorry."

She takes off her sunglasses to stare at him and he flinches, his dark brown eyes mirror her own.

"What's your name?" he asks.

"Like I'm going to tell you my name." She clenches her fists but doesn't break her gaze.

"How old are you?"

"How old do you think I am?"

He looks away from her, back out across the valley, his eyes following a kestrel as it hovers in the sky. "I think you're approximately nineteen years and…" he does some mental arithmetic, "four months?"

She holds her breath and closes her eyes. Nothing happens. When she opens them again, he's standing in front of her. "If I hand over this suitcase to you, am I going to get my daughter back? Fiona…" he adds hastily, to avoid any confusion, "in one piece? As in how she was before any of this started?"

Lily puts her sunglasses back on. She looks away from him, beyond him, across to the valley. "She'll be returned to you unharmed, unchanged, they said."

He offers the suitcase to her, holding it in one hand, his arm fully extended. "Here's the money. When will I see Fiona?"

Lily bites her teeth into her lips as hard as she can. "Tonight."

"I'll be waiting. You tell your friends if she's not back by 6pm, I will report them to the police." And he turns on his heels and strides out through the gate away from her, back down the hill.

Lily's lips are dark, bruised from the cold. Her fingers are too cold to roll a cigarette. She concentrates on the tree halfway down the valley, that looks like it's been blown sideways. It's spent its life in gale-like winds and yet it clings on. What kind of life is that; to exist at ninety degrees?

Lily is surprised to see Stuart standing in front of her. "We saw his car leaving at the bottom of the hill," he says. "We've been waiting ages."

He sits down next to her on the bench and puts his arm across her shoulders, trying to pull her into his embrace, but her body is rigid, frozen like the grass. "Lily, tell me what happened."

Lily continues to stare at the tree.

"Lily?"

Lily speaks in a flat monotone. "He knew who I was and he didn't ask me anything. He handed me the money like I was some kind of prostitute. All he cared about was whether Fiona knew who I was." Her gaze is unwavering, fixated on the tree; its branches pushing back against the wind.

"He's fucked up; look at the life he has. His wife treats him like a doormat, he's living a lie." Stuart gingerly strokes her hair. "He's not worthy of you. You have so much more courage. All he has in his life is Fiona, and she'll leave sooner or later, and then he'll have nothing and he knows it. That's why he's scared, he's scared of losing her same as he lost you."

Stuart stands up and holds out his arm to Lily. She hesitates and then allows him to pull her up to standing. He threads her arm through his and together they stroll back down the hill, blinded by the sunlight. Fiona is leaning out of the car window, her balaclava pushed up to her brow. When she sees them round the bend, she calls out, "How did it go?"

Lily opens the car door and climbs into the front passenger seat, next to Jo. She stares out through the windscreen. "All he was bothered about was that Fiona doesn't find out who I am."

"Did he know who you were?" Fiona asks.

"Yes."

Stuart climbs into the back seat of the car. Fiona looks to him, waiting for an explanation. He shrugs his shoulders. She turns to Lily again. "He knew you were his daughter?"

Lily continues to stare at some indistinguishable blot on the landscape. "He knew who I was."

"How do you know?"

Lily speaks in a monotone. "Because he asked me how old I was and I said 'guess,' and he said 'nineteen years and four months.'" A surge of irritation rubs over her, making her itch.

"But…"

"He knew who I was, now drop it."

"And he didn't…" Fiona falls silent as Stuart shakes his head and puts his finger to his lips. The colour drains from her face as she pulls the balaclava off the top of her head.

Lily examines her fingernails. "But I got the money… Shit! I've left the money."

"What?" says Jo.

"I left it by the bench."

"And my bike," says Stuart.

"I don't believe you two," says Jo, as she turns the key in the ignition and hurtles the car back up the hill. She brakes so hard the tyres screech, as she pulls up outside the churchyard gate. They all turn to look at Stuart. He dives out of the car and into the graveyard. The suitcase still stands on the ground by the end of the bench. His eyes scan his surroundings before he grabs the case and runs back to the car.

"Come on, let's get away from here," he says as he jumps back into the car, sweat beading on his forehead. "I'll pick my bike up tomorrow."

It takes Jo several attempts to turn the car around in the narrow lane. "Come on," says Stuart, "Get a move on."

Once Jo has got the Mini pointing back down the hill, Stuart flicks the suitcase open. Jo glances behind her and screams as the Mini veers across the road. When she regains control of the car, she shouts, "Eighty-five thousand smackers."

Chapter 26

Once she's parked the Mini in the car park round the back of Stuart's flat, Jo leaps out of the car, opens the rear door and takes the suitcase from Stuart. The others follow her into the flat and up both flights of stairs into the attic. She sits on the double bed in Andre's bedroom and opens the suitcase. She removes one of the neat bundles; one thousand pounds, and fans herself with it, before putting it to her nose and inhaling. She whistles. "Direct action, in action. Who says crime doesn't pay?"

Stuart looks over her shoulder. "Wow, that's a lot of money."

"Look Lily," says Jo. "You're rich."

Lily shrugs her shoulders.

"You're owed it, Lily," Stuart says. "It's rightfully yours."

Lily sits on the floor by the small garret window, looking down on the street below. She watches a couple arguing across the street. "By the way," says Lily, "he said if you're not home by six he's ringing the police. I think he meant it."

Fiona sits on the floor near the door. She stares at the suitcase; it has a sticker on the side that says 'Hotel Oleander' and another with a picture of the Hilton in Cairo. "We went there last year."

"Where?" asks Jo.

"Cairo. I rode a camel and Dad got gastroenteritis. I am not going home."

"We've been through this, Fiona," says Jo. "We can't take eighty-five thousand pounds off him and then not give you back. That would be seriously bad karma. You don't have to stay, but you do have to go home."

Fiona's bottom lip juts out. "I want to stay with you guys."

"If you don't go home you won't be able to stay with us, because we'll all be in prison." Jo starts to count out the bundles of money.

"He won't know where to find us."

"Look." Jo slaps her hand on the top of the suitcase. "You can't kidnap someone, demand a ransom, get it and then not release the person you kidnapped."

"Why don't we ask for more money?"

"You've got to go home, Fi," says Stuart.

"It's not fair. What am I going to do? You want me to go home and pretend like everything's fine? What am I going to say to him? I have to tell him I know." Fiona starts to cry. "I hate him."

Lily crosses the room and sits down on the floor next to Fiona. "I don't want you to go either." She leans into Fiona so that their heads rest against each other. "But we have to return you. He deserves to know you're ok. You can leave again, but you should tell him you're leaving. We'll drive you back and we'll wait for an hour or two if you like. But you have to tell him you not kidnapped anymore."

"It's all here," says Jo. "Eighty-five k."

"You promise you'll wait for me?" Fiona asks Lily.

"I promise."

"So I can just go in, say I'm not kidnapped anymore, and then you'll bring me back here?"

"Yeah."

Fiona nods. "Ok." Lily hugs her.

Jo divides the money into piles: seventy-five piles for Lily, two for Fiona and eight piles for Jo. "Have you got any carrier bags?"

Stuart goes downstairs and returns with a handful of plastic bags. Jo places two bundles in a Morrison's bag and hands it to Fiona. Fiona shakes her head. "Give it to Lily. She deserves it more than me."

Jo shrugs and starts stuffing Lily's money into the largest carrier that has 'Bag for Life' written on the side. She adds one of Fiona's thousand pound bundles to it. "Are you sure you don't want some Stuart?" Jo asks, waving Fiona's other bundles in the air. "I feel like we owe you big time, even if it's just to pay you for all the food we've been eating?"

Stuart shakes his head. "I don't think I should profit from blackmailing my girlfriend's father. I'm going to have enough explaining to do as it is."

Fiona gives him a watery smile. Stuart jumps to his feet. "Does anyone want a cup of tea? I'll put the kettle on."

"We haven't got time," says Jo, adding Fiona's other thousands pounds to her own carrier bag. "We need to get going. Who's coming to Skipton?"

"Me," says Lily.

"I can't," says Stuart. "I'm on the late shift tonight and I'm already in the bad books for missing Saturday."

"I will if I have to," says Fiona. "But I'm not stopping."

"Right then," says Jo, as she pulls herself up of the bed and picks up the two carrier bags. "Why don't you two say your goodbyes, while me and Lily get ready downstairs."

"I want to get a shower," says Lily.

While Lily showers, Jo prowls around the first floor of the flat, checking the clock that hangs in the hallway every five minutes. As she paces back and forth, a creaking floorboard catches her attention. Using a knife from the kitchen she prises it loose. "Perfect."

Jo fetches the two bags of bank notes, stashes them under the floor and then replaces the floorboard. She adjusts the position of the settee and then glances again at the clock. "We need to be going, Fiona!"

Fiona appears at the top of the attic stairs, her eyes red rimmed.

"Bang on the bathroom door. Tell Lily we need to get moving."

The journey back is quiet and subdued. The sisters sit in the back seat, mute in each other's company. As they drive into Skipton, they pass the grammar school, and Fiona shudders.

Jo parks at the far end of Primrose Glen. It is already dark. She checks the time; three minutes to six. Jo jumps out of the car and holds open the back door, like a chauffeur. Lily and Fiona unfurl themselves and climb out. They inch along the pavement, arms linked, until they are a few hundred yards away. Jo holds out her arm and they stop.

"Wait for me," pleads Fiona as tears start to stream down her cheeks.

"We'll be here. If you can't stand it, just come out and we'll be waiting." Lily struggles to keep her voice normal. "What will you tell him?"

"Don't know." Fiona looks up the street at her home. "I won't know till I see him. Promise you'll wait for me?"

"Promise. We'll be here 'til eight o'clock. If you don't come out we'll go to Stuart's. Ring us there tomorrow morning, whatever happens. We'll come back for you anytime, won't we, Jo?"

"It's six o'clock," says Jo.

Lily puts her arms around Fiona's shoulders. "Go on then. Off you go and grass me up." Lily does her best to force out a laugh, but Fiona cries harder and clings to Lily, her arms tight around her sister's waist. Lily closes her eyes for one moment, trying to imprint the smell to memory, and then she pushes Fiona in the direction of Newlands. "Take care, you."

Fiona drags herself towards her house.

"Fi?" Lily shouts after her. "If you decide to stay, will you still ring? Or, if you can't ring, write to me? I'll leave Stuart my address."

"I'm not going to stay."

Half way along the street, Fiona turns back and looks at them both with a pleading expression. Lily smiles, points her arm in the direction of Newlands and bites her lip. Fiona continues, exaggeratedly scraping her feet along the pavement, until she reaches the iron gates. She enters the code with one hand, waving at them in the darkness with the other. Lily and Jo can make out her profile in the light of the street lamps, but then the gates open, Fiona disappears, and the street is still.

Chapter 27

Lily and Jo wait until half past eight but Fiona doesn't appear. Jo stubs out the spliff, sits higher in the seat, and turns the key in the ignition. "Come on, it's time to go."

"You don't think he's hurting her do you?" Lily asks, before taking a drink from the hip flask. "What if he's locked her in against her will?"

Jo rubs her eyes. "If she doesn't ring tomorrow, we'll ring the police and say we're scared she's being abused or something, but I'm not going in there now, Lil." Jo starts the car. "It's over, at least for tonight."

In Lancaster, Jo and Lily have to run from the car park to Stuart's flat, as rain starts hurling down at them. Stuart isn't back from work and the flat is cold and dark.

Jo lifts the floorboard and counts the money again, while Lily tries to work out how to turn the central heating on. By the time the boiler starts to make reassuring operating noises, Jo has replaced Lily's share of the ransom under the floorboards. She cradles her own carrier bag like a baby. "Do you fancy coming to Kirby? I need some clean clothes and we're almost out of dope."

"No," says Lily. "You go if you want. I could do with a night on my own anyway."

"You sure? I want to get this little lot in the bank before my bank manager sues me for his mental health problems. You sure you'll be ok?"

"I'll be fine, I could do with the rest."

Lily sits down on the settee and starts to unlace her boots. Jo runs up the attic stairs into their shared sleeping quarters, and before Lily has managed to pull the second boot from her foot, is back carrying a holdall and her coat.

Jo chucks the tobacco tin at Lily. Lily misses the catch and it hits her on the side of her leg. "That's the last of the dope; there should be enough for a couple. I'll be back tomorrow. You sure you're ok?"

"Stop fussing, I'm fine already. Go." Lily stands to give Jo a hug. "Drive carefully and say hi to your mum."

As soon as Jo is gone, Lily makes herself a cup of tea and goes upstairs. She flicks through Andre's meagre record collection and puts Madonna's 'Like a Prayer' album onto the small turntable. She sets the volume so low she can only just make out the words, and then rolls down her trousers, stepping on them to help extract her legs from the tightness of the cloth. Then she climbs into bed, arranging the pillows around her to prop up her upright, as she rolls herself a spliff. She hears Stuart come in around midnight, hears him call out, "hello" on the first floor a couple of times, and pulls the duvet up under her chin.

She doesn't expect to sleep, but when she next opens her eyes it's daylight. She lies in bed trying to guess what time it is, until she remembers that Fiona promised to ring, whatever happened, this morning. She picks her trousers up from their heap on the floor, puts them on and goes downstairs. Stuart is already dressed, standing at the cooker with a wooden spoon, stirring a pan of something. "Hello," he smiles at her, "I made you breakfast. Where's Jo?"

"She went back to her mum's, to put her money into the bank and wash her clothes. She'll be back later today."

"I hope you're hungry."

Lily sits down as Stuart places a plate of scrambled eggs on toast in front of her. As the smell reaches her nostrils her stomach turns and she frowns. "You're up early."

"I'm on the lunch shift today – I'll be back by four. What will you do?" He passes her a knife and fork. "You could come down the pub if you like, it's normally pretty quiet."

Lily prods the scrambled egg. "Thanks. I think I'll have a bath and just wait for the others."

"Would you like salt?" Stuart hovers over her, waiting for her to eat. "What others?"

Lily places a forkful of egg into her mouth. It feels rubbery and alien. She tries hard to swallow, but her mouth is dry. "Jo."

"You said others, plural."

"I'm just going to make a cup of tea." Lily stands up and rushes over to the kettle. "Maybe Fiona might come back today?"

"Maybe." Stuart sounds doubtful. He pulls on his coat. "You've got a key? Right, see you at four."

Lily follows him into the hall. She leans on the banister to watch him run down the bottom flight of stairs to the front door. When she hears the front door close, she goes back to the kitchen and scrapes the congealed mass of scrambled egg into the bin before lighting a cigarette. She stands with her back against the worktop, silently smoking until the kettle boils. When she's made herself a cup of tea, the tea bag still floating in the milky liquid, she wanders through to the bathroom and turns on the clunky old taps above the bath. It takes her all her strength to move them, and even when she's twisted them as far as they will go, the water hardly gushes, despite the optimistic gurgling sounds coming from the ancient plumbing system. She closes the toilet lid, sits down and smokes another three cigarettes while waiting for the bath to fill.

When she finally turns off the taps and climbs into the tub of water, she's unnerved by the absence of sound. She holds her right leg out of the water and wonders whether she should start shaving. The hairs are blonde and soft, but thicker than she remembers. But then, shaving your legs only matters if you're going to wear a skirt or have sex, and she can't decide which of the two is less likely. She settles for washing her hair, examining the array of toiletries lined up against the bath. One of the reasons for her dreadlocks, was she'd got sick of washing her hair in washing up liquid; her mother having given up on expensive luxuries like shampoo.

Once she's washed her hair, she stands up and wraps a towel around her body, before stepping out of the bath and looking at herself in the mirror. It still seems strange to see herself without dreads; she feels naked, vulnerable. She rubs a handful of Jo's mousse through her hair and tries to spike it up a bit. It still insists on falling back around her face in soft curls. She tuts at her own reflection and starts to get dressed.

After she's washed the breakfast plates and plumped up the cushions on the settee, Lily squirts a bit of polish from the spray tin she found in the cupboard under the sink, into the front room. It takes her a few minutes to realise the unpleasant smell is coming from her clothes, and another twenty to work out how to open the washing machine. She goes back to the bathroom and picks up her damp towel from the floor. She sits wrapped in it again, as she watches the two changes of clothes she has with her, roll around in the machine. When the telephone rings, at a quarter to two, Lily leaps from the settee and the towel drops to her ankles. She runs to the hall table and grabs the handset. "Hello?"

"Hi, what's happening?" Jo's voice sounds croaky.

"Oh. Jo, hi." Lily crouches down on the floor, feeling the icy draft coming up the stairs, on her bare skin. "Nothing, just doing the laundry, you know. When are you coming back?"

"I just got up. I didn't get here till nearly three. And Our Ste's coming over this evening, bringing his new girlfriend, so my mum wants me to stay. I think she's worried they might start shagging under the dining table. Do you mind? I mean if I stay another night? Are you ok?"

"Yeah, fine. Did you put the money in the bank?"

"No, that's another thing I've got to do today."

Lily shivers.

"You sure you're going be ok?"

Lily looks up at the ceiling. "Yeah, I'm fine I said."

When Stuart arrives home at ten past four, Lily is sitting in the front room, an empty packet of milk chocolate digestives and a half bottle of vodka in front of her, watching Ricki Lake. The curtains are almost closed, and the room is thick with smoke.

"Hey."

"Hey." Lily doesn't turn around.

"How was your day?"

She shrugs her shoulders. "Ok."

"Did Fiona ring?"

Lily shakes her head.

Stuart picks up the remote control and switches off the television. "Why don't you get a nice warm bath and I'll make us some food?"

"I already had a bath this morning."

"It'll make you feel better. I'll go and turn the taps on." He picks up the vodka bottle off the coffee table in front of her, screws the top back on and takes it with him. Lily waits a moment and then fires the remote control at the television.

Ten minutes later Stuart is back. He moves around the settee, switches the TV off at the set and stands in front of it, his arms folded across his chest.

"What?"

"Bath. Go on, it's run. What time's Jo coming back?"

"Tomorrow."

155

When she gets out of the bath, her head wrapped in a towel, Stuart has set the table, opened a bottle of wine and a candle burns from an old wine bottle in the centre of the table. He has Tracy Chapman on the stereo and is wearing an apron with 'don't mess with the chef' written on the front. "I've made us baked bean lasagne. Sorry, the cupboards are a bit bare. I hope you're hungry."

Lily has never done this before in the whole of her life; sat down to eat with one other person, facing each other. There's something so intense about it, she's not sure she's up to it. "Where did you learn to cook?"

"My mum, she's the best cook."

Lily tries to imagine her mother passing on any recipe tips. 'So, you need to take one box of fish fingers, weigh out one packet of oven chips, add a pinch of salt and...' Lily takes a seat at the table and starts fiddling with her cutlery. The kitchen is warm, the worktops are clear and the washing up done.

Stuart places a full plate of lasagne in front of her, garnished with a side salad of rocket leaves and baby tomatoes. Lily takes a first tentative bite. What if she hates it? She's scared she might choke, her mouth is dry and the thought of trying to get something down her throat, terrifying. She lays down her fork and reaches instead for her glass. Red wine. She takes a huge gulp to try and steady herself. In the background 'Baby Can I Hold You' plays. Absent-mindedly, Lily sings along, the tune so familiar to her, she knows the words without thinking. "Forgive me, is all that you can't say. Years go by and still, words don't come easily." She looks up briefly and sees Stuart staring at her, with such a gentle look in his eyes, that she forgets for a moment to be scared. She picks up her fork and puts it to her mouth and this time she enjoys the sensation, the taste. She takes another mouthful of wine. "Why hasn't Fiona rung, do you think?"

"They've got a lot to sort out," says Stuart. "She's always been a daddy's girl. They'll have to work it out, one way or another. She won't be able to stay mad at him for long."

Lily's chin drops a couple of inches. "Oh."

"I mean, she'll give him hell, don't worry about that. Having to acknowledge that what her dad's done to you challenges everything she believes in. Her dad was always the one that stayed home. Her mum is a complete workaholic. It's weird; she's not interested at all in what Fiona's up to, whereas her dad's obsessed. "

"Do you think she'll have told him what happened? That it was me?"

Stuart sits down at the table opposite her and Lily moves her head so that her eyes are turned to the door. "I think you should prepare yourself for the fact that if she hasn't already, sooner or later she will. Fiona's honest to the point of brutality. I think it's been really good for her, all this. I mean apart from gaining a sister, because her dad's fallen off the pedestal she always had him on."

Lily rubs her forehead and reaches for her wine glass.

"It's good for both of them," Stuart says. "They'll have to have a more grown-up relationship now, and I'm sure they will. Now she knows he's flawed. That's no bad thing."

"I know why you're pleased she's not such a daddy's girl anymore."

Stuart's cheeks flush as he takes a mouthful of wine. "We've been seeing each other for over a year. Although 'seeing each other' is a bit misleading; her dad rarely lets her out of his sight anyway."

Lily holds up her hands. "It's none of my business. Sorry I shouldn't have said…"

"We probably shouldn't have done it." Stuart stands up and takes his hardly touched meal over to the sink. He leans his back against the worktop and runs both his hands through his hair. "I know it was only two days ago, but a lot's changed since then."

"It's obvious she has no regrets, so you shouldn't have either. I wish my first time had been like that." Lily tries to laugh. "I'm surprised I ever had sex again."

Stuart looks at her, waiting for her to say more.

She takes another mouthful from her wine glass. "I don't want to talk about it. Can I have more?"

Stuart's brow crinkles into a frown.

"Wine," she shrieks. Stuart smiles and fills her glass. Lily takes another gulp of wine. God she's shit at this conversation stuff. Lily forces a forkful of lasagne into her mouth, trying to push the food around her plate to make it look like she has eaten more than she has. "Wow, that was delicious. Shall I wash up?"

"No, let's go and sit down for a bit." He ushers her through to the front room and lights a few more candles, while Lily flops onto the settee, undoing the button on her tight black trousers.

"So," he says coming to sit beside her, bringing with him her glass of wine, "you're a woman of substance now. What will you do with the money?"

157

Lily sighs. "I don't know. I guess this is my inheritance. My mum didn't leave me anything, so I should be a bit sensible. I might go on holiday. What would you do with seventy-five thousand pounds?"

"Oh something boring, probably. I'd use it as a deposit to buy a house. Stop me having to hand over all my hard earned cash to a money grabbing landlord, who does nothing in return."

Lily's struck by the decisions that lay before her. Where would she buy a house? She has no ties to anywhere really. Will she go back to Leeds and carry on where she left off? Accrington is hardly appealing. She realises how alone she is, and her throat tightens.

Stuart puts his arm around her shoulders. "Hey, don't get sad. It must be so weird not having family, even though all mine do is drive me crazy. Don't think about it now. There's too much to take in. You can stay here as long as you want you know. I was wondering what I'd do for Christmas, it's only a week away."

"What about your parents? Don't you have to go and see them?"

"They've gone to stay with my sister in Mexico. She emigrated about eight years ago, and now she's married to a Mexican guy. They had a baby girl this year. My mum and dad are over the moon about their first grandchild. There's no way they'd miss her first Christmas. They've gone about three times over the baggage allowance with toys. God knows what Mexican customs will make of them."

"So you've got no one to spend Christmas with either?"

He shakes his head. "Graham, that's my eldest brother, is skiing and George, my other brother, is backpacking in Thailand."

"Blimey. You're all well travelled."

"Well, my dad's a journalist, so we were dragged all over the place when we were younger, and I guess it becomes a habit. But before your heart breaks, don't feel too sorry for me. There's an invitation from my Aunt Dorothy, to go round to theirs for turkey and the trimmings. But my cousins are probably the most boring kids you're ever likely to meet. Tom plays the viola. Have you ever met anyone who plays the viola?" He shakes his head. Then a thought occurs to him. "You could come with me if you like though. It might be fun if you were there."

"Well, I don't know."

"Or, we could just stay here. Maybe persuade Fiona and Jo to join us after they've done their family bit. Just don't leave." The words fall out of his mouth too quickly. He takes a deep breath. "I mean, I don't want you to go yet. I've been preparing myself for a lonely few weeks, and then you three arrived and now I don't want to go back to being lonely again."

Lily looks up at him and something happens in her stomach. She may be about to be sick. "Shit."

Stuart stares at her for a long time and then he leans forwards and kisses her, on the mouth. It's more of a brush with his lips than a kiss at first, but Lily is so scared of what will happen when it stops, that she starts kissing him back. They kiss for a long time, Lily's eyes tightly closed.

She pulls away. "Fuck, what are we doing? Stop."

"I absolutely love you." He stares unwavering into her eyes. "I know I shouldn't, but I can't help myself. I've never been moved by anyone, the way I am with you. The first time I saw you on the front street, the way you walk…"

Lily's eyes are itching; no one's ever told her they love her before. She curls into a ball. Stuart pours her another glass of wine. "What about Fiona? You're her boyfriend." She sits up to accuse him. Men, they're all the same. Always want what they haven't got.

"I know." He closes his eyes, head tilted to the ceiling. He sighs. "I think she's great. She's spirited and energetic and ready to take on the world. She's had everything you haven't, Lily. And before I met you, I thought I loved her. I do love her, but it's not like I love you."

"Stop saying that." She pulls a cushion over her head.

"I love you, Lily."

"You don't know me," is Lily's muffled response.

"I didn't choose to feel like this." Stuart stands up. "It would be much easier for me if I didn't feel the way I do about you, but I do. I can't help it. I've tried hard to ignore it, but it's hopeless. And I don't think Fiona's going to be broken-hearted, I truly don't. She's only fifteen. It was never going to be forever."

"You're not going to tell her." Lily jumps up from the settee. "You can't tell her."

"Of course I'm going to tell her." Stuart puts his arm out to her. "I don't have to tell her about this, but I do have to tell her it's not there between us. She'll know anyway."

Lily wishes she lived in olden times. She would just faint right now. It's all too much, sensory overload, system malfunction. She needs to shut down.

159

Chapter 28

Lily's tongue is stuck to the roof of her mouth and her head hurts. She opens one eye and sees the back of Jo's dark head on the pillow next to her. Lily lifts her head a little higher on the pillow, hoping the headache will subside if she sits up. A wave of nausea runs through her body. She looks to the side table for her bottle of water. It isn't there. Neither is the bedside lamp; it's been replaced by a radio alarm clock she doesn't recognise. Lily turns to Jo, and as she turns her head, a thought strikes her. Jo's hair isn't dark, it's bright peroxide white, and anyway, Jo is in Liverpool. A sound, somewhere between a yell and scream fills the room, and it takes Lily a moment to realise it came from within her own body.

"What?" Stuart sits up, bare-chested, looking for the cause of Lily's scream.

"Oh fuck," says Lily, pulling the sheet up and being briefly reassured to see she's still wearing her T-shirt.

"Don't worry. You fell asleep on the sofa, I carried you in here. I didn't want you to wake up alone."

Lily swings her legs out of bed. They are bare. She shakes her head.

"Ok, I didn't want to wake up alone. So I carried you here. Nothing happened."

The sound of the telephone breaks the silence. Lily flings herself out of bed, momentarily embarrassed to be seen in her knickers, and kicking out of her head the thought that she should have shaved her legs. She runs out of the door, forgetting to take into account the fact that Stuart's bedroom door is much closer to the stairs than her own. She meets the stairs much faster than she imagined she would. Half-falling, half-jumping down the stairs, she slams into the wall at the bottom and grabs the telephone from the hall table.

"I'm at the train station in Skipton," says Fiona, not waiting to hear who has picked up the phone. "Will you come and collect me?"

"Hi," Lily shrieks. 'Too much, tone it down' she thinks. Her cheeks flush. She tries to remember how her voice really sounds. "What happened? Is everything alright?"

"Will you come and get me please?"

"I can't, Jo's not here. She went back to Liverpool, but I think she's coming back today. Hang on, let me ring her and see what's she's up to. Are you ok?"

"I'm ok." Fiona says in a voice that implies someone else isn't. "I'll tell you all about it when I see you. I can't wait here for two hours." She sighs heavily. "I'll have to get the train. I think there's one in twenty minutes. I'm coming to stay for a few days."

"Right!" Lily tries to stop her voice sounding like a screech. She takes a breath. "I'll meet you at the station."

As soon as she puts the phone down, Lily picks it up again and rings Jo.

"Hi, Lily love," says Jo's mum. "She's still in bed."

"Would you mind waking her up? It's kind of important."

"What are you girls up to? I get the feeling there's some big secret."

"Nothing." Lily sits down on the floor and puts her head between her knees. A couple of minutes later Jo comes to the phone.

"Fiona's coming back."

"What happened?"

"She didn't say. Just that she's coming back."

"Does her dad know…"

"I don't know. I don't know anything."

"Does she need a lift?"

"No, she's going to get the train. I just thought… you should know. She's coming back. When are you coming back?"

"I'll set off in about half an hour," says Jo.

Lily puts the phone down and stands frozen for a moment. Then she turns and runs back up the stairs, two at a time. Stuart is in the bathroom. Lily can hear the sounds of the shower spitting out water. She fights the urge to throw open the door, and sits instead on the edge of the bed, picking at a loose flap of skin round her thumbnail. It starts to bleed.

She practises sentences in her head, but they all sound like clichés from soap operas. "Last night was a mistake." Or, "It can never

161

happen again." Or for top marks, "I can't lose my sister when I've only just found her."

In the end Stuart saves her the trouble. He emerges from the bathroom, his dark hair damp. "I've got to run. I'm on earlies again. I'll be back about four." He puts his hand on the top of her arm, and stares into her eyes.

"Fiona and Jo are on their way back. They'll be here by lunchtime."

"We'll sort this out, Lily. Don't worry."

She's aware she wants to kiss him again. He doesn't give her the chance.

"I've got to run." And he's gone. Two minutes later the emptiness hits her. She wanders around the flat, marvelling at her own triteness. After all the events of the past few days, her mind chooses to focus on a kiss, replaying it over and over in her mind, until her insides are tied in knots.

At the train station, Lily tries out various poses as she waits for the train from Skipton to arrive, trying to remember how she would normally stand. Hands in pockets or on hips? A minute after, the train pulls in, Fiona runs over to Lily and almost knocks her off her feet. Lily closes her eyes as she hugs her sister back.

Fiona looks exhausted; her eyes are puffed up and red. After spending the week of the kidnap wearing a mixture of Jo, Stuart and Lily's clothes, or the new clothes she bought in Lancaster, she looks odd wearing her own clothes; an olive green leather jacket that Lily hasn't seen before, and a pair of blue jeans. Her hair has been cut short and styled, making her look elfish.

"So, how was it?" Lily pulls back from Fiona.

Fiona shakes her head. "I'll tell you when we get home. Can we get a pasty? I'm starving."

Jo is pulling up in the mini when they reach the flat. "So go on then, don't keep us in suspenders, tell us what happened." says Jo, as they sit down in the front room with a tea tray. Jo starts to roll a spliff.

"It was awful." Fiona flops down on the settee, the back of her hand against her forehead.

"Well, go on then," says Lily.

Fiona raises herself a little in the seat. "First he was really pleased to see me, obviously. Mum was out. I was like 'what do you mean she's out?' and she's in London for the week because she's got some big case on. Court of Appeal, apparently. Anyway, then Dad

Chapter 29

Lily ducks. She's not sure why, but it's what her mother used to make her do when the Rent Officer came calling. It serves little purpose in a first floor flat, except Lily feels safer closer to the floor. Stuart picks up the overflowing ashtray, his eyes darting round the room for a suitable place to hide it. Fiona is on the settee, hugging a cushion, with her thumb in her mouth. Jo has gone as white as the walls, her mouth open; she appears paralysed. Lily crawls over to her and taps her on the knee, but she doesn't respond.

Lily starts to laugh. The carrier bags she was holding are lying on the floor, a wad of ten pound notes and a pair of knickers having spilled from the top. Lily tries to stand up but she's laughing so hard she can't. She looks to the others. The sight of Stuart still holding the ashtray with both hands, proffered like a gift, makes her laugh even more. The doorbell rings again.

Crawling on her hands and knees, body still wracked with laughter, Lily leaves the room. In the hallway, she stands up straight and tries to stop giggling by biting down hard on the inside of her mouth. She bounds down the stairs, two at a time and throws back the front door, "Daddy."

In front of her stands her father, in the freezing December rain, wearing jeans and a black anorak, looking smaller than he did in the graveyard. His hair is plastered to his head and splashes of rain obscure his glasses. "Lily."

The rain continues to fall, unaware of the tension. From upstairs, the sounds of frantic running around, bumping and scraping of furniture, drift down. Lily knows she should give them some time, but she can't think of anything to say except, "Would you like to come in?"

told me he'd told her we'd had a row, and I'd gone to stay at Caroline's for a few days." Fiona glances at Lily, and then Jo, and then back to Lily again. "I was kidnapped for six days and my mother doesn't even know."

"Oh," says Lily, aware Fiona is waiting for a response.

"When I asked him why he'd told her that, he looked really shifty and said it was because he didn't want her to worry. So I said, 'well, are you going to tell her the truth now?' And he said he'd rather we didn't. And then I said didn't he think that I'd want to tell my own mother about the torture I've suffered at the hands of these evil people? And he said 'Fiona, they didn't torture you' and I said how did he know. And then he said 'well, did they?' and I said no, actually I'd been quite well looked after. Then he turned and opened the fridge, and without looking at me, he said did I find out anything about the kidnappers? And he was just so scared, not that I'd been tortured, or whatever, but that I might have found out."

Fiona's eyes fill with tears and her voice shakes as she continues, "And he just looked so pathetic, so old and so pathetic, and I found myself thinking, you're not my dad. You're not the dad I left behind. You don't even look like him. And then the phone rang and he said, 'that'll be your mother. She wants to talk to you.' And he answered the phone and told Mum I was in the bath, while I was stood there, right in front of him, and he told her I'd ring her back in ten minutes. And then he begged me to tell her I'd just been staying at Caroline's for six days, even though I have never stayed at Caroline's for more than one night in all my life. And so, I didn't know what to do, so I rang her and she asked if we'd made up and I said 'I guess'. And then she started going on about this bloke in the court case who's doing everything he can to avoid paying maintenance for his kid, even though he's a top lawyer. And I thought, 'my mother doesn't know anything about me.' I was like, 'Mum, I've just been kidnapped by my own sister.'"

"Did you?" says Jo.

"No, I went to bed."

"So what happened yesterday? Why didn't you ring?" asks Lily.

"Well, Dad had taken the day off work and we went to Gargrave, to this pub we sometimes go to. And then we, well, we went shopping, and I got my hair cut and he bought me some new clothes, including that leather jacket." She nods to the armchair, where the olive green jacket she was wearing at the train station, now lies draped. "I've wanted that for ages. And then he suggested we watch *Dirty Dancing*, which I love and he hates."

"Ok, now I'm feeling sorry for him," says Jo. "Joke, kind of," she adds as Fiona frowns at her.

"And then this morning he was being all jolly, like he knew he'd got away with it all. And he said, 'Don't forget your mother's coming back today. I'm sure she'll want to know what you and Caroline got up to.' And then he asked me if I wanted cereal or toast. And I just said to him, "Dad, I know you know who kidnapped me.""

Fiona pauses. Lily is sitting on the edge of the settee, "And?"

"And he dropped the carton of juice he was holding, and it splashed all up his trousers. It looked like he'd wet himself."

Fiona reaches for a cigarette from Jo's packet.

"Then what?" asks Lily.

Fiona lights the cigarette and exhales a plume of smoke. "I asked him if Mum knew about Lily and he said no. So, I said, 'I want you to tell Mum, or I will.'"

"Shit."

"And then I told him I was going to stay with my sister, who's lovely. And I said, 'if you want to speak to me, you'll have to speak to her, because we come as a pair from now on.'" Fiona smiles at Lily. "And that was pretty much it."

Lily lies back on the sofa and closes her eyes. "Oh my God."

"Oh, and I told him we're staying here."

Lily springs back upright. "What?"

"What can he do? I'm sixteen in three weeks. If he does contact the police, they're not really going to do anything, and anyway he's not going to contact the police, because what's he going to tell them? I was kidnapped and he didn't tell anyone, not even his own wife, for fear that I may have been kidnapped by his other secret daughter and he didn't want to look bad?"

"But he might come." Jo dashes over to the window, looking down on the street below.

Fiona's cheeks redden. "I might have been being tortured by evil paedophiles and he didn't do anything, because he was too scared people might find out he told a lie."

"Fuck, Fiona," Lily says. "He might come here at any time?"

"I can't believe he didn't tell my mum I'd been kidnapped," Fiona's voice has a whiney quality to it.

164

"He knew it was me, that's why," Lily snaps at Fiona. "He from the beginning. I said he would and now he might just t wanting his seventy-five grand back. Sorry, eighty-five gran God."

Jo sits down on the settee next to Lily. She reaches for hand. No one speaks. The sound of the front door opening them all lean closer to each other. They hear footsteps on the Lily puts her head into the front of Jo's jumper. The front roor opens and Stuart appears. The sound of his voice makes the rush to Lily's face and she's glad no one can see her. She kee head buried in Jo's lap. "It was a quiet day, so I begged for t off. The suspense was killing me. What's happening?"

Fiona takes a deep breath, ready to recount her story aga Lily cuts in. "She's told him she knows it was me and she's to we're all here."

The colour seems to drain from Stuart's face, and when stands up to hug him his body is stiff. "Oh, Christ." He pushes to one side, and goes to the window and draws the curtains.

"Let's get out of here," says Lily. "We can go to my mu mean, my house." Then she looks at Stuart and she can't b thought of taking him to that house. "Or Leeds maybe?"

Jo nods and stands up. "Let's get packing."

"Ok." Lily rushes from the room, Jo close behind her.

"Oh," says Fiona, looking like a deflated balloon. She si down on the sofa and looks up at Stuart. "Do you want to rur too?"

"I don't know. I'm not overly excited at the idea of seein dad. What do you want to do? Did you tell him about, you kno

"About us having sex?"

Lily bursts back into the room with a carrier bag in each each with their contents spilling over the top. "Are you ready?

Stuart and Fiona glance at each other. Lily waits for an a And then the doorbell rings.

165

He nods, just as a raindrop makes it to the end of his nose. His nod causes the droplet to fly off his nose and it catches Lily in the eye. She rubs it with her sleeve. Then she slowly turns to lead the way up the stairs. "Close the door behind you."

As she reaches the first floor hallway, furious shuffling noises still emanate from the front room, so Lily pushes open the kitchen door. "Do come in. Please, have a seat. Let me take your coat. Would you like a cup of tea?"

Her voice sounds nothing like her voice, even to her. The giggles rise up in her throat again, and she has to turn her back to him as he takes a seat at the table. She thinks, at this rate it won't be long until I'm apologising for the china and asking whether it's one lump or two. She switches the kettle on and starts opening and closing cupboard doors. Half a packet of chocolate hobnobs fall out at her, so she starts to arrange them in the shape of a flower, each biscuit a petal. She breaks one in half to form two leaves and turns to offer her father the plate. Rain drips from his hair and his hands are red from cold.

"I'm sorry, Lily."

The words hang in the air for some time. "Sorry for what?"

He doesn't answer.

"For leaving?"

He nods.

"Or for lying?"

He opens his mouth to speak, but she's too quick for him. "For hoping you'd never have to see me ever?"

He rubs his face with his hands.

"For writing that you had no desire to communicate in capital letters and underlined?"

"For-"

"For not considering my feelings for one minute ever in your whole, deceitful life?" she shouts, so loudly it strains her throat.

"For everything."

"Oh, neat." They listen to the kettle reaching its climax. "Now," says Lily, "what did I do with that teapot?"

"How's your mother?"

She whips round to face him. "How's my mother? You don't know? You don't even know?" His eyebrows knot across his brow. "Fiona didn't tell you?"

"Tell me what?"

"She's dead."

167

"Oh God." The blood drains from his face and Lily allows herself a smile. Her father looks up at her and asks, "When?"

"She died of a broken heart."

"Oh don't, please." He rests his head against his hands, like he's praying.

"If you're looking for absolution, you've come to the wrong place. She never, ever recovered from what you did to her. She died the day you left her, that's what Aunt Edie says." When she is certain he is crying, from the shudder of his shoulders, Lily pours the tea. "Sugar?" She puts the mug down in front of him without waiting for an answer and lights a cigarette, inhaling deeply on her first drag.

She's almost smoked it down to the butt when he finally moves, takes a handkerchief out of his pocket and removes his glasses. "When did she die?"

"You ruined our lives. I hope it was worth it."

"When did she die?"

"September."

"September? I thought you said…"

"When you left her, she stopped living. It took twenty years for her body to get the message."

"Why did no one tell me?"

"No one knew where you were," Lily screams at him. "And when I did finally manage to track you down… you had no fucking wish to communicate."

"It wasn't," he says, the quietness of his voice a contrast to hers. "Worth it, I mean. There's Fiona, but that's all there is. If it wasn't for her, well…" his voice trails off. "I loved your mother." He looks down at his hands. "I still do."

Lily frowns and shakes her head. "You've got a funny way of showing it."

"I made a mistake and Pam, your mum, wasn't big on forgiveness. You must know that. I begged and begged for another chance and she was like stone."

"You made a mistake? Oh well, that's ok then. You made a mistake." Lily lights another cigarette, her hands shaking. "What 'mistake' did you make?"

"The mistake all men make." He stares at the table.

"I want to hear it." Lily takes another deep lungful of smoke. "I want to hear it all."

He sighs. "Oh, God."

168

"I need to know."

"It's past."

"Maybe for you; it's my inheritance. I lived the life I did because of you. I need to know."

He takes a swig of scalding hot tea and flinches from the pain. "I was working in a recording studio, nothing glamorous, I was a session musician. A band came in, the lead singer was… female. We recorded together for a few days. She had this amazing, soulful voice. I found out her husband had left her and she'd moved down from Northumbria and didn't know anyone. So, I asked her to our house a few times, your mum made her tea, that kind of thing. They got to be quite good friends and everything was fine."

"Go on."

"And then your mum, well, she was expecting you. We always said we weren't going to have children. We were happy, the two of us. I know this doesn't paint me in a very good light, but I felt left out. She was so wrapped up in her pregnancy; I barely got a look in. She didn't want to go out to the pub anymore because it was too smoky, didn't want to go dancing because she was too tired. She started going to bed at seven. I suppose I was jealous. And then there was the Christmas party at the studio, and I had a bit too much to drink and well, one thing led to another."

"You had an affair." Lily hurls the accusation at him.

"Well affair's a bit strong, I kissed her. That's all, I swear. I kissed her." He runs his hands through his thinning hair.

"Liar." Lily doesn't know how she knows, but she knows. She stands with her hands on her hips, glaring at him. "Don't you dare waste my time-"

He starts talking again, the words falling over themselves in a bid to be heard. "And then I met up with her another night and we went out for a drink together."

Lily gasps like she's been stabbed. "How could you?"

"And we kissed again, a few times."

"You cheated on her. You cheated on us."

"But that was it, I swear it."

"You lying, cheating, low-down-"

"I was jealous; you had each other, I had nothing."

"…miserable, pathetic excuse for a-"

"Course your mum wouldn't believe me."

"You're all the fucking same-"

"She went through the roof when she found out."

169

"You told her?" Lily winces. Their brown eyes lock and a flicker of understanding passes between them.

He stands up and turns away from her, to stare out of the window. "Worse than that, bloody Freda Matthews saw us and she told your mother. Pam was so heavily pregnant, I thought she was going to have the baby right there and then. She went off to her parents', your grandparents. Are they still around?"

He turns back to look at Lily. She shakes her head. David turns back to the window. "He never liked me, your granddad. Never approved; musician? I might as well have said murderer. Your gran had a soft spot for me though."

He watches the rain drip down the glass. "And then, all bloody hell broke loose. Your grandparents went bananas. They'd always thought your mum had married beneath herself; maybe they were right. I felt so bad, for a while I believed what everyone was saying; that she was better off without me. I didn't even find out you were born until days later. I went round to Edie's and she said, 'You've got a beautiful baby daughter.' And that was it. I tried and tried to get to see you. I rang a hundred times and your mum put the phone down on me as soon as I spoke. Then she changed her number. I wrote letters, and they all got sent back. I'd open the envelope and the pieces would fall out like confetti. She moved house and no one would tell me where she was. And then I got a letter saying she wanted a divorce. And I thought, 'she'll have to see me then,' so I went along with it so I could see her in court. Only she didn't turn up, sent a lawyer instead, and before I knew where I was, I was divorced."

"And then you married that bitch. You couldn't have been that heartbroken." Lily stubs out her cigarette and reaches for another.

David looks confused. "I didn't marry Anne, I never even saw her again. I lost my job, I had nothing."

"You had more than we did."

"I didn't. You had each other, I was alone."

"You can't have been alone for long."

"I was hopeless on my own. And then I met Fiona's mum, and well, I didn't tell her about your mum. Or you."

"Pathetic."

"I didn't think we'd be together long enough. And then… a small white lie-"

"A small white lie?" Lily screws up her face.

170

"Turns into a much bigger er, thing, because well, we got married. And I never found the courage to say-"

"So whose is the other baby?"

"What other baby?"

"God, you're compulsive. Aunt Edie told me. You had another kid the year after I was born. I'm guessing you've not told Fiona about that one either, huh? Which poor cow did you get up the duff that time?"

David seems to deflate in front of her. He becomes physically smaller, like his bones have turned to jelly and won't hold him up straight any longer. "That was Ruth too."

"So, where's-"

"The baby died. Cot death they call it now, but in those days it didn't have a name. I hadn't known Ruth very long when she, well, when Daniel came along. He died when he was five weeks old."

"Oh," says Lily, feeling suddenly uncomfortable as tears start to stream down her father's face.

"Ruth couldn't cope with it. She threw herself into work and I never dared tell her about you. I thought it was my punishment from God for what I... for losing you."

Lily can barely make out his words between the sobs. She sits down at the table and puts her head on her hands. Her father stands staring out of the window, talking so quietly, Lily can barely hear him. "I was so afraid at being by myself again."

He takes a deep breath and turns towards her. "And then Fiona was born and I felt like I'd been given a chance to make things up. That if I could be a really good dad to her, it would somehow compensate for you. I never even saw you once."

"So why the no desire for contact, underlined, capital bleeding letters, when I came looking for you?" Lily smashes the palm of her hand against the table, causing her father's mug of tea to spill.

"I panicked, I was so scared of losing Fiona, I didn't think-"

"Where's Anne now?"

"Anne?" It takes her father a second to remember who Anne was; the woman who had destroyed Lily's family. "I haven't the slightest idea."

"Does she know what she did? Does she know she destroyed my family?" Even as the words spew out of her mouth, Lily recognises her latent misogyny. Jo would never forgive her. 'Men,' she would say, 'you just never stop covering for them.'

171

Lily picks up the milk bottle from the kitchen table and sends it flying across the room to the door. It smashes and the milk gushes out, drenching her and her father.

Moments later Stuart throws open the door. "Are you ok?"

"Great, the cavalry," mutters her father, removing his spectacles and wiping them with his handkerchief.

Stuart doesn't glance at him. "Are you all right, Lily?" He tries to make eye contact with her but she's staring at the floor.

Fiona joins them. "What's going on? What's happened?" She rushes to Lily's side. "Lily?"

David stares at his two daughters, Fiona's arm around Lily. He stands a little straighter.

"Have you made up?" Fiona asks Lily.

Lily looks up at Fiona, sees the hope in her face. "Fiona, how can we make up? We never fell out. He didn't stick around long enough for us to fall out in the first place."

Fiona's face falls. "Oh."

Jo appears in the doorway. "Come on Fi. This isn't 'Surprise, Surprise'. You can't expect Lily to forgive him for what he did."

"It was only a kiss," David mutters.

"Yeah and only bears shit in the woods," says Jo, her hand on her hips.

"Who are you?" David asks.

"I'm Lily's only friend."

"I'm Lily's friend too," says Fiona. "And Stuart's her friend as well, aren't you, Stu?"

"I…" Stuart's cheeks start to glow, "I… yes… I mean…"

"Look," says Lily, anxious to divert attention from her friendship or otherwise with her sister's boyfriend, "it's alright, we've made up."

Jo frowns at her. "What?"

"It doesn't matter," says Lily.

"Yes it does," says Jo.

"Really?" Fiona looks over to her dad for the first time. "Oh, that is so great." She throws her arms around Lily and then beckons for her father. "We can all be a family together."

David moves towards them awkwardly. Fiona puts her arm around him. He clears his throat. "Well, let's not get carried away. There's your mother, she…"

"She'll come round," says Fiona. "When she's had the chance to… come round. Do you think Lily could live with us?"

David groans. "Listen, your mother, she isn't going to want us to be a family all together. I can tell you that now, even if we were to tell her."

"You are going to tell her," says Fiona. "And we are a family, whatever she thinks. Lily exists. She's your daughter, my sister. We are a family."

"Christ," says their father, mopping his brow with his handkerchief.

Chapter 30

Fiona releases David and Lily from their uncomfortable embrace and grins broadly. She appears not to notice the unbending stiffness in either of them. "I'll clear this mess up," she gestures at the spilt milk and broken glass, "and make us all a nice cup of tea. You go into the front room and make yourselves comfortable."

Jo leaves the room, but the other three remain rooted like dandelions. "Go on," Fiona says to her father and sister who are still standing next to each, their bodies turned slightly, so that although they are next to each other, the distance between them seems vast. "You have so much to talk about."

This surprises Lily, as she can't think of a single thing to say. Fiona walks behind them, shooing them out of the kitchen. Stuart is still standing by the doorway. "I'll make the tea, Fiona."

She shakes her head at him, reaching up to kiss him as she pushes him through the door. "Go on."

"It's my kitchen."

"You're the host," she says. "You have to make sure conversation flows. I'll be there in a minute."

Stuart trudges into the front room to find Lily and Jo sitting together on the settee, with David perched on the edge of the 1950s armchair. A vacant seat remains on the settee, at the end closest to David. Stuart elects to sit in the upright chair, by the window, at the far side of the room.

"So, do you think it will snow for Christmas?" Jo asks the room. All heads turn to the rain lashing at the windows. Lily picks at the loose piece of skin on her thumb.

"So," David clears his throat. "Fiona says you're at university?"

Lily looks at him, her face blank.

"Studying politics?"

"Oh, yeah," she tries to think of something to add but can't. "Politics."

"Are you enjoying it?"

Lily considers this question for a moment. It's hard for her to remember Leeds. Her life feels like a film she watched a long time ago.

David rubs his forehead. "Do you have a favourite subject?"

"We've enjoyed 'Feminism and Gender'," says Jo. "Have you read any Dworkin? She thinks all men are-"

"Jo." There's a warning note in Lily's tone.

"...rapists. But I think she's wrong actually. I think all men are cowards. Miserable, lying, cheating cowards."

"Bit of a generalisation," says Stuart, but his voice tails off as Lily looks across the room at him.

Fiona bounds through the door, tea tray held high. "I've found biscuits," she announces. "Chocolate ones. How's everyone getting on?"

Stuart goes cross-eyed at her from the other side of the room. No one says anything.

"What?" Fiona sets the tray on the coffee table and takes the seat next to Lily, forcing Jo to squash up into the corner. Fiona extends an arm across Lily's shoulders and smiles at her father. "Isn't this great?"

Her father doesn't reply, but tries vainly to return her smile.

"Don't you think she looks like Hannah?" Fiona asks, as she takes a bite of chocolate biscuit. Crumbs spill from her mouth as she continues, "And guess what, Dad? Lily wanted to be a librarian when she was little, same as me."

"Don't talk with your mouth full, Fi."

"And she supports Liverpool."

Lily nods and lights up another cigarette.

"How long have you been smoking?" asks David.

"And The Stone Roses played at Leeds Poly last term. Lily says if they play again she'll get me a ticket."

"Yes, you can come and stay with us whenever you like," says Jo. "We'll have a blast."

"Well, GCSEs first," David says. Fiona frowns at him. "But after that, I'm sure you'll have a wonderful time. It would be great for you to see what student life is like. You may even start getting an idea of what degree you'd like to do."

"Oh, I think I may be able to find a spare evening before July, Dad. You know what they say about all work and no play. You wouldn't want me to burn out now, would you?"

"Heavens, is that the time?" says David glancing over at the clock on the wall, which hasn't worked since the day the girls arrived. "I'd better be going. Fi, can I have a word with you before I go?" Fiona nods. "In the kitchen, Fi?"

As soon as the kitchen door closes behind them, David turns to his youngest daughter. "I want you to come home with me."

"I'm not coming home until it's all out in the open," Fiona says. "I want my mum to know what's been happening in my life, I want her to know I'm not an only child anymore. I have a sister. I want us to spend Christmas together, go on holidays together, get to know each other as a family."

Each of her requests lands on her father, as if it were a hammer banging in a nail. "Fi…"

"Do you know she's never been abroad?"

"Why don't you come home with me now and we can tell your mother together?"

"No way, it wouldn't be fair on Mum." Fiona looks up at her parent, her eyes filled with a mixture of pity and anger. "You have to tell her yourself or she'll never forgive you."

"What about school?"

"We break up on Friday. It's only a couple more days and it's not like we learn anything in the last week of term."

"It's an important year."

"What've you told them? Bet not that I was kidnapped by my half-sister."

"You can't stay here with Stuart. You're too young. I won't allow it."

"You can't stop me."

"Why don't you go back to Lily's house? If you want to spend some time getting to know each other, you don't need him around."

"I want him around." Fiona folds her arms across her chest.

Her father sighs. "He's too old for you. You need to be with a boy your own age."

"He's eighteen, Dad. He's three years older than me. Mum's eleven years older than you."

"But I didn't meet your mum when I was fifteen, Fi. We were both grown up."

"I'm sixteen in less than a month. And I'd be more grown up if you stopped treating me like a child the whole time."

"Men his age have different agendas, want different things."

"You're too late, Dad." Fiona juts out her chin as she stares at him. "I already know about those different things."

His eyes fill with tears. "Oh, Fi."

"You've got to let me grow up," Fiona shouts at him, as he turns away from her and to the worktop for support. "I've been going out with him for over a year. You should be pleased my first time was special, and with someone I love, because Lily's certainly wasn't."

David pulls out a kitchen chair and sits down. "I could call the police. Have them all arrested for kidnap, extortion, God alone knows what else."

"I'll tell them I went of my own accord. As a matter of fact, it was me that suggested demanding a ransom. You should see where she grew up. She has nothing. I thought you owed her."

"Well, I've paid her. I don't begrudge her the money, Fi, really I don't. I would have gladly paid child support, had anyone ever allowed me the opportunity. Why don't we go home and talk this all through?"

"I'm not coming home till Mum knows. I refuse to live a lie."

David puts his head in his hands. His shoulders start to heave.

"Dad, don't, please. Everything will be all right, really it will." Fiona leans her head against his back, and winds her arms around this torso. "School's finished for Christmas. I just want some time with Lily. Please, Daddy. I still love you."

David stands in the doorway, his arm around Fiona's shoulders. She has both her arms around his middle. She looks at Lily, Jo and Stuart; all sat together on the settee and says, "I can stay til Sunday."

"That's great," says Lily, checking her father's face for a sign he thinks so too. David glares at Stuart with ill-disguised contempt.

"Don't worry, we'll look after her for you," says Lily.

"Good. That means no smoking indoors." David nods at Lily's fingertips, and Lily stubs out her cigarette.

"I want you to promise to eat properly and don't stay up too late. And remember Fiona is only fifteen. I don't mind her having the odd glass of wine, but no spirits and no drinking to excess. Agreed?"

"Agreed," Fiona and Lily chorus.

David glares at Stuart again. "And I think it would be best for all concerned if you girls shared a room."

Stuart's face turns red.

"Dad," Fiona stretches the word in the way that only teenagers can, so it sounds like it consists of two syllables.

"Why don't we all have a drink now to celebrate?" says Lily, desperate for something to take the edge off.

Jo is up off the settee before anyone can say a word. "There's a bottle of white wine in the fridge."

"No, wait," says Stuart, leaping up from the settee almost as quickly as Jo. "I've got something much better. At least it should be, it cost me forty quid." He darts out of the door.

"I'll get the glasses," says Jo.

It seems to take an inordinate amount of time for Jo and Stuart to reappear with five wine glasses and a bottle wrapped in Christmas paper. Stuart unwraps it to reveal a 1982 Château Ducru-Beaucaillou. David glances at him and inclines his head. "Good choice, they've been having some problems lately."

"It's my Aunt Dorothy's Christmas present," says Stuart. "They invited me to spend the day with them, so I thought I should splash out. But, well, I think we deserve it more."

"Just a small one, Fi," says David.

"I don't want any," says Fiona. "You guys drink it."

It's a deep, red wine, smooth and warm. Lily takes small sips, allowing the wine to stay in her mouth, to flow over her tongue. By the time of their second glass, Jo is making David laugh with her Cilla Black impression. And when Lily and Fiona collapse in a heap of giggles together on the settee, David pats Lily's head.

An hour later, David stands. "I ought to get going," he says with the air of someone who has a root canal appointment.

"Hang on," says Lily as she topples off the back of the settee. "I want to give you the money back. I'm sorry…"

David holds up a hand. "It's yours; legally, morally. You've earned it and you should have had it a long time ago. If I'd have known where you were…"

Lily looks across at Jo. Jo appears as if she is holding her breath.

"But do something useful with it," David continues. "Use it to buy a house, or invest it wisely. I can probably put you in touch with someone who could advise you. Anyway, I hope it goes some way to making amends…"

The four of them accompany him down to the front door and stand on the pavement to wave him off. The rain has stopped and it's already dusk.

"Ok. Well, I'll ring you when it's safe to come home." David ruffles Fiona's short hair. She reaches up to hug him. He closes his eyes as if trying to infuse himself with her courage. Then he opens his eyes and turns to Lily.

He offers his hand to her. She shakes it, as she wishes him good luck. "It was, er, nice, meeting you."

"Look after her… everyone for me," David says to Stuart, without making eye contact.

"I will," says Stuart.

"And, er thanks for the wine."

"Thanks for, er, coming."

"Ok, bye Jo. And remember, smoke on the doorstep. It's not even raining anymore." David glances up at the dark, foreboding rain clouds overhead. A few drops of rain spatter back down on him.

"I love you, Fi," he murmurs into the ear of his youngest daughter, as she hugs him again. "I'll pick you up, Sunday morning." He glances at Lily one last time, a half look and a slight nod of the head. They wait for him to drive off before filing back up the stairs.

"Shall we open that bottle of white?" Jo asks.

"No," says Lily, "it would be like drinking toilet water after that last one. I may never drink cheap wine again."

"I can stay." Fiona holds up her hands and jumps into the air. "Give me a cigarette." Fiona snatches the one Jo is about to light.

"What do you think your mum's going to say?" Lily asks.

Fiona frowns like she doesn't understand the question.

"To your dad?"

"Oh," Fiona thinks for a second, her eyes screwed up against the smoke. "She'll kill him."

The knot in Lily's stomach tightens. "Will you roll us a spliff, Jo?"

"I can't, Stuart flushed it down the toilet when your dad arrived." Jo's aggrieved tone suggests this wasn't a mutual decision.

"I know," says Fiona, "let's have a Christmas party; a proper Christmas dinner. Today's Wednesday. Can you believe it's only been a week since you kidnapped me? Thanks to you two I'm not bored out of my brain in double chem right now. Let's have a dinner on Friday. That will give us chance to prepare and recover. Come on. It's time to celebrate. I'll cook." She laughs as Stuart pulls a face and puts her arms around him. "Obviously, you may need to guide me a little. I'll go shopping tomorrow. We can have turkey and those little sausages with bacon wrapped round them. Oh and chocolate log. I know, let's get a Christmas tree."

"I'll come with you," says Jo. "This is the first year since I was about twelve that I can afford Christmas presents. What about you, Lil?"

"No, count me out," says Lily. "I hate Christmas shopping. Besides I need some time alone." Jo raises an eyebrow. "Just, you know…" Lily doesn't meet Jo's eyes. "I need to calm down, I'm all over the place."

"What about you?" Fiona asks Stuart, as she wraps her arms around his neck and presses her body against him. "If you're very good you can choose your own Christmas present."

"I can't, I'm working the day shift tomorrow." Stuart puts his hands on Fiona's hips and pushes her a few inches backwards. "Why don't you come down for a drink when you're done shopping?"

Chapter 31

The house is in darkness. Ruth opens the door and steps inside, stooping to take off her brand new Italian shoes as soon as she crosses the threshold. Even in the gloom, she can see that blood from her heel has seeped into the stitching. She throws them both in the waste paper basket in the hall, before turning right into the dining room and switching on the light. At the drinks counter in the corner, she pours herself a double gin and tonic and then continues through to the kitchen.

"Oh!" She flicks a switch and the kitchen is illuminated, revealing David, wearing his coat and sitting at the table. "You frightened me. What are you doing sitting in the dark?"

"Hello, Ruth."

"What's happened? Don't tell me you've had another row." She opens the freezer and takes out a tray of ice cubes.

"No. It's... it's rather a long story."

The ice cubes splash into the gin. "Go on then, let's hear it."

"Would you like me to run you a bath?"

"Story first I think."

He stands up and moves to put the breakfast counter between them, before turning to face her. "I'm sorry I haven't told you before, but I have another daughter. I'd never met her until today."

Ruth looks at him as though he's speaking a foreign language. The gin and tonic remains in her hand, halfway between the counter and her lips.

"A few weeks ago, she, my daughter, tracked me down, through a Missing Persons service. I told them I didn't want any contact, so she, er, kidnapped Fiona and demanded a ransom, which I paid. But now Fiona knows she's got a sister, a half-sister, and she's refusing to come home until I tell you the truth."

Ruth appears frozen. The glass still hasn't moved. David's neck starts to itch. "Because she wants Lily to be included in our family."

"Lily? I'm sorry, who's Lily?" Her voice is cold, as frozen as the ice cubes on the counter.

"My daughter," he says. "My eldest daughter."

Ruth coughs to clear her throat. She raises the glass to her lips and drinks the entire contents without pause. "Get me another drink, would you darling, a large one."

He takes the glass from her and hurries from the room. The moment she is alone she grabs hold of the counter to steady herself, and then turns towards the sink, as her stomach threatens to throw its contents onto the hand-quarried slate she had imported from Argentina. She holds her hair back from her face and then splashes some cold water on her face.

David re-enters the kitchen bearing another gin. She straightens her shoulders, turns to face him, and takes the glass from his hand. "Cheers. Aren't you joining me?"

He shakes his head, resumes his position on the other side of the breakfast counter, and waits for her to speak.

She takes a sip of gin, savouring the taste of it on her tongue, before swallowing. "Is this a joke? If it is, it's remarkably ill-timed, darling."

"It's not a joke."

"Is she illegitimate?"

He starts to nod his head and then says, "Actually, no. I was married before I met you."

"You were married before you met me," Ruth echoes. "That is interesting. And where is your first wife now?"

"She's, er, she's dead."

"My commiserations. You were widowed?"

"It's complicated. She didn't die while we were married."

"She didn't die while you were married. So, were you also divorced before you met me?"

"Yes." He grimaces. "Well, nearly. I was divorced after I met you."

"After you met me, but before we were married?"

"I-"

"Does anyone else know of her existence?"

"Well, my parents, obviously, Sue and Norman-"

She shudders and holds up one hand. "I meant friends or colleagues?"

182

He shakes his head.

"And you've had no contact with her, your daughter?" she asks as she makes mock inverted comma gestures with her fingers, glass of gin still in her hand.

"None, until this week."

"Or your first wife?"

"Absolutely none. I didn't even know she was dead."

"You didn't know she was dead. How strange, because I didn't know she was alive."

"I am sorry."

Ruth holds up a hand again, a policewoman stopping traffic. "Have you ever taken a paternity test?"

"No."

"Acknowledged the child in any way?"

Wrinkles appear on David's brow.

"In writing?" Ruth clarifies.

"No."

"Is your name on the birth certificate?"

"I don't know, I wouldn't think so."

"Ok. Well, I suggest you tell our daughter," she stresses the word our, "to get her teenage backside back in this house immediately. You can also tell her that Lily has as much chance of being included in this family as Mother Theresa. Now, I am quite certain we will discuss this in greater depth at a later date, but for the moment, it's been a terribly long day and I have some calls to make."

Ruth pulls her briefcase onto the counter and clicks the lid open. She looks up to see David still standing at the other side of the counter, staring at her. "Was there anything else?"

"No." David turns and heads towards the door. As he puts a hand on the gold plated door knob, he hesitates and turns to face her again. "Actually, yes. Yes there is. You want your daughter back; you ring her and tell her. She's at her boyfriend's."

Ruth holds a bundle of papers, tied with a red ribbon in her hands. "I thought we agreed she wasn't going to have boyfriends until after her exams?"

David takes a bunch of keys from his pocket and starts fiddling with the ring. He steps towards her, and throws half of them across the counter. "His name is Stuart. His telephone number is in the address book, under Robertson."

"Robertson, Stuart Robertson?

"That's him."

"His father's Brian Robertson, the journalist?"

"Goodbye, Ruth."

"Where do you think you're going?"

"Enough, I'm leaving you."

"How dare you? How bloody dare you? After what you've put me through? You've lied to me, your whole family has lied to me, for the past eighteen years, and now you expect me to welcome another daughter into our lives? We haven't room. You're already obsessed with the one that we've got. How will you find the time to fit another one in?" she screams at him. "You're a coward; a lying, cheating, pathetic coward."

He shrugs his shoulders. "You're not the first woman to call me that."

"Get out then." She pushes him towards the front door, jabbing at his chest with her fingers. Without her shoes on, the top of her head barely meets his chest. He stumbles backwards down the hall way, trying not to laugh. "And don't think you're getting the house. This is my house, I paid for it. Mine."

"I don't want the house," he mutters, mainly to himself. "I never liked this house."

"You can find some other mug to buy you the life you've become accustomed to. You're not getting a penny from me." He opens the front door. "You pathetic man." She manages to make man sound even more of an insult than pathetic.

He strides down the gravel drive into the darkness without a backward glance. A few moments later, an empty gin glass whizzes past his left ear. He climbs into his car and locks the door from the inside. As he starts the engine he leans across the passenger seat and reaches into the glove compartment, pulling out a cassette box. He puts the tape into the car radio and 'Dark Side of the Moon' starts to play as the gates sweep open for him.

Chapter 32

"Lily? Is that really you? Oh, sweet Lord."

"Who is this?"

"He said not to ring you before eleven. I've had ants in my pants all morning."

"Who is this?"

"It's your grandmother. Oh I can't wait to see you."

"Oh my God." Lily tries to wake herself up by scratching herself, her fingers making red lines along her forearms. "Hi. Sorry. I didn't recognise…" she stops as she realises there's no way she could be expected to recognise a voice she's never heard. "I mean, Fiona's told me a lot about you."

"Oh, I can't wait to meet you. David says that you're beautiful, and too thin."

Lily feels a bubble of excitement rise up through her windpipe She twists the telephone cord around her fingers. "Did he? So is, has, did he tell…"

"Oh, he's told her alright. He turned up here late last night without so much as a clean vest."

"Oh." The smile on Lily's face dies. She sits down with a bump on the bottom step.

"Now, don't you go worrying yourself about Ruth. Is Fiona there?"

"No, I don't think so. I don't think anybody's here." Lily cranes her head to see into the kitchen. "I think they've gone shopping."

"Well, I'll tell you a secret, child. Just between you and me. Never did like Ruth, although don't tell your sister I said that, she is still her mother. But intelligence without wisdom – it's not worth a penny. Oh I can't believe I'm talking to you. I've thought about you so often."

"I was asleep," says Lily.

"How are you feeling?"

"I don't know, different. Is David…"

"Don't worry about him. You've done him a favour. Ruth too probably, in the long run. What?"

Lily hears the low thrum of male voices in the background.

"Well she has," Lily's grandmother says to someone else. "Talk about, 'marry in haste, repent at leisure'." She turns her attention back to Lily. "Come for lunch, we have so much catching up to do. David says you're beautiful. Not that I'm surprised, mind. Your mother was always a looker."

Lily looks up to the ceiling, holding the phone an inch away from her ear. She has to blink several times. When she returns to the conversation, her grandmother says, "I'm sorry about your mum."

"Thank you."

"Will you come for Christmas Day?"

Lily hears more background conversation.

"Ok then, Boxing Day," the older woman says to Lily. "Wednesday. Six days."

"Well…"

"Promise?"

Lily scratches the back of her neck. "Ok."

"Promise?"

"Promise."

Lily's grandmother gives a small gasp of pleasure. "Perfect. I can't wait to meet you. I haven't seen you since you were five days old."

"Could I speak to Da… David, please?"

"Of course, he's right here. So, I'll see you on Boxing Day, about eleven?"

"Eleven? Well, I'll have to find out about trains."

"Well, let me know if you're going to be late. Hang on, here's your father. God love you, Lily."

"Hi, Lily," David's low voice hums down the line.

"Hi, er, hi." Silence fills the telephone. "Are you…ok? How did… Fiona's mum take it?"

"I should really speak to Fiona. Is she there?"

"No, she's out shopping. I don't know when she'll be back."

"Well, could you just tell her she might want to give her mother a couple of days to calm down before she rings her."

"Days?" Lily tentatively teases him, ready to pretend she's misheard if it backfires.

He gets the joke. "Maybe weeks. I'll see you soon, Lily. Boxing Day it would appear."

Lily puts down the receiver and hugs her bare, knobbly knees to her chest. She lies back on the staircase, her face to the ceiling, and shouts up the stairs. "Anybody in?"

The silence echoes around her. In the kitchen Lily finds breakfast dishes on the table and a note from Jo and Fiona. 'Gone shopping. Back after lunch. x'. Lily flicks through the shelf of vinyl records in the front room, selecting 'This is the Sea' by the Waterboys. As soon as 'Don't Bang the Drum' starts, Lily starts to dance.

Lily fills the kettle and reaches for a cigarette, but the packet is empty. She glances at the clock on the kitchen wall. It's ten past twelve. While she waits for the kettle to boil, she washes the dirty plates, singing as she does. 'I wandered out in the world for years. While you just stayed in your room. I saw the crescent. You saw the whole of the moon'.

Jo and Fiona burst through the door at half past three, with arms stretched to the limit by a dozen carrier bags. Lily is still in her pyjamas, but the kitchen is spotless.

"Wow, you've been busy," says Fiona, as she heaps a clutch of bags onto the kitchen table. "We've got paper chains."

"Fiona, er, you'd better sit down. Your dad rang. He's staying at your granny's house for a few days." Lily anxiously watches Fiona's face for signs of trauma.

"Oh. Well at least he's told her. Mum, I mean." Fiona pulls a tinsel fairy with purple wings from one of the carrier bags. "Isn't she gorgeous? She's for the top of the tree."

"What tree?"

"It's being delivered later," says Jo, as she rummages through her own collection of carrier bags. "And we got fairy lights."

"Did you get cigarettes?"

Jo throws Lily a packet of Marlboros across the kitchen. "Stick the kettle on, Lil. We haven't stopped. I'm knackered."

The telephone rings while Lily is pouring the tea. Jo goes out into the hall to answer it. Moments later she kicks open the kitchen door, while speaking into the handset in a foreign accent. "Ah, no, no, me no speaka..." She beckons to Fiona, holding the phone in her palm, her fingers tightly clasped over the mouthpiece. "It's your mum."

Fiona shakes her head. "I'm not in."

Jo pulls a face and raises her eyebrows at Lily, her hand firmly pressed against the mouthpiece. She holds the telephone out to Lily. Lily moves away from the proffered phone as if it were an undetonated hand grenade. "I'm not speaking to her." She turns to Fiona. "She's your mother."

They all stare at each other for several seconds, until Fiona reluctantly moves into the hallway and takes the telephone from Jo. "Hi, Mum." Lily can hear Fiona's mother's tirade from the other side of the kitchen; exploding down the receiver like firecrackers.

Fiona holds the telephone a good thirty centimetres away from her ears. Jo stands with her back pressed against the kitchen door, holding it open so that Lily can see Fiona on the telephone. She keeps opening her mouth to speak, but never getting as far as forming the words; all the time a thin, tinny rant buzzing from the receiver. Eventually the noise stops and Fiona carefully hangs up the phone. She turns to Jo and Lily. "Well, that went well."

Lily spits out a mouthful of tea in a spray across the kitchen table. Jo laughs.

"She's looking forward to meeting you both," Fiona says as she starts to laugh too.

"She'll come round," says Fiona, once the laughter has subsided.

"What did she really say?" asks Lily. "Does she hate me?"

"No. Let's talk about something else. I was getting tired of doing what I was told to do anyway."

"Oh, Fiona, do you think you should-"

"And don't you start telling me what to do either," Fiona says to Lily. "I know what I want."

"Come on," says Jo, "we've got decorations to put up."

"God, I wish we had a spliff." Lily puts her forearms on the kitchen worktop and lays her head on top.

"There's wine in the fridge."

"I don't want to drink that cheap shit anymore."

"Well, you have seventy-five thousand ways round it."

Lily lifts her head slightly. "What?"

"Lily, you have seventy-five thousand pounds under the floorboards," says Jo, "you can afford a bottle or two of expensive wine, if that's what you're after."

Half an hour later Lily is dressed, and the three of them are in Oddbins. They choose four bottles of expensive wine; red, white, rose and sparkling. The bill comes to one hundred and thirty-three pounds.

When Stuart arrives home that evening, having worked a double shift, the flat is unrecognisable. Tinsel adorns every surface, including the banisters, and a brightly coloured cardboard montage of Father Christmas and his eight reindeers, flies across the hall wall.

Chapter 33

Friday morning, the morning of the Christmas party, Fiona wakes up in bed with Stuart next to her. She watches him sleep for a moment, smiling at his long sleeve T-shirt. That had been the compromise; he had wanted her to sleep in Andre's room, with Jo and Lily, and she had wanted to sleep with him. They had eventually agreed on sleeping together, but clothed. She even had to keep her socks on because he's always had a thing about her feet. She bends down and places a kiss on his dark curls.

He stretches in his sleep and opens an eye. Fiona kisses his cheek. "Hey."

"Hey." He opens both eyes. "What time is it?"

"Ten past six."

"In the morning? Oh, Fiona." Stuart groans and pulls the duvet over his head.

"You can't go back to sleep, we've got so much to do." She bounces off the bed to open the curtains, and then claps her hands together. "Oh look, snow." Another muffled groan comes from under the bedclothes.

Fiona stares at the lumpen mass for a moment and then shakes her head. She runs down the stairs, pulling on Jo's boots and grabbing her coat from the bottom banister on her way down. When she opens the flat door, the street is deserted, and the snow is virgin. Looking up to the skies, she sees heavy white clouds hanging low above her, promising more of the same. Fiona picks up a handful of snow, rolls it into a ball in her hands, and throws it high up in the air.

Three quarters of an hour later, Lily is dressed and making tea and crumpets for breakfast. Stuart is sitting at the kitchen table writing

190

down the instructions for Christmas dinner. Jo peers over his shoulder as she enters the room in her dressing gown, her hair sticking up at right angles to her head. "2pm, switch oven on?" she reads. "Aren't you going to be here?"

"I'm at work until four."

"So we've got to cook without you? Christ. Pass us a fag, Lil."

"You'll be fine. Just follow these simple instructions, you can't go wrong." Stuart starts a second sheet of paper.

Fiona is sieving flour into a bowl. Jo scowls at her. "Fiona. It's seven o'clock in the morning. What are you doing?"

"I'm making the pastry for the mince pies."

"And why are you dressed?" Jo asks Lily.

"I'm going to go into town at eight. I've got to get in there before the crowds or I'm a dead woman. I suddenly realised it's the weekend tomorrow, and then Monday is Christmas Eve. If I don't go today it's all over."

Jo flicks her ash into the sink and then opens the bottle of Harvey's Bristol Cream she and Fiona bought yesterday. She adds a liberal capful to the bowl of mincemeat next to Fiona. "Well, suppose I'd better get dressed."

Lily has only one carrier bag, but it's heavy enough to make the veins stick out in her forearms, as she climbs the stairs. Jo and Fiona are both in the kitchen, with the radio playing Christmas carols. Jo is wrapping chipolata sausages in strips of bacon and Fiona is peeling sprouts. Lily stands unnoticed in the doorway, marvelling at how life has changed. Fiona swears under her breath as she catches her thumb on the knife she's using. "I'm going to wrap a few presents," says Lily. "I'll help out in a bit."

Fiona waves a hand but doesn't look up from her duties. Lily slips from the room. Half an hour later she hears a scream.

"What's up?"

Jo is red-faced and crying with pain. "It can't be supposed to be this hard."

"What?"

"Cream. I'm trying to whip the frigging cream, my arms are on fire."

"Jesus, I thought something was seriously wrong."

"Something is seriously wrong," snaps Fiona, sweat dripping from her forehead. "We're two hours behind schedule. This sucker was supposed to be in the oven at half past two."

Lily eyes the large turkey, "What are you doing to it?"

"I'm stuffing it," says Fiona. "What does it look like? Only I'm not sure it's meant to be frozen."

"Hello," shouts a voice from the hallway. "I'm home, how are getting on?" Stuart opens the door, his gaze sweeping the room as the smiles on his face fades. The sink is so full of washing-up; the girls have started piling dirty crockery on the floor. Vegetable peelings, spilt milk and broken egg shells festoon every surface, Fiona's hair looks grey with flour, and a lump of pastry hangs from the ceiling.

"What have you been using this for?" Stuart asks as he points to the blender.

"Don't ask," Jo and Fiona shout simultaneously. Then they look at each other and laugh. Stuart takes off his coat and starts to roll up his sleeves.

"Oh," says Fiona. "It was supposed to be a treat for you."

"I love cooking; it is a treat for me. Just let me get some of these dishes out of the way first." He puts on his apron, the one he wore the night he cooked for Lily. Lily's face reddens, but in the heat of the kitchen, no one notices.

Fiona grabs a tea towel and rushes to the oven. "Shit, I mean sugar, the chocolate log."

"You haven't baked a Swiss roll, have you?" asks Stuart.

"No," says Fiona, her tone suggesting she's offended by the question. "We were defrosting it." She opens the oven door and four faces peer inside. The chocolate cake has melted and dripped through the rungs of the shelf. It lies in a sticky heap on the oven floor.

"Ah well," says Jo. "At least there's trifle."

It's almost nine o'clock before they sit down to dinner, having pulled the small, red Formica topped table into the living room. The settee and armchairs are pushed back to the perimeter of the room, and Fiona has covered the table with silver wrapping paper.

"Would you like to pull my cracker?" Jo asks Stuart. "Oo-er, missus."

Wearing a crooked, crêpe paper party hat, Stuart carves the turkey at the table. "This is delicious," says Lily, already full from the prawn cocktail starter she's just eaten. "Last Christmas we had turkey sandwiches; only they'd run out of turkey at the Spar so it was actually chicken."

Fiona stands up. "I'd like to propose a toast," she says, as she sways slightly. "To my sister. The best Christmas present ever."

Stuart and Jo stand to raise their glasses. "Speech, speech," chants Jo.

Lily tries to rise to the occasion, pushing her chair back. She bumps the edge of the table with her hip and knocks her glass of red win over. "Shit."

Jo and Fiona both dab at the spilt wine with red napkins. "I just want to say I love you all," says Lily, her words slightly slurred. Stuart's dark eyes meet her own and Lily blushes.

After dinner Fiona insists they play charades, "We have to, it's traditional."

"Maybe in your family," says Lily.

Jo's attempts to mime 'Dirty Dancing' have Lily laughing so much, she holds up her hand and pleads with her to stop. "I've got to wee." Lily runs out of the room. When she comes down the stairs from the toilet, Stuart is waiting for her at the bottom with a bowl of crisps in his hand. He nods his head at the limp bunch of mistletoe hanging in the hall. "It's tradition."

Where's the harm in one Christmas kiss? She takes two steps towards him, her head slightly tilted to one side, aiming for a light brush of his cheek with her lips. He steps forward too, so that they are closer at the point of meeting that she had anticipated. As their bodies almost collide, close enough that she can feel the heat of him through her belly, Stuart turns his head towards to her and kisses her on the mouth. His lips taste of red wine and brandy sauce and chocolate. Lily closes her eyes and doesn't notice Fiona stepping out of the front room. The first she is aware of her presence is when Fiona coughs. Lily steps back and pushes Stuart away.

"We were under the mistletoe," says Stuart. Fiona turns to Lily; the look of confusion on her face makes Lily want to cry. Fiona stands staring; waiting for an explanation for about five seconds, and then asks Lily, "What's going on?"

Lily stands with her mouth open, two bright spots of crimson for cheeks, still saying nothing, so Stuart takes Fiona by the arm. "Let's go for a walk," he says.

Fiona allows Stuart to take her by the elbow and guide her down the stairs, out of the flat door. The fact she doesn't say anything all the way down the stairs, makes Lily feel scared. Stuart unhooks his

193

black ski jacket from the banister, on their way down the stairs. They walk in silence until they reach the castle, and there Stuart sits her on a low wall and stands in front of her. As he looks into her eyes he says, "I've fallen in love with Lily."

He watches the truth register on her face, and the tears build in her deep, brown eyes. He pulls her towards him, holding her head against his chest, blinking back his own tears. "I'm sorry, Fiona." She rests her head against him, pressing her nose against its warmth, fighting back the tears. "I wish there was something I could do," says Stuart, "to make it not hurt you."

Then she hits him. She jumps down off the wall and hits him again, as hard as she can. He puts his arms up to stop her blows landing on his face. Running at him, she punches him so hard he steps backwards and trips over the low wall. She flings his coat on top of him and runs off into the darkness.

Stuart sits up and touches his fingers to his skull, feeling the warm wetness of his own blood. He looks behind him and sees the stone he hit his head against. Standing up, he calls for Fiona, but there is only quiet. He listens for a moment, but he can't hear her footsteps. As he jumps back over the wall, he lands awkwardly, going over on his ankle. He starts to run, then limps down the street, unsure of which way she has gone. A number of side streets offer themselves as possibilities. "Fiona," he shouts into the darkness, "let's talk about it. Don't do this." All he can hear is the wind.

Chapter 34

Stuart runs as best he can, his coat in his arms, back to the flat. As he rounds the corner he sees Lily is on the doorstep, the glow of a cigarette tip hovering around her like a firefly. As he passes a street lamp, Lily sees blood on Stuart's face and she flicks her cigarette onto the floor, sparks flying.

"She ran off," he calls as he approaches her. "I don't know where she is."

"Oh, God. What are we going to do?" Lily turns to Jo, who is sitting on the bottom step in the doorway to the flat, shivering in the cold.

"We'll have to find her. Let's try the pubs," says Jo, as she pulls herself up from the step. She doesn't look at Stuart. "She's got to have gone somewhere warm."

Without speaking, Lily and Jo climb the stairs to get their coats, and the three of them spill out onto the street, the dark December night enveloping them. Flecks of snow start to fall as they make their way through the residential area into town, the houses' warm amber light glowing against the freezing, black backdrop.

Seven pubs later, they make their way from The Crown, towards The Crossed Keys, when Stuart spots two policemen on the other side of the road, their bright yellow coats reflecting the street lamps. Stuart nods over to them. "We're going to have to ask for help."

"Fuck off," says Jo. She turns to Lily. "We can't ask representatives of the fascist state to help us. We'll manage..." Jo realises Stuart is already jogging across the road towards them. She starts to run after him.

"Excuse me, can you help us?" Stuart calls out.

Jo puts on a spurt of speed to catch him up. "We've lost our friend," she calls out, already out of breath from her exertions.

"We've had a bit of a row and she's run off and we're worried because she hasn't got a coat."

The older policeman rubs his greying beard, his eyes streaming in the cold night air. "How long has she been gone?" he asks.

"Over an hour," says Stuart.

The policeman removes a black leather glove to check his watch. "Give her another couple of hours. If she's not back by midnight, phone the station. They might put out a description."

"She's only fifteen," says Jo.

"What does she look like?" asks the younger policeman, his blonde hair just visible beneath his policeman's hat. He turns to his colleague, "We can keep an eye out for her."

"She's got short hair," says Stuart, "and she's wearing a denim skirt with black tights and a blue top, with some kind of pattern around the top."

"Roses, it has roses round here." Jo gesticulates to her chest.

"Ok. Well, stick together." The blonde policeman nods towards Lily, who hovers, still on the other side of the road, then he looks at Jo. His blue eyes glint under the light of the street lamp. "You should have a hat."

Jo touches the shaved sides of her head. "I know."

"Give us your telephone number, then if we see her, we can let you know she's safe," he says. Stuart recites his number and Jo scrawls it in the policeman's notebook; her fingertips so frozen the number covers a full page. When she's finished, he snaps the book shut and replaces the pen. "Have you tried all the pubs?"

"That's what we're doing now."

"Ok. Well good luck, and remember, call the station if she's not back by midnight."

Stuart and Jo cross back over the road to Lily. Stuart shakes his head and says, "We're going to have to ring her dad." Lily leans against the wall and closes her eyes. "She may have rung him already," says Stuart. "Got him to pick her up. We could be looking for her all night while she's safely tucked up in Skipton."

Lily's hangover is starting to form. "Oh, God."

"It's not your fault," says Jo to Lily, while looking at Stuart. She puts an arm around Lily's shoulders.

They return to the flat and Lily finds the telephone number her grandmother gave her. She tries to hand the scrap of paper to Jo, but Jo shakes her head, "It's got to be you, Lily."

"It's half past ten. What if everyone's asleep?"

Neither Stuart nor Jo answer, and Lily reluctantly takes the phone from Stuart's hand. Lily's father answers on the third ring. "Hi, er, David. It's me, Lily. I'm fine, thank you. Um, how are you? No, it's about Fiona. She's not with you is she? It's like, we had a bit of an argument and she's run away. No. About two hours ago. It's complicated. No. It's just, it's so cold. Do you think she might have gone home? I mean to her mum? Yes. Right. No, ok. Bye."

The dial tone sounds in her ear. Lily turns to Jo and Stuart. "He's on his way."

Stuart kicks at the cupboard. "It will take him an hour to get here. I'm going to go and have another look for her."

"Hang on," says Jo, "we'll all come."

The weather has worsened, the fine flakes of snow have turned to icy sleet, coming at them horizontally. The town square is filled with drunken revellers, making their way to one of the two clubs in town. Men in shirt sleeves shout and push each other, while groups of women watch from the sidelines, huddled together like nesting penguins.

"Let's split up," says Jo. "We'll stand a better chance of finding her, before her dad gets here. I'll check out Woolies and round there, see if she's curled up in a shop doorway. I'll meet you both back at the flat in an hour."

"I'll go back to The Kettledrum," says Stuart. They'll be finished up there soon. Roy and Bill might help look for her."

"Oh, ok," says Lily. "Where will I go? I could try the bus station?"

Jo nods, "Good idea."

"See you back at the flat." Stuart jogs off, leaving Lily and Jo together.

"Will you be ok?" Jo asks as she pulls up the collar of her duffle coat. Lily nods and Jo waves as she starts towards Woolworths. Lily watches her walk a few paces and then turns in the opposite direction.

Jo only walks a few hundred yards before a voice shouts to her. "Hi there. Did you find your friend?"

Jo turns to see the policemen, still walking the beat. She shakes her head and curses the tears that prick at her eyes.

"Come on, we'll help you look for her," says the blonde one. He turns to his colleague, "We've nothing else on. Let's try down the Shelters."

197

An hour later, Lily and Stuart meet back at the flat. "There was a bus to Skipton an hour ago," says Lily. "Maybe she was on that."

Stuart pulls a face, rubbing his hands together to try and increase the circulation. "If she was going home," he says, "she would have gone to her dad, not to her mum. And I'm sure she would have rung him and got him to pick her up. Unless she feels too ashamed to tell him what's happened. Oh, God, I don't know." He runs his hands through his hair. "Where's Jo?"

"Dunno," says Lily. A second later the doorbell rings. "Maybe that's her."

"Still no sign?" asks David as Lily opens the front door. He's wearing a sheepskin coat which makes him look like a shady trader from 'Only Fools and Horses'. Lily shakes her head. He pushes past her and starts climbing the stairs. "Right then, where have you looked?"

Stuart is standing at the top of the stairs in the hall. He nods hello to David, but doesn't make eye contact. "I've tried work," he says, "and Lily's been to the bus station. We've tried every pub we can think of."

"There was a bus to Skipton," says Lily.

"What about the hospital?" asks David.

"No," says Stuart, "we didn't try there. You don't think…"

David stamps the snow from his boots. "The train station?"

Stuart shakes his head and looks at Lily.

"Taxi firms?" David asks. Silence. "McDonalds?"

"Jo might have tried there," says Lily. "She said she was going to the high street."

"Well, that's ridiculous," says David. "The last thing we need right now is people going off on their own. I need to ring the hospital. You two wait in the kitchen. You can make me a cup of tea while you're in there."

Stuart leads Lily through to the kitchen. Lily sits at the table, staring at the floor and smoking a cigarette, while Stuart boils the kettle. Stuart clatters cupboard doors. "God, he's so smug."

If Lily hears him she doesn't reply. She doesn't even look up when David throws open the door and steps into the kitchen. "Ok," says David, "the police have radioed her details to all foot patrols and they're going to get someone in Skipton to meet the bus, so if she's on it we'll know."

"What about-"

"She's not at the infirmary." David sighs heavily. Lily senses it's an exaggerated sigh.

Stuart shuts the fridge door with his foot and nods his head at the cup of tea on the worktop. "That's for you."

"Good," says David. "Right, I want you both to visit every single place you've been with Fiona. Everywhere; cinemas, sports centres, coffee shops. She will have gone somewhere she knows. Lily, you come with me. We will try the bus, train station and taxi firms. We will meet back here in ninety minutes. No one is to do anything alone, clear?"

Lily and Stuart both nod. "I'll just get my, things," says Lily, running up the attic stairs as she's remembers the new packet of fags that are up there. Jo's got the old ones.

"I think I can hear Jo," says Stuart, as Lily leaves the kitchen. He follows behind her, running down the bottom flight of stairs. "I'll see you in an hour and a half." The front door bangs behind him.

David watches Lily as she steps down the attic stairs. "So, what happened?"

Lily stumbles on the last few stairs and lands upright at his feet.

"Never mind," he says. "Let's just get going."

"Haven't you a hat or gloves?" he asks outside, as he pulls his own hat firmly down over his ears. Lily feels an inappropriate flush of excitement that he cares that she's freezing. She looks up and down the street. There's no sign of Jo or Stuart. David doesn't seem to notice. He starts walking in the road, where car tracks have made the snow less thick. Lily follows in his footsteps, trying to get the words of 'Good King Wenceslas' out of her head; 'heat was in the very sod, which the saint had printed.'

Stuart jogs into the town square and sees Jo talking to the same two policemen they had seen earlier. Jo looks up, spots him, turns and says something to the police and then runs over to him.

"They're going to have a look down by the canal. And there's a place that does soup and stuff."

"Well, we've got to go to every place we've ever been to here with Fiona. Even places that are shut."

"Can't we go with them?" She gestures towards the policemen. "I mean, they're trained in this kind of stuff."

"No, David said..."

"He's here?"

Stuart nods. "And he's pissed off with us all. Obviously. He said we've got to stick together. He's gone with Lily."

Stuart starts marching down the street. Jo shouts over to the policemen, "I've got to go, see you later." She catches up with Stuart and matches her steps with his own as they walk along for a minute or two in silence. "So, is it true? Do all men think with their dicks?" Stuart doesn't answer. "You see, I thought you might have been different."

"I love her, Jo."

"Who? Lily? Or Fiona?"

"I love both of them."

"So do I. Doesn't necessarily mean I have to shag them both."

"I shouldn't have slept with Fiona and I haven't slept, I haven't had sex, with Lily. But then maybe you shouldn't have encouraged one emotionally fragile sister to kidnap the other. So don't start on me, I'm not in the mood."

Chapter 35

David strides down the road, leaving Lily trotting in his wake, like a three-year-old child. He barely speaks to her, apart from barking the odd instruction. "If you see an all night garage, remind me to buy a street map."

As they turn the corner into King Street, a group of women out on a hen night are lurching down middle of the road. David calls over to them, "Excuse me."

There doesn't appear to be a sober one amongst them, and Lily flinches with embarrassment as one of the women starts shouting, "Ignore him, he wants to get his leg over, you're spoken for."

"I just wanted to ask you ladies whether you've seen a young girl, on her own, without a coat." He acts oblivious to the dozens of inflated condoms, safety-pinned to their dresses. No one has seen Fiona. As the women stagger off, David turns to Lily, "I should have brought a photograph."

"I've got one," says Lily excitedly, glad to be of some use at last. She pulls the picture of her and Fiona on the log flume ride, out of her wallet.

"You went to Blackpool?" David asks, his brow creased.

"Yeah, we, er…" Lily lights a cigarette.

"Do you have to smoke so much?" They watch two drunken men career into the road outside the train station, to be screeched at by an oncoming taxi. The taxi swerves up onto the pavement and the driver winds down his window and shouts obscenities.

"Have you not read anything on attachment theory? I smoke because my early childhood needs weren't met by my loving parents." Lily mutters as an afterthought, "We studied it in 'Youth and Crime'."

"It must be great for you having someone to blame for everything that's wrong with your life." David's face is clenched against the sleet. They cross the road in front of the station in silence. A homeless man asks them for 20p for a cup of tea. David shows him the photograph and gives him a fifty pence piece..

The man shakes his head and asks, "You couldn't stretch to a fiver could you? I'm supposed to be meeting a friend but I've lost my train ticket."

David strides past him, and out of the station. He takes off a glove and wipes the cold from his eyes. "Wait a minute. Let's try in here."

Lily follows his gaze to the church next door. A banner above the door advertises a midnight carol service. The snow is coming down thickly now and settling on the ground. Her breath hangs in the air.

David pushes open the heavy door. The church is empty, but still warm from the memory of the late night carollers. Huge candelabras at the front of the church are still lit, and Lily notices a teenage boy in a white smock, working his way along the front of the church, extinguishing each candle with a snuffer. He moves slowly, methodically. He snuffs out another flame, before turning round and making eye contact with Lily. Then he nods to a corner pew, and as David makes his way down the central aisle, Lily sees her, a small bundle, hunched over, the bare skin at the back of her neck, red with the cold.

Lily runs down the side aisle as David works his way down the pew towards her. Lily comes in from the other side and they meet at Fiona. Her lips are tinged blue and her eyes are swollen. David takes off his sheepskin coat and wraps it around her shoulders. He pulls her towards him, trying to warm her body against his own. "Oh, baby, you had me worried."

Tears start to pour down Fiona's face and Lily is struck by how young she looks.

"What's up, titch? Did you girls fall out?" He looks at Lily now, acknowledging her for the first time this evening. "That's what happens with sisters, you know. Think about Hannah. She's always fighting tooth and nail with Kate. It drives Auntie Sue mad."

Fiona leans her head against her father's chest as he strokes her hair. "Do you want to tell me about it?" Fiona doesn't answer. David turns to his eldest daughter. "Lily?"

Lily shakes her head and Fiona looks up. "You can bet she doesn't want to tell you." Lily sees the bottle of vodka by Fiona's feet. She picks it up. "Where'd you get this?"

"I bought it."

Lily shakes her head. "You didn't have any money on you."

"What do you care?"

"What's going on?" David asks, the relief that had made his voice soft, melting into something more akin to anger. "Come on, someone's got to tell me."

Fiona tries to focus on Lily. "Go on, you tell him."

Lily closes her eyes and wishes to be anywhere else but here. For the first time she regrets finding her father; wishes she'd left it alone. Wishes her mother wasn't dead. She opens her eyes. Fiona and her father are still there, looking at her, waiting for her to speak. "It was only a kiss for Christ's sake."

The 'for Christ's sake' comes out too loud and reverberates around the church. The choirboy turns his head for a moment before continuing with his task. The smell of extinguished candles has filled the front of the church.

A puzzled frown crosses David's face. "I know, I told you that."

"No, I kissed Stuart under the mistletoe. Just a Christmas kiss, but Fiona saw us and…" she raises her hands, trying to pass it off as a gross overreaction from the kid sister.

"He says he loves her," Fiona interrupts, her words slurred and her head lolling as she speaks. "He doesn't just love her, he's 'in love' with her."

Lily feels her stomach turn over with excitement. She squashes the feelings down. "No he's not. That's not my fault. It doesn't matter. All that matters is you. Honestly, Fiona." Lily slides down the back of the pew in front, so she is sitting on the floor at Fiona's feet. Her voice shakes as she speaks, "Finding you has changed my life. You have no idea. Before I met you, family was a word I didn't understand. There's been no one else in my whole life, ever. He shouldn't have said that because it doesn't matter. Nothing's going to happen, Fiona, please."

"Do you love him?" says Fiona in a small voice.

Lily doesn't answer.

"Do you?" asks David.

"It doesn't matter," Lily half whispers.

"It matters to me," says Fiona.

"It doesn't matter, because I love you." Lily's voice rises so that the last three words ring out in the church. Never having said, 'I love you' to anyone before, it now feels like a curse, a prison sentence. She stands up, her nose running. "I shouldn't have kissed him. I'm sorry, I wanted to know what it felt like to have someone who cared."

"Look, let's talk about this some other time. Please," David begs. "Things will look different in the morning."

"Please, Fi." Lily's touches Fiona's arm.

"I always said he wasn't good enough-"

"Shut up!" Both sisters turn on their father at the same time.

"I want to go home." Fiona sways as she stands up. As soon as she hits the fresh night air she vomits. The sick hurtles to the pavement, splashing half way down David's trousers. Fiona's legs buckle beneath her. She groans and says, "I don't feel very well," before collapsing at her father's feet.

Chapter 36

'Tis the season to be jolly, and violent and drunk. Casualties of the festive spirit lurch around the streets. Lily watches a window being boarded up, sees the broken pint glass that smashed it lying in the middle of the street. Fiona is slumped, barely conscious. Lily and David try to march her up and down the church path, but her legs trail along the floor. David calls 999 three times, the third time yelling, "My wife's a lawyer" into the phone. The ambulance takes nearly forty minutes to arrive.

Fiona is admitted straight away. Because Accident and Emergency is full of drunks with cut heads and broken limbs, Fiona is taken to the paediatric ward and Lily and David have to pace it out in an empty waiting room with stencils of Winnie the Pooh on the wall. David strides up and down the centre of the room, under the fluorescent lights, while Lily sits in a blue plastic chair, her arms folded across her chest.

Half an hour of pacing later, David turns to his eldest daughter. "You've really gone and fucked up my life haven't you?" he says through clenched teeth.

Lily continues to stare at the floor.

"You kidnap my daughter, blackmail me, take my money, renege on your promises, destroy my marriage, and now my daughter's in hospital, having overdosed on vodka. All because you were jealous."

"It's not my fault. If you'd just written me a letter, instead of having no fucking wish to communicate-"

"I've explained that."

"Yeah, well explaining it doesn't make it any better. I live with the consequences every day." Lily stands up. "I am what I am because of you. Same way Fiona is. She's bright and well adjusted

205

and lovely, and I'm fucked up, hopeless, a mess. That's what you get when you did what you did to me."

"Do you ever take any responsibility for your own life? I fail to see how having an affair with your sister's boyfriend can be construed as my fault."

"It was just a kiss," Lily shouts.

"Yes. Well. Maybe that makes us even."

"How dare you compare... I'm not married. I haven't got a pregnant wife. I'm not about to have a baby."

"Kissing your sister's boyfriend is the moral high ground?"

A nurse appears around the door. "Could you keep it down in here please? Or I'm going to have to ask you to leave. There's a ward full of children right next door."

"Sorry," says David, not meeting the nurse's eye.

"I should think so. Now, don't let me have to come in here again." The nurse turns on her heel and leaves the room.

"I'm sorry," says Lily after some time. She sits down again and puts her hands over her face. "I didn't ever mean it to be like this. You know it was Fiona who first told me we were sisters. I hadn't even realised being your daughter meant she was my sister."

David sits down in a chair on the other side of the room, facing Lily. He looks at his watch and groans. "I should ring Ruth."

"We spent weeks watching you, you know, before the kidnap. Watching Fiona in her pigtails and knee socks, glowing like the Ready Brek kid. You're right. I was so jealous. I didn't see her as a person; I just saw a way to get at you. And then we kidnapped her and she was so indignant, so absolutely sure we'd got the wrong man 'Daddy would never do that'. And I loved showing her the wedding album, the pictures of you and Mum. You should have seen the look on her face."

Lily can't help a small smile at the memory. She stands and walks over to the window, lays her head against the glass. "She was more pissed off with you than I was. She wanted to make you pay and I thought great, this is going to be a piece of cake. But then she said she'd always wanted a sister, and that was the first time I realised." Lily looks over to David. "She never held it against me, you know, that I'd kidnapped her. She was so cross and so outraged by the injustice of it all, that I started thinking, if she's this good a person then you couldn't be all that bad, because you'd raised her. She thinks the world of you."

206

Lily becomes aware that David has followed her across the room. She turns to face him. "In her eyes you're like Father Christmas and Superman all rolled into one."

David is standing in front of her. He reaches out to her and takes her hand. He pulls her to him, so firmly Lily's nose gets squashed against his chest. He smells of soap and pine needles. Lily bites down on her lip until she can taste the blood, but the pain doesn't help. A wave of sickness rises up inside her; her eyes are hurting and she tries to stop herself crying out, by holding her fist against her mouth. Her father strokes her hair and says, "I'm sorry."

Lily collapses into his arms. She feels the wetness run down her cheeks, and she cries harder. David pulls her down to a chair and sits next to her, holding her tightly to his chest. As Lily cries, she can hear his heart beating.

"Mr Winterbottom?" A young doctor stands in the doorway. "You can see your daughter now."

David doesn't let go of Lily. "Is she…"

"She's going to be sore for a few days. We've had to pump her stomach, which involves a rather invasive procedure to her throat," the doctor smiles, "but she will be fine."

"This is Fiona's sister, my eldest daughter. May we both go?"

The doctor nods. "But just a few minutes. She's going to need to sleep."

Fiona's face blends with the hospital pillow, her dark eyes sunken and her lips pale. David hesitates, stands by the door, trying to blink back tears. Lily stands at the side of Fiona's bed and reaches out to touch her hand, which has a plaster across the back of it.

Fiona opens her eyes, "I feel dreadful."

David hovers at the foot of the bed, while Lily tells Fiona to shush. Lily wipes Fiona's fringe from her face and tells her to rest. Fiona struggles to lift her head an inch off the pillow, to look for her father. Her eyes fill with tears as she sees him by the door, "I know I've been stupid."

"No, it's me that was stupid," says Lily. "I'll never forgive myself." She sinks into the chair by the side of Fiona's bed, her hands clenched in fists.

David steps forward. "Stop it now, both of you. Fiona, you need to sleep. Everything will seem different in the morning."

"I'm sorry, Daddy."

"I said, no talking. Everything's going to be ok." He plants a kiss on Fiona's forehead. "Now, close your eyes and rest."

"Time to go," whispers a nurse, "you can see her again in the morning."

The snow has settled and the moon spreads a translucent light across the deserted streets, as David puts an arm across the small of Lily's back, and they make their way back to the flat.

Stuart and Jo are waiting for them; Lily rang them from the hospital to tell them Fiona was ok. Jo opens the door and leads them upstairs. Stuart is waiting in the hallway. He doesn't meet David's eyes as he asks, "Would you like a hot chocolate?"

"Thank you," says David, taking off his coat. Stuart turns towards the kitchen. "Er, Stuart? I have a favour to ask. Would you mind if I spent the night on your settee?"

"No, not at all. It's the least I can do."

"I'll make the hot chocolate," says Jo, putting her arm through Lily's. "Give us a hand, Lil."

Stuart has his back to the wall, as he watches Jo lead Lily into the kitchen. He glances at the attic stairs. Fiona's father stands at the bottom of them, blocking the entrance. "I've got a sleeping bag upstairs." David doesn't shift his position. Stuart breathes and looks him in the face, "I'm sorry…"

"It's not me you need to apologise to."

"I know," says Stuart, looking at the floor.

"I think, I think we all have lessons we can learn from this." David stands to one side to allow him to pass.

"Thank you," Stuart mumbles as he climbs the stairs.

Jo and Lily are sitting on the settee when Stuart comes back downstairs with a royal blue sleeping bag that has badges sewn onto it. Four mugs of hot chocolate stand on the coffee table and David has taken his coat off and boots off. Stuart lays the sleeping bag over the back of the settee. "It was right at the back of the wardrobe."

Jo stands and picks up two of the mugs. She hands one to Stuart. "Right, we're off to bed," she says as she nudges Stuart towards the door. Then she turns back to Lily and David and adds, "Not together obviously. Think we've had enough of that kind of thing for one night."

David actually smiles as Stuart stares at Jo with a look of horror on his face. "Thanks for that, Jo," he says. "Right. Night everyone, see you in the morning."

As Jo leaves the room she turns on the lamp on the sideboard and flicks off the overhead light, leaving David and Lily in the half-light. The gas fire creaks. Lily picks up her hot chocolate and takes a mouthful, and then spits it back into the mug. "Aah, hot, hot."

"You look so like your mother. She was about your age when I first met her."

"How, I mean where, or when, did you meet her?"

"I used to play in a band. Just kids stuff really. And we played a gig at these awful discos they used to put on at the Church Hall, and she just came up to us afterwards and started talking. All the lads were hoping she was interested in them. Well, she was a bit older than us and so beautiful. We'd been at the same school together, but she'd never noticed me. I couldn't believe my luck when she asked me if I wanted to dance."

"Aunt Edie said you were a plumber."

"I was, kind of. I didn't really know what I wanted to do when I left school. Actually I did," he laughs. "I wanted to be a rock star, but there weren't many vacancies for rock star down at the job centre and my father, he was a plumber, and he had always wanted me to go to work with him. So I did but I didn't much care for it. I wasn't very good at it either."

"So, what happened?"

"Well, your mum, she always saw me as a musician. I was fifteen when we got together, eighteen when we got engaged. She gave me the confidence to tell my father I didn't want to be a plumber, and she found a job advertised for session musicians for a recording studio, and I got the job. I mean, when I say job, it was very sporadic, some weeks I didn't get paid a thing. But Pamela never minded about money. She was working and she earned just enough to make sure the bills were paid."

"My mum had a job?"

David nods. "She was a typist in a legal firm. She didn't really like it, but she never complained. And she used to organise gigs for the band, The Recluse we were called. Stupid name."

"Did my mum want a baby?"

"I guess she must have done, I just didn't realise. I know it sounds selfish, but we were so happy. I didn't want a baby spoiling things. I was young. I didn't know then that babies grow up fast and become incredible human beings. I just thought it would keep us up all night, screaming."

209

"Do you think she regretted it? I mean when she told you she was pregnant and you weren't pleased, do you think she wished she wasn't pregnant?"

"No. That was the thing about your mum. She was always sure; she wasn't the type of woman to regret things." He strokes Lily's cheek. "She didn't tell me at first, she wanted to wait until she was twelve weeks, but she couldn't wait. She was glowing with this great big secret and she, well you know what they say about pregnant women, she was absolutely blossoming, like a flower; she never looked more beautiful."

"What did you say when she told you?"

"Oh Lily. I didn't say very much. I mean I tried to pretend I was pleased, but not much got past your mum. But she didn't seem to mind. She was completely sure I would come round, which of course, I would have done, if..."

"If things hadn't turned out the way they did."

"She used to call me Rock Star." He laughs softly to himself, his eyes shining.

When Lily climbs the attic stairs that night, the sounds of her father zipping himself into the sleeping bag follow her up the stairs. The Velux window at the top of the stairwell casts a red glow over the stairs, as the new dawn breaks in the sky.

Chapter 37

Jo brings Lily a cup of tea at eleven o'clock the next morning. Lily, having had only four hours sleep, raises herself on one elbow and asks, "Where's Da... er, Fiona's..., David?"

"Fiona's David is downstairs, bleaching all the ashtrays. I can't believe you slept through his telephone conversation with the hospital at seven thirty-three this morning."

"Is Fiona..."

"Fiona's alright." Jo takes out a packet of tobacco from her bra. "She's being discharged this afternoon."

Lily takes a mouthful of tea and then jumps out of bed, still wearing her clothes from the night before. She pulls an extra jumper over the top, and opens the door. Jo looks up from her hand rolled cigarette. "Where are you going?"

"Just, you know, to see what's happening."

David is wearing Stuart's apron and a pair of rubber gloves when Lily enters the kitchen. It seems he has all the contents of the cupboards lined up on the worktop next to the sink. "Ah, Lily. You're up at last. Did you get your cup of tea? I've made porridge, there's still some left on the stove. Give me a moment and I'll heat it up again."

"How's Fiona?"

"The doctor says she's doing as well as can be expected. I'm going to pick her up in an hour. You may come with me if you like. He did say she's a bit down, but that's perfectly normal in these situations."

"Are you going to stay?"

David nods. "I've asked Stuart if he'd mind putting up with us for a couple of days. I don't really want Fiona's grandmother to see her in this state, or her mother for that matter. Besides, there's not really

211

the room at my mother's. She only has a spare single bed. So, Stuart has offered to sleep on the settee, Fiona can have his room and I've bought an air bed this morning, so I can sleep in with Fiona, until she's fully rested."

"Have you been to bed?"

"One day, when you have kids, you'll understand."

At the hospital, Fiona is sitting up in bed, but when she sees Lily and David she closes her eyes and pretends to be asleep. The doctor who discharges her tells David she must spend at least two days in bed, resting. David carries her like a child, her legs bent over the crook of his arm, to the car. Lily carries Fiona's possessions in a hospital issued plastic bag; one set of damp clothes and an empty vodka bottle.

Stuart is at work, but Jo is waiting for them, having been to the shop for tins of chicken soup and bottles of banana milkshake. David has already pumped up the air bed and placed it at the foot of Stuart's bed. He's careful not to step on it as he lays out his youngest child on the double bed. He covers her with a duvet and rearranges the pillows behind her. Throughout the whole procedure, Fiona doesn't open her eyes once.

"Can I get you anything, Fiona?"

She doesn't answer. He stays sitting on the other side of the bed next to her for half an hour, but she doesn't open her eyes. When David goes downstairs to make a cup of tea, Lily is waiting for him.

"You can go up now, but only for a few minutes. She's not speaking. I think she just needs to rest."

Lily runs up the stairs into Stuart's bedroom, banishing memories of the last time she was in there. "Oh Fiona, I'm so glad to see you. How you feeling?"

Fiona is lying prostrate on the bed. She makes no attempt to move, to sit up.

"I'm so sorry Fiona," says Lily. "I will never forgive myself."

Tears seep through Fiona's closed eyelids.

"Oh Fi, please don't cry. I bought you some magazines." Lily lays a copy of Just Seventeen and Smash Hits on the bed next to Fiona. Fiona turns her head towards the wall.

"Would you like me to read them to you?" Still Fiona doesn't look at her. "Come on, Fiona. Say something."

Ten minutes Lily goes back downstairs. Fiona remains mute the rest of the day.

212

On Sunday morning Stuart, Lily and David are in the kitchen eating breakfast. "It's my fault that she's in such a state," Stuart says. "I should be the one to talk to her."

David wipes his fingertips on his handkerchief. "I think you've upset her quite enough already. I'll have another try."

As he stands up, Jo comes back through the kitchen door, carrying Fiona's untouched breakfast on a tray. Jo shakes her head at them and says to Stuart, "I think you need to grovel some more."

"Come on Da... David," Lily says. "Let Stuart go and see her. We're not getting anywhere."

David looks at Stuart and says, "Five minutes."

Stuart climbs the stairs and knocks on his bedroom door. There is no answer, so he pushes the door. The room is dark, the curtains drawn, blocking what little light the day contains. He creeps inside, trying to adjust to the gloom. "Fiona?"

Fiona flicks on the switch without moving, the flex of the bedside lamp coiled in her hand. Stuart jumps, and screws up his face against the sudden influx of light. Fiona stares, unblinking at him, her dark eyes emphasized by the dark shadows underneath.

"I don't know what to say... except I'm sorry."

Fiona narrows her eyes at him. He adjusts his weight as his legs start to weaken, but he doesn't look away.

"Did you mean it? Do you love her?"

He nods.

"Are you in love with her?"

"Yes I am."

"And you don't love me?"

He looks up at the ceiling. "I do love you, but I'm not... it's different."

Fiona sinks down into the duvet, and pulls a pillow over her face.

"Oh please don't cry Fiona, you're fifteen." Stuart sits down on the edge of the bed and tries to stroke her arm.

She removes the pillow, shrugs off his touch, anger suffusing her face and neck. "Don't you dare..."

Stuart holds up his hand. "What I mean is, you were never going to stay with me for long." She opens her mouth to argue, but he's too quick for her, "You've got 'A' levels, and university. And travelling; you've always said you wanted to see the world."

"I meant with you."

"No you didn't. You've got it all in front of you. You've just found your sister."

"So has Lily."

"You don't need me."

"And Lily does?"

"Yeah, I think she does."

"I think that's patronising. You're patronising me and you're patronising her. You make it sound like you're doing this because she needs you more than me, but I need you."

"You don't. You know you don't. I don't think Lily does either. I think with you and your dad and all your family, she's got what she needs. It doesn't matter anyway; she's never going to let herself love me, because she loves you too much."

"Good."

"I'm sorry, Fiona. I thought I loved you, honestly I did. And I did, kind of." He doesn't notice her wincing at his words. "But then, when I met Lily, I started having these feelings and I realised…"

"What?"

"I realised that what I felt for you, well it wasn't love, not true love."

"Get out."

"I'm sorry."

"Get out."

"You were never going to stay with me for long," he says, ducking as a rolled up copy of Smash Hits hurtles through the air towards him. He opens the door and leaves as the bedside clock crashes against the doorframe.

"I never want to see you again," Fiona shouts at the closed door. She climbs out of bed and opens the door. The stairwell and hallway below are empty. "You're pathetic. Do you know that?"

Her father opens the front room door and steps into the hall. "Did you call me?"

"No." Fiona slams the bedroom door closed and throws herself across Stuart's double bed, sobs wracking her body.

An hour and a half later, Lily edges into the room, with lunch on a tray. "How are you feeling?"

Fiona turns away from her to face the window, the back of her hand against her forehead. "Sick."

"Try and eat something, Fi. It will make you feel better."

"I can't. My throat hurts too much." Fiona watches Lily set the tray down on top of the set of drawers next to the bed. "So, do you love him?"

Lily closes her eyes, her back to Fiona. "I told you, it doesn't matter."

"It matters to me."

"I don't know. I've only known him just over a week, during which time I've kidnapped a sister I didn't know I had, blackmailed my own father, made more money than I've ever seen, and drunk the best part of about fifteen bottles of vodka. I don't know anything, except nothing's going to come of it."

"So you promise you won't start seeing him? You won't have any contact with him after this?"

Lily turns to meet Fiona's gaze. "I promise," she says.

"How do I know I can trust you?"

"Because the stakes are too high," says Lily. She sits on the edge of Fiona's bed, the same spot where Stuart sat. "What if I did start seeing him behind your back? Where would it go? All that would happen is that I'd be found out, and I'd lose everything. I've got no one, Fiona. No one. I'm not going to risk it am I? Not on a man I've known less than a fortnight."

Fiona closes her eyes for a few moments. Then she sits herself a little higher up against the pillows. "I might be able to manage a few sips of water."

Lily jumps up to pour her a glass of water from the jug and holds the glass to Fiona's lips. Fiona takes a sip and groans a little as the water passes down her throat. She nods towards the door. Lily stands poised next to her, the cup in her hand. "Do you mind?" says Fiona, nodding towards the door. "I want to be alone."

Lily puts the cup down. "Shall I take the tray away?"

"No leave it there. I may feel like something a bit later."

Fiona watches Lily leave the room, waits a few moments, and then reaches for the bowl of soup and the hunk of soft white bread.

Chapter 38

Lily closes the bedroom door behind her and exhales. She starts slowly down the attic stairs. Halfway down she sits down on the middle step. A flash of memory of her granddad; what was that rhyme? 'Not at the bottom and not at the top'. The more she reaches for the memory, the more it dances away from her. The strains of the 'Only Fools and Horses' theme tune, filter up from the front room. Lily sinks her head into her hands.

When she opens the door to the front room a few minutes later, Stuart and David are sitting in matching armchairs, each with an opened can of lager in front of them. Lily asks, "Where's Jo?"

"She's gone out," says Stuart without shifting his gaze from the television screen.

"Where to?"

"She didn't say," says Stuart, as David laughs out loud. On screen Granddad is upstairs in a stately home, unscrewing an enormous chandelier, while Rodney and Del stand on stepladders in the room below holding out a sheet, braced to catch it. Granddad hits the peg out, and a second chandelier in the room behind Del and Rodney smashes to the floor.

"Classic," David mutters, banging his palm on the arm of his chair.

"Stuart?" says Lily. "Will you help me find the tea tray?"

"It's in the cupboard underneath the sink."

"Stuart," Lily repeats, a warning note creeping into her tone.

Stuart tears his gaze from the television and looks at Lily for the first time since she entered the room. As she pulls a face at him, he understands. "Ah." He gets up and follows her into the kitchen, leaving David chuckling to himself. "What's up?"

"I've just promised Fiona that I won't see you again."

216

"Oh." The silence is broken only by the sound of David's laughter. "Do you want me to leave?" he asks. "Or are you going to wear a blindfold?"

"Don't try and be funny."

"But why-"

"I didn't have much choice."

"Why don't-"

"I need you to help me. This is the first time in my life I feel like I belong somewhere. Don't let me screw it up, please." Stuart steps towards her as Lily takes five steps back.

"Oh, Lily."

"Please." Lily backs into the sink. She puts her hands behind her back and holds onto its edge to keep herself upright. "Don't ruin my life."

Stuart looks at her, sees the tears threatening to fall. He studies her face for a moment and then he says, "Ok," turns 180 degrees and leaves the room.

It's another twenty four hours before Fiona pads, barefooted down the stairs. It's already dark outside, even though it's not yet four o'clock. She stands outside the front room door for a moment, drawing breath before throwing open the door and stepping into the room, shoulders back and her head held high. The sleeveless top with black embroidery she bought on her Christmas shopping trip with Jo, and the skin tight jeans she's lifted from Lily's room, emphasize the fact she has lost a few pounds during the last few days.

It takes Fiona a moment to realise the room is empty. She cocks her head and hears voices coming from the kitchen. Quietly, she places a hand on the door handle, her bright pink nails gleaming, and pushes the door ajar. Inside, she sees Stuart standing with his back to her, sleeves rolled up, using a rolling pin on something. Jo is washing up at the sink and Lily and her father are both sitting facing each other at the kitchen table. Lily is peeling potatoes. She can't see what her father is doing, as he has his back to her. 'God Bless Ye Merry Gentlemen' plays on the radio.

Fiona stands unobserved for a moment before Lily catches sight of her. "Hi, Fiona."

David turns in his seat and smiles at his youngest daughter. "Baby, oh I'm so glad you're feeling brighter. Come and sit down."

He takes a pile of recipe books off the chair next to him. "You can be in charge of timings. The responsibility is too much for me."

Jo winks at Fiona. "You look great. I like what you've done with your hair."

"What are you all doing?" asks Fiona.

"Well," says David, "we thought, because you've been feeling so poorly, we thought we'd all stay here for Christmas, so we're making dinner for tomorrow." He sees the puzzled expression on her face. "It's Christmas Day tomorrow."

David's eyes are bright, his shirtsleeves are rolled up and he has flour down the front of his trousers. He follows Fiona's gaze to the open bottle of Château neuf-du-Pape on the table and shrugs his shoulders. "I've been making truffles. It wouldn't be Christmas without truffles."

Fiona notices plasters on each of Lily's forefingers. "What happened to you?"

"Terrible accident with the potato peeler," says Lily. "Don't worry about me. I have more fingers."

"Aren't you supposed to be in Liverpool?" Fiona asks Jo.

"I thought I'd stick around. I've made a deal with my mother." Jo raises an eyebrow. "Don't ask, but I don't have to be home until Boxing Day."

Fiona stands nonplussed for a few more moments. The others watch her without speaking. Stuart smiles at her. "Well," she asks, "what can I do then?"

"You can squash five pence pieces into this," says Jo, lobbing a Marks and Spencer's wrapped pudding across the room. "For luck."

Fiona catches it in both hands.

Chapter 39

Fiona sits up in bed on Christmas morning, switches on the lamp and sees her father asleep on the air mattress, like a guard dog at the foot of her bed. "Daddy?"

The heap of blankets stirs.

"Will Mum be coming over? It's Christmas Day."

"What?" says her father, as he tries to raise himself on one elbow, his eyes screwed up against the light.

"Mum, I was wondering whether…"

"Oh darling, I don't think so. Your mother is very upset with me at the moment, understandably so. But she still loves you, obviously, and I'm sure she'll want to spend some time with-"

"Oh my goodness." Fiona's attention is caught by the sight of a bulky red stocking hanging at the foot of her bed. She grins at her father and asks in mock-amazement, "How did Father Christmas know where to find me?"

Her father lies back down on his mattress. "Oh, we sent him a last minute fax. Go back to sleep. It's too early."

"Rubbish. It's nearly six," says Fiona, diving across the sheets.

Her father groans and pulls his blankets up over his face. Fiona pulls the first present from the stocking and is about to rip the paper off, when she stops and asks her father, "Do you think I should wake the others?"

David lifts the blankets a couple of inches so that he can see his daughter. "They said I wasn't to let you open so much as one tiny corner, without them being here."

Fiona claps her hands together and leaps out of bed, jumping down onto her father's air bed and nearly catapulting him across the other side of the room. He listens to her knocking on the next door and shouting, "It's Christmas," her voice filled with excitement. David smiles to himself as he hears Jo swear.

"Come on Stuart. Wake up," calls Fiona, as she clatters down the stairs. Stuart appears in a T-shirt and boxer shorts, rubbing his head. Minutes later they are assembled in Stuart's bedroom. Lily climbs into the double bed next to Fiona, and pulls the duvet over her legs. Jo clambers onto the foot of the bed.

"Chuck us a pillow. Come on Stuart, there's room for another here." Jo indicates the portion of the bed next to her.

"And you Daddy." Fiona squashes up next to Lily.

"I'm perfectly alright down here."

"No, you're not, you can't see properly. Come on." Fiona pats the mattress next to her. "Has no one else got a stocking?"

The others all shake their heads. "Obviously you're the only one who's been good enough this year," Jo says. "I don't know what I could have done wrong, unless it was the whole kidnapping thing."

"Oh, I feel terrible being the only one with presents," Fiona says, as she rips the paper off the first present out of the stocking. It's a soft brown teddy bear with the words 'I can't bear to be without you' embroidered on its belly. "Who are all these from?"

"Father Christmas," comes the chorus.

Each item in the stocking is wrapped and decorated with curling ribbons. Fiona unwraps lipsticks, chocolates, mousse for her hair, scented candles and a silver charm of two children, holding a bucket between them, a spade in each of their other hands. "That's beautiful; I've got a charm bracelet."

"Go on," Lily urges, "there's still more."

Fiona unwraps the 12" version of Eurythmics' 'Sisters Are Doing it for Themselves', a small book of William Blake's poetry and the photograph of Lily and Fiona on the log flume ride, in a silver plated frame. Finally, at the bottom of her stocking, she finds a bag of gold chocolate coins, a tangerine and a packet of hazelnuts.

"Wow," says Fiona as she lies back against the headboard, the bed almost completely covered in wrapping paper.

The phone rings. Stuart goes to answer it and comes back a moment later. He looks at David. "It's for you."

David pulls back the bed sheets and climbs out of bed, his pyjamas still bearing the creases from their packaging.

Lily picks up the book of Blake's poetry. "I've never heard of him." She flicks open the pages and reads out loud.

220

He who bends to himself a joy
Doth the winged life destroy
but he who kisses a joy as it flies,
lives in eternity's sunrise

David re-enters the room. "Your mother wants to come and see you."

"Crikey, she's coming here?" Fiona looks at the four of them, squashed into bed, with its wrapping paper eiderdown.

Her father ties his dressing gown around his waist. "Yes, I'm under strict instructions to vacate the premises, and take my issue with me. By that she means you," he says to Lily. "She'll be here between two and three thirty, when she has to leave because she has to get back to Skipton by six to meet a client."

"A client? On Christmas Day?"

"So, Lily and I will get an hour and a half in the pub, while you lot get the dinner ready together." David stretches. "It's not such a bad life."

"But I thought she wasn't going to speak to me until I promised not to see Lily again," says Fiona. No one speaks. "I mean, obviously, it'll be... nice to see her."

"Ok, ok. Time for a cup of tea," says Stuart. He smiles at Fiona. "And time for someone else to open a present."

In the front room, a haphazard pile of presents teeters under the potted Christmas tree. "Oh it looks lovely." Fiona claps her hands again. "I feel terrible, I haven't bought any presents. Who's that big one for?"

"That's for Lily, from me," says Jo. "Open it."

Lily drags the box into the centre of the room and pulls off the paper, as Stuart lights the fire. "A Nintendo Game Boy?"

"My brother's mate got it from America. They're not even out here yet."

"That's a very generous present, Jo," says David, "You students, always moaning you haven't got enough money."

Jo's cheeks redden. "I just thought it would be good when we're back in Leeds."

"It's great, thank you." Lily gives Jo a hug and then crawls under the Christmas tree and pulls out a small suitcase, with a silver gift bow stuck to the side. She hands it to David. "Ok, more presents, this one's for you."

"If that's what I think it is, I don't want it."

221

"You've got to take it. I can't live with it. I'm too young to handle the responsibility. Please. I can't live with money I blackmailed off my own father, by kidnapping my little sister, scalping her and threatening to kill her. Have some respect for my karma."

David smiles. "You deserve it to make up for all the things you didn't have."

"Please, you could keep it for holidays for us or something, but I really, really don't want it."

"Ok, thank you." He reaches out for the case. "Technically it's not actually mine, but it may be the closest I come to a divorce settlement."

"There's a slight problem," Lily says as her cheeks fill with colour. "It's not quite all there, we had some, er, expenses."

Jo is reading the instructions on the side of the Game Boy box intently.

David holds up his hand. "Don't worry. And thank you. It's certainly better than the customary tie I was expecting," he jokes, and then his face falls as he sees the crestfallen look on Lily's face as she hands him another, smaller, tie sized package.

"Oh, gosh. I'm sorry…"

Lily throws her head back and laughs. "Joke. This one's yours." She replaces the small package under the tree, and picks up a thin, square parcel.

He opens his gift to find a 1979 limited edition picture disc of 'Sgt. Pepper's Lonely Hearts Club Band. "Oh wow, this is great. I used to really love this album. How did you know?"

"I just thought you'd like it."

"I have something for you too." He reaches under the Christmas tree and hands her a small package. "I bought it for you a long time ago. My mother has been keeping it safe. I never got the chance to give it to you."

Inside is small blue box containing a tiny silver bracelet, meant for a child, but with a silver clasps that allows it to expand as the child grows older. Lily's hands start to shake as she pulls it out of the box. She sees the engraving 'Lily Ann 3/8/70 I think of you always.'

Lily leans over Fiona on the settee and kisses her father on the cheek. "I love it."

"I can't breathe," squeaks Fiona.

"Will someone go and put the kettle on?" asks David.

"I guess that's me and you. Come on." Stuart says as he pulls Jo to her feet. They leave David with his daughters.

"I just want to say, girls, this is the best Christmas I could have wished for."

"Enough with the touchy feely stuff already," laughs Fiona, as she crouches down to the Christmas tree again. "There's loads more here."

When Jo and Stuart return with the tea tray, they eat Danish pastries and chocolate croissants, while opening the rest of their presents. Jo gives Fiona tickets to see Jasper Carrott in concert, and David has bought Jo a copy of Allen Carr's, *The Easy Way to Stop Smoking*. It's gone eleven o'clock by the time everything has been opened. While Lily and Fiona take turns playing Tetris on the Game Boy, Jo nips upstairs and gets dressed. When she returns to the living room, she is wearing her coat.

"Where are you going?" asks Lily.

"I said I'd nip down to the Shelter, help them serve the tea and mince pies."

Lily gawps at her, waiting for a punch line.

"Just for an hour or two." Lily's mouth is still open as the front door slams.

At quarter past one, David gets his coat on and he and Lily depart for the pub. David turns to Stuart. "You're welcome to join us."

Stuart turns to Fiona. "I'll stay with you, if you want me to."

"Yes, please," says Fiona.

"If you're sure you wouldn't like some time on your own with your mum? You haven't seen her for ages."

"No. Thank you," says Fiona, politely.

Chapter 40

Stuart opens the door to Fiona's mother. She glances up and down at him. "So, you're the boyfriend are you?"

"Well, er, I'm-"

"It's a simple enough question."

"I-"

"Your father is one of the few journalists in this country who can string an intelligent sentence together."

"Ah, yes, thank you. I mean-"

"A shame he hasn't passed his talents on to you. I've come to see my daughter."

"Yes, er, would you like to come in, Mrs Winterbottom?"

"It's Ms Hurst, and yes, thank you, I would."

Fiona is waiting in the front room. She can hear Stuart trying to make conversation, and her mother's curt responses as they climb the stairs. Fiona pours herself a quick sherry in the glass her dad left earlier on the coffee table. She is draining the glass when her mum enters the room.

"What are you drinking?"

"Sherry. Would you like one?"

"Your father said you'd almost overdosed on the stuff. Haven't you learnt anything?" Ruth takes off her gloves and scarf and hands them to Stuart. "When are you coming home?"

"I don't know where my home is anymore."

"Don't be so dramatic. You sound like a teenager." She hands Stuart her coat. "It's where it's always been."

Stuart leaves the room as Fiona asks, "What about Dad?"

"Your father and I have a lot to sort out."

"I want to live with him."

"Well you can't. You must come home. What about school? You've already missed a week, which will be difficult to catch up so close to your GCSEs."

"I haven't got you a Christmas present. I'm sorry."

"You can't live with your father. He hasn't got a house. And your grandmother hasn't got enough room."

"Dad will get a house."

"On his wages he'll be lucky to buy a garden shed."

"I don't care about the house, so long as there will be someone in it. You're never there. Who would look after me?"

"Fiona, when I was your age, I was working full-time to put myself through college."

"Well then, if I don't need looking after, I don't have to come home."

"Fiona, you're being silly. You have to live somewhere."

"I'll live with Dad then."

Her mother opens her mouth to argue further, but Stuart stands in the doorway. "Perhaps this is a conversation for another day. Would you like a cup of tea Mrs, Ms Hurst? Or a glass of sherry and a mince pie perhaps?"

"Tea will be fine." Ruth inspects the settee, and swipes at it a few times before sitting down. As Stuart leaves the room, Ruth turns to Fiona. "He's lied to me all these years, Fiona; he's lied to you too. Doesn't that make you really angry? How can you trust him again?"

"I think he's sorry and he's willing to make it up to Lily. You should meet her, Mum, she's great."

"Over my dead body."

"She wants to get to know Dad. Her mum's just died. She hasn't got anybody else."

"Oh, Fiona. She's probably witnessed our standard of living and decided she'd like a slice of the pie. How do you know she is his daughter? She could be making the whole thing up."

"I've seen her birth certificate. And the wedding album."

"The wedding album." Ruth stands up again. She walks over to the window and looks down on the street. "What was she like? His ex-wife, I mean."

Fiona shrugs her shoulders. "You need to talk to Dad about that."

"I will never, ever, forgive him for what he's done. He's made a complete fool of me."

"He must have been suffering all these years too you know, having to live a lie."

225

Ruth turns to face her daughter, her fists clenched at her side. "You sound like the stupid client I had in my office two days ago. Standing in front of me with a black eye and half her front teeth missing, making excuses for her big bully of a husband; I've heard it a thousand times. I will not be one of those women."

"Dad would never hit you," says Fiona.

"It's not about violence. It's about trust; breach of trust. It doesn't matter whether it's through lies or fists. The result is the same."

"But it's happened; we can't just pretend it hasn't."

"Fiona, I spent most of my childhood watching my father beat the living daylights out of my mother," says Ruth, turning to face her daughter. "So don't talk to me about forgiveness."

"I didn't-"

"I lived in fear of him killing her. Not because I'd miss her; that thought didn't even cross my mind. I lived in fear of him killing her because I was terrified that if she wasn't there to soak up his fists, he might start on me. And she always, always, forgave him. Stayed with him right until he died; pathetic."

Fiona sees the tears glisten in her mother's eyes and it hits her like a slap across the face. Her cheeks burn. "I didn't know…"

"Yes, well, you don't know everything. Which brings me back to my original point." Ruth collects herself with lawyerly efficiency. "You have to come home. Please, Fiona. Try and see this from my point of view. I'm not certain he was even divorced at the time of our marriage. Can you imagine how embarrassing this is for me, professionally? I will have to instruct solicitors in my own marriage."

They hear Stuart whistling 'Jingle Bells' loudly to warn of his arrival. The door opens and Stuart steps inside with a cup of tea and a hunk of chocolate log on a plate. "Do you take sugar, Ms Hurst?"

"No."

Stuart places the cup of tea in front of Ruth and then sits down on the settee next to Fiona. "Was it a difficult journey?" he asks Ruth. "To get here I mean."

Ruth doesn't answer. Fiona stares at the carpet.

Stuart stands back up again. "Do you two want to be alone?"

"Yes," says Ruth. "Please."

"Did you want a cup of tea, Fi?"

Fiona looks up at Stuart as if she's only just noticed him. "No, I'm fine."

"Stuart, please leave us alone for five minutes," says Ruth.

"Fi?"

Fiona looks up at him again. "Fine," she says, unsure as to what his question is. Stuart almost runs from the room.

Lily's face is flushed red from the cold as she and David make their way back to Stuart's flat. "Stuart said she only stayed an hour," says Lily.

"You mean we needn't have had those last three pints? Shame," says David, as they let themselves into the flat with the spare key. Stuart and Fiona are in the front room, lying together on the settee. Fiona is in her pyjamas, her hair damp. They're watching a 'Miss Marple'. "Your mother didn't stay long," says David. "Was everything ok?"

"Yeah," says Fiona, without removing her eyes from the screen.

Lily hovers by the door. "I'll just go and switch the oven on."

"Would you put the kettle on while you're there?" asks David, taking off his coat and settling into the armchair. "What's happening? Aw, we've seen this one before, haven't we?"

Lily slips out of the room and shuts herself in the kitchen. She switches on the oven and takes off her coat. "I'm really lucky," she says out loud, to the foil wrapped turkey, "I've got a whole new sister and a whole new dad. I don't need anyone else."

Lily glances at the instructions Stuart wrote out last night, so that they could all assume equal responsibility for the preparation of Christmas dinner. Lily's remit is the turkey and Brussels sprouts. "I can't covet every bit of her life. She's been generous to share her dad, I don't know if I would have been the same. And she's forgiven me for snogging her boyfriend."

"He's yours."

Lily starts and turns around to see Fiona is standing behind her. "I didn't hear you come in."

"Consider him my Christmas present to you," says Fiona.

"Shut up."

"I mean it. He loves you and he deserves a beautiful girlfriend."

"Ok, too weird," says Lily, stuffing the bird into the oven. She wipes her hands on a tea towel. "You're freaking me out."

"It makes it fairer. I don't have to feel guilty for being the one that had a dad. I took one man away from you and now you've taken one from me. We're even."

"I said, you're freaking me out," Lily shouts, pushing the oven door shut with her foot.

227

"But that's it. Do it again and I'll kill you."

"Shut up."

"It's up to you. But I think you should give it a chance."

Lily puts her hands over her ears and starts singing, "La la la la la," at the top of her voice. Fiona shakes her head and goes back into the front room. Five minutes later, Jo appears in the kitchen, her cheeks flushed with the cold, her hat pulled down over her ears.

"You've been gone hours. Where have you been?" asks Lily. "You were supposed to be in charge of stuffing. Have you read the schedule?"

"Alright. What's up with you?"

"Nothing."

Stuart is carving the turkey three hours later, when the doorbell rings. Lily goes down to answer it.

"Jo?" Lily shouts up the stairs. "There's someone here for you."

Jo appears at the top of the stairs, wearing a red V-necked T-shirt that Lily hasn't seen before, and a beaming smile. The blonde policeman from the night Fiona disappeared is standing at the bottom of the steps, clutching a bottle of wine and a box the size of a brick, wrapped in gold paper.

"Hi. Come on up. Everyone, this is Andy. Andy, this is everyone."

Stuart comes out of the kitchen and joins Fiona and her father at the top of the stairwell. Lily looks up at Jo, with her mouth open. Jo giggles. "I said he could come for dinner. Is that alright with everyone?"

Chapter 41

Alice stands in the bay window of her front room, watching the robin take the crumbs she put out onto the bird table this morning. A Jack Russell sits at her feet, its hopeful gaze shifting every few seconds, between a ragged tennis ball and Alice's face. Alice absent-mindedly kicks at the ball again, and the dog scoots off after it, bringing it back less than five seconds later. "Go away, Tess. Can't you see I'm busy?"

When she sees David's car pull round the corner into the cul-de-sac, she takes one quick glance around the front room, and plumps up the cushions on the settee.

"You're late," she says as she opens the front door. David is leading the way down the short garden path. She shoos him out of the way, so that she can watch her two granddaughters, arm in arm, as they make their way from the car to the front gate. Tess bounds out, racing up to Fiona and jumping up at her, getting its little body almost up to Fiona's chest height.

"Where have you been?" says Alice to David, as she watches Fiona fuss over Tess.

"Sorry," says David, lifting the bags across the threshold. "We had a very late night." He winces as his mother cuffs him round the back of the head, despite the fact she's more than a foot shorter than him. "Don't, I've got a bit of a headache."

Alice opens her arms to Lily; her hands shaking so much the silver bangles on her arm jangle a tune. Lily allows herself to be embraced, breathing in the scent of lavender. "Let me look at you," says Alice, stepping backwards. "My goodness."

"This is all I could have wanted for Christmas," Alice says, as she directs the girls into the kitchen. Tess keeps jumping up at everyone, desperate for attention. Alice turns to David, "Put the dog in the garden, will you? And take those bags upstairs. Did you remember the air bed? Why don't you blow it up now so it's done with?"

"I thought I might have a cup of tea-"

"Oh go on, then I get some time with my granddaughters before your dad gets back from the shop." David sighs and climbs the stairs.

Alice joins the girls in the kitchen. "I sent your granddad to the shop. I wanted a little bit of time with you on my own first. Would you like a mince pie?" She pulls the oven door down and pulls out a tray of freshly baked mince pies. "Isn't this wonderful, Fiona? You will never be lonely again, ever. You will always have someone to talk to."

"Well if you'd have been more honest with me, Granny," says Fiona, "I'd have had someone to talk to a long time ago."

Her grandmother's cheeks flush red. "I know, I know. But what could I do? It was your foolish father. I could have killed him for what he did." She brandishes the fish slice she was using to lift the mince pies. "I would have done, if he hadn't have been so heart-broken. I was very sorry, Lily, to hear about your mum."

"Thanks," Lily says, shaking her head as her grandmother offers her a mince pie.

"Are they here?" calls a voice from the hall.

"That'll be your granddad," says Alice. She raises her voice, "In the kitchen."

A tall, handsome man with white hair and eyes that are bright blue enters the room, carrying two large bags of shopping. He puts the shopping on the counter and places a hand on Lily's shoulder. The heat sinks into Lily's body. "It's been a long time," he says. "You probably don't remember."

Lily wrinkles her nose. He tightens his grip on her shoulder and pulls her into his chest, patting her back so hard she fears it may break.

"Did you remember the cream?" asks Alice, spreading the contents of the shopping bags over the worktops.

Arthur breaks his hold on Lily, stepping back to smile at her. "They'd sold out. Can't think why so many people are buying cream, what with it being Christmas and all."

"Oh, that's just typical. Right, everybody out of the kitchen," says Alice, just as David joins them, "too many people. Front room

230

everybody. There's a fire lit. David, will you bring another basket of logs?"

David mutters something under his breath and leads the exodus from the kitchen. He heads for the back door as the others wander through to the front room.

"And how are you feeling, little one?" Arthur asks Fiona, as he unbuttons his coat.

"Well, I'm still a bit upset no one told me…"

"Aye, well if there's one thing I've learnt in this life, it's not to get involved when there's women on the warpath. What's that saying? Hell hath no fury? Hell, they got that right."

The light from the fire is reflected in the glass baubles on the Christmas tree, like fairy lights. Fiona picks up a photograph from the mantelpiece; it's of her grandmother, twenty years younger, holding a bundle of blanket. A scrap of red face can just be seen emerging from its swaddling, jaws wide. "I've not seen this before."

Alice wipes her hands on her apron. "That was the only time I ever saw Lily."

"So why didn't anyone keep in touch with her?" asks Fiona, putting into words the question that's plagued Lily all her life.

"It was difficult. Pam moved without telling anyone. We weren't close."

"One way of putting it," says Arthur from his armchair by the fire.

"They were a different class to us, that's all," says Alice. "I think it's fair to say, Lily, that when your mum and David married, most folks weren't particularly pleased with the match. I think your grandfather, your mum's dad, wanted more for her."

"More money you mean," Arthur grumbles.

"Your gran had a bit of a soft spot for David. But then he packed in a perfectly good apprenticeship and started up with his music business," Alice raises her eyebrows.

"No one understood what he was playing at, still don't," says Arthur. "He was making a good wage."

"And then David, well, then it happened." Alice stresses the word 'it', "That was the end of it. All bloody hell broke loose. I think they thought we were all as bad as each other…"

At that moment, David comes into the room, carrying a basket of logs. "What?"

"Nothing," says Lily.

David kneels at the fire, adding half a dozen logs to it, stoking the wood until big orange flames start to lick up the side.

"I've got you a present," says Alice, walking over to the sideboard. She hands Lily a long slender package.

Lily opens it to reveal a brass coloured toasting fork. Her eyebrows knot as she looks across to her grandmother. "Thank you."

"It's tradition," says Fiona, as she takes another toasting fork from the side of the fireplace, its prongs blackened from years of use. She pulls a small footstool in front of the hearth, and then another one for Lily. Her grandmother hands her a packet of marshmallows and the two girls sit in front of the fire, watching their marshmallows turn to blobs before adding them to their hot chocolate.

"So what's the plan for you all?" asks Alice. "Will you be going back to Leeds, Lily?"

"I don't know." Lily stares into the flames, mesmerised. It takes a moment for her to realise people are waiting for her to expand. "The only reason I went to poly was because I was desperate to leave home. I don't know what made me pick politics. It's not like I want to be a politician or anything."

"Thank goodness for that," says Arthur. "Bunch of self-serving, power mad hypocrites, every last one of them. Not interested in the working man."

"Everything's changed," says Lily, as she tears her gaze from the fireplace and looks up at her grandparents. "Don't think I'm relying on you or anything. It's been great to meet you all, but even if I never saw any of you again, I'm different now. And I want to do something different."

Her grandmother strokes Lily's cheek. "Well, don't think you're going to get rid of any of us in a hurry," she says. "What about you, Fiona?"

"I can't live with Mum on my own," says Fiona quickly. David opens his mouth to argue but Fiona raises her voice and continues. "Come on, Daddy. You know I might as well be living on my own. She's never there. I'd have to do all my own cooking."

"You will have to come to some arrangement with her, Fiona," says David. "She is your mother."

"I know. I'm just not going to live with her that's all. I want to live with Dad and Lily," she says as the turns to her grandmother.

Her father snorts.

232

"Why not? It could work."

Everyone in the room looks at David. He takes his handkerchief from his pocket and cleans his glasses. "There's nothing I would like more," he begins. Fiona shrieks with excitement but he holds up his hand. "But, let's not get carried away. We haven't got anywhere to live and it could take a long time to arrange somewhere. I'll have to look into it. And in the meantime, Fiona, you have exams to think about. This is a very important year."

Fiona shakes her head and stands up, toasting fork clenched by her side. "I'm not going back home. No way."

David looks exasperated, "Fiona…"

"I don't even want to do my exams. I hate school."

"What if Ruth calms down and decides she can make room for Lily?" says Alice, standing up to place herself between her youngest granddaughter and her son.

David shakes his head quickly, indicating the subject is closed.

"Well if you're not going back, you can't expect me to either." Fiona shakes off his arm and puts her hand on her hips.

"It seems simple to me," says Alice. "You must all stay here until you get something set up."

"Thanks Mum. That's a very kind offer, but it might take months for me to organise…"

"That doesn't matter."

"You don't have the room."

"Oh silly me," says Alice, lifting her hands off her lap. "How we managed to raise three children here, I simply can't imagine."

"I may not even be able to get a big enough mortgage."

"We'll manage," says Alice. "Please. It would make me, it would make us both so happy, wouldn't it Arthur?"

Arthur lowers his newspaper and nods his head. "You'd be like a breath of fresh air."

"We could get twin beds in the spare room. I'll clear out the study. No one ever uses it."

David shakes his head. "It's too much to ask."

"Can't you see what it would mean to us? We've never had the chance to know Lily. Stop being so bloody selfish."

David looks over to Lily. "What do you think about all this?"

Lily can't stop a grin from stretching itself across her face. "I think it would be great."

233

David holds up his arms in defeat. "Well, if you two can put up with sharing a room and not tearing each other's hair out, then why not? Obviously, we'll have to clear it with your mother."

Fiona runs across to him and throws herself at him, knocking him back into the settee.

Chapter 42

The 11th of January falls on a Friday. Lily tiptoes across the bedroom. It's so dark that even though the distance between the two single beds is less than six feet, negotiating the obstacle course of discarded clothes, shoes, the flex of the hair dryer, bottles of nail varnish and other debris is almost impossible. She stands on a plastic hair slide and shouts out in pain. Fiona wakes up.

"What are you doing?" she mumbles sleepily.

"Happy Birthday, sweet sixteen!" says Lily, rubbing her foot. "I was trying to surprise you." She puts the present she was carrying onto Fiona's single bed and pulls back the curtains. Daylight shows what she was up against. "Maybe we should tidy up a bit."

Fiona lifts her head up off the pillow to look at her present. "I'm not tidying up on my birthday. It's a special occasion. Means no chores."

"I thought you doing chores would make it a special occasion," says Lily, only half joking. She hasn't seen the floor of their room since David built the flat pack single beds two weeks ago. Lily's used to mess, but only her own mess. She's never shared a room before. In fact when she was a child she had the whole top floor of the house to herself, as her mother got too fat to climb the stairs. The cramped quarters of her grandparents' house are taking some getting used to. "What time's Stuart coming?"

"He said he'd meet me after school. Do you want to come?"

Lily shakes her head. "No, I promised Gran I'd take Tess for a walk. What time do you think he'll go?"

"You can't just avoid him."

"I don't want to see him today, that's all. Open your present."

"I told Mum we'd go there for tea," says Fiona. "She's actually finishing work early. So you're safe, he won't be coming here."

235

Fiona sits up and pulls the present onto her knee. "Mmm, heavy," she says, nodding appreciatively.

Tess scrabbles down the side of the hill, chasing after the scent of rabbit. Lily follows a few hundred yards behind, turning away from the lake and into a section of the park she hasn't been to before. By the time she catches up with Tess, they've left the park, over a small bridge over the river and onto a cobbled road Lily hasn't seen before. She's just about to turn round and go back, when she notices one of the houses has a 'To Let' sign in the garden. It's a small, stone built cottage, with a small dormer window in the roof. All the curtains are drawn and there's no car outside, so Lily walks down the drive and round the side of the house. A long, narrow garden backs down onto the woods. At the end closest to the house is a tumbling down garage, and what may have been an outside toilet. Lily turns to face the back of the house and sees old wooden French doors, in need of a coat of paint, which lead onto a small stone patio. She walks back to the front of the house and commits the name of the letting agent to memory. "Jarvis and Jones," she recites to herself all the way home.

When the details for Fern Cottage arrive in the post the next day, Lily is on her own in the house. Fiona had rung last night to say she and Stuart were staying over at Ruth's house. She'd sounded quite touched at the lengths her mother had gone to to celebrate her birthday. Apparently, she'd taken them both out to the poshest restaurant in Skipton and told them they could order anything they liked, much to Fiona's delight. So Lily had had her first night sleeping alone since Boxing Day. Bizarrely, after feeling desperate for her own space, she'd hardly slept at all. Kept waking up drenched in cold sweat and not knowing where she was. Awful dreams where she was paralysed, or in a coffin being buried alive.

David had gone round to Newlands first thing in the morning, possibly sensing the thaw in relations, and hoping it might be a good time to sort out a few issues. Lily had overhead one telephone conversation a few days ago, where she'd gathered that if David didn't return the ransom money by the end of the day, Ruth would involve the police. He'd disappeared with the suitcase less than half an hour later.

Alice and Arthur had left after breakfast to visit friends over in Gargrave. Lily spends most of the day smoking cigarettes in the tiny back garden and burying the stubs in the rosebeds. When David turns up, in the late afternoon, Lily waves the prospectus at him almost as soon as he steps through the door. "Look at this."

David takes it out of her hands and opens the page.

"What do you think?" asks Lily.

David nods his head as he reads the particulars. Since Ruth demanded the return of the ransom money, it makes sense to rent somewhere. A teacher's salary doesn't go far, particularly when you have a daughter used to the finer things in life, like tennis lessons and skiing holidays. Ruth made it quite clear that she wasn't going to be funding their new abode. At least Lily doesn't expect much. "It looks good. Give them a ring, let's go and see it."

Lily's heart is beating too fast as she rings the agents. "It's still available," she shouts from the hall as she puts the phone down. She comes back into the kitchen. "I said we'd meet them there Monday, after school. Where's Fiona?"

"She's spending the day with Stuart and her mother. Apparently Ruth is taking them to London to see Starlight Express, as a birthday treat." His tone is peevish.

"We could get a video," suggests Lily, anxious to offset his loss. "Gran and Granddad won't be back til late. Or we could go to a show. I'll pay." Her overdraft might just stretch to it.

David smiles and puts his arm loosely round her shoulders. "A video tape will be just fine. So long as you promise not to get *Dirty Dancing*."

They meet outside Fern Cottage at 4 o'clock on Monday. Lily walks round with Alice and Arthur and Tess. David had offered to pick Fiona up from her school on his way from his, but Fiona insisted on getting a taxi so she wouldn't be late. The cottage is unfurnished and could kindly be described as 'old-fashioned'. With the five of them, the estate agent and the dog, it feels like it's bursting at the seams, but it has three bedrooms on the first floor and a room in the attic, which Lily falls in love with. They sign the lease on the spot. David pays the deposit. "I'll get a job," offers Lily, in a moment of rashness. "I'll pay my share of the rent."

"Well, we're alright for the moment," says David. "You need to take some time to figure out what you want to do."

"The first thing I need to do is go back to Accrington," says Lily. "I have to hand the keys back, sort out a few things."

"I'll come with you," says Fiona.

"You can't, Fi. You've got school," says David, as he walks round the front room checking for electric sockets.

"School's boring."

"Thanks, but it's something I need to do it on my own," says Lily.

"How long will you stay?" asks Fiona.

"Don't know. A few days; there's a lot to do. I might go to Leeds as well, clear up there."

"Well, if you need anything," says David, "just ring."

Two days later, Lily pushes open the front door of her mother's council house and steps over the stack of mail that's built up in the hallway. She closes the door and drops her bag on the floor. The house smells of stale fish and chips, joss sticks and that other lingering smell that Lily doesn't like to think about. It's so cold Lily can see her breath. She picks up the stack of mail and goes into the front room. Fiona's school blazer is still on the bed and the newspaper fish and chip wrappings from that first night are screwed up on the floor. The room looks like someone just ran out of the back door, which of course they did, a month ago. She's travelled so far in a month, Lily doesn't recognise these reminders of her past life. Strands of Fiona's hair still lie on the floor. Lily can't remember what she looked like before they cut her hair off. That gawky schoolgirl they spent so much time stalking never seemed to materialise. It's impossible to equate her with the Fiona she knows now.

Lily puts the tokens she stopped off at the SPAR to buy, into the electric meter. The bulb in the ceiling lights up and the fridge starts to hum. There's no point getting the gas reconnected but she's going to freeze her ass off while she's here.

She takes the stack of letters into the kitchen, opens all the ones addressed to her mother or 'the occupier', and sorts them into two piles on the worktop. There are three letters addressed to her, which she puts to one side, unopened. One of the two piles she picks up and drops into the half full bin liner, that's lying against the back door. The smell makes her recoil. She ties the bag and puts it outside the back door.

Once she's made herself a cup of tea, she writes to all her mother's creditors, her fingers blue gripped around the pen, before turning her attention to her own post. A card from Aunt Edie, a letter from Leeds Polytechnic, asking whether she intends to return

238

to her course, and a letter from a firm of solicitors asking her to contact them, 'with regards to her mother's estate'.

Lily lifts the receiver but there's no dial tone. She puts her coat on and walks to the phone box at the edge of the estate. She rings Aunt Edie first, and after apologising for disappearing, arranges to go round for tea. Next she rings the solicitors and speaks to an elderly-sounding receptionist, and makes an appointment for Monday morning. Then she walks back to the house, grabs the roll of bin liners she bought from the SPAR and heads for the loft. She's guessing David has no use for a pair of beige chinos with the crotch missing.

As she picks up a copy of *Brave New World* a photograph slips from its pages and flutters to the floor. Lily picks it up and sees her parents sitting on a scooter, David at the front, wearing a thin black tie and a shiny grey suit, his hair spiked, while Lily's mum peers out behind him, her arms wrapped tightly around his waist, wearing a helmet and a broad grin. Lily puts the photograph in her pocket and scoops everything else into the bin liners.

When Lily has moved all the contents of the loft down to the front room she lugs the Hoover she's borrowed from Mrs Delaney at number 34 up the ladders and sucks up all the cobwebs.

The next day, she sugar soaps walls, trying to scrub off the nicotine stains, scrubs the bathroom, crow bars the planks of wood they had nailed across the window of her old bedroom, and boils hundreds of bucketfuls of hot water. All her mothers' tent-like clothing she bags up, and drags to the recycle bins at the local supermarket, and grins when she sees she's donating it to the Salvation Army.

On Friday Lily is invited to Aunt Edie's for tea. She puts her mother's small wooden jewellery box into her backpack, and catches the bus across town, her arms aching from a day of scrubbing the greases stains from the kitchen.

"Aw, thank you, pet," says Aunt Edie, opening the empty wooden box.

"Sorry there wasn't any jewellery."

"But it's nice to have a keepsake. You're looking well, child; you've finally got a bit of meat on your bones."

"That's thanks to Alice, my grandma." Lily experiments with the words. "I have a dad, a sister, a gran and a grandpa. I've got aunts and uncles and five cousins too, but I haven't met them yet."

239

"Yes, well, you want to watch that one, Alice. Marjorie never took to her."

"I know, Alice said they were disappointed Mum married David. Apparently they thought she married beneath her."

"Poppycock. Your granddad might have thought that, I don't know, but I can tell you Marge wasn't the sort to look down on other people. We weren't exactly the Rockefellers when we grew up."

"Well, whatever, it's all in the past."

"Your mother never liked her either."

"My mum didn't like anyone unless they were carrying pizza."

"Don't be too hard on her, Lil. She did her best."

"You weren't saying that when she was alive."

"Aye, well," Aunt Edie bristles. "If there's one thing I've learnt it's judge not, unless thee thyself want judging."

Chapter 43

Lily stands in the doorway between the kitchen and the front room, the smell of bleach in her nostrils, and she slowly nods to herself. It's taken her five days of working like a dog, and the muscles in her arms feel warm and tight, but it's done. She moves across to the kitchen window and pulls the clasp to close it. It took nearly a full day to scrape the fat splashes from the wall next to the cooker, but now the tiles, which she'd always thought were beige, gleam creamy white in the morning sunshine. Walking through to the front room, she bends to pick up her rucksack which contains some clothes, including Fiona's school blazer, a couple of photographs and a hand mirror from her mother's bedroom, which used to belong to her granny. Everything else has been burnt, tipped or donated. Lily takes one last look around the front room, before stepping out into the crisp January air, pulling the front door firmly to behind her.

It's only when she's handed in the keys at the housing office on the edge of the estate, that the relief she feels in her head translates to a light feeling in her chest. She adjusts the weight of her rucksack and sets off into town. As she rounds the corner at the bottom of the street, she almost trips over a manky black cat, its right ear missing.

The red paint is faded and peeling off the front door of the solicitor's office. Lily checks the piece of paper in her hands, and steps inside. Her appointment is for 9.30am. It's not quite twenty past. An elderly receptionist in a floral cardigan stands to greet her, pink lipstick not quite running to the edges of her thin lips. "Lily Appleyard, we've been expecting you," she says.

Lily looks around the small waiting area, with its tattered magazines piled neatly on a small coffee table, and suspects she's the first client they've had in this week, possibly this year, although it is only January. She follows the receptionist through a narrow corridor to the back room, where an old man is bent over his desk.

"Miss Appleyard," he says, standing up. His shoulders are so hunched that his head faces downwards, so that Lily feels his eye level is somewhere around her knees. He holds out a gnarled hand. "Thank you for coming. Please accept my condolences."

"Thank you," says Lily softly.

"Please." He gestures towards the only other chair in the room. Lily shrugs the rucksack from her shoulders and sits down, folding her hands on her lap. Once seated, she makes eye contact with the old man. He stares at her for a few moments, before speaking. "Would you like tea or coffee?"

"I'm ok, thanks."

"Just a tea for me then please, Miss Farnley," he says to the old lady as she shuffles from the room, closing the door behind her. The solicitor lowers himself down into the well worn leather chair opposite Lily's. "It's a pleasure to meet you, young lady. Thank you for coming. Now, about your mother's estate."

"I wanted to ask," Lily inches forward in her seat. "Can they make me responsible for her debts?"

"They may be able to claim against your mother's estate, but there would be little value in doing so, as your mother, I would imagine, had very little in the way of assets. Did she leave a will?"

"Not that anyone's said."

"I heard a little about her over the years. The world is a small place and Accrington smaller still. I promised your grandfather I'd keep an eye on her. I would assume she has no estate to claim against."

"I got a letter from the council saying I could inherit the tenancy, but I, well I said I didn't want it." Lily's voice falters. "I hope that was ok?"

"Sometimes a clean break is for the best," says the old man, as Lily fights the tears she feels threatening to spill into her eyes.

"So why do you want to see me?"

"Well, Miss Appleyard, may I call you Lily? You won't remember me, but we have met. You were about three years old. Lily, I was a friend of your grandfather's. He was a great man; I miss him to this day. I was executor of his will and, as you may or may not be aware, his estate was left in a complex trust." He pauses, his statement really a question. Lily shakes her head.

The old man continues. "His reasoning being that he didn't want to leave his estate to your mother, in light of her…" he spends several seconds searching for the right word, "difficulties. He stipulated that; in the event your mother failed to meet the criteria necessary for her to benefit from his last will and testament…"

Lily fidgets in her chair. She wishes she'd had a fag before she came into the office, as she has this feeling that she might be there a while, especially at the speed the old man speaks, each word carefully considered, chosen and expressed.

"On her death, it would pass to you."

He pauses, waiting for a reaction. Lily nods, her attention caught by the ticking of a large, old-fashioned wooden carriage clock on the mantelpiece.

"So, you are now set to inherit your grandparents' estate."

"Ok," says Lily.

"Which amounts to, let me see," he pats at the pieces of paper in front of him, but Lily has the feeling that, despite his advanced years, he knows exactly how much, down to the nearest penny. "This may not be an exact figure. The money is currently held in trust and interest will need to be calculated, but somewhere in the region of one hundred and thirty-seven thousand."

"Pounds?" asks Lily, suddenly feeling too warm.

"Pounds Stirling," the solicitor says, as he sits back in his chair and smiles at her, a slender black fountain pen in his gnarled hand.

"But where did they get that much money from?"

"It's not a terrific sum."

Lily pulls a face.

"There was the sale of their house, some unit bonds, stocks and shares, that sort of thing. The money has been invested these last fifteen years, cautiously, yet yielding some return. You may have to pay tax on the sum, but I can put you in touch with an advisor who will be able to guide you through that process."

"Wow." Lily sinks back in the chair and lets out a long low breath. "Did my mum know the money was there?"

The solicitor nods his head. "Your grandfather attached certain stringent conditions to his last testament; conditions that your mother would have to have met in order to benefit from his estate."

"What kind of conditions?"

"There were several, including but not limited to, being in full-time employment or registered on a full-time educational course."

"What did my mum think about that?"

The solicitor throws his head up, so that Lily catches a glimpse of his face. "Not a great deal. In fact I think Miss Farnley is still recovering, and she was in the outer office at the time."

"And did she ever…?"

The solicitor understands the question without Lily needing to finish the sentence. His voice is quite gentle as he speaks, "Once she had the facts spelt out to her, I never heard from again."

"How did you know she was dead?"

"I saw the notice, rather the article, in the newspaper."

Lily nods. 'Ten pallbearers needed to carry couch potato'. She had seen the headline too. She rubs her forehead, feels a trickle of sweat running down her shoulder blades. "So, I'm going to get one hundred and thirty-seven thousand pounds?"

"It will take some time to organise, but yes. It's a lot to take in but I'm sure your grandfather would be pleased to know it's with you now. I have an influence on how the money should be spent until you come of age."

"Come of age?"

"Turn twenty-one. After that you are on your own, but I can't think we will have any problems. I'm a reasonable man, providing you don't want to bet it on the horses." He starts to laugh at his own joke, but it turns into a wheeze. He takes a moment to recover his breath. "I think we'll be able to come to some arrangement."

Lily's head is in a daze as she follows him through to the front room. She carries her rucksack on one arm. "Right then," she says, not sure what she's going to say. Not sure how to act, what to do with her arms. She sees the open door and feels drawn towards it.

Miss Farnley looks up from her small desk. "Dear, we need to take some details. Your address…"

Lily turns in the doorway. "Oh yes, actually I'm staying with my grandparents at the moment, my father's parents."

The solicitor is standing behind his receptionist. "Your father?" His voice betrays little emotion, and when he's standing it's difficult to read his facial expression without crouching, and Lily feels that would be rude.

"Yes, it's a long story. We've only just met."

There's a long silence. The old man holds onto the back of Miss Fernley's chair. When he does speak, his words are measured, well chosen. "I would advise caution, Miss Appleyard… Lily. I don't wish to perpetuate ill feeling, but I feel I should inform you. Another of the conditions of your grandfather's will was that your

244

mother would vow never to have any contact with any of your father's side of the family ever again."

"Oh. Well, if he's up there listening, he might be pleased to know she kept to that one. Doesn't take my feelings into account much though, does it? What if I'd wanted to know who my family were?"

"Your grandfather would have spent a great deal of time considering the best course of action."

"Yes, but the best course of action for who? Anyway, there's nothing to worry about. My dad's been great, so far. And I've got a sister."

"Lily, I urge you to be careful."

"Right, well, thanks for everything. I guess we'll be in touch."

"It's been a pleasure to meet you my dear. May God bless you."

It's not until Lily reaches the bus station that she remembers where she last heard that phrase. It had been on the bottom of the letter from the Salvation Army.

Chapter 44

Lily shivers and pulls her jacket tighter round her. The lukewarm sun makes the frost on the gravestones glisten. She makes her way up the hill to the north of the graveyard, past the mounds of disturbed earth, to her mother's final resting place. On the ground lies a headstone waiting to be erected. Lily reads the script, 'Pamela Appleyard. 28.4.44 – 28.9.89'.

Lily pulls a SPAR carrier bag from her rucksack and takes the two bottles from it. Then she puts the bag on the floor and sits on it. She takes the top off the orange Fanta and pours a third of it out, then she pours the half bottle of vodka into it. It's her first drink in over a week, and her mouth salivates at the sight of it. She raises the bottle to the heap of earth. "Cheers."

She takes a swig, feels the heat slide down her throat, and stares at the mound of frozen earth. "Well," says Lily, "your dad doesn't sound like a bundle of laughs. 'Full-time employment or education', what's that about? Didn't he know you had a child to look after? Jo would've have put him straight, 'What is it with men? They think if you spend your day in an office, it means you've achieved something.'"

Lily watches a groundsman wheel his barrow between the gravestones. She hears the faint sounds of his whistled tune. "If only it were that fucking easy."

The warmth of the vodka spreads like a fire through her belly. She feels her shoulders relax half an inch. "So, I've met Dad," she says, feeling suddenly bold. She pauses, half expecting her mother's spirit to rise from the ground and start berating her. 'That bastard' she can almost hear her mother screaming. But after a moment or two she realises there is only silence.

"I can see what you saw in him, I think. I mean he's good looking and he's being really kind to me now. Jo's not so keen. But then she hates all men, so what can you do?" Lily rubs her nose and realises how cold it is. She takes another drink.

"And I've got a sister. She's cool, pretty, knows her own mind." The image of Fiona standing up to David in the kitchen, that first time he came round, pops into Lily's head. Fiona with her hands on her hips saying she wasn't coming home until Lily was accepted into the family. "So you don't have to worry about me, because I'm not on my own. Just in case you were. I'm really happy, so don't worry," she says again, as tears burn at her eyes and start the long slow journey down her face. "I just wish I had someone to talk to, that's all."

"It's like, all the time I was with you, I was dreaming of knowing the other side of the family. And now I'm with them, I'm wishing I'd got to know you. And I wonder if the problem's me. I can't ever be with the people I love because in my head I'm always somewhere else."

She sits and drinks silently, allowing the sadness to well up and flow out of her body. "I met this guy. He was really nice. And now I suppose, I understand what it's like to want to be with someone and then not be. And I only knew him a couple of weeks. I don't know him, not like you knew Dad. Aunt Edie told me you were only seventeen. Anyway, it's never going to happen, so there's no point going on about it."

Lily watches a robin hop along the ground, trying to peck something from the frozen earth. "Do you know what he said? He said we were both addicts; me and you. You chose food, I chose spliff and vodka." She takes another drink and wipes her nose on the back of her sleeve.

"All this time I've been so busy blaming you, I never really noticed that I'm just the same." The sobs rack her body and Lily covers her face with her hands. "I was a shit daughter. I spent most of my energy hating you."

She wipes at her running nose with the back of her sleeve and takes another mouthful of vodka. "Do you remember that school report, where it said I wouldn't ever achieve my potential because I never applied myself? That stupid cow, Mrs Hunt? In fact you called her a stupid cunt. I remember because I'd never heard you use that word before. You went mad, saying how could they write me off at thirteen, and maybe it was something to do with their

247

boring lessons; it was their fault if I wasn't engaged and you said you were going to tell them, and I knew you never would, but it didn't matter."

The cold has seeped into her bones. Her shoulders are rigid, like a brace around her neck, and she's lost the feeling in her bum and legs. The heat of her tears feels like steam under her eyes. "I miss you, Mum. I really, really miss you."

Lily feels a hand on her shoulder. She looks up to see Bert, standing there in his awful plastic coat and a bobble hat that looks like it's been knitted by the basket weavers, down at the day centre on the estate.

"Hey, Bert."

"Lil."

Lily puts her hand on the cold grey slab of the headstone. "I'm going to get her a new one. Beloved mum. Rest in Peace. Something like that." She looks up at him and nods at the brown paper bag he's holding. "What's in the bag?"

"I just thought she might like the smell. It's a Big Mac." He lays it down on the mound of earth, tenderly, like a lover would lay a single red rose. Lily closes her eyes and silently tells her mother she loves her. She can't see through the tears when Bert eventually pulls her up to standing, and leads her away from the graveyard.

Chapter 45

As the National Express Coach pulls into Leeds bus station on Tuesday, Lily catches sight of the new Playhouse, built on the site of the old Quarry Hill flats. The building seems to have sprung from nowhere, making her realise the city never stays the same. She's only been away for a few months, and yet already she doesn't recognise it. And she's not even off the coach yet.

Lily's skin feels dirty, probably from spending the night on Bert's sofa, and she thinks she's been bitten by fleas, as she walks past the market, into the city centre. She decides against taking the bus when she sees the queues at the bus stop for Headingley. Instead she continues up past the Odeon and the new Morrisons, which has scores of students lined up with their carrier bags waiting for taxis, and out north of the city to Leeds Polytechnic, which towers above the top end of town.

Mr Strange is kneeling on the floor in his office, his shirt sleeves rolled up, as he unpacks a stack of new textbooks from an oversized cardboard box. Lily fights the urge to offer to organise them on his shelves. Instead she holds her thumbs and tells him she wants to withdraw from the course. He offers little resistance, although he does offer to keep her place open for a year, in case she changes her mind. Lily thanks him, at the same time as knowing there's no question she'll come back to study politics there. She isn't the same woman anymore.

It's dusk as she strolls back through the park, her favourite time of day, as the colours bleed into a single lilac haze. Lily remembers the countless drunken stumbles through the dark on her way home; the time she laughed so much she was sick through her nostrils; an occasion when Jo had chased off an old guy who'd had the misfortune to choose her to flash to. They'd laughed so much Lily had ended up wetting herself right there in the middle of the park.

The house is empty and freezing cold. The front room curtains are still drawn and there's a collection of beer cans on the coffee table. She spends five minutes trying to get the ignition on the gas fire to light before it finally throws out a steady blue flame. Lily keeps her coat on while she waits for heat to take some of the bite out of the air. Her bedroom is next door to the living room, across the corridor from Jo's. As she opens her bedroom door she recoils from the smell. Empty bottles, cans, cigarette packets. There's a plate of something that may once have been mashed potato. Heaps of black clothes lie on the floor, so dirty and damp that when she picks up her favourite black shirt she notices mould all around the collar.

She switches on her electric bar fire, realising for the first time how dangerous the wires look, the flex badly frayed, and sits on the bed until the room starts to warm up. But as the warmth spread the smell seems to get worse, until at last she can stand it no longer. She finds a roll of black bin liners in the cupboard under the sink in the kitchen and sighs to herself as she begins scooping her possessions into them. She finds a handful of scrumpled lecture notes under her bed and stuffs them in there too.

The carpet is just about visible again, when she hears the front door open and close and footsteps on the stairs. A voice calls out. Lily freezes, recognising the voice as belonging to one of the two chemistry students that live on the second floor. Moments later, there's a knock on her bedroom door.

"Hi." The door opens and the one she thinks is called Joel appears in her doorway. "You're back," he says rather obviously.

"Yeah."

He stands with his foot against the door, his puffed up anorak making him seem three times the size she remembers him. "I'm sorry, you know, about what happened. Your mum."

"Yeah. Thanks." She waits for him to leave, but he doesn't. She tries to encourage him on his way. "So, I'm just trying to clear this mess up."

"Do you want a hand?"

"No, thanks." Still he doesn't leave. "So, I'd better get on."

"I didn't know whether to ring you, but I didn't have your number."

"Would have been difficult then," says Lily, her tone unkind. She remembers how much time Jo and her had spent slagging these two off now. Talk about nerds.

"It's just, I really enjoyed, you know."

Lily doesn't know but as he stares at her intently, a memory stirs and she feels the colour race to her cheeks. She squashes her memory back into its closed box. "Do you mind?" she almost spits at him. "I've said I'm really busy."

"Oh, right. I'm sorry. Maybe we could meet up later?"

Lily walks over to the door and pushes it closed. "Maybe," she says to his disappearing face. "Or maybe not," she adds as she leans against the closed door. She pulls the privacy bolt across and wonders whether she'll ever have the courage to leave the room again.

She's still sitting on the floor with her back against the door an hour later when there's another knock. Lily feels her body tense. "Lil? S'me, Jo. Let me in."

The tension rushes from her body and Lily stands up and pulls back the bolt. "Jo, thank fuck."

"Wow, I hardly recognise the place. It's looking great. Hurrah, you're back." Jo throws her arms around her friend's shoulders. "And you've put on some meat. Double hurrah."

"Did I have sex with that scrawny geek from upstairs?"

Jo giggles. "Don't blame me. I told you not to." She opens her canvas bag and pulls out her tobacco tin. "How was Christmas with 'the family?' I've missed you. Term started last Wednesday, but there was hardly anyone around. I've been covering for you."

"Jo, I've withdrawn from the course."

"Oh." Jo plumps herself down on the bed. "What the fuck will I do without you? Hey, I just saw a sign in The Fenton. They're looking for bar staff."

"I'm going to live with Fiona and my dad. We found a house."

"You're going to live with your dad?" Jo couldn't sound more horrified if Lily had said she was considering voting Tory. She doesn't look at Lily, but instead opens the lid from her tin and takes out a packet of rizlas. She glues three together and Lily notices her fingers are shaking.

"Soz." Lily sits on the edge of the bed next to her. "You're the one and only thing I'm gonna miss. But I feel like I've got this one chance; it's now or never. I've got to find out what it's like."

"What what's like?"

251

"You know," says Lily looking at her fingernails. "Normal. Family."

"Normal? You want to be normal?" The disbelief in Jo's voice is clear.

"Well, I don't mean, oh God, Jo, I don't know."

"You won't be able to smoke."

"Well, it's probably not such a bad thing for me to cut down a bit. I've been smoking since I was eleven."

"What about me?" Jo looks at Lily for the first time and Lily sees the tears welling up in her eyes. "I'll hate it here without you."

"Maybe I'll just do it for a few months. I can keep my room on here. I'll pay the rent."

"Yeah? Planning another kidnap?"

"I don't need to. I just found out. I inherited some money from my granddad. Can you fucking believe it? I'm a trust fund kid."

Jo tips her head against Lily's shoulder and Lily puts her arm around Jo. "Don't be sad, Jo. Please. I can't bear it."

Jo does her best to smile though the tears are now running freely down her cheeks. "I'll miss you so much. You're sure you're sure about this, Lil? I mean, your dad's a bit-"

"I know. He'll probably drive me crazy in a few weeks and I'll be back here looking for a job."

Jo leans her head against Lily's shoulders again. "I just don't think he deserves you, Lily," she says.

Lily jumps as another knock sounds on her bedroom door. "Oh no, it's that fucking Joel again."

"Jo?" calls a voice.

"'S alright," says Jo. Her cheeks seem pinker than a moment ago as she pulls herself up off the bed and checks her reflection in the chipped mirror that's attached to the chest of drawers. "It's, er, it's Andy."

"Andy, as in representative of the fascist state, Andy?" Lily smiles.

"Yeah, so what?" says Jo as she reaches to open the door.

252

Chapter 46

Alice is sitting on the blue bench as the bus pulls in to Skipton bus station. Lily meant only to stay one night in Leeds but it turned into three. Deep circles underline her eyes and she'd almost fallen asleep on the bus. Alice hugs her. "Have you been eating? You look tired."

"I'm fine," says Lily, a feeling like pleasure that someone notices her enough to know she looks tired. "Where's the others?"

"Your granddad's gone to a meeting at the town hall. Something to do with the historical society. And David and Fiona are still at school."

Lily looks up at the clock on the bus station wall. It's only two o'clock. It feels later, maybe because she's so tired. Alice links arms with her and they leave the bus station. "They got the keys to the new house yesterday. David's talking about moving in next weekend."

"Cool. How's Fiona?"

"Ok. She's going to Ruth's for tea. They seem to be seeing a bit more of each other. Apparently Ruth's finishing work earlier so they can spend some time together. A case of 'you don't know what you've got til it's gone' I think."

"So, Fiona's not coming home after school?"

"Well, in fairness, we didn't know you were coming home today."

When they're back at the house, Lily glances up at the kitchen clock. "I'm going to meet Fiona from school," says Lily.

Alice having pulled the rucksack from Lily's back, is busy stuffing all her clothes into the washing machine. "I'll just make it, if I run. Just to say hi, before she goes to her mum's."

"Fine. Will you pick up a pint of milk on your way home?"

Lily runs down the street. They live on the other side of Skipton now, and the walk to school takes over half an hour, so Fiona catches the bus most mornings. Lily arrives outside the gates as school-children are already pouring from the building. Lily's pretty sure Ruth won't be meeting Fiona at school, but all the same she tries not to draw any attention to herself. She stands against the wall, watching the students swarm by, but there's no sign of Fiona. She waits until the last stragglers have left the playground and then runs to the bus stop three streets away. There are children from the school hanging around, chewing gum and clutching files, but Fiona is not among them.

Lily climbs on the bus, remembering to pick up a pint of milk from the corner shop when she gets off.

"How was she?"

"Don't know. I didn't see her. The bell had gone by the time I got there. I must have missed her."

Upstairs she unpacks the rest of her worldly goods and spreads them on her single bed. Two photographs of her mother, a mirror and her small collection of books and LPs. And an envelope sandwiched between the pages of 'The Unbearable Lightness of Being', which contains a print out of a statement of her grandfather's trust fund, totalling just over one hundred and thirty seven thousand pounds.

She hears footsteps on the stairs and immediately folds the piece of paper back between the pages of the book. David knocks on her door and then opens it. "Hi, you're back. We missed you. Did you have a good trip?"

"Yes, thanks. I sorted out the house in Accrington, and withdrew from my course in Leeds."

"Well, we can talk about that later. There was an article in the Times Ed while you were away; the universities with the best graduate employment records. You know you could always resit your A levels. It's never too late you know."

"I feel like I need to decide what I want to do first."

"Ok. Well, like I said, we can talk about it later. Did grandma tell you we got the keys for Fern Cottage? We can move in whenever we want."

"Cool."

"It won't be like living in your student digs in Leeds, you do realise that, don't you? I am your father and there will be rules. Not smoking indoors, for one."

"I'm cool with that. So long as you remember I'm nineteen and don't expect me to be in by nine every night."

"Oh goodness no. I was thinking ten o'clock might be reasonable on a Saturday night."

Lily hits him with a T-shirt, catching him on his hip. "Come on," he says, "Granny told me to tell you tea's ready."

Try as she might to stay awake, Lily's fast asleep by the time Fiona gets home, lulled to sleep by the smell of freshly ironed sheets and a stomach full of homemade rhubarb crumble.

"Right," says Lily, zipping up her holdall. "I'm done. I'll see you there. You sure you don't want me to ride the bike round?"

"No, you go in the van and I'll dawdle and then hopefully you'll have unpacked it all by the time I get there."

"Gee, thanks." Lily takes a last look around their bedroom. The two single beds have already been dismantled and are now in the van outside. Fiona's belongings are still strewn around the floor.

"Give us a hug, sis," says Fiona. She holds onto Lily tightly.

"It feels like I haven't seen you in ages," says Lily, a little taken aback by the ferocity of Fiona's embrace. "Why don't we get fish and chips and a video tonight? Celebrate our new house and catch up."

"I feel sad, leaving this place." Fiona's eyes look bright.

"We're only twenty minutes away, and we'll still visit, you soft lump."

"I just feel like I've moved a lot these last few weeks. I've only ever lived at Newlands. And then in the last six weeks, I've been all over the place."

"Well, your mum's not moving anywhere is she? You've still got your room there. You've spent three nights in it this week. How is your mum?"

"She's really changed. Well, actually I don't know whether she's changed or I'm just getting to know her better. Did you know she had a baby that died? Our brother. Now isn't that weird? He died of cot death when he was only two months old."

Lily isn't sure whether she should say that she already knows, so she starts fiddling with the zip on her hold all instead. Fiona sits on the floor surrounded by piles of clothes. "I think that's why she starting working like she did. She said she felt she'd failed. That it was her fault, something she'd done or not done. Not as much was

255

known about it then. I feel sorry for her. She didn't exactly get great parenting tips from her parents."

David beeps the horn in the van outside. Lily looks through the curtains and sees David and Arthur sitting in the front seat. Her grandparents have both volunteered to help with the move. She waves at them. "Right, I'd better go." She swings her bag over her shoulder, "I'll see you round there in about half an hour."

"We've forgotten tea-bags," says Alice as she opens the front door of their new house to them. Her long grey hair is tied back off her face and she's dressed for the business of cleaning, in a blue nylon house-coat, that's similar to something Aunt Edie would wear. "And the phone's not connected. It's so dusty in here, I'm gagging for a brew."

"I'll go back and get some," says Lily. "It'll only take me ten minutes if I cut through the woods."

"Take a coat," shouts Alice. "It's about to chuck it down."

Arthur and David are manoeuvring the first single bed out of the back of the van as Lily walks back down the drive. "Where do you think you're going?" asks David.

"Mercy mission. No tea bags," says Lily. "I won't be long."

Great black storm clouds hover, as Lily crosses the road and walks into the cul-de-sac where Alice and Arthur live. Lily gets to the garden gate before noticing Fiona, her back to Lily, locking the front door. Fiona is wearing a backpack that is almost as big as herself. "Fiona?" Lily opens the small wooden gate. "You can't ride a bike with that on. Why didn't you put it in the van?"

Fiona doesn't turn around for ages. Lily walks up the path towards her. "Fiona?"

Fiona turns round slowly. Her face is pinched and white. "I'm not coming."

"What do you mean, you're not coming. Where are you going?"

Fiona shakes her head and purses her lips. She draws a deep breath and as she exhales, her shoulders sink an inch. "I've got a job."

"What?" says Lily.

"In Paris."

"You've got a job in Paris?"

"Oh God, I know I should have told you, but I just couldn't. I'm going to Paris. For a year."

"What job?"

"An au pair. With a nice family."

"Are you nuts? What about school? And what about Dad, the house?"

"You'll have to tell him."

"No chance. You can't leave like this. What are you thinking?"

Fiona squares her shoulders and looks at Lily's face for the first time. Because she's still standing on the step she's an inch or two taller. "You've found your family, and I'm really pleased for you, but I feel like I've lost mine. And I've always wanted to travel, and I thought I'd never be able to, because being the only child, well, you know what it's like. But now, I'm not an only child anymore."

"You can't just leave, not like this. What about Dad? Granny? You'll break their hearts."

"Don't you dare start guilt-tripping me."

"What about school?"

"I hate school. I keep telling everyone and no one listens to me. I haven't been to school since the day you kidnapped me. I told them my parents have split up and I've moved to Portsmouth."

"Fiona." Lily's face is contorted with disbelief.

"Don't start telling me how to live. You're not exactly an advert for doing the right thing."

"Have you told your mum?"

"Yes. She thinks it's time I learnt to stand on my own two feet. She got me the job. She says I've relied on a man for everything and he's let me down. She says this could be the making of me."

Lily rubs her chin. "What were you going to do? Leave a note?"

Fiona doesn't answer.

"What about Dad?"

"He'll be ok, now he's got you."

"But I don't want to live with him, without you. I want to live with you, that's the whole point. You're my sister."

"Don't give me that either. You weren't the slightest bit interested in me; all you wanted was a dad. All those weeks of you watching us, you never thought about me, just him. You wanted a dad and now you've got one. Personally, I'm a bit tired of having a dad, of always having to do what I'm told the whole time."

"Fiona, have you gone mad? We've just rented a house."

"It'll give you time to get to know each other, without me being in the way."

"I don't want him, not without you. I want to be with you."

Fiona shakes her head. "I need to be on my own. Please, Lily, don't make this hard. I've thought about it. It will give you and Stuart space to see whether you want to be together."

"I don't want Stuart," says Lily, her voice rising with desperation.

"He wants you. He tries hard, but all he's thinking about is you. He's like a love-sick puppy. You should ring him."

"I told you, I promised you I won't ever see him."

"There's no point not seeing him. He loves you, whether you love him or not. He's yours."

"Is that what this is about?"

"No, I need to think about what I want from my life. Please don't spoil it for me."

"But why didn't you talk to me? What were you going to do, just disappear?"

"I didn't want a scene."

"A scene? You think you can move to Paris and there won't be a scene? Dad will flip his wig."

"Mum said she'd explain it to him."

"Oh, that'll go down well."

"This is my chance. I've got to take it." Fiona pushes past Lily and walks down the path.

"Fiona, please. Wait. At least tell them yourself."

Fiona opens the gate and steps outside onto the path. She closes the gate behind her. "I can't. I'm really sorry but I can't. There's a letter inside. You give it to them."

"Fiona," Lily curses the tears that are spilling down her cheeks again. Having not cried once for as long as she can remember she now feels like a leaky tap.

"Don't, Lily. Please. Please understand. I'm not going forever, but I need to do this. I'll write to you." Fiona's already half way down the path by the time she gets to the end of her sentence. Lily notices for the first time the minicab waiting a couple of doors down.

Lily watches her sister waddle down the street, her slender frame leaning backwards under the weight of the rucksack, and wonders whether she'll get back to Fern Cottage before the clouds break.

"Where are you? Have you got the tea bags?" her father's voice sounds grumpy.

"I," Lily walks into their new kitchen diner taking off her coat. Alice is standing behind the breakfast bar, five mugs lined up. Arthur and David are wrestling with the flat pack set of drawers they bought yesterday from MFI. When Lily doesn't speak, the two men look up at her.

"How's Fiona getting on?" asks Alice. "Any sign of my bedroom carpet yet?"

"She's not coming. She left a note."

"I beg your pardon," says David, standing up and reaching his hand out for the white envelope Lily is holding out. There's a printed picture of kitten wearing a bow tie on the front. He reads the note, the colour draining from his face as his eyes scan the letter. "I don't sodding believe it."

He looks around the room. No one has moved. "Her mother's put her up to this. I bet my life on it."

Alice steps around the breakfast bar, but David shouts at her, "She's gone to Paris. I've never heard anything so fucking stupid in my life. Give me the phone."

"It's not connected," says Alice, her voice timid.

"Come on, son," says Arthur. "Calm down."

"I need to stop her. Where's she flying from?"

"I don't know," says Lily. "She didn't say."

"You mean you saw her?"

"She got a taxi."

"And you didn't stop her?"

"Well, I tried," begins Lily, feeling the colour rush to her cheeks.

"You tried?"

"What can I do? She's sixteen. I can't force her to come."

"So you gave up? Well, you are your mother's daughter."

Lily feels like her face has just been slapped.

"You just sat and watched her get into a cab without even asking where she was going?"

"Don't you dare bring my mother into this," says Lily in a very quiet voice.

"David, please," begs Alice.

"Did you plan this? Did you want Fiona out of the way? What is it? Are you jealous? You have to steal her boyfriend and destroy her family?"

"You know what," says Lily. "You can fuck off. Say what you like about me but not my mum. Because you know what, at least my mum stayed. She was there. She might not have been a teacher or a lawyer, but she was actually fucking there. And she listened. Perhaps if you listened more and talked less-"

"That's enough." David's voice is steady. "I don't want to hear any more from you."

"I think we all need to calm down," says Arthur. "There's no sense-"

"What are you going to do?" says Lily to David. "Send me to my room?"

He looks at her with such anger, such dislike that Lily suddenly can't bear to be in the same space as him. Her place is in Leeds, with Jo. She turns and runs from the room. Her hold-all is lying in the hallway, at the foot of the stairs, waiting to go up. She grabs it and runs out the front door. Fiona's bike is lying where she left it, at the gate. David follows her out of the house. "Wait, Lily."

But Lily shakes her head. "I can't do this. I'm sorry."

"You've ruined my life." David slams his fist against the wooden door frame.

She puts the hold-all on her back like a rucksack and mounts the bike. As she pushes off out of the gate, she notices that the clouds don't seem so heavy anymore. She speaks quietly, almost to herself. "Well, then I guess that makes us even."

"What am I supposed to do in this house, on my own?" he calls after her.

Lily is half way down the small lane. She turns in her saddle and shouts to him, but she's so far away she's not sure he will hear her. "You'll figure it out. I had to."

She sits back down on the seat and concentrates on crossing the T-junction ahead.

260